Ollie Quain lives in London. She has worked for Ministry of Sound, The O2, a load of fashion mags and also done a bit of telly. She is a fan of techno, Jason Orange from Take That, Citalopram, white leather and black liquorice. She hopes for global harmony, but wishes one of her exes wasn't so annoyingly fit. She loves her cat, Eddie—even when he sneezes in her face—and hates writing about herself in the third person. *How to Lose Weight and Alienate People* is her first novel...the second is on its way. Follow her on Twitter @olliequain.

Ollie QUAIN

how to
lose weight
and alienate
people
A Novel

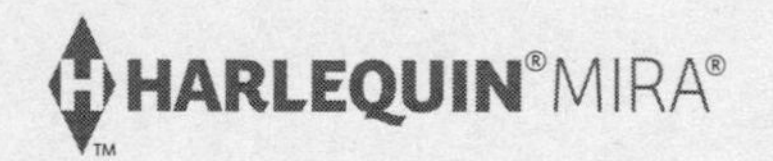
HARLEQUIN® MIRA®

Published in Great Britain 2014
by Harlequin MIRA, an imprint of Harlequin (UK) Limited,
Eton House, 18-24 Paradise Road,
Richmond, Surrey, TW9 1SR

ISBN 978-1-848-45333-3

58-0614

Harlequin (UK) Limited's policy is to use papers that are natural, renewable and recyclable products and made from wood grown in sustainable forests. The logging and manufacturing processes conform to the legal environmental regulations of the country of origin.

Printed and bound by
CPI Group (UK) Ltd, Croydon, CR0 4YY

This book is dedicated to Mummy Q.
She is the best.

PART ONE

CHAPTER ONE

I am aware that learning my lines on the loo is not the classiest way to prepare for an audition, but it works for me. The gentle trickle of a cistern filling up, the hypnotic whirring of an AC unit in the background; it helps me concentrate. I often imagine what other actresses get up to in the toilet. I picture them:

a.) Sticking Post-it notes on the shoots in *W* magazine they would like their stylist to draw inspiration from.

b.) Tweeting a *supposedly* self-deprecating, goofy 'selfie' in which they actually look fabulous.

c.) Plotting how to raise awareness of their worthiness and humanity by raising awareness of worthy humanitarian causes.

d.) Using their visit as me-me-*me*-time to consider their brand extension. Maybe – right now – somewhere in the Hamptons in a WASP-y 'new minimalist'-style bathroom, Gwyneth Paltrow is coming up with a low-GI (but highly condescending) spelt-based agave-nectar-infused muffin recipe for her latest cookbook.

***

I doubt I will ever get to confirm d.), though, as Gwynnie and I don't mix in the same circles. Unlike her, I am not a super-successful thespian with my fingers in other financially rewarding (gluten-free) pies. I am a hostess at a private members' club in central London called Burn's. I act when given the opportunity but I am certainly not at risk of suffering from 'exhaustion' due to a relentless schedule of back-to-back projects. My own fault – I have some focusing issues – but honestly, I am not *desperate* to become a huge star. Besides, I don't do 'selfies' and I reckon I'd struggle with the worthy humanitarian angle.

I leave the loo and head for a meeting with Roger, my boss. It still feels weird calling him this because over a decade ago we started out as waiting staff together. We always used to request the same shifts so we had the same hours off to party and go on the pull. We went for the same type of guy, too: those with directional haircuts and an enticing after-the-club-shuts attraction at their apartment, like an ice box full of premium vodka or tandem-functioning disco lights and surround sound. But then Roger met Pete and our late nights out together? They petered out.

'Hi, Rog,' I say, loitering outside his open office door.

He looks up from his desk. 'Come in, Vivian. I saw you in that advert for the Sofa World *Spring Clear Out!* last night. To be fair, you made that cream leather recliner look very tempting indeed. The way you flopped down on to it in your sensible office separates without spilling a drop from your glass of *vin rouge* – I was abso*lutely* convinced you'd been grafting at work all day … not a look of yours I'm particularly familiar with.'

We both laugh as I enter the room. Like the rest of Burn's it is painted in an understated off-white Farrow & Ball paint and the furniture is a mixture of ultra-contemporary pieces and perfectly worn classics. Ten years ago, when the club first opened, this schizophrenic new-meets-old look was reasonably fresh. Now you can't move in London's hospitality industry without tripping over an angular chrome footstool and landing on a tattered leather sofa.

'Anything exciting?' he asks, pointing in the direction of the manuscript I am holding.

'*Surf Shack.* The audition is tomorrow. It's a new kids' show for a late-afternoon slot, so even if I get the role and deliver a performance with Tilda Swinton-esque intensity, it'll probably only be seen by some homework-dodging ten-year-old in between mouthfuls of reconstituted poultry "nibblets" and ketchup.' I pass Roger the script and sit down on the Eames office chair in front of his antique desk.

He flips open the first page and reads out loud. '*"CHARACTER: DEBBIE. Debbie is a neurotic yet stubborn and antagonistic mother. She takes echinacea, spinning classes and life very seriously. In the scene below (taken from Episode 1) Debbie is nagging her daughter to do her homework instead of hanging out at the local water sports club, the eponymous Surf Shack."*' Roger gasps sarcastically. 'Ooh, nail-biting stuff. I'm already envisioning an end-of-series drowning or a story line involving a stranded dolphin. It's got Emmy Award written all over it.'

I yawn and rub my eyes. 'Did you actually want to see me about something to do with Burn's, Rog? Or did you just want to remind me how insignificant my contribution is to global entertainment?'

'Both really.' He grins at me. 'This morning, Fiona on the board told me she still hasn't found a suitable candidate to take over my role as Head of Staff when I get made General Manager in six weeks. You're easily the most experienced person on the floor, so I'm pretty sure if you made yourself available she'd give you the position. Shall I lie and tell her how industrious you are?'

I take a good two seconds to consider the offer. I covered for Roger once before – when he had his wisdom teeth removed – and found myself having to do some work. 'Thanks, Rog, but nah.'

'*But nah*? Is that it?' He gives a deflating lilo of a sigh. 'Think about this seriously, Vivian, it's obvious you need some motivation. If you had some extra duties it would inspire you to take more of an interest in how Burn's operates. You'd be organising all the private functions, doing the rosters, liaising with the committee over membership, structuring and monitoring the deliveries …'

I zone out temporarily at this point as I notice a glass jar of truffles on Roger's desk. Each chocolate is individually wrapped in yellow metallic paper. I think of Keira Knightley wrapped in gold lamé at the second *Pirates of the Caribbean* première. A classic noughties' moment. Bitchy bloggers accused her of appearing 'emaciated'. I think the intention was more …

'You'd be silly not to consider it,' Roger is saying. 'You would even have this office all to yourself …'

… ethereal.

'And you would finally be part of the management. It's your chance to stop winging it, Vivian.'

I re-engage. 'Newsflash, Rog … most of the staff at Burn's are "winging it". None of us grew up with a burning ambition to provide mouthy media executives with Long Island ice teas and fresh towels. It's just a means to an end until we get into our chosen career.' This is true. Amongst the 'floor' team are various hopeful thespians, writers, fashionistas and musicians. When clearing up at night, you can guarantee someone will break *Fame!*-like into an impromptu song-and-dance routine using their mop as a microphone.

'Look …' Roger sighs again. 'I *really* do *not* mean this in a patronising way …'

'Which means it will sound exactly that.'

He laughs. 'Okay, fair enough … it might do. The thing is, you're not in your twenties any more. There comes a time in life when you have to accept the *reality* of your situation and simply make the best of it. I'd say you are unequivocally at that point, Vivian, given you are *thirty-five* years old.'

'Don't exaggerate, I'm thirty-four.'

'Thirty-five on Saturday; and since that is only two days away it's time for you to create a more secure life for yourself. Because, face facts, *this*,' he taps my script, 'is not exactly lining the coffers and it's showing no signs of doing so in the near future. At this rate your breakthrough lead role is going to be the sequel to *Driving Miss Daisy.* Question: do you know what a PEP, ISA or Tessa is?'

'The more precocious characters from a Dickens novel?'

I joke, but I shift a little irritably in my seat. I don't want a conversation about the future. I'm not done with the present. The only time span I am totally done with is the past, but I am not going to talk about that either.

'I'm only saying this because I'm your mate, and I understand your situ,' explains Roger. 'I used to be a hot mess too, but I had to change when things got serious with Pete ...' He glances fondly at the framed picture of his husband – a garland of flowers round his neck on their honeymoon in Hawaii – that takes pride of place on the desk. 'Because he had this crazy idea about wanting us to have *security*.' Roger looks back up at me and grimaces. 'But guess what? Earning then saving *can* be fun. Having a few quid in the bank means that should you ever want to shake things up a little and do something out of the ordinary – *just for you* – it's possible.'

'Rog! Are you suggesting I might want to go and *find myself*? Ha! Count me *out*. I've seen *Eat Pray Love* ... What a load of bollocks. Trust me, any woman who spends six months scoffing pasta, pizza and traditionally manufactured Italian ice-cream, then another six months in an ashram thinking about the amount of white flour, wheat and trans-fats she has consumed would end up in a mental institution. Not Bali.'

He tuts. 'There's more to life than getting trashed in London every weekend, Vivian.'

'I know. That's why God invented budget airlines ... so that from the beginning of May to mid-October for less than the price of a round of drinks in one of our capital's leading nightspots we can go and get trashed in Ibiza instead.'

'Does that mean you're going there *again* this summer?'

Depressingly I can't, as I am the poorest I have ever been. I don't know where my money goes. Okay, that's a lie. I know exactly where it goes: nights out, minicabs on the aforementioned nights out, St Tropez (the tanning mousse not the luxury French seaside resort), Grey Goose vodka (the lowest carbohydrate content of all the brands but the most expensive) and ASOS. I am addicted. It's the crack pipe of the online fashion world. Every time I enter my three-digit security code I tell myself that it is my last hit but two days later I'll find myself buying another load of basic vests and skinny-leg trousers... *in the style of Tyler Momsen.* I am too embarrassed to tell Roger the truth, though, so I blame him.

'I won't be heading to the White Isle this year, actually. Since my once reliably up-for-it GBF won his man but lost his sense of adventure,' I fix him with a pointed look, 'I haven't made any plans. I'm assuming you and Pete are already booked into a four-hundred-euro-a-night boutique hotel in Mykonos.'

'Turkey, actually. Greece is too much of a cliché.' He smiles at me. 'Seriously, at least take Fiona's number and have a chat with her.'

I get out my absolutely knackered old Nokia from my back pocket to show willing. Roger laughs loudly when he sees it.

'Piss off, Rog, I will get round to upgrading at some point.'

'Vivian, since you last mentioned you were going to do that, London has bid for the Olympic Games, won the honour to stage them, built the Olympic Park, staged the event and the athletes are now in training for 2016. But if you do, *obviously* get the new iPhone. It's genius, I can't live witho…'

I zone out again and get up from the desk, taking one last glance at the truffles. Ethereal. *Ethereal.*

Roger cocks his head at me. '*Vivian?* I was saying I'll text you her number.'

'Ace. You do that …' I tell him. 'Now, can you quit with the concern and return to your usual light bitching – you're freaking me out.'

He repositions his Joe 90 spectacles and glances down again at my manuscript for *Surf Shack. 'A neurotic yet stubborn and antagonistic mother'*, eh? Well,' he grins, 'you'll have to dig deep on the maternal angle. But other than that, you should be fine.'

*

It's only early evening but the atmosphere in Burn's is what British *Vogue* once described as 'expensively buzzy'. For many of our members – now that summer is here – Thursday marks the end of their working week. Tomorrow they'll either head off to a music festival with VIP laminates dangling round their necks or jet off on a European city mini-break. Those with kids will jump into their 4x4s and motor down to the West Country for a relaxing weekend at their second home – usually some sort of traditional fishing cottage, which thanks to a chi-chi interior designer (based in Hampstead, naturally) is now free of any sense of sea-faring tradition bar a Cath Kidston table cloth bearing an anchor motif.

In addition to the restaurant there are four other floors at

Burn's. It's a similar layout to Shoreditch House – our main competitor – except they have a rooftop pool. Our basement has a cinema, the top floor has a spa and a gym, the first floor has a cocktail bar and alcoves for private dining, whilst the second floor is used as a lounge area. This can be used for business meetings, reading the papers, playing games … whatever. Some members spend *all* day and *all* evening here until 2 a.m. when Roger has to ask them to leave so we can close. These die-hards always look panicked when they get booted out, as if the prospect of fending for themselves for the next five hours (until we re-open at 7 a.m. for breakfast) without instant access to Molton Brown toiletries, a decent Caesar Salad and an antique backgammon board is really quite daunting. My job is to flit unobtrusively between all these floors making sure that everything is running smoothly and that all members are happy. They usually are, but today, one of them looks even happier.

'Oi, Vivian! Over 'ere a sec, sweet'eart.' The genuine cockney bark of Clint Parks resonates around the restaurant. The letter 'h' has no place in his vocabulary.

I wind my way through the tables and give him a kiss on the cheek. As always, he smells of *Envy* by Gucci and over excitement. 'How are you, Clint? I haven't seen you for a few days.'

'I've been in Tenerife on a nice little freebie, as it 'appens … judging some beauty contest for a chain of 'otels. Naturally, I made sure the fittest bird came second so I could cheer 'er up in my suite afterwards.' Everyone at the table giggles. Clearly, they aren't picturing Clint hammering away at some desperate wannabe with vacant eyes.

As the loud, crass, womanising gossip columnist for *News Today*, you would have thought that Clint is exactly the kind of punter who would have his application for membership at a swish private club like Burn's revoked as soon as it came before the selection committee, but actually he and his friends are just the kind of punters we need. It's simple. Clint and his mates rack up huge bills on booze, then go to the toilet to rack up huge lines of cocaine and then they return to the bar to rack up even bigger bills on booze. If we turned him away he would only go to any of the other members' clubs in London, then Burn's would miss out on his custom and all the free promotion we get from being mentioned repeatedly in *Clint's Big Column.*

He can be a handful, but I like Clint. Without him I wouldn't have my job at Burn's, and he's saved me from being sacked a number of times. (*'If you tell 'er to 'oppit, I'm 'opping off to Shoreditch 'ouse.'*) When I first met him I had left drama college and was working in a scuzzy basement wine bar. We were open from *5 p.m. until My Boss Was Drunk Enough to Ignore All Laws Concerning Sexual Harassment in the Workplace and Would Start Pestering Me to Sleep With Him.* Clint bowled in one night, celebrating his first major splash as a junior reporter: revealing the three married Premiership soccer stars behind a series of roasting orgies. He got so plastered he left without his laptop; it contained all his leads and contacts. I made him sweat a couple of days then called him at *News Today* saying I had found the computer. He immediately asked what he could do for me in return. I told him I was desperate for a new job; somewhere with a bit more pizzazz and finite working hours. Clint had the answer; he had just been asked to become a member at a brand-new private club in West London. He put a word in for me and I was hired instantly. So, I slept with my boss one (more) time, then handed him my resignation.

'So, 'ere's the score, Vivian ... we need some of that quality Krug. Something very special indeed 'as 'appened.' Clint rolls up the sleeves on his jacket – a pale blue silk bomber with the word *'Parksie'* emblazoned on the back in diamanté studs. 'The wife's only got a bleedin' bun in the oven. She's *preggers*!'

'Wow,' I say.

After this initial response, I have time to practise my 'I'm thrilled for you' face, as one of his cronies – a depth-free harridan called Sophie Carnegie-Hunt, who runs *Get On It!* (a celebrity management and promotions company) – returns from the loo. As usual she is wearing a hat tipped at a jaunty angle and a guitar band gig T-shirt. That's her *thing*. Today it's a woven tweed shooting cap with a top from the Strokes *Is This It?* tour. She sits down without acknowledging me and rubs Clint's back in that overly earnest way induced by a recently ingested substantial line of coke.

'You really *bloody* deserve this blessing, angel.' She nods. 'You'll be a bloody *amaaaaaaaaaa*-zing father. My daddy is a bloody ama*zing* man ... genuinely philanthropic. I think I got the desire to nurture and support people from him.'

Clint rolls his eyes at the rest of the table. 'That'll be the nurture and support our Sophs offers at a standard rate of thirty per cent of all future earnings, eh?' They all laugh and he turns back to me. 'She's right, though. With me as a dad, Junior will want for nothing …'

'Except maybe regular visits from Social Services.' I smile at Clint. He snorts loudly and winks at me. 'Anyway, let me get that champagne sorted. You wanted the Krug Grand Cuvée?'

'That's the one. Three bottles to get us going. Bung 'em on my tab.' No one else at the table gives me another option for payment. 'Right, I'm off to the khazi.' He pulls away from Sophie's hand, which is still pawing his back. 'Oi, Sophs, you got my nonsense?'

She passes him her handbag. 'In there somewhere, angel.'

I *pretend* not to notice, but the truth is none of the staff at Burn's would ever stop anyone from doing drugs. The police never come in anyway. Years back, they did show a bit of interest after Sadie Frost's sproglet was reported to have found an ecstasy pill to nibble on in another leading members' club, but these days serious knife crime quite rightly takes up more of their time than preventing go-getting career professionals from bellowing self-aggrandising crap at one another for hours on end.

Clint heads off upstairs. Our members tend to eschew the lavatories on the restaurant level for coke snorting as the futuristic egg-shaped toilet bowls jut out of the cubicle wall. There is no visible cistern or anywhere to get a *purchase* on, unless you use the loo seat … which they would consider using a bit … well, *druggie*. So they go upstairs. There, the roomy art deco influenced unisex conveniences have the required air of decadence and purpose. In fact, they may as well have been designed in consultation with regular visitors to The Priory or Promises. Every surface in the loo is mirrored, including a heavy back shelf – which is also under-lit, so every last grain of gak can be accounted for.

I wave over to Dane, one of the waiters. He also plays guitar in a folk rock band … *sort of Mumford and Sons-ish but with more of a message.* Despite this, he's an all right guy. He walks over.

'Parksie's having an ickle tiny kidlet,' Sophie tells him in a baby voice. (Another of her 'things', it's not just because of the subject matter.) 'Bloody-wuddy amazing, no?'

'That's cool, man. Pass on my congratulations, won't you?' Dane smiles sweetly, whilst I'm thinking how much I would like to plunge a fork into her hand. 'Champagne all round, then?'

'Three bottles of Krug,' I instruct him. 'Cheers, Dane.' Then I mooch off …

… to do more mooching around the restaurant; checking that orders are being taken, glasses filled, bills issued and tables turned over swiftly. The air is thick with braying voices regaling industry anecdotes. Our members are a mixture of those with glamorous jobs in the media (movies, music, television, journalism, advertising), the fashionably creative (designers, artists, photographers), plus a few of the more urbane City boys and girls. Everyone wears conspicuously on-trend outfits. For the men this means sharp suits and smart-casual wear from fashion-forward labels available on Selfridges first floor, or an ironically hip talking-point garment like Clint's *'Parksie'* jacket. For the girls it's bang up-to-date designer gear mixed smugly with decent high-street copies, vintage pieces, and a 'statement' handbag (usually a Mulberry or a Chloe). A statement that they hope says emphatically: *I have it all!* But what it actually says is, *I have a very negative image of myself but forking out nine hundred quid on a single accessory every season has a temporarily positive effect.*

As a hostess I have to wear black. Within this remit I can choose clothes that are stylish enough to give the place an aspirational vibe and slightly intimidate the non-members coming in, but not *so* stylish that I make the regulars feel like they are losing *it* or that the venue is too of-the-moment. I can get fully ready – tan, outfit, face, hair – within two hours. This may sound like a long time but as well as wanting to get my look right for work I have *always* stuck to a simple grooming statute: I will never leave the house unless I wouldn't mind bumping into anyone who I went to school with. Obviously, when I say *any*one, I mean *some*one.

'What a gorgeous evening. Summer really is on its way,' trills Tabitha, the receptionist, as I am walking into the foyer to check on ... not much. (Tabitha always has everything under control.) 'We're going to be busy bees ...' She rearranges her tartan headband. 'The restaurant and alcoves are all fully booked and the first-floor bar has been chock-a-block since lunchtime.'

Tabitha is in her mid-twenties but accessorises as if she was still nine, and likes to send group emails to us all of YouTube footage showing different breeds of animals unexpectedly befriending one another. She sees the good in everyone and is always irrepressibly cheery. So much so that at first I thought this might be a front she puts up to hide a much darker side, but then I bumped into her having a night out with her friends. Were they similar to Tabs? Let's say it would be safe to assume not one of them will go to the grave knowing how filthy an amphetamine comedown on a Wednesday can be.

'Oooh, it's your b'day on Saturday, isn't it? How exciting!' she squeals.

'Very,' I lie. I'm not excited. Birthdays make me uncomfortable.

'Have you got the whole weekend off?'

'No, I've got to do the breakfast shift on Sunday morning.' Roger's idea of a joke – making me drag my sorry carcass into work with a hangover.

'Me too. But since I won't see you on the special day itself, let me give you your gift now.'

She reaches under the desk and pulls out a white cardboard box. I flip open the lid. Inside are six mini fairy cakes decorated with pink icing and crystallised jelly hearts.

'Ah, thanks a lot, Tabs ... you shouldn't have.' She *really* shouldn't have. Later they will be placed in the big black wheelie bin outside the club. 'So, who's in tonight? Anyone interesting?'

She grabs the reservations clipboard and holds it to her chest. 'Ooooooooooh, has no one told you?'

'About what?'

'About who has arrived for supper?' She claps her hands repeatedly like a delighted seal. Tabitha *still* hasn't got her head round the whole pretend-to-be-utterly-unimpressed-by-all-celebrities that is a given amongst staff working in the high-end hospitality market. 'My tummy totally did a flick-a-flack when he walked in.'

'Who is it, then?' I ask distractedly. I could do with a Nurofen. The raspberry-tinged scent of the freshly baked cakes hovers in the air between us. I bet Tabitha loves eating pink food. Personally, I stick to green, white or brown. Everyone has their nutritional colour rules, don't they?

'Hello? *Vivian?* Reaction, please!' Tabitha claps again. 'I said, it's MAXIMILIAN FRY! He must have literally *just* got out of rehab … Oooooh, he is sooooo cute in the flesh. Even *cuter* than he was in *The Simple Truth.* Un-be-l-*iev*-able to think that what's-her-name *actually* cheated on him. I tell you, if given the opp, I would never ever *ever* be unfaithful to him. Honestly, I wouldn't.'

I smile at her. 'Very decent of you, Tabs.'

Dane trots down the stairs holding a giant ice bucket with bottles of champagne poking out the top.

'Did you see Maximilian Fry up there, Dane?' Tabitha grins. '*How* gorge is he?'

'Yeah, yeah … but it's what's inside that counts,' says Dane. 'You know he's a Buddhist? Always cool to hear people embracing a sense of spirituality … whatever the origin. I'd love to play him some of the band's tracks.'

'I think he's had more than enough to deal with this year,' I laugh. But then something occurs to me. 'Dane, how come you saw him? You only went up to the bar. Isn't he dining in one of the private alcoves?'

'Nope, he's at the bar.'

Tabitha checks her yellow Swatch. 'I seated him there ten

minutes ago … he said he'd prefer to wait there until his guest arrived.'

'Great. Clint Parks went upstairs about five minutes before that to use the loo.'

'What's the issue*?'* she asks, furiously batting inch-long (natural) eyelashes as she senses impending drama.

I take a deep breath. 'It was Clint who broke the story about Zoe Dano doing the dirty on Maximilian Fry. It was also Clint who printed those pictures of Fry heading off to treatment. He's going to walk straight out of the toilet and slap bang into the one person who wants to kill him. Well, one *of*. Trust me, it will kick off.'

I run up the stairs to the first floor. There is a long line of people sitting at the bar on stools all with their backs to me, but I recognise Maximilian immediately because of his footwear: textbook A-List-actor scuffed hiking boots. (All generations wear them off set. Depp, Pitt, Farrell, DiCaprio, Butler, Cooper, Franco, LaBeouf, Lautner, Lutz, etc.) As I detect the shoes and approach Maximilian, the door of the unisex loo opens on the other side of the bar. Clint Parks bowls out looking *refreshed*. He immediately spots his nemesis.

'Well, well, *well!* If it ain't Max—' is all he manages to say before Maximilian shoots off his stool and charges towards him.

'You fucking noxious lump of shite,' snarls Maximilian. 'How dare you screw over my life to sell your contemptible whoring rag?' Which is language he definitely did *not* use when last interviewed on the red carpet for *E!* by Giuliana Rancic.

Then everything seems to move in slow motion. Maximilian steams into Clint, knocking him back through the lavatory door; women at the bar start screaming, grab their drinks and jump off their stools. Tabitha and Dane come running up the stairs behind me, our head barman drops his silver cocktail shaker and tries to hurl himself over the bar in an attempt to split up Maximilian and Clint. But I get there first and find myself wedged between them. I don't even get a fleeting glimpse of Maximilian's face before his fist comes hurtling towards me.

It says a lot about how strange that day eventually turned out to be when the weirdest thing that happened to me was *not* getting punched in the eye by an Oscar nominee.

CHAPTER TWO

I open the door to the flat, automatically sling my keys in the glass fish bowl on the hall table and hang my leather jacket on the back of the door. I have been trained to do this by my flatmate, Adele, who has a zero-tolerance policy to household mess. For example, dirty clothes have to be washed, transferred to the dryer and put back in the wardrobe in quick succession – not lcft to 'lingcr unnccessarily' on the radiator. Smoking is strictly prohibited (even on the patio) and the fridge is constantly monitored for decaying comestibles. The chances of a bio-yogurt drifting past its best-before date are very slim indeed. Adele was only half joking when she once said to me, 'Those bacteria may be friendly now, Vivian, but who knows when they might turn?'

A lot of people would find Adele's idiosyncrasies a nightmare to live with but I am not really in a position to complain. I am lucky to be living in such a nice apartment in Bayswater, with a big clothes cupboard and the added bonus of a flatmate who travels abroad whenever she has time off. For some unfathomable reason Adele is never happier then when she is tramping through some Third World country under a spine-crunching backpack. I don't see the point of travelling to far flung places myself, unless it's to stock up on hardcore downers and speed-based diet pills, or to catch dysentery – the ultimate detox – then all the hassle would be worth it. Anyway, she bought this flat after she'd quit the drama college we were both at to become some sort of money broker. I was shocked when she told me she was giving up her dream of being on stage, and remember asking, 'Do you think working in the City will be that rewarding?' The answer turned out to be 'yes'. Last year, her *basic* income (she wouldn't tell me her bonus) was two hundred grand. She has an extensive shares portfolio, two sports cars, a buy-to-let in the Docklands and this place, which – after the installation of a hi-tech new kitchen – has been valued by a number of local agents at just over a million.

I feel like a bit of a fraud for living here. I always avoid saying hello to the upstairs neighbours – a German couple with their own architectural practice – and if I ever see them I pretend to be deep in conversation on my mobile. Stupid really, what are they going to do? Drag me into the upper maisonette and interrogate me using a Philippe Starck brushed-steel anglepoise lamp until I admit Adele lets me live here for a minimal rent? One thing is for sure, without her generosity I would be living in a much lesser flat somewhere a lot further west ... like Wales. So, what does she get in return? Well, someone to stand by her, I suppose. Or more specifically, someone who is on standby 24/7 with a box of man-size Kleenex to mop up her tears. They fall quite often. Adele may have her working life neatly squared off, but her love life is a pentagram of doom.

I pick up an ASOS package off the hall table. It should

contain five vests, four grey marl and one nude, plus two pairs of skinny-leg trousers, one black, one grey. It is the second ASOS parcel to arrive this week.

I can hear Luke in the kitchen, opening then banging cupboards shut, still trying to work out where things are. I have been letting him stay here whilst Adele is trekking across the Himalayas with her latest boyfriend, James. They met in Asia doing voluntary work at a wildlife sanctuary for endangered species. She has already hit a new record with him: they've been together since the end of last year and she hasn't cried *once*.

'You're back early,' shouts Luke.

'Yes, I am,' I shout back. 'Five hours and thirty-three minutes earlier than I should be, if you need the exact timings for your log book.'

'Thanks, I'll jot those figures down.'

I hear him laugh as I walk into the lounge. The usual organised debris that appears whenever Luke is within a ten-metre radius is all present and correct. A half-drunk two-litre bottle of Dr Pepper, headphones, laptop logged onto beatport.com and back copies of dance music magazines are lined up on Adele's African chest, which doubles up as a coffee table. In a pile on the floor next to it are his hooded grey sweatshirt, gaffer-taped work boots, thick mountain socks and a plastic bag from an electrical wholesaler. It's full of electrical leads.

'Luke!' I yell. 'Why have you bought *more* cables?'

'Because I need them.'

'Christ, how could you? Your bedroom floor already looks like the snake pit in *Indiana Jones*. By the way, Adele gets back tomorrow so we need to clean up this mess. It's a tip in here.'

I sit down on the sofa and notice a Kentucky Fried Chicken bucket on the floor the other side of the arm rest. Luke must have bought a snack from there at teatime on his way home from the building site. I peer inside the container at the gnawed, withered drumsticks and find myself thinking about Angelina Jolie's leg poking out of her dress at *that* Oscar ceremony …

'This isn't a tip,' says Luke, walking into the lounge holding a plate of more food. 'Mine and Wozza's place is a tip. What you're looking at is just *surface rubbish*, which admittedly has shock value, I'll give you that. But it's easy to get rid of. Although, I still can't find the bin in there.' He nods towards the kitchen.

I smile. To be fair, Adele's recently installed kitchen is a complex set-up. You feel pressurised cooking in there … it's like competing in an episode of *The Cube*. Fortunately, that – preparing and assembling dishes *or* game shows – is not something I like to get involved in very often.

Luke sits down next to me and puts his dinner on the leather chest. He has made himself a grilled lamb chop with salad and potatoes.

I find Luke's approach to diet interesting but baffling. On the one hand, he is quite content chomping his way through the types of dishes laid out in front of the obese person on the first episode of *The Biggest Loser* to serve as a reality check. On the other, he could name most superfoods (probably not the goji berry, though), and more often that not always has his five-a-day. He eats what he wants, when he wants it. His approach to exercise is the same. He doesn't bother with a gym schedule, but if he fancies some fresh air he goes for a run. Not that he needs to burn anything off; there is no 'excess' on him. The combination of doing manual labour and a ridiculously high metabolic rate keeps his body hard and angular. It's like sleeping next to a bicycle.

'So why did you sack off the rest of your shift?' he asks, leaning over to give me a kiss. Then he clocks my blackening eye and leaps back. 'Jeeeeeeeeeesus, who the fuck did that? I'll *kill* them!'

I burst out laughing. Luke is the least confrontational person I have ever met. If he found a spider in the bathroom he would negotiate with it to leave as quietly as possible and put in a polite request that any *flamboyant scuttling* is kept to a minimum.

'It was an accident,' I explain. 'A couple of the customers had a run-in; I tried to split it up and got whacked by mistake. It looks a lot more painful than it is.'

'Ouch.' He peers at the bruise. 'That's a shiner. Why didn't you call me when it happened?'

'Because I was flat out on the floor.'

'Afterwards, I mean. I could have come to get you.' He picks up his fork and motions at me to try some of his meal, but I pull a face and shake my head. This is our standard procedure. 'You might have got delayed concussion on the way home and passed out on the pavement.'

'Well, I didn't, did I? I'm here.'

'You never phone me in a crisis.'

'That's because in the year I have known you there hasn't

been a crisis to report. It's not as if one has occurred and I have made a point of not informing you. Besides, this wasn't a *crisis* it was a *drama*.'

His face crumples slightly. It always does when I have a verbal jab at him. First his forehead creases, then his cheekbones sink and his mouth turns at the corners.

'At least, let me get you some ice,' he says.

'No way, I want it to look really bad for tomorrow. I may be able to elicit some sympathy at my audition and get a call-back because they feel sorry for me. Desperate times call for desperate measures.'

'Don't be stupid, you'll get a call-back because you're talented not because you're injured.'

'Luke!' I nudge him on the leg. 'What have I told you about being overly supportive of my non-existent career?'

'Sorry, I'm afraid it's in my genes. Despite inventing the drinking game, *Show us your rack, Sheila!* ...' He smiles pointedly at me, knowing full well it winds me up when he uses Australian slang. '... us Aussies are extremely sensitive. It's a fact.'

But I smile back at him, because here's the thing. Despite the obsessive timekeeping, low-level buzz of neediness and his place of birth ... Luke is hot. If he was in a boy band, he'd be the tall one at the back who never gets to sing lead vocal but is on hand to do some decent break-dancing moves and point at the fans a lot. He was born in the eighties, at the nineties end ... so when he was in a cot, I was in a bunk, not a grown-up bed. He would be even hotter if he cut his hair, used some basic grooming products on his skin to protect it against the elements, and wore some better clothes. I don't mean expensive, but just something that fitted properly, with possibly a hint of tailoring or edginess. Just because he has an athletic physique, doesn't mean that sweatshirts should be the only option. I don't badger him about this sort of thing, though, because I wouldn't expect him to change himself for me, as it's not as if I would change myself for him. I think that's why it's lasted twelve months. We're together, but there isn't any grand plan for us; we're having a laugh. When we stop having a laugh we'll go our separate ways.

'Did you know the person who clobbered you?' he asks, as he chews.

'Kind of. It was Maximilian Fry – the actor.'

'Maximilian Fry?' He repeats his name out of surprise, not because he is remotely impressed.

'Uh-huh. He was trying to have a pop at Clint Parks.'

'Who's that?' Luke doesn't look at any of the tabloids. He buys the *Guardian* and reads it on the building site at lunchtime.

'The gossip columnist on *News Today.* As soon as Maximilian saw him leave the Gents he pelted towards him, I jumped in the middle and *pow* … he thumped me.'

'So did the cops pitch up and bundle him into the back of a police van?'

'God, no. His PR rep arrived within minutes and ushered him through the fire exit into the back seat of an air-conditioned people carrier.' I had missed all of this, though, because I had to go and look after Tabitha who was upset about seeing me get hurt. 'Have you fed Monday?'

The second I say that, my cat's big orange face appears

in the doorway. He does one of his mammoth over-exaggerated yawns (similar to how a cobra dislocates its jaw to swallow a whole deer), and then blinks slowly as he scans the room, assessing the current situation. Monday has got blinking down to a fine art. He can say so much simply by shutting his eyes and opening them again. If he is feeling particularly narked he also raises his eyebrows. For example, if someone offers him fish. He can't stomach seafood.

Luke nods. 'Yeah, he's been fed, but I think he may have been upstairs for a snack first because he smelt of bratwurst. Anyway, I got him some chook from that butcher's round the corner. You know, the posh one where they pride themselves on the non-stressful conditions the animals are reared in? Apparently, this particular bird was allowed to hang around in the barn all day wearing his dressing gown and playing the most recent *Grand Theft Auto* on the Xbox. Wasn't it, little mate?' He gives Monday a thumbs-up. Monday pads over to him and rubs his head on Luke's shin.

Luke adores Monday and Monday seems to like Luke a lot too, which is saying something as in the eleven years since I collected him from the Cat's Protection League he has found fault with most of the men I've been with. Yes, I'm aware that the words, 'Men I've Been With' aren't likely to inspire Danielle Steel's next romantic bestseller, but it's the closest I can get to describing the connection I make with members of the opposite sex. I am *with* them, and then I am not. Not in the way that Adele is. She is an emotional car crash. I've never even come *close* to having a minor prang let alone careered into a major pile-up. This is because I am always in the driving seat and plan exactly where I am going. Adele instantly hands over the keys and never bothers with GPS.

'That Fry bloke … was he on speedo?'

I make a face at Luke for using another annoying Aussie-ism. 'Speedo' is what he calls cocaine … because it *speeds up time*.

'No, he's just come out of rehab.'

'But he managed to apologise for hitting you?' asks Luke.

'Nah …' I shrug my shoulders. 'I wouldn't have expected him to.'

He laughs. 'Oh right, is that one of the rules of joining a private members' club, then? You have to behave as rudely as possible at all times? I would sign up myself but I may only be able to manage "faintly offensive" during opening hours. "Wholly insulting" could take some practice.' Then he mutters to himself, 'What a pretentious wanker.'

This is classic Luke. Maybe it's because he grew up on the beach in Sydney where life was one long fun-packed family *barbi*, but he is so grounded. He is entirely unaffected by everything that everyone else I know *is* affected by. He doesn't concern himself with what people do, how they live or what they look like. He doesn't care what anyone thinks about what he is doing either, as long as he is content within *himself* and sticks to his plan. Case in point, he graduated from university in Australia with a first-class degree, and then worked for five years in an ultra-dull-sounding recruitment job, just so he could save up for a deposit on a property in Sydney to keep as an investment for the future. Then he travelled over here to fulfil his ultimate dream: becoming a DJ. Not because he eventually wants to be the idolised centrepiece of wild parties where the crowd scream his name and supermodels nosh him off behind the decks – which I thought was the whole point of deejaying – but because he is genuinely into the music and wants to 'share' this passion. It goes without saying that when we very first met, I warned him that his plan was unlikely to work out. After all, for nearly two decades it has been mandatory for every bloke under thirty inhabiting the hipper UK towns to know how to mix, run club nights *and* produce their own tunes on set-ups in their bedroom. *Everyone* is a DJ, or a promoter, or a producer; other typically young male-dominated industries have suffered as an effect. You can't get a decent plumber for love nor money over Hackney way. Anyway, Luke ignored what I said, found work on a building site so he had a reliable job that required no overtime and then set about finding some gigs.

To be fair, he has managed to land a few. Mainly through his flatmate, Warren, who knows *everyone* in Clubland and also throws the odd party himself at an underground venue in South London. (That's underground as in literally *below street level*, not underground as in madly cool.) But Luke always has to play the thankless slot at the very beginning of the evening when punters are thin on the ground. It's the bar staff turning up for their shift who tend to congratulate him on his set. This does not bother him in the slightest; he's thrilled to be part of the environment. For me this would be like meeting someone for a drink at Shoreditch House who enjoyed full membership all year round, whilst you were still waiting for your application to be processed and approved. Which I am. Small acorns have grown into large oaks since I've been on their sodding waiting list. Roughly, twice a year I get to the top and am offered a contract, but I can't afford the fee because I will have just spent/be planning to spend an eye-watering amount of euros at the Ibiza opening/closing parties. So, I go back to the bottom.

'Are you hyped for Saturday night, then?' asks Luke, as he puts his knife and fork together and pushes his plate away. He hasn't eaten all his potatoes.

'That depends on what we're doing.'

'We're celebrating your birthday.'

'Yeah, I know. But *how*?'

'It's a surprise,' says Luke, then he winks at Monday. 'Isn't it, little mate?'

Monday blinks at him and kneads the carpet with his two pristinely white front paws.

'A surprise …' I repeat.

'Yeah, a sur*prise*!'

'Putting an inflection on the end of the word doesn't make it sound more appealing.'

'Everyone likes surprises,' Luke argues.

Not me. I don't even put my MP3 player on 'shuffle'. In fact, I like surprises even less than birthdays. *Combined?* No, thanks.

'I'd prefer to know where we are going, Luke.'

His face crumples slightly but he pulls it back. '*And the award for most ungrateful reaction to the news that someone has gone to the trouble of organising a nice treat goes to … Vivian Ward!* Jesus, you can be such a witch sometimes.

You'll have a great time, I promise, not that you deserve it,' he says, and pulls off his T-shirt over his head. 'Now, I suggest you make some amends by getting your kit off.'

'Why is that?'

'Because I want to have some of that really bad nookie we're so good at.' He reaches into his pocket, fishes out a condom and Frisbees it into my lap.

'Ok-*aaaaay*.' I pick up the sealed plastic pouch faux-wearily and shove the trunk with my foot to get the leftover potatoes out of my line of vision. One of them has a large blob of mayonnaise next to it. 'But please, let's make sure it is a whole different level of unsatisfactory this time. Dull, perfunctory humping only. Do you mind if we have the TV on in the background?'

'Nope, we'll switch it on when we've finished … then we've got something to look forward to,' says Luke, dexterously unbuckling his belt and jeans with his left hand. With the right he throws his T-shirt towards the doorway where it drops on Monday's head, making him look like a furry-legged ghost. 'Sorry, little mate, this is not for your eyes.'

I wriggle out of my skinny-leg trousers, which are almost identical to the ones that arrived today, and lie back on the sofa. 'Let's press on. Try to keep it under five minutes, yeah? Then we can actually enjoy what's left of the evening.'

'Got it.' His jeans come off.

And then so are we. No awkwardness, no hesitation, no more admittedly fairly laboured sarcastic build-up, which I am *well* aware is only funny if you are us, just no-holds-barred, relentless shagging accompanied by some slightly feral grabbing, licking, sucking, biting and maybe a bit of light (non-scab forming) scratching. This is certainly not the Calvin Klein approved, black-and-white *lurve*-making that goes on in advertisement for *Eternity.* It's full-on fucking; the purely-for-pleasure stuff my mother would warn me against as a child. Corinthians Chapter 6 Verse 18; *Flee fornication. Every sin that a man doeth is without the body; but he that committeth fornication sinneth against his own body.* There is no gentle whispering or delicate contemplation, just ecstatic yowling and frenzied gulps for breath. It's been like this since the moment I met Luke; one knock-out session after another. The sort you might want to record for posterity … so on occasion, we have. When I watch the footage back, I am always amused – and rather impressed – by the assorted surfaces we manage to utilise.

Tonight, we end up on the new island unit in the kitchen, possibly the most uncomfortable material in the flat – no, Europe – but Luke likes it. Probably so he can give me a knowing smile whenever Adele is using it to assemble one of her authentic ethnic dishes, as if to say, *We both know it's not just cumin seeds that have been pummelled up there* … It's good. Really good … and when it's over, we stay sprawled on the granite, the endorphins that are pelting round our bodies easing the pain in Luke's spine and my cruciate ligaments. That's when I look across at him – his unkempt hair in an (entirely unintentionally) sexy mess – and at that very moment I think about what a nice addition he is to my life right now.

Then I look over to the fridge and stare at the photograph stuck to the refrigerator of Adele and James grinning manically as they cradle an orphaned baby orang-utan in the Bornean rainforest. It reminds me that I must must *must* remember to remove her stone-coloured Max Mara tank top from its dry-cleaning cellophane, unpin the yellow ticket from the care label and replace it in her wardrobe. Ditto her LnA white V-neck tee. And grey Equipment shirt. (Adele's closet is a haven of high-quality basics that I like to borrow – without asking – on a regular basis.) I also need to sweep up the fag butts on the patio, buy some Pantene shampoo and conditioner to put in the shower so she doesn't think I've been caning her Aveda Colour Conserve, and then I need t—

'Vivian?'

'Mmmm?' I twist to face Luke. '*Christ!*' His eyes are one centimetre away from mine. 'You gave me a shock.'

'Sorry.' He pulls back a little awkwardly. 'I was figuring out whether I should talk to you about something. Something quite … *serious*.'

'*Serious?* Like what? You've acquired an STD …'

'Ha! No, nothing like that.'

'You've got a wife back home in Australia and she drives a "yoot"…' I smile.

'I don't.'

'You've been to prison?'

'Would that be a turn-on?'

'Possibly, if it was an act of selflessness that got you sent down – like Wentworth Miller in *Prison Break.* But if it was manslaught—'

He interrupts me. 'What are your feelings about reproduction?'

'Reprod …' I tail off.

'… uction. Reproduction.' He visibly relaxes as he says the word a second time and stares directly at me.

I tense and look away. 'The heavy wooden French furniture, you mean?'

'Not that, Vivian. *Human reproduction*, as in the creation of another being. It's something that I've been meaning to get your thoughts on for a while,' he says, as if he were casually requesting my opinion on which actor has been the most convincing James Bond. 'Well, not a while as in ages and *ages*, we've only been together for a year so it would be pretty scary if I had been thinking about it for *too* long. Don't panic, I'm not some sort of psycho-sperminator who's simply been biding his time for the right moment to impregnate you.' *Definitely not Pierce Brosnan – too self-conscious. Or Timothy Dalton – too self-righteous.* 'And even though I said it was a "serious" subject, it doesn't mean I "seriously" want us to think about doing it right *now*, but it would be good to know your feelings about the subject, generally.' *I know this is controversial but I wasn't mad about Sean Connery – too hairy, and I can't even remember the name of the actor in* On Her Majesty's Secret Service. *George someone?* 'I can tell you're a bit surprised, but I've surprised myself by even wanting to approach the whole issue. I certainly didn't think I'd be asking you about it tonight, but …' *Lazenby! George Lazenby, that was it. As for Daniel Craig – way too shaggable. Distractingly so, it's impossible to concentrate on the plot.* '… sometimes it's hard to plan when you're going to talk about the things in life that need the most planning, and you don't get something that needs more planning than a … *baby.*'

ROGER MOORE! There's your answer. He was the best 007. Yes, he was cheesy, but I like cheese. (The sentiment not the dairy product.) Plus, he made my favourite movie of the entire franchise …

Luke shakes his head at me. 'Aren't you going to say anything?'

'*Moonraker.*'

CHAPTER THREE

'Eh? Moon-*what*?'

Luke is confused. I go into the lounge and stand in the nude for a few seconds staring aimlessly round the room, before grabbing his grey hooded top and putting it on. It's long enough to reach past my mid-thigh but I still feel weirdly *bare*, so I find my knickers and put them on too. When I return to the kitchen Luke is aimlessly opening and shutting cupboard doors.

He stops when he sees me and smiles, tentatively. 'I'm guessing by that reaction you would have preferred it if I was actually diseased, hitched or an ex-con. I've caught you unawares, haven't I? Maybe it would have been best to wait.'

'Wait?'

'Yeah, *wait*.'

Or rather … weight. Because that's what you *actually* gain, isn't it? As well as a child, I mean, you gain weight during the storing and development of the foetus. Even if you have the dollars to pay an illegitimate Miami surgeon to perform one of those sneaky Caesareans where Junior gets whipped out six weeks early to avoid Mom piling on the last trimester of bulk, for the other six and a half months hormones will send your taste buds loony tunes. Some women are lucky. They get savoury cravings along the lines of pickled onions or gherkins. (At least over-consumption can have a laxative effect.) Some not so, and spend the entire gestational period with their head in a catering-sized pot of peanut butter. Or maybe even that special variety – based on Satan's own recipe – which comes with swirls of milk chocolate spread woven through it. After the expulsion of the fully formed anthropoid, the only way they are going to 'ping' back to their pre-baby size is to surround themselves with a crack team of nutritionists and exercise specialists like the top models do. Miranda Kerr's were *fucking* efficient. When she stalked down the catwalk at Paris Fashion Week for Balenciaga eight weeks after giving birth, she didn't even look as if she'd had a bowl of porridge, let alone a son.

But obviously I don't say any of this to Luke. He wouldn't understand what I was saying. Nor would I want him to try. Because then he may try to understand something else. *Me.* I clear my throat to buy myself some time to think. I am baffled as to why he would have even thought to approach this subject. At some point, I must have started behaving in a way that has triggered him to start seeing 'us' in a way that was not intended. This unnerves me, because none of the other 'Men I've Been With' have misread the signals. I am angry with myself. So, obviously, I channel the anger towards him.

'Are you completely fucking un*hinged*, Luke?'

He doesn't reply to my question. He shakes his head at me and stomps into the lounge. I follow him in and watch as he puts on his boxers inside-out, yanks on his jeans and buttons them up incorrectly, then puts on his T-shirt back to front.

'And you reckon you could handle a nappy?' I taunt.

'Forget I even mentioned it, Vivian. We need to clean up. I'll turn the sofa back round and you do the cushions. You'd better get a cloth too. There's Dr Pepper all over the carpet,' he mutters.

'Don't sulk, Luke. You can't just blurt out that you want to get me knocked up—'

'*Knocked up?* Nice choice of words.'

'Whatever you want to call it … and then go off into a strop when I don't immediately suggest we start stocking up on sterilisation equipment.'

'That wasn't what I was saying. You weren't listening properly. It was only meant to be a discussion *about the subject.*' He pushes the couch back on its legs and turns round. His face is fully crumpled. 'Jesus, Vivian. You can be such a …'

'… witch. We've already established that.' I make a concerted effort to soften my voice. 'Okay, I'm sorry, go from the beginning. What made you start thinking about all this?'

'I suppose it was because your birthday is coming up.'

'My birthday? Well, it was really sweet of you to consider the gift of life as a present option but vouchers for Space NK are fine … then I can get some decent eye cream. Adele doesn't keep hers in the bathroom any more – so selfish, how am I meant to stand defiant in the war against puffiness and dark circles on my rubbish wages?' I force a laugh, but Luke's face remains crumpled. 'Sorry, sorry, *sorry* … again. Go on, *explain*. I'm listening.'

He sits down on the sofa and sighs. 'I suppose I've been thinking about you turning thirty-five.' He shrugs. 'If you wanted to have kids, then I figured now would be the time you would be starting to examine what's involved. Clearly, you have a very thorough understanding of the initial phase …' He manages a small smile. 'But the rest of it can be more complicated, especially as you get older.'

'Older?' The word judders through me. 'Cheers, Luke. That's the second time today someone has brought up my advancing years. Roger was going on at me earlier for not having a pension plan. I had no idea that come Saturday I am an official shambles if I haven't got the blue print for the rest of my time on earth signed off.'

'I'm not saying that at all,' he replies plainly. 'I was thinking realistically. The fact is it *does* get more difficult and dangerous to have babies after thirty-five. It's basic biology.'

'That's bollocks. Jennifer Lopez didn't have hers until she was thirty-nine. *Twins*.'

'They were probably IVF.'

'Actually, they weren't. Going down the in vitro route would have been entirely against J Lo's strict beliefs. She's publicly said as much. Fortunately for her, though, she didn't have any ethical guidelines in place about accepting a whopping six-figure fee for supplying pictures of the tots to *People* magazine … ha!'

But this information does not throw Luke off track. He simply picks up where he left off.

'Actually, irrespective of your current age, I sort of assumed you might have already thought about the whole parenting thing. Without getting too deep, it's a pretty common thing for people who have difficult relationships with their own parents to want to create a more secure *unit* themselves.' He pauses. 'What with you not having that much contact with your mum, obv—'

'I do have contact with her.'

'I know, but not *that* much.'

'She's busy with the church and her catalogues and … stuff,' I retort. 'It doesn't mean she doesn't care about me or vice versa.'

'Vivian, I make sure I *see* mine three or four times a week and she lives in another continent.'

'That's different, you Skype her. I'm not going to go to all the hassle of utilising visual communication technology to contact my mother when she lives the other side of Milton Keynes.'

'And you *never* see your brother or sister.'

'Because we don't get on. Oh, and believe you me, if you'd seen any of my sister's children when they were babies, you wouldn't want to risk me having one. I've seen more attractive beasts carved into the stone of French cathedrals. I might carry the same genes.'

Luke laughs and I think he is about to drop the subject. But he doesn't.

'Okay, but there's the issue of your father.'

'What issue? There is no issue. I've told you he's not around.'

'And that's where the discussion always ends. Why?'

I hold my hand up. My face feels hot and my neck is itching. 'Right, the cod psychology stops here, Luke. We don't need to talk about family stuff. It's boring … and pointless.'

'Not when they are the people who have shaped you.'

'I *shaped* me!' I snap. It's definitely time to re-route this conversation. I flop down onto the sofa, put my head on Luke's shoulder and change tack. 'Look, I know I'm handling this chat quite badly, but you have to admit it was a bit of a curveball. Let's face it, we're hardly in a practical position to think about a, er…'

'Baby,' he says, putting his arm around me. 'A *baby*. You won't get pregnant by saying it.'

I smile, equally pleased he has been drawn away from the subject of my family and is loosening up. 'Whatever you want to call it. How could we consider having *one of those* when we've only been seeing each other a year?'

'I agree,' he says simply. 'It would be ridiculous, which was why I was only *approaching* the issue. It was you who went off on a tangent. Kids would obviously be some way down the road …' *Not if I'm driving!* '… after we've lived together for a while.'

I feel uncomfortable again; as if I'm lying on the island unit, my joints pressed into the marble. 'Where would we do that?'

'Why not here?'

I burst out laughing. 'Luke, hell would have to freeze over before Adele let you do that. In fact, hell would have to freeze over and then maybe a few years later sometime after an entire winter theme park with snowboarding facilities and an ice hotel had been built on top then maybe she would consider a trial period … as long as you didn't bring your records, music equipment *or cables*.'

He tilts my head up towards him. 'We could always get our own place – just you and me. It wouldn't be as big as this place but—'

'Monday would find downsizing hard,' I interject quickly. 'It wouldn't be fair on Warren, either.'

'Since when have you cared about Wozza? You called him "tragic" last week.'

'He is. But he's a tragedy who has done you a lot of favours recently. If you moved out he'd really struggle to fill your room. I doubt he'd get too many responses from an advert on Gumtree: *AVAILABLE! Tomb-like space in dark basement flat on very rough road in Shepherds Bush (usually cordoned off by police) – must be okay with dark Berlin techno and basic communication with other tenant. General knowledge of hydroponics and GCSE chemistry Grade C or above a plus…*' I lean up and kiss Luke's cheek. 'You can laugh now. Go on, I know you want to.'

He doesn't. Which makes me feel odd, because that's why I thought both of us were here – *to have a laugh* – and now Luke isn't laughing. But what is even odder is that I'm sorry that *I* am the reason he's not. I genuinely am. More than I thought I would be.

CHAPTER FOUR

A full English breakfast is not something I would ever *choose* to make. There are too many individual components. Personally, I think that three is a *more* than sufficient number of items for *any* dish. But the following morning, I feel I ought to get up at the same ridiculous time Luke always has to (on week days) and do something *he* would consider a nice gesture. So I pop a Nurofen and cook.

Things appear to be fine between us. We potter about the kitchen bantering with each other as normal. He in his favourite T-shirt, the one with a picture of a large cartoon fish wearing a pair of headphones underneath the words, *Cod is a DJ*. Me wearing his boxer shorts and sweatshirt. As he grabs his car keys from the fishbowl, I attempt to pull him back in the flat by his rucksack.

'Stay for a bit longer,' I tell him. 'Just for a few minutes … I'll make it worth your while.'

'Really? How would you go about doing that?' He turns round and prises my fingers from his bag. 'Actually, don't answer that. I've got to pick up Kevvo en route and I'd prefer to do that without a hard-on. I mean, he is a fellow Aussie and, admittedly, we have got a lot closer recently, but …'

I laugh. 'You always *used* to stay when I asked you.'

'That was an isolated period of a few weeks, before I got a job. I can't be late … it's not fair on the others. When we *all* put in the effort we get more done.'

I roll my eyes at him and push him out into the corridor. 'Tsk, no one ever got anywhere by having a strong work ethic and a dedicated sense of teamwork, Luke. You should remember that.'

Smiling, he rolls his eyes back at me, then backs off down towards the front door. 'Play a blinder at your audition. Shall I come round later?'

'Nah, Adele will be back. I ought to spend the evening with her and feign interest in her endless camcorder footage of imposing mountainous terrain.'

'Well, look after yourself and don't get into any more fights.' He bends down to stroke Monday who has wandered out into the hallway and is doing that feline slalom thing; twisting in and out of Luke's legs. 'Make sure you have a productive day, little mate,' laughs Luke. But when he stands up his expression is serious.

I feel that marble surface digging into my joints again. 'What's the matter?'

'About last night …'

'Last night?'

'Yeah, last night. I've been thinking … about what happened.'

'What about it?'

'I think you should know something. Something very important—'

'Which is?' My voice goes up a nervous octave as I interrupt him.

Luke repositions his rucksack, but doesn't stop staring at me; his mouth is fixed in a sombre straight line. I swallow hard. I really can't be doing with another heavy conversation.

'I think I … well, I've got a bad feeling about something.'

'A bad feeling about *what*, Luke?'

He pauses, then suddenly, grins. 'I *may* have thrown away that condom in a cutlery drawer … not the bin. That new kitchen set-up is a total mind-fuck.'

I burst out laughing.

I am still laughing as I dispose of the offending article in the *actual* waste unit … along with the breakfast leftovers. I squirt these remains with washing-up liquid and then finish my necessary chores throughout the flat. In the background, I can hear an American actress being interviewed on some morning TV show, talking openly about how she doesn't let Hollywood's obsession with size double zero concern her – yeah, right, *treadmill face!* Then I do my *Barry's Boot Camp* DVD and collapse on the sofa. Monday is already on there enjoying a snooze, clearly not having had enough quality shut-eye during the twenty odd hours he slept yesterday. I lie down next to him and scroll through a load of programmes I've stored for viewing. I plump for the last series of *90210.* The opening scene on the beach in the first episode is entirely stolen by AnnaLynne McCord's ribcage. It is so prominent I wonder if it has hired its own publicist during the down time between seasons. My mobile bleeps. I don't recognise the number.

'Hello?'

'Vivian Ward? Barb Silver …' She sounds a bit like Streisand. 'Publicist. I represent Maximilian Fry. I got your number from the manager at Burn's. I'm assuming you've seen what's happened?'

'Er, no.' I try to sound slightly irritated, as though getting calls from tough-talking industry players is a regular part of my daily routine.

'You haven't been online yet this morning?' she asks, aghast. 'Freakin' hell, it's half past nine! *Silver's Golden Rule Number Twenty-six: Get down with your day before the day gets you down …*'

I turn down the volume on the television.

'So listen, kiddo,' she continues, 'Clint Parks has conjured up a load of bull in his column about what happened last night … that Maxy got mad and lashed out like a crazy person.'

'Which *is* what happened.'

'Ha! Details, details. Anyway, there's no doubt Parks will try to eek the most he can out of this non-story so he'll probably come waving his grubby chequebook at you. You're a sensible girl, though … am I right?'

No, not really, but selling a story to the press about a celebrity who had come into Burn's would immediately result in me getting the sack. In fact, once word had travelled no private members' club would ever employ me again. I could even end up employed by a *chain* of 'lifestyle' bars – collecting empty pint glasses and clearing up piles of pistachio shells as privately educated ex-school boys grapple each other whilst singing faintly racist/homophobic/misogynistic songs in front of giant screens beaming live sport. *Shudder*.

'You don't have to worry about me talking to anyone. It's not my style, Ms Silver,' I say toadily. 'I know the score with these situations. Besides, I *also* do some acting myself.'

'That's neat,' she replies. In the way that Rafael Nadal might react to someone who enjoys the odd gentle knock-about during the summer when the weather permits telling him they 'also' play tennis.

'And besides, Clint wouldn't put me in an awkward position. We're mates.'

'Mates?' Her voice becomes thicker. 'You're close?'

'Yeah, kind of. He's always looked out for me. We met years ago when I was working as a wait—'

Barb interrupts. 'Listen, I've had an idea. Why don't you come and see Maxy at his place? I was going to apologise on his behalf but it's occurred to me that you deserve a *direct* apology from the man himself. He actually suggested this to me earlier. I guess it's a Buddhist thing … they dig all that sackcloth and ashes shizzle.'

'I think that's the Catholics.'

'Ha! I bet it is. Makes more sense … attention-seeking as usual,' she cackles. 'Meet me outside The Lansdowne public house in Primrose Hill at two p.m. Don't be late.' She hangs up without waiting for my answer.

One hundred and fifteen minutes later, I have exfoliated so rigorously that my entire upper epidermis is probably sitting in the drain, and have applied a dense layer of St Tropez Whipped Bronzing Mousse all over my face and body. My tan is developing nicely. I'd say currently somewhere between Natural Cedar and Rich Teak on a generic DIY wood stain colour chart. After blow-drying my hair to a wavy mess, I switch on my special ghd straighteners with ultra-hot ceramic blades (not available over the counter – I bought them from a session stylist on an advertisement shoot) and the real work begins; parching each strand of any natural moisture or oils to get it poker straight. I'm also pleased with my make-up (all by MAC except Yves St Laurent Volume Effect mascara and Touche Eclat under-eye concealer), which I have applied then reapplied with Shu Uemura brushes in twenty-minute stages to achieve a natural yet hermetically sealed finish. Outfit-wise I have gone for a pair of my new grey skinny-leg trousers from ASOS and a brand-new Stella McCartney putty-coloured silky racer-back vest that I found in Adele's cupboard. It's baggy on me but that doesn't matter because the Stella *look* is all about the billowing top, isn't it? I also 'borrow' some barely worn flat gold sandals. Heels would look as if I had made too much effort. The last thing I want Maximilian to think is that I am some wide-eyed fan who is in any way overawed by the situation. To make absolutely sure of this I spend fifteen minutes in front of the mirror planning a nonplussed greeting. Next, some research. I go into the lounge to find Luke's laptop.

Yes, I am aware that I am probably the last inhabitant in the developed world who does not own a computer themselves, but a long time ago my chunky Hewlett Packard was stolen as I travelled up the escalators at Oxford Circus tube station. Obviously, it wasn't insured. Who takes out insurance on *anything* in their twenties? Actually, I haven't got anything insured now, but anyway … I didn't replace it. It was the right thing to do. I'd developed a problem with the internet. My days had become consumed by celebrity images, the hours nibbled at by Google Alerts, but I wanted to digest *more*. This over-consumption hit a high in the mid to late noughties … as it did with a *lot* of women. I dread to think how many times that decade – as a nation – we double clicked on 'Nicole Richie' to observe her head getting comparatively more enormous until it was perched on top of her delicate body like a Scotch egg on a cocktail stick. So, now I have a rule. I'm only allowed to use other people's computers. Limited access is healthier. More people should give it a go.

I flip open Luke's laptop, have a quick squizz at the 'New In' section on ASOS and then I do a search to find Maximilian's account on Twitter, but I only find fake ones. Hardly a surprise, Maximilian Fry falls into the Jude Law/Robert Pattinson camp of scandal-embroiled/fiercely private actors who would shun any sort of social media. So, I log on the Internet Movie Database for some career statistics.

The son of glamorous diva Violet Carrington and millionaire playboy Harvey Fry, Maximilian Kavanagh Fry's big break into movies came whilst he was studying at the illustrious Sturrow School for Boys, when he beat hundreds of young actors to play the young D. H. Lawrence in A Son and a Lover, *by British director Charley Naylor. His acclaimed performance led to a place on the now iconic*

Vanity Fair *gatefold cover of nude teen actors – 'Naked Ambition' – and a 17-million-dollar deal to star in the blockbusting trilogy based on the fantasy novel* The Orc's Progress *by Irish writer Donal O'Hare. Fry then honed his skills in a number of small independent films including anti-war docu-drama* Victim X, *which caused controversy in the US. But he was soon propelled back into the spotlight as special agent Jack Chase in* The Simple Truth – *a low-budget action thriller that became a mega box-office hit on both sides of the Atlantic. The role secured him his first BAFTA Award and an Oscar nomination. Previously engaged to the American model Zoe Dano, Fry is currently single.*

This is typical. The IMDB always concentrates on the career of the star as opposed to their private lives. '*Previously engaged to the American model Zoe Dano, Fry is currently single*' was the succinct and non sue-able way of saying; '*After years of persistent speculation that Maximilian's fiancée Zoe Dano – labelled Zoe Can't Say (Da) No by British tabloids – was sleeping with half the iTunes download chart she finally left Fry after an affair with Rick Piper, soap dodging guitarist from Seattle rock band Squalor, who were touring the UK at the time. Devastated, Maximilian Fry turned to drink and drugs. Following an arrest for disorderly conduct and an incoherent acceptance speech at the BAFTAs, he checked into a Swiss rehabilitation centre. Zoe Dano joined Squalor on their world tour where she appeared on stage with the band performing mercilessly weak back-up vocals and was booed by fans ...*'.

Clearly, she's a *total* bitch, but it has to be said – I Google image her – she does have to-die-for hair. Thick, long, defined, strong, glossy locks. I'd go as far as calling them *tresses*. According to *Glamour* magazine, the volume isn't boosted with any extensions, either. The popular girls at school all had 'tresses'. I can picture their blonde ponytails swinging like gold pendulums as they skipped down the corridor giggling. Swish, swish, *swish.* I focused on the longest ponytail – always in the centre of the coven – the one that belonged to Kate Summers … and kept a safe distance behind.

CHAPTER FIVE

At 1.50 p.m., I am sat on a wooden bench outside The Lansdowne having a single vodka on the rocks and sucking on Smints. At the table next to me, a couple are enjoying a relaxed alfresco pub lunch. I can smell pork belly. Did you know, Cameron Diaz stopped eating pig when she read an article that swine have a mental capacity similar to a three-year-old child, and can master very basic maths?

Since I have been here only two cars have gone past: a retro convertible of some sort and a vintage Jaguar. There is no noise bar the gentle burr of conversation and laughter emanating from the pub. This is typical Primrose Hill. It came as no surprise when Barb told me that Maximilian lived here. If a bomb was dropped on this villagey part of North London it would decimate the British film-making community. Richard Curtis would literally have no one left to star in his heart-warming ensemble pieces except possibly Emma Thompson, who no doubt would survive the explosion thanks to her British fighting spirit and thick helmet of hair. Bayswater – where Adele and I live – is hardly slumming it, but Primrose Hill has an air of effortless sophistication and moneyed calm. Luvvies *love* it.

The couple next to me finish their main courses and ask

for a dessert menu. It looks extensive … and gooey. I am pulling a pack of cigarettes out of my bag when a black people carrier draws up on the pavement. The electric window whirs open and I immediately recognise Barb Silver in the back seat wearing her bug-eyed sunglasses and trademark vampiric blood-red lipstick. The PR mogul looks no different to how she did back when she was directing movies. When I was at drama school, I remember an interview with her in an industry magazine where she said, *Most freakin' film stars aren't actors, they're simply professional narcissists…* She is gripping an iPad and shouting into a BlackBerry.

'Problems? Maxy's problems are *over*, for sure. You know you can trust me, JP, we've got history. I wouldn't be telling you the kid was ready if he wasn't.' She pauses briefly. 'He's *not* a risk. Last night, last *shmite*! Minor hiccup, and you know it. He's good to go. End of.' But clearly it isn't because then she adds, 'Look elsewhere and you'll regret it, big time – you'll kill the franchise. Maxy *is* Jack Chase. Wait there …' She pauses again, peers out of the window over the top of her sunglasses and squints at me. Her forehead doesn't move. 'Vivian?' I nod. 'Barb Silver. Get in the car, kiddo, and don't you dare fire up that freakin' death stick.' She points at my packet of Marlboro Lights. 'I haven't spent forty thousand dollars on surgery to smell like a goddamn ashtray.' She shuffles along the seat and gets back to her telephone conversation. 'Don't disappoint me, JP. Let's nail this today.'

She hangs up as I get in the people carrier. Safe to say it is far more comfortable than Luke's car, which is always knee deep in club flyers, plastic bottles and discarded snack packaging. This vehicle has a cream leather and walnut finish, pleasantly squidgy seats with television monitors on the back of each headrest and a selection of newspapers and film magazines fanned out on the back shelf. Actually, it's far more comfy than Luke's actual flat. As soon as I am sat, Barb hands me *News Today* open at *Clint's Big Column*. STIR CRAZY FRY HITS ROOF AND DEFENCELESS WAITRESS! screams the headline.

'That Parks is a cretin,' she says. 'He should get his facts straight.'

'He's not a cretin, but yeah, he should get his facts straight,' I tell her. 'Clint knows *full* well I am a hostess, not a waitress. There's a big difference between the two. The waitress has to take the drink order, then the food one, deliver both to the table, check what condiments are required, continue to monitor the customer requirements throughout their meal, clear away the crockery, make coffee, organise the bill and prepare the table for the next set of diners. The hostess just watches.' I laugh.

Barb snatches back the paper. 'I wasn't referring to your job title. I meant the way he's making out my Maxy is madder than a box of frogs. We really don't need this kind of bull at the moment.'

'I thought any publicity was good publicity.'

'Not these days, kiddo. The money guys are nervous about expensive over-runs and rescheduling. In the old days, a bit of chaos was part of the fun. When I worked on set I didn't care what my leading man was doing – usually *me,* ha! – as long as he delivered. Everyone is so precious now. Which reminds me, you need to sign this before you see Maxy. It's a confidentiality agreement … regulation procedure with the big stars. But I guess you'd know that,' she smirks, 'what with you being *in the industry* yourself.'

I cringe as she pulls out a document and a gold fountain pen from her red Hermès Birkin bag. As I'm signing, her BlackBerry buzzes and she checks the caller ID. I glance at it too. It says 'Achilles'.

'Woah, someone's keen.' She cackles satisfactorily but then zaps the call with a scarlet fingernail. 'I'll make him sweat, though. Some model I met last night,' she explains. 'I've got a good feeling about this one.'

'Boyfriend material?'

'Sheesh, no! I've got handbags older than him. The prognosis for relationship age gaps is never good in the entertainment industry … no matter how much the more mature party spends on cosmetic surgery. I mean look at Demi Moore. She looked *younger* than Ashton Kutcher by the time they hit their fifth wedding anniversary, but he still celebrated it in a Vegas hot tub with someone other than his wife.' She cackles harder. 'I meant I've got a positive hunch about the kid's career.'

'Is he an actor too, then?'

"Course he is, *all* models are actors. At least, they all *think* they could be. Trust me, if I had a dollar for every clothes horse I've screwed that wants to play a misunderstood junkie in some leftfield art-house movie opposite Chloe Sevigny I'd be a lot richer than I already am.' She removes her shades and raises her eyebrows at me. Well, judging by the expression in her eyes I assume that's what her brows would be doing if the surrounding area wasn't paralysed with Botox. 'Take us round the back, sugar …' She taps the driver on his left shoulder. 'There are paps outside the front gate.'

'But you think this one does have talent, Barb?' I ask.

'From what I've seen so far? I reckon he'd be hard pushed to show grief at a funeral. But you know what, sometimes they don't need any real ability for a crack at a screen career. Okay, so in shelf-life terms we're not talking canned goods, but they can make a few dollars. Way more, if they *really* luck out. Enter stage left, Channing Tatum!'

'Did Maximilian ever model?'

'No goddamn way … Besides, he's more than an actor.' Her voice becomes serious. 'He's an *artist*. *What* he does is *who* he is.'

She inserts a piece of gum into her mouth and as she breaks it in we drive down a road lined with stucco-fronted five-storey white houses, then turn down a back street behind them and stop outside a wide iron gate. The driver jumps out of the car, enters a code into a security box and the gate swings open to reveal a decked garden full of exotic-looking flowers and a big lily-covered pond with its own fountain. Next to the pond is a giant bronze Buddha.

'Just what this house needs,' I deadpan. 'A tranquil point of worship to help combat against the surrounding chaos and disorder of Primrose Hill.'

Barb smiles. 'I bought Maxy that statue. Personally, religion gives me the willies. I used to sneak out of Sunday School and go to the flicks. But hey, if it provides him with a little tranquillity then I'm not going to argue.' She turns to the driver. 'I'm going back to The Dorchester in a couple of hours, so you might as well wait here.' He nods and doffs his cap at her. 'Payton, *sugar*, how many times do I have to tell you not to do that? I'm not the Duchess of goddamn Cornwall. Chill!' She beckons to me. 'Come with me, kiddo …'

I follow Barb as she stalks up a decked pathway, round the pond, across a flagstone patio and into the house through a set of French windows at the side. She glances at me over her shoulder.

'So, this is my Maxy's place …'

CHAPTER SIX

I immediately notice two things about 'Maxy's place'. Firstly, it looks like something out of the hardback book on hip hotels that Adele bought for the upstairs neighbours last Christmas; full of expensive design details like marble flooring, leather padded walls, giant neon crystal chandeliers and the odd piece of slightly risqué art – including a semi-nude photograph in the hallway of Zoe Dano, only her ridiculously long, lustrous, unassisted hair retaining her modesty. Secondly, it is spotless. Not in a quick-whip-round-with-some-antibacterial-spray-on-a-wet-cloth kind of way but clinically clean, like a hospital operating theatre. Every surface is bare and all the walls are painted white. As Barb guides me down the hallway into an immaculate kitchen with pristine stainless-steel worktops I get the impression that Maximilian Fry clearly feels that the home shouldn't necessarily be where the heart *is* but more somewhere you could potentially transplant one.

'Right,' says Barb. 'You stay here, kiddo. I'll go and find him.'

She leaves the room, her heels clip-clopping across the marble. I walk over to the kitchen window and look out onto the garden. From this angle I can see an ivy gazebo sheltering a raised multicoloured platform where there is another Buddha on a podium. It is scattered with flower petals. That's probably a meditation area. This thought makes me squirm a bit. There's something rather embarrassing about celebrities who are seeking a higher meaning – especially those who wear a wristband to prove it. Luke was right. *What a pretentious wanker.*

'Yeah, yeah, I know … I'm a pretentious wanker.'

I spin round. Standing in the doorway of the kitchen wearing a pair of worn grey tracksuit bottoms with a T-shirt tucked in the pocket and a white towel draped round his neck is … Maximilian Fry. Now, I had always thought he had shown potential – even as a 'wolf-boy' in *The Orc's Progress* and badly wounded in *Victim X* – way before *everyone* fancied him as Jack Chase in *The Simple Truth.* But nothing could have prepared me for this … the *live* version. Like all actors he is smaller than he looks on film, probably no more than five foot ten-ish, but he is a lot broader and his features are much more intense. His eyes are a velvety brown. His cheekbones are sharper, his jawline is squarer and the jagged scar that runs down his right cheek is much deeper, giving his face a kind of brooding darkness. He has obviously just finished some sort of exercise session because his body is covered in a thin sheen of perspiration, making him look sort of … not simply sweaty, more *basted.* My eyes fall to his torso. Parts of it are so defined that I never even knew were an official muscle group. I force myself to jump past the pelvic area and scan down to his feet. Like the rest of him they are immaculately groomed – the nails on each toe are buffed and shaped to perfection, a world away from the pterodactyl-like claws that most men tended to reveal at the beginning of every summer. A lemony, woody scent fills the space between us. I have a feeling it's Issey Miyake. The visual and nasal stimulus is so intense that I totally forget to do my (heavily rehearsed) casual greeting, cowering as if I am expecting him to hit me again. Instead, I find myself giving him a wave as if I'm setting off on a cruise. He gives me a confused but half-hearted wave back as though he is unsure as to *why* I am departing these shores, but isn't that fussed if I *do* go.

'A pretentious wanker?' I repeat.

'Well, that's what the press makes me out to be, isn't it?' His voice is posher than I was expecting, but it isn't luvvie-ish. It's got a kind of lazy lilt to it.

'But that doesn't mean *everyone* accepts what they say.'

'Most people do.'

'Why do you think that is?'

'It's easier to take the piss out of someone than to try to understand them. Any form of spirituality is only wanting to be at peace with yourself and the world around you, but it's hard to explain that without sounding even more of a …' He drifts off, as if he can't be bothered.

'Why talk about it, then?'

'I wish I hadn't, but I had to give them something. They need those sorts of details to manufacture the image of … "*the*" Maximilian Fry.'

I pull a face at him. 'Did you just place an italic 'the' before your name and imaginary parentheses around it?'

'Not purposefully,' he replies. 'I'm severely dyslexic – so that all sounds rather complex.'

I realise the lilt in Maximilian's voice is not laziness, it's guardedness mixed with arrogance … plus a tinge of self-persecution. Or possibly self-righteousness. Definitely self-indulgence.

'Give them something else, then,' I tell him. 'Lose the spiritual stuff and find another party piece.'

He peers at me.

'You know, a prop, a talking point, a gimmick …' I explain. 'What about a pig? George Clooney used to bang on about his pot-bellied one the whole time and everyone always says what a regular dude he is. Make sure you opt for traditional swine like him, though, those tiny micro ones are way too 2010 and dubiously bred. You wouldn't want animal rights groups on your back.'

Now, he yawns. We stand in silence, and I really mean *silence*. It feels weird, being in London and hearing no sound whatsoever. Actually … what's *that?* I hear a very faint humming noise. Possibly the buzz of anxiety from a neighbour running low on Prosecco or Jo Malone candles. Then I realise it is coming from Maximilian's gigantic steel fridge.

'Well,' I say. 'This is, er, … *fun*.'

He drains his bottle of water, then crunches the plastic container into a ball. 'It wasn't my idea, it was Barb's,' he replies, flatly. Irritability now edging past the guardedness and arrogance.

'Charming.'

'But obviously, I am glad you're here.'

'Oh, *clearly* you are. Although, I have to say you were a *lot* more convincing as a wild dog human hybrid in *The Orc's Progress* than you are now as the welcoming host in your own home.'

He gives me the faintest hint of a smile. 'I would say *touché* but then the "pretentious wanker" badge would be a done deal, wouldn't it?' He pauses and throws the crumpled bottle of water in the direction of a steel column by the door that leads out onto the terrace. Annoyingly it sails over my head and lands perfectly in the slot at the top. 'Look, I'm not great at entertaining, never have been. Not a very attractive trait, I know …'

It is impossible to put into words how attractive he looks as he says this. His sudden body movement has caused beads of sweat to slide down between his pectorals and then *one, two, three, four …* they trickle over his *eight-pack* as if they were driving over speed bumps, and consequently disappear under the low-slung waistband of his tracksuit. But just as a new batch of droplets are about to begin their journey, he ruins the show by yanking out the T-shirt from his pocket and putting it on. I force myself to speak.

'Don't worry, you're doing okay. I wasn't expecting to arrive and find you setting up for a game of Twister. But I suppose if I was being *really* picky, you could have said "hello".'

He rubs his head with his towel and I notice a small 'Z' tattoo on the inside of his wrist. I'm surprised he didn't have it lasered as soon as he found out Zoe had cheated on him.

'Didn't I even do that? Fuck … sorry. Let me get you some tea or something.'

'What's the "something"?'

He goes over to the fridge – I can almost *taste* the trail of Issey Miyake he leaves in his wake – and opens the door. Every shelf is packed with row after row of Fiji water, each bottle placed perfectly in line with the label turned out.

'Is that the only choice for "something"? I ask.

'Yes, this would be the "something".'

'Well, you've redeemed yourself a little bit in the pretentious wanker stakes. I was fearing coconut water.'

He starts opening cupboards randomly, briefly reminding me of Luke in Adele's kitchen.

'Bet I lose points for not knowing where the glasses are kept, though … the housekeeper usually leaves some out.'

'I'm fine with the bottle,' I tell him, although I am intrigued to see what he keeps in those cupboards; whey powder, protein bars, supplements … no *real* food. Interesting.

'Who the fuck drinks coconut water, anyway?' asks Maximilian.

'Celebrities. It's the showbiz refreshment of choice … especially post work-out. You must know that? Everyday there's a picture on the TMZ website of some ambitious personality vacuum leaving a West Hollywood studio gripping on to a yoga mat and a carton of the stuff.'

He shrugs. 'I've never used the internet.'

'You *what*?' I try to imagine the self-control and the complete indifference to modern culture that must require. It is mind blowing. 'Aren't you remotely curious?'

'No. Barb does my official site, but I've never looked

at it. Occasionally, I look at a computer screen when my financial advisor is here … but I don't even have an email address.'

'And you've never Googled yourself?'

'Why would I need to do that?' His eyes focus directly on mine for the first time. 'I've got a pretty good idca of who I am.'

I'm still considering how to reply to this when Barb clip-clops in. She winks at me, then nudges her client in the stomach and pretends she has hurt her knuckle on his rock-hard abdominals.

'That's what you call marketable goods, right, kiddo?' she gushes. 'Bet you've never seen anything like it.'

'Him,' mutters Maximilian. '*Him.*'

'Yeah, you, er… must have a really good team of trainers,' I say casually, in a bid not to sound as if I am agreeing too wholeheartedly. 'Or do you just have one *really* mean one?'

'I don't have *any*,' he says, his voice flattening again.

Barb's BlackBerry vibrates. She checks the caller ID and immediately answers it.

'Yeah, it's me. Shoot … uh huh. I'm listening.' She covers the phone with her hand and glances over at Maximilian. 'It's JP. I'm going to take this in the study and put him on speaker with Nicholas. FYI, Maxy, Vivian was telling me she also acts.'

As she leaves the room, I shake my head at him. 'When she says I "act", she doesn't mean I act in the way that *you* act.'

'What way would that be?' he asks, indicating to me to

sit down at the large glass table in the centre of the room. 'Acting is acting. Either you *are* or you're *not*.'

'I mean, I haven't hit *that* level … doing movies and stuff,' I tell him. 'I've appeared in lots of commercials. Have you ever been in an ad?'

'No,' he says emphatically. 'I don't *do* advertising.' He adds this in the same tone as Martha Stewart might insist she has never bought pancake mix. 'We're talking about you, though. What about television drama … done any of that?'

'Yeah, a fair bit.' I sit down in a Perspex dining chair. 'The best role I've had was the first one I landed after college: a prostitute in *Prime Suspect.* I featured prominently in the first two-hour episode but then I was garroted and dumped in a lock-up.'

'You got to work with Dame Helen Mirren?' comments Maximilian. 'Many actresses would kill to work alongside her …'

'… and more often than not *pretend* to have been killed too,' I laugh, but he only reciprocates with another tiny flicker of a smile. 'Have you ever died on screen? I mean, acted as if you were passing away, not been crap in the role.'

'I nearly died in *A Son and a Lover* of pneumonia.'

'Oh yeah, I remember. You were *skeletal* …'

All the papers reported on Maximilian's dramatic weight loss for the role, especially as he was still only a teenager. It seemed extreme then, but not so much now. Since then, actors such as Christian Bale, Matthew McConaughey, Michael Fassbender … they've all been allowed to damn nearly starve themselves to death to play a movie character. It's weird how actresses never get to go that far on screen. (They're expected to look skinnier in *real* life.) Even when supposedly suffering from malnutrition in *Les Mis*, Anne Hathaway merely looked as if she was on the Attack phase of the Dukan.

'How did you reach your target weight?' I ask casually. But specifically so.

Maximilian shrugs at me. 'Incredibly, I ate less and exercised more. It wasn't a big deal. I'll do whatever a role requires to convince an audience I am that character. I love what I do and get paid stupid amounts of money to do it. Ultimately, total dedication is what the crew who surround me and the audience who pay to come and see me deserve. It's no more or less fucking complicated than that.'

'Wow, that's a particularly *un*-pretentious and non-wankerish thing to say. Didn't you mean, *I believe in becoming one with my art*?'

He ignores my quip and sits down opposite me, his eyes focus on mine again. 'So, tell me, Vivian, how far would *you* go?'

'Erm ... oh, I er ... *well* ...' I look at my lap. 'To be honest, the sort of parts I audition for don't require *too* much application.'

'There's your answer, then.'

'Answer to what?' I ask, suddenly noticing a loose thread on the bottom of Adele's vest. Shit. I must have snagged it on something.

'Why you haven't hit "*that* level",' explains Maximilian. 'Decent casting directors can sense a lack of commitment.

They can smell it the moment you walk in the room. You should approach every part wanting to *feel* that person; give everything, do everything, *be everything that they are* … because that's what acting is. The ability to reach inside yourself and pull out *a* truth …'

He pauses. I glance up. He is staring at me. I stare back.

'But you won't be able to do that until you know *the* truth,' he continues, his eyes penetrating mine. 'Until you know *your* truth … who *you* really are, you can't pretend to be someone *else*.'

'O-*kay*. Thanks for the career advice. I'll bear that in m—'

He interrupts me. 'Oh, that wasn't just career advice, Vivian. That was advice for *life*.' He holds my gaze for a few moments longer, then his eyes dart to the side. 'Barb?'

I twist round to see her head cocked round the door. She is chewing her gum even more vigorously.

'Maxy, we need to have a quick pow-wow with Nicholas.' She beckons at him with a heavily jewelled hand and then beams at me with an overly generous smile, one that I haven't seen yet. 'Apologies, kiddo. We won't be long.'

As they leave she pulls the door behind them, but it swings back open.

'Okay, Maxy,' I overhear her say as they disappear down the corridor. 'I'm going to give you this straight. JP has bailed. He's looking to cast elsewhere for *Truth 2*.' She doesn't give him a chance to react. 'Am I surprised? Not really. Your train hasn't exactly been pulling into Good Press Central recently, but hey, I've never let you come off the tracks. You know I'll get you to your final destination.'

'Barb, lose the clunky metaphor. I've already told you, I'm not going t—'

She interrupts him. 'You'll do what's required, Maxy. You hear me?' Again, she doesn't give him time to reply. 'By the way, how did you get on with that Vivian?'

'Why?'

'She could be useful.'

Then a door slams and I can't catch any more.

I sit back in my chair. Useful? *Really?* I'm not usually. Most of what I do on a daily basis could easily be done by someone else. I like the idea of being considered useful, though. Definitely a step up from simply serving a purpose and a world away from being wholly surplus to anyone's requirement, something which I used to feel every day when I wasn't so …

CHAPTER SEVEN

... normal.

Obviously, now I am. Aren't I? But I was not a normal child. I had a sort of ... dark side. I wasn't born with it. One day the darkness descended and before I knew it, that's who I was: someone who preferred to hide away in the shadows. Nowhere was this more noticeable than in the framed photographs that decorated the corridor of my family's home. On the wall, you could see my football-fanatic brother scoring goals, celebrating with team mates and waving his club scarf at away games. My teen-model sister was pictured (professionally) frolicking in paddling pools or through sprinklers for leading homestore retailers or leaping off a diving board for travel brochures. There is no photographic record of me after I hit double figures. I avoided cameras.

Obviously, my parents were not oblivious to my downward spiral but they dealt with it in different ways. My father said nothing. My mother asked Jesus to help me. (As in the Son of God – our local GP was not an immigrant Mexican.) She encouraged me to pray as well ... up at the jagged crack in the ceiling of my bedroom, which according to her had been created by God with a thunder bolt to create a clear pathway of communication to Heaven. Clearly, all the crap that was stored in the loft kept getting in the way of my prayers, because my mood did not improve. So then – on advice from her church group – my mother screwed a full-length mirror to the wall, on the opposite side to the other one that was already there. They thought it may help if I could look at myself from a different perspective. But it only gave me a new angle from which to question myself. …. And now I could see *exactly* why Kate Summers thought she had all the answers.

After the second mirror was installed, no matter where I stood in my bedroom I was reflected, so being horizontal was key. I would get under the duvet on my bed and place my hands straight down my sides, in an attempt to make myself as invisible as possible. I used to lie there for hours and hours and hours; day and night, in exactly the same position. But one day – not long after finishing school for good – I woke up to find my hands placed across my chest, not down by my sides as they usually would be. It was as if I was about to be buried. My bed had become a coffin, my bedroom was a morgue. I could see myself lying there. *I still can.* I was dead. Yeah, I know, I know … I told you … *dark side!* Anyway, I left home that day. Ironically, the next time I saw any of my family again was actually at a funeral.

I hear voices coming from the corridor.

'You know as well as I do we've had worse freakin' bull to deal with than this,' says Barb. 'It won't take too much to get him back on top. Maxy isn't just a ripped torso with a twinkle in his eye … he's got *talent*.'

'He's also bloody *temperamental* and *testing* my patience.' A flat male voice that I don't recognise interjects. 'Look, Silver, like I've always said: I certainly don't give a singular monkey's bollock whether Fry is *respected*. To misquote that bell-end in *Jerry Maguire*, "*S*how me the sodding money*!*" All I am asking you to do is make him popular and bankable again *and fast*. It's getting ridiculous. Your face has had more work than Fry has over the last year. I don't care if they spit his name at the Royal Shakespeare Company as long as every sad female singleton wants to screw him, every moronic alpha male wants to be him and he delivers the wonga. Now, where's this waitress?'

Barb appears at the kitchen door with a sharply dressed man in a grey suit with a silk striped shirt and matching tie. His thick blond hair is swept back to show off an angular although not entirely unattractive face. He marches over to me.

'Nicholas Van Smythe,' he says, flashing a set of brilliant white veneered teeth. 'Fry's agent, visionary, evil overlord … depending on which rag you read.' He kisses me on both cheeks. 'Pleasure, darling.'

'Hi,' I stand up. 'I'm Viv—'

He interrupts me. 'Not to worry, darling, there's only one thing I'm worse at than remembering names and that's small talk, so I won't bother with that either. Silver and I have got a proposal for you.'

Barb motions at me to sit back down at the kitchen table. 'We thought we'd have some fun, kiddo. The Great British Youth Awards, sponsored by *News Today*, take place at lunchtime on Saturday. Usual drill: a bunch of adolescents who have fought against the odds get to go up on stage in a top London hotel to receive a trophy from a celebrity and the editor of *News Today*. The ceremony raises money for a children's charity, is broadcast live and the paper always does a huge pull-out in the *Sunday News*. It's a good marketing tool … it makes the celebrities look more sympathetic to their fans and the editor more sympathetic to his readers. Everyone's a freakin' winner.'

'Except the courageous youngsters, of course,' laughs Nicholas. 'Who get to experience the charmed life of the rich and famous for just a few precious hours, before being herded on the early-evening train back to their insignificant lives in some depressing backwater of the UK.'

'Really? There was me thinking everyone stayed in touch after those sort of events,' I say sarcastically.

Nicholas smirks at me. 'I think we all know that the whole point of celebrity charity work is to get *recognised* for it, not to do it on the quiet so you don't get anything out of it for yourself. There's a reason why Madonna takes a full sodding camera crew to Malawi; free children and additional downloads. I jest! I *love* that old crone. She's an icon.' He taps the table. 'Let's get to the point, Silver.'

'So, kiddo,' she continues, 'we've decided to throw an olive branch to *News Today* after all the recent hoo-ha in *Clint's Big Column*, by getting Maxy to present an award at their ceremony. It'll be a good coup for them, what with it being Maxy's first public appearance since rehab, and of course, if you came too we could show everyone that …'

'… despite what happened,' I continue for her, 'Maximilian and I are *great mates*. Maybe even inspire

Clint to write a little piece on what *great mates* we now are. Do you really think people are that gullible?'

'The readers of *News Today* and the *Sunday News* are,' confirms Barb, her voice thickening. 'But, kiddo, this isn't all about Maxy. It would be a nice little bit of exposure for you and that acting work you were telling me about. I don't know what kind of performer you are – you could be shit or you could be shit hot, but either way no one is going to find out unless you get some roles. You're not getting them at the moment because no one has a freakin' clue who you are. In this day and age there is no such thing as a lucky break, everything is engineered by a relentless PR machine. Hype is everything. *Silver's Golden Rule Number Forty-three: There's no such thing as a squirrel … he's just a rat with a better tail and a good publicist.*'

'She's right,' adds Nicholas, twisting the gold Rolex on his wrist. 'No offence, darling, but at your age you need all the help you can get. As far as the industry is concerned, as a woman in her mid-thirties—'

'I'm only thirty-four.'

He smirks again. 'As I said, *mid*-thirties … your career is pretty much *finito*. This is a good offer. We're not asking you to snog some reality TV chump at a suburban night-club, we're asking you to attend a top-flight awards show at a five-star hotel with *the* Maximilian Fry …' Clearly, this is how they *all* refer to him.

With perfect timing, Maximilian walks into the kitchen pulling a grey hooded sweatshirt over his head. I can tell that the top is fashionably distressed, i.e. it's brand new but *looks* as if it has been damaged whilst the owner was engaging in some kind of heavy-going manual labour. (Not like Luke's one that looks that way because he has been doing precisely that.) Maximilian gets another water bottle out of the fridge and swigs it back without looking directly at me. The expression on his face is exactly as it was when I arrived.

'Come on, kiddo. It'll be fun …' pushes Barb.

'Not for me,' I tell her. 'Rubbing shoulders with celebrities is not everyone's idea of a perfect day out.' She looks confused, as I expected. 'Anyone who works in show business always finds this hard to believe. I mean, most of you assume any normal member of the public would sell a kidney to catch a glimpse of Kristen Stewart buying acne wash in Sephora, but it really isn't the case. Besides, I see enough famous faces at work so when—'

Nicholas butts in and stands up. 'Look, I don't want to hear the labour pains, darling, I just want to see the baby. If you're not up for it, fine. Obviously, this is the pro-active go-get-'em attitude that has resulted in you clearing dirty dishes off restaurant tables at thirty-four years old.'

I look across at Maximilian and wonder whether he will apologise on his agent's behalf, but he is concentrating on peeling off the label from his water bottle. *Arsehole*. Suddenly, I find myself thinking about the scene at the very end of *The Simple Truth* where Jack Chase leaves the exquisite Arabian princess (who is also a spy and a professor of metaphysical engineering) he has been shagging. By this point, the two characters have escaped from the desert and are back at the ornate Persian palace owned by the now-dead leader of the rebels who was also the princess's husband. After a steamy session in her four-poster bed with the silk curtains billowing in the breeze as per movie-set-in-a-dust-bowl standard, Jack Chase waits until the princess is asleep, slips out the window and shins down the side of the building, onto his next adventure. When the princess wakes up at dawn, she touches the pillow next to her, realises Jack has gone for good and then smiles. *She smiles.* This is a woman who has betrayed her own people, committed adultery, got her husband killed, lost her job – and at one point nearly her right leg – all for some bloke. *Who has now deserted her.* But is she pissed off? Does she immediately get on the phone to a girlfriend and have a good moan about the chaos-causing non-committal toss-pot? No, she walks over to the window and stares into the horizon all gooey-eyed … *because he is Jack Chase.* Well, I'm not such a sap.

I stand up too. '*Actually*, for your information, I don't remove any plates. That is the waitress's job. I'm a hostess, so technically my role is to look after the cust—'

But suddenly, I stop. My hands become clammy and my heart races. This can happen in the aftermath of a minor flashback. What Maximilian said pings back into my head. *Until you know your truth … who you really are, you can't pretend to be someone else.* I look up, and consider attempting to continue what I was saying … but I don't bother. I know when I've lost an audience. Even *I* don't want to hear what I have to say.

CHAPTER EIGHT

Losing an audience is also a familiar feeling for every one of the thirty-something females hovering around at the East London studio, waiting to be seen by the casting director and producers for the *Surf Shack* audition. I recognise nearly all of them. For over a decade we have been competing against each other for the same parts. In chronological order these have ranged from *sassy graduate* to *sexy love interest* to *wise-cracking singleton* to *office gossip* and now (gulp!) *trendy mum*. Much further along the line, *woman of the people* (with some sort of all-consuming job in the federal civil service) will be up for grabs, then *plucky divorcee rebuilding life*. The thought of getting to the stage where we are vying for the role of *crime-solving gardening enthusiast* makes me shudder.

The atmosphere is exactly the same as it always is on these days, with everyone being pleasant and encouraging to each other. Good-luck hugs and supportive smiles are dished out without being meant in the slightest. I try to bypass the main throng without getting caught up in any chit-chat but am stopped in the hallway by Harriet Morgan. She was at drama school with me and Adele.

'Vivian … *hi*!'

'Oh, hi … how come you're here?' I ask. 'I thought you were still shooting *Nurses*?'

Harriet plays 'Angela', the sensitive doctor with a crush on 'Danny' the married night porter. I've been in that show before. I was the first victim of a three-way suicide pact. It was a rubbish part – I got the least camera time out of the three corpses because at that point my demise didn't appear to be part of a bigger plan, merely unfortunate.

Harriet sniffs acridly. 'I'm being written out. *Apparently*, Angela can't handle the pressures of hospital life. She's going to deal with a horrific RTA at Christmas – drunk driver, natch – then lose confidence and leave to open a beautician's. Bastards.'

'That's such shitty luck.'

I grimace, but I am not feeling too sorry for her. I auditioned for 'Angela' too. The casting director asked if I would put on a few pounds for the role. The character needed to appear more 'comforting', supposedly. I was extremely annoyed. Why can't a thin person be seen as sympathetic on the screen? Surely, when you don't revolve your day around mealtimes, you're more flexible with the time you can give others? But that's British TV for you. You wouldn't get that in the States. Over there, if an actress has a strong stench of a disordered approach to eating and/or exercise about her she's more likely to smell success.

'Yeah, really shitty …' agrees Harriet.

'Maybe you should go on one of those soap chat-rooms to moan,' I tell her. '*Surely, there was far more to come from the Angela/Danny/Danny's wife plot-line? I for one would adore to see the love triangle reignited after Danny nips into Angie's Spa for a seaweed wrap.*'

She shoots me a withered look. 'Piss off, Vivian. I don't think I'm quite ready to laugh about it yet. Nice shiner, by the way.' She points at the bruise under my eye. 'I read about your little incident on Perez. Did Fry apologise?'

'Kind of.'

'He did it through his agent, you mean. Bastard. Don't give a fuck, do they?' (*They* being our alias for anyone enjoying exceptional standing within the world of entertainment.) She eyes the packet of Marlboro Lights in my bag. 'God, I'd kill for a fag.'

'Help yourself.'

'Nah, I'm crapping myself about wrinkles. Do you think I look older than when you last saw me?'

I pretend to examine her face. 'Well, you're hardly Yoda … but I think we both know you haven't got a portrait up in the attic.'

'Piss off,' she says again, laughing. 'Anyway, I never knew you smoked.'

'I like to have some on me, just in case …'

'Of what?'

I shrug. 'You know, *stress*.'

'Yeah, I *do* know. Agh, I WANT ONE! But it's a sad fact that no one can get away with puffing cigs at our age. Even Sienna Miller will struggle.'

'That's true,' agrees one of the girls further down the queue who has been ear-wigging our conversation. 'She's already got sallow looking.'

'Mmmm, sort of pasty and "lived in",' says another.

'Oh, stop!' grins another.

But they carry on, because this is how they kill time before any audition: gunning down Sienna Miller. It's been like this on the circuit for a long time, and there is no sign of a ceasefire. It may sound a negative thing to do, but actually it has a positive effect on morale for the regulars to have at least one actress they hate more than each other.

I sneak off to the loo, my place of comfort. I've always liked toilets. A locked cubicle is a good place to escape the potential uneasiness of any communal area. Once inside, I read through my script one more time. On the last page, I find a message from Luke. He must have written it while I was making his breakfast.

Since I'm not allowed to say anything encouraging about your acting I thought you should know that there are many other areas you excel in. I won't list these areas in case you stop excelling in them on purpose to wind me up but rest assured, on a scale of one to ten ... one being someone with a single niche party talent (e.g., swallowing whole fist or very low limbo-ing) and ten being bonzer across the board, I'd say you're a nine. Good luck.*

**You lose a point for not being able to swim.*

Luke has started to leave me more and more messages like this. He uses them to say the stuff he has realised I am uncomfortable with him saying to my face, i.e. Aussie-isms and slushy stuff. The messages are never texted or emailed; they're always handwritten on random bits of paper. Given that all other males born at the nineties end of the eighties have fully rejected the concept of communicating through either the medium of handwriting *or speaking* in favour of tapping a screen … well, it's quite nice, really.

Prior to Luke, the only 'secret notes' I'd ever been written were at school. They would be slipped into my pencil tin, often with an added gift of spit globules, bogeys or pubes. I knew who the perpetrators were and who they were led by. Their leader never ran out of names to call me but never had the guts to sign hers.

I don't audition for *Surf Shack*. Twenty minutes after arriving I am on my way back to the Underground; hands clamming up again, heart racing faster. As I walk, I realise Maximilian Fry was wrong about me lacking commitment. I don't. I am wholly committed to playing one role: 'me'. The thing is that sometimes leaves me too exhausted to play anyone else.

CHAPTER NINE

Adele is home. I would know this even if her backpack wasn't sitting in the corridor because I can smell something spicy wafting from the kitchen. She brings back some kind of pungent brew from each trip abroad and can't wait to tell me the ludicrous myth behind its production, like it was originally ground from the bark of a hallowed oak tree and rubbed on the bleeding feet of Taoist monks during long pilgrimages. But no matter what the mystical back story to the leaves, the finished drink *always* tastes like piss with a hint of cinnamon.

I drop my keys in the goldfish bowl and creep into my bedroom to get undressed and hide the things I nabbed from Adele's wardrobe this morning.

'Vivian, is that you?' she calls from the bathroom, in her resolutely middle-class Home Counties accent.

'No, I'm a masked robber with a spare set of keys to the flat,' I shout, clicking back into 'me' mode with ease. (Years of practice.) 'I'm going to fleece the spare room first, then the lounge. Is that okay?'

'Fine. Do your worst … as long as you don't call it the *lounge*!'

I strip out of the Stella McCartney vest, chuck it under my duvet, kick off the sandals under the bed and manage to pull on Luke's sweatshirt seconds before she appears in the doorway.

'... or the *living room*,' she says. 'Repeat after me ... *sitting room*.'

'It's been seventeen years, Dels. I think it's about time you accepted I'm a bit common.' I smile. 'Wow, you look fantastic.'

I am not being sycophantic. She has got a post-vacation *zing* about her; the type that comes from two weeks spent at one with nature and yourself. She is *refreshed*. Personally, I have never quite grasped the concept of a health-boosting break. If your internal organs aren't really feeling it, what's the point? Once, as I was sunbathing on the final day of a *heavy* trip to Ibiza, Roger told me I looked like that *Roswell alien laid out on the autopsy table...*

Mind you, except when she's sunk too much white wine, Adele *always* looks fresh and expensively demure. Today, her bouncy bracken-coloured curls are neatly held back with a beige silk scarf and she is wearing a white smock top with an ankle-length white tiered skirt. I think it's all Anna Sui. It's gypsy chic but done in an off-duty high-powered career-girl kind of way; a look that says more, 'This cost me a fortune!' as opposed to, 'Can I read your fortune?'.

'Ah, thanks,' she says, pushing her scarf further back off her forehead. 'I feel *great*. Nepal was amazing. Such an intriguing country and the people were so kind and generous.'

'Good, good ... but most importantly did you remember to get me some super-strength sleeping pills that have definitely *not* been authorised by any medical governing body, during your stopover in Bangkok?' Adele always manages to get me the strongest downers without prescription in Thailand – presumably the Thai people need easy access to medication like that to help them zone out from the constant flow of gap-year students in Billabong T-shirts called Josh invading their homeland. I rub my hands together. 'Please, tell me they're as powerful as that batch you got me at Christmas? They could have felled an ox.'

She grimaces guiltily. 'I didn't get any. I'd planned to get them on the way back, but then … well, *something* happened. I got distracted and totally forg—'

'Dels! Nooo! I took the last one after going clubbing while you were away assuming you'd replenish my stock.'

'You shouldn't take downers after doing uppers, anyway, or vice versa,' admonishes Adele. 'You're asking for a cardiac arrest. If it's any consolation, I did get you some Napalese black tea. I'm brewing a batch on the stove. It's good stuff – packed full of antioxidants. In the old days, the villagers in the foothills filled pouches of—' But then she stops, distracted by something on the floor.

I follow her line of vision to the carpet where one of her gold sandals is sitting. It didn't quite make it under the bed. *Shit.*

'Sorry, Dels, I really needed a pair of smart-ish summer shoes f—'

'Don't panic.' She smiles. 'Anything else you took whilst I was away? Confess now and we'll leave it at that. Call it a flatmate amnesty.'

I peer at her suspiciously. 'Seriously?'

'Seriously.'

'No repercussions?'

'You have my word. I won't even confiscate any of my Aveda products from the shower as punishment, so you won't have to use your *decoy* bottles of Pantene.' She carries on smiling. 'I do *know* they are a decoy, by the way.'

Nervously, I peel back my duvet to reveal her Stella McCartney top. 'It still had the price tag in it.'

'Again, it's not an issue,' she says breezily. 'Just get it dry-cleaned.'

'Dels, have you lost the plot? You hate it when I *stea* … borrow without asking.' I grab the vest and show her the loose threads. 'Look, it's snagged, beyond repair probably, and you haven't even worn it yet.' Something else odd occurs to me. 'Hang on a sec, you haven't even mentioned Luke's music equipment littered around the lounge.'

'*Sitting room.* Personally, I don't think he's left enough. I was hoping to come back and find it rigged up to rival Madison Square Garden.' She carries on grinning at me as she curls a tendril of hair round her finger.

I step closer to her. '*And* you haven't told me off for filling the bathroom bin with latex gloves.' I use them for tanning. Adele always moans that it makes her feel like she is living with a full-timer carer.

'Sod all of that, Vivian.' Her eyes are glassy. 'Something *incredible* has happened. It's actually *happened* …'

'It has?'

She nods and my chest clenches. Obviously, her membership has been accepted for Shoreditch House. Before mine. For years, she never saw the point in shelling out for any other private clubs as she always came down to

Burn's for free. But just before she met James, Adele panicked that she wasn't casting her net wide enough to meet Mr Right and filed requests to all the other leading clubs in town.

'I can't believe it. But it's only been six months.'

'Just over. I *know*. Crazy, isn't it?' She grins, her eyes filling up even more.

'Congratulations, Dels …' I reply, stoically, as I try to blank out the image of her plonked on a sunlounger by Shoreditch House's famous rooftop pool, caipirinha in one hand, Factor-30 suncream in the other. 'Perfect timing too, now that summer has arrived.'

'Don't be silly,' she laughs. 'I'll never have enough time to organise it for *this* summer. We'll aim for December at the earliest. Hopefully it will snow. How fab would it be to have a white wedding?'

I cock my head at her. 'Eh? Who's getting married?'

'Earth calling Vivian!' She shakes her head. 'Have you not heard anything I've said? It's *me*. *I* am getting married. Me! Well, me and James.'

'You're *what*?'

'Getting married. *James asked me to marry him!*'

'Christ! That is *such* fantastic news! I thought that you had got your … Oh, it doesn't matter what I thought.' I rush over to hug her. 'Dels, that is *so* amazing. You must be so pleased and …'

'Shocked, yes. Very. It's still sinking in.' She steps back and looks at me. 'I am engaged, Vivian. *Engaged!* Can you believe it? After the quagmire of relationship *sewage* that I've waded through – the *crap* excuses, the cheating *turds*, the full-of-*shit* arses on dating websites – I never thought anyone would propose to me.'

'Oh, ye of little faith. I *always* knew someone would.'

She bursts out laughing. 'That is such a whopping lie.'

'Yeah, I did. Actually, I thought it might happen last year, with oh, you know, that guy who got so pissed during dinner at your parents' house, your mum came down in the morning and found him asleep in the dog basket. What was he called? He actually sounded as if he *could* be a dog … ha! Was it Spike?'

'Rex,' she says, sounding less amused. 'Anyway, look at the ring. The ring! *My* ring!' She thrusts her left hand about a millimetre away from my face. 'Look, look, *look at it*!'

'I'm looking. *I'm looking*! That is *some* rock, Dels. So how did James propose? Did he get down on one knee?'

'Eventually. But there was a bit of a build-up.' She grins. 'He asked me on the final leg of our trek through the Himalayas. Funny thing was I had been in a strop with him that day, because after breakfast he pelted off at a fast pace and left me with the dawdlers. But as dusk came and the peak came into view I could see everyone in the front pack holding up a massive sign with the lyrics of "Ain't No Mountain High Enough" followed by MARRY ME, ADELE!' Then as I made my final climb to the top, James got in position and everyone serenaded me with the whole song. How romantic is *that*? No prizes for guessing what retro classic I'm walking up the aisle to.'

'"Smack My Bitch Up" by The Prodigy?'

She punches me in the shoulder a little harder than is

necessary. 'I'm *obviously* having "Ain't No Mountain High Enough" by Marvin Gaye and Tammi Terrell.'

'I was only mucking about. Come here, you …' I give her another hug. 'Congratulations, Dels, you're getting *married!*'

'Yes, I am. I am engaged. I am going to get … *maaaaaaaaaarried!*' she screeches, directly into my left ear. 'Married. *Married.* Me? Me! Getting MARRIEEEEEEEEEED!'

I jump back. 'Ouch, volume!'

'Eek, sorry …' Her eyes glaze over as she reties her scarf. 'I guess it's still sinking in.'

'Of course, it is. We should go out and celebrate.'

She fans her cheeks with her hands, and watches as her ring glints in the light. 'Not tonight, James and I are having supper with my parents … to tell them our news. We need to visit James' foster family too, but they live in Leeds.' She says this as if it would be more difficult to arrange a couple of days in the North of England than one of her month-long treks across another continent. 'We'll have to get something in the diary soon. God, there is so much to organise …'

As Adele chatters away I am distracted by Monday appearing in the doorway. He stares at me in utter bewilderment. Clearly, having heard me get home ten minutes ago he is now wondering why the *hell* I am not preparing his tea. If he owned a wristwatch he would be tapping it with a single claw. I tell Adele to come and talk to me in the kitchen.

She pads after me. 'Anyway, if we're aiming for a Christmas do, I'll need to step on the gas to arrange everything in time. Twenty-four weeks is nothing.'

'I'm sure you'll be fine, Dels. Bob Geldof organised Live Aid in less than that. At least you won't have the added hassle of trying to perfect the most ambitious international satellite television link-up *ever* for a global audience of four hundred million.'

'Very funny. I'm certainly going to need to be focused,' she says, pouring herself a mug of her stinky brew. 'On the plane yesterday, I had already come up with the idea of a winter wonderland theme … possibly at Burn's … Luke could DJ … but we'd also have world music to encapsulate mine and James' love of travelling … and possibly some sort of tribal entertainment. That was *before* the cabin crew had finished their safety demonstration. We hadn't even taken off!' She giggles, but a little uneasily. 'Joking aside, Vivian, do you think ethnic drumming whilst canapés are being served is too much?'

I laugh and suck in a sharp intake of breath. 'I'd be very careful with bongos, Dels. They really are the Nicki Minaj of the percussion world – quite fun for five minutes but they'll do your head in any longer than that.' I get a serving of organic goose and venison chunks in gravy out of the cupboard.

'Ha! Okay, no bongos.'

'Or children,' I add. 'Too distracting, noisy, messy, demanding and unpredictable.'

'And an added expense.' Adele nods. 'Thank you, Vivian. That's *exactly* the sort of solid advice I will be needing from my chief – and *only* – bridesmaid.'

I stop peeling open the sachet. From between my legs, Monday looks up at me and mews, his face a picture of panic and confusion. I stare at the slimy cat food for a few seconds then return to removing the foil and scraping the contents into his bowl. I don't put it down on the floor, though, because then I will have to turn round and react to what Adele has just said.

'You heard right, by the way,' she says. 'I did *just* ask you to be my bridesmaid. Well, I-asked-you-slash-*told*-you.'

I half twist round. 'Oh, Dels, that's *so* …'

'So?'

Monday mews again. I put his food down on the floor and immediately his distress signal turns into a joyous high-pitched chirrup, all his years of experience informing him how tremendous the next few minutes are going to be. I stand up and turn to face Adele properly. She smiles at me.

'It's all right, Vivian. I know what you're thinking, and quite rightly so. You're thinking I've gone back on that deal we loosely made …'

'Erm, I think you'll find we *shook* on it. We said that—'

'I know what we said,' she interrupts. 'We said that after the age of twenty-nine, if either of us got married we would never do all that following-each-other-up-the-aisle, telling-each-other-what-to-wear nonsense, because being a bridesmaid …' I wince as she says the word again, '… in your thirties is a bit embarrassing.'

'A *bit*? Dels, they've even made a blockbuster movie about how embarrassing it is since we had that conversation. The agreement was that we help each other organise *everything*; hen do, dress, venue, etc., but we're not officially *one of them*. I'll do anything else you want me to that wasn't on that list too – within reason. I'll even do a reading from the Bible.'

'Don't be silly, you don't believe in God.'

'Neither do you and you're the one wanting to get married in a church.'

She giggles. (I don't.) 'That's not the point, Vivian. Look, I didn't realise I was going to feel this way, but now I am actually going to be a bride, I want to do things the right way on my big day. All my other close girlfriends are married so they aren't *allowed* to be bridesmaids. You *aren't* so you *are*.'

With that she puts one foot firmly in that metaphorical stirrup, ready to mount the moral high horse I can tell she will be riding right up until the big day. Why can't people get married *properly*, like Penelope Cruz did in *Blow*? Off the cuff (and off her head) in Vegas wearing a purple jumpsuit. I had expected more from Adele, but like a shocking number of females who have made a point of swerving dry customs their *entire* lives she has turned into Anne of Green Gables now she has got a wedding to organise.

'Fine, I'll do it. But you better make sure this is the one and only time …' I smile back at her as I sit down. 'And you can forget about me wearing anything ten swatches in front of *or* behind "dusky peach" in the fabric sample flip book.'

She bursts out laughing and idly picks up the pepper grinder from where it is still lying on its side from, er, *last night*. I watch Monday as he finishes his meal, licks his whiskers, does a few feline press-ups and strolls out of the kitchen without thanking anyone. When I turn back to

Adele she has stopped laughing. Her eyes have gone watery again.

'Stop that.' I tut at her. 'You're not allowed to cry today, or this week, or this month. You've shed enough tears over the years. In fact, I am going to lay down a non-negotiable rule now. You are not allowed to blub for your *entire* engagem—'

'Stop! Stop being so lovely, Vivian. Look …' She stares into her tea. 'There's something else that I … I don't know how to tell you. I've been dreading this moment so much.' She stops to take a deep breath. 'Okay, I'm going to come straight out with it. God. Oh God. Oh *God* …'

'Oh God, *what?'*

Another deep breath. 'The thing is, I … well, *we* … as, in James and I … we've had a lot to talk about since he …' She flashes her ring hand at me. 'And moving forward, we've decided to use his place as our base whilst we look for a, er, *forever* home. Or, at least what I *hope* will be our *forever* home … as long as I don't make a total mess of this relationship like I have done all the others … I mean, he could cheat on me or turn about to be a …'

'Compulsive liar?' I raise my eyebrows at her. 'Christ, remember *that* one? The psycho you met in that wine bar who told you he was a professional polo coach, and then freaked out when you organised a date horse riding in Hyde Park. Now, what was *he* called?'

'I never got to find out his *real* name, did I?' she says, slightly boot-faced again at the mention of a previous amour. 'But listen, about the flat …'

I reach across the table to her. 'It's fine. I know what

you're going to say; I need to find someone to move in. Don't worry, it won't be too hard. Dane could be up for it. He mentioned the lease on his place is com—'

'Vivian! Let me finish. Look, I'm sorry, *so* sorry ... but you're going to have to move out. I'm selling up.'

'Selling?'

She nods solemnly. 'It's time.'

'When are you going to put it on the market?' I really don't like the way she is forced to take yet *another* deep breath as I ask this. This one is more of a desperate gulp for air.

'When the work has been completed. To get the best price I need to install another bathroom so there is one for each bedroom. It's what young professionals expect ... so I'm getting a wet room installed.'

'Where?'

'Your clothes cupboard. I'll be staying here to keep an eye on the builders, but you won't be able to stay in your room with all the work going on.'

'How long have I got?'

'Three weeks.'

'*Three weeks?* Christ, Dels, I've spent less time getting ready to go out on New Year's Eve.'

'Trust me, I feel awful about the timescale, but the builders who did such a good job of installing the kitchen here and doing my place over in the Docklands had a cancellation, so I wanted to book them in.'

She pulls off her scarf and hangs her face in her hands. When she looks up, I can see a tear is about to slip over the edge of the lower lid under her right eye. I get up and put my arm round her, fully aware that she needs to remember this day as the one she threw her happy news out to the world … not the one I threw Himalayan tea over her.

'Dels! Remember the rule. No tears.'

'I feel dreadful for doing this to you.'

I squeeze her tighter. 'Don't worry about me, I'm extremely resilient. And besides, being made homeless is not the worst thing that can happen to a girl at thirty-four years and three hundred and sixty-four days old.'

She wipes her nose. 'It isn't?'

'Nah …'

'W-what *is?*'

'Being made a fucking bridesmaid.'

'Vivian!'

CHAPTER TEN

When Luke realises who has buzzed the bell, he flings open the door, picks me up, swings me round, then snogs me for more than a minute.

I untangle myself from his arms. 'I see you haven't got round to reading that treat 'em mean, keep 'em keen manual I ordered for you.' I bend down and pick up the squashy bag I have brought with me containing his laptop, magazines, cables and sweatshirt, as well as the grooming tools I will need in the morning. 'Adele got back and was being narky about your stuff littering up the lounge so I thought I would bring some of it over.'

'Ha!' he laughs, straight at me. 'I see someone *else* hasn't got round to reading the manual I ordered for *her* on coming up with decent excuses to cover up for the fact that she really wants to spend time with me. Besides, I think we both know that if I was *that* into you, I would have got rid of these by now.'

He points at the trousers he is wearing. They are my most hated item of all his clothes: knackered army-surplus combats that have a side pocket long and wide enough to hold a family-sized tube of Pringles. Today a red tube is peeking out. *Paprika.*

'Yeah, but—'

He interrupts me. 'The "yeah" is all I need.' With that he picks me up, throws me over his shoulder, leans down to grab the bag and carries me down the corridor. 'So, how did the audition go?'

'I won't get the part,' I say with *absolute* certainty.

'You reckon? I'm sure you were m—'

'Stop!' I reach down and wallop him on his concrete-hard backside. 'Don't even try to make me feel better.'

'Okay, okay. I'm saying nada.'

He kicks open the kitchen door and plonks me down on the floor. The room is a tip. The sink is full of dirty crockery, the bin is overflowing with empty takeaway cartons, the floor is littered with cardboard pizza boxes and all the surfaces are covered in a thick film of biscuit crumbs. It's like a Disneyland for *real* mice.

'Christ, Luke …'

He shakes his head at me. 'Don't give me grief. I try to keep it clean but you know what Wozza is like having his mates over the whole time to party. It's like living within the eye of a storm. I haven't been around the past few weeks to contain things, have I? Let's get out of here and grab some dinner.'

'It's Friday … eating is cheating. Besides, we're having dinner tomorrow.'

'Oh yeah, I forgot. Having dinner on consecutive nights is a crazy Aussie thing, isn't it? You only have it once a week in the UK.'

'Exactly,' I say, pleased he is making a joke. 'Besides, I had something earlier.'

'Earlier today, or earlier in the month?'

'Don't nag, I had a proper meal.'

'A proper meal from whose point of view? An adult human or a baby marmoset?'

Now I can tell he isn't joking, and I am not particularly amused either. The anti-congratulatory way in which he refers to my neatly calculated portion control pisses me off. On *The City*, Allie Crandell's boyfriend never said anything about her weight, despite her being so waifish she often wafted into scenes like an apparition. I did eat tonight. I had an Atkins bar. Then I did an hour of *Jillian Michaels – Body Revolution.* Then I had a vanilla Skinny Cow ice-cream.

'I don't know what you're so worried about, anyway,' continues Luke, shrugging. 'There's nothing of you. Put on a few kilos and there'd be more of you to do *bad* things to, which could only be a *good* thing. Guys like something to grip onto.'

I nod as if I am taking on board what he is saying. I am not. He's speaking like a larger lady who is trying to convince herself that she is happy with her size. Next he'll tell me that Beyoncé is 'bootylicious' (read: bottom heavy) or that Jennifer Hudson looked better with 'more junk in the trunk' (she didn't) or that Christina Hendricks's curves are 'old Hollywood' (i.e., not so helpful when getting roles in *this* century). But I don't bother repeating any of this. I can feel them – the thoughts from earlier – lining up, ready to start running through my head again.

'Why don't we go clubbing?' I suggest. 'Ask Warren to bung us on the guest-list somewhere. He'll have some gear too, right?'

Luke raises an eyebrow at me. 'You want to get stuck into the speedo?'

'You know I don't do *that* any more.' I may have stopped purely not to hear him say that *beyond*-irritating expression. 'But I …'

'… wouldn't mind *doing something* to let the wheels come off?'

Yes, I would like to. Maybe an E, but *not* because I want the wheels to come off. The opposite. When I *occasionally* use drugs, it is as a tool to get myself back *in* control. I see it like this: being yourself and convincing other people of this self is a mental marathon. One that does not have a finish line. The stop watch will never go back to zero. Nor will you be wrapped up in a heavily branded silver foil blanket. There is certainly no medal. It's a hard slog. So sometimes you need time out from the race. For me, that's what drugs are about: a reprieve from thinking. It's a trick. Not a treat.

'Why not?' I say to Luke, reaching into the bag I brought with me. I get out a bottle of Grey Goose vodka and some beers for Luke (which he will probably ignore in favour of a Dr Pepper). 'And stop looking at me like that.'

'Why don't you just tell me what's the matter? You've obviously had a shit day.'

I prickle, wrong-footed. 'I haven't. I simply want to go out and have fun. That's *all.*'

'Fair enough, but I can't stay out late; I'm working in the morning.'

'I thought the whole point of your job was that you didn't do weekends or overtime.'

'I could do with some extra cash right now.'

'What for? More cables to add to your viper's nest?' I huff. 'Look, I won't keep you up for hours. Warren has got some Valium' – another necessary trick – 'hasn't he? It'll knock me out as soon as we get back.'

'You're really not dressing this up as A Night to Remember.'

'Christ, Luke … *live a little*.' I add another huff and untwist the cap on the vodka bottle.

He huffs back at me, then opens the freezer compartment for a bag of ice and half fills two pint glasses with cubes. I pour at least three measures of Grey Goose into one of the glasses. He reaches into the fridge for a bottle of Dr Pepper. When he turns round I can see his face could be about to crumple.

'Why do you always have to lash out at me like a cut snake?'

I figure this is not the time to pull him up on his usage of Aussie slang. 'I don't mean to.'

'Try harder.'

'I *am* trying.'

'Yes, you *are* … *very* trying.'

'Why do you bother with me, then?' I nod at my glass. 'More ice, please.'

He looks at my glass, then at me, chucks the ice on the table, and gently pushes me back against the fridge. 'Why do I bother? I wish I didn't feel I had to. But unluckily for me I find your combination of short temper and long legs extremely attractive.'

'How attractive?'

'On a scale of one to ten?'

'Yep.'

'With one being reasonably do-able if there was no one else around who I fancied the look of and ten being *this much*?' He grabs my hand and places it firmly over his crotch. 'I'd say you've got yourself full marks there.'

So, we don't go out. Luke keeps me entertained in his bedroom. He entertains me on the floor, in the chair, against the door, by the wardrobe and over the mixing desk – we video that bit. Basically, we do it everywhere except the bed because the frame is about to collapse. You can sleep in it but that's about it. Bar the rickety bed, Luke has made a real effort to make the room comfier over the past year. Although the floor is still covered in cables, he has filled the shelves with candles (bit corny, I know, but the original ceiling light could have been used to perform laser eye surgery), painted the walls, acquired new bed linen (black to hide my fake tan smudges), stripped the floorboards and covered them with a fluffy rug from Ikea, bought a miniature fridge and kettle so I don't have to go into the kitchen in the morning, and he's had the window fixed so it can open and his boyish smells aren't allowed to fester. He also keeps it pretty spotless. Okay, so it's still not going to merit the cover feature in *Architectural Digest* but it's a world away from the dank, putrid cave that is Warren's bedroom up the corridor.

Before we go to sleep, Luke gives me an early birthday present; not clothes, thank God. Hair straighteners. He says they are for me to keep in his bedroom so I don't need to bring mine over every time I stay. The tongs are made by ghd, but they are the pink ones, which means that a certain amount of the purchase price will go to a breast cancer charity. Typical Luke; reminding me that having hair with a propensity to kink if left to dry naturally is not the most life-threatening condition that can affect a woman. They make me smile, and a few seconds later I find myself telling Luke about Adele's engagement and asking him if he minds me staying with him for a short while when I move out of her flat. He reacts as a young spaniel might having just been told he is the new quality-control manager in charge of road-testing products at The Squeaky Ball and Throwable Stick Company. He is as ecstatic as it is possible to be without risking further structural damage to the bed ... and I have to admit, that as I lie there under the more than adequately togged new duvet but with just the right amount of cool breeze drifting in through the window, I don't think it's the *worst* idea in the world. Just until I get myself sorted, anyway.

CHAPTER ELEVEN

'Oi oiiiii! Wozza's in the hooooooooouse. Time to get the mother-fuckin' clown car out the rave garage! Vroom vroooooooooom! *Oooooooooh,* this gear is *mental*. MENTAL! It's mental continental Avis four-door hatchback seven-day rental chicken orientaaaaaaaaal!'

At seven o'clock the next morning, Luke's flatmate Warren – the only living organism to make Scott Disick look complicated – returns home from a night out with his mates. Banging dance music starts pounding through the wall. Simultaneously, the washing machine in the flat above kicks into the planet's clunkiest spin cycle, so I give up trying to sleep and make a cup of tea. Luke has stuck a note on the kettle.

Happy birthday! As they say in The Outback, 'Rinse it like a drongo!' So here's the plan. From now until 8 p.m. I want you to remember you're awesome, because you are. Then, at 8 p.m. meet me outside that Spanish place round the back of Bethnal Green Road. We're going for tapas …

I freeze and immediately stop reading. Christ, *really*? Tapas is a ridiculous way of eating. Multiple dishes come to the table at random times and nothing on the menu is straightforward, i.e., plain brown, white or green. Bar the olives, I suppose, but even they could be stuffed with an insurgent pimento. I take my tea back to bed and pull the duvet around me. Luke's room hasn't got the same kind of feel about it in the cold light of day, with no twinkling tea lights or post-coital glow to bathe in. (Spotting the almost full tape in my video camera makes me cringe slightly.) I listen to the bass pounding away through the wall, and as much as I wouldn't want to be hanging out with Warren and his gang, I am jealous that they have all been out having fun. The thought of not going to Ibiza this summer – the Promised Land of Fun – makes me disgruntled.

I look over to the mantelpiece. Propped up behind a photo of Luke's family is the acting card my agent, Terry, uses to send out to casting directors. For someone who resolutely avoided a *single* picture to be taken of them between the age of ten and twenty, it's weird how relaxed I appear. The shot is in black and white and I am looking directly into the camera whilst pulling my best smiley yet pouty, serious but light-hearted, angelically devilish face … to show I have a fantastically varied range. I lean forward and try to figure out how old I look in the picture but it's difficult to tell. I certainly don't look my age, but then I'm not, not really. According to my birth certificate I am thirty-five today, but in a sense I'm only twenty-five. That *dark side* period … it obliterated a whole decade of my life. Losing me to it, looking for me, giving up on me to create the new me, getting used to this me … took close to ten years.

My eyes wander back to the picture of Luke with his family; he is laughing as his father pretends to plonk a large prawn on his mother's head with some barbecue tongs. He must be seventeen, nearly eighteen, at the time that picture was taken – round about the same age I was when I left home. The scene looks like something out of a summer TV commercial for outside grilling equipment, with Luke's parents cast as the perfect mum and dad. But then Luke thinks his parents *are* perfect. One of the first things he ever said to me was that the greatest lesson he learnt from them was to be honest with yourself … because then you will be honest with other people. I murmured something resembling an agreement – as I do every time he imparts any other words of wisdom his 'folks' have bestowed upon him – because it's the easiest thing to do. But frankly, their inspirational fridge-magnet approach to life doesn't sound that far up the well-meaning-but-delusional scale from my mother's biblical one. Proverbs Chapter 10 Verse 9: *Honest people are safe and secure, but the dishonest will be caught* … She couldn't have been more wrong.

*

I flop back against the head rest. The bed snaps in two like a Venus fly trap, ensnaring me in the middle and sending my tea flying. Wriggling out, I catch my hair on one of the broken springs, which causes unhelpful tangling. So I switch on the do-gooding styling irons Luke gave me last night. But even after a minute they don't heat up to a level anywhere near as powerful as my own ones that I bought off that stylist. It just goes to show you can't save lives *and* achieve a catwalk-ready look. I crawl over some electric leads to get my own straighteners out of my bag. But whilst rummaging, I stop, grab my Nokia instead and quickly scroll down the list of received calls. I find the number I need and before I give myself a moment to change my mind, I phone it. The call is answered on the third ring – I knew she would be up.

'Ha!' cackles Barb Silver. 'You *do* have a bit of freakin' ambition after all, kiddo. Maxy will be freakin' pleased you're coming. Listen, I'm mid Gyrotonic … I'll shoot you over the details in five minutes.'

They ping through in three. I am back at home in forty. I am ready in two hundred and twenty-six … and waiting by the window in the lounge for my cab. Whilst I am there, I text Adele, tell her I'm going to a party and ask if I can go into her closet and borrow some accessories – namely, the ones I have already stolen. Monday watches me from the sofa, blinking. He blinks a few more times then wraps his big orange tail tight round him, and settles down amongst the cushions with his back to me.

CHAPTER TWELVE

The Rexingham Hotel car park is teeming with coordinators and assistants buzzing around wearing Prada pumps, headsets and stoic expressions at having a job that is so all consuming it would make a student nurse feel positively overrun with leisure time. A bank of photographers are positioned either side of the entrance steps, where they are being monitored by security guards in dark suits. Not that the press are likely to get out of hand today. On an event like this, which is supposedly *not* about the stars, there probably won't be any outrageous outfits on display for the paps to get in a frenzy over, which is a shame. I like female celebrities to always go the whole hog – I want to see them sucked in by Spanx, splattered in Swarovski crystals, feet scrunched into podiatrist-baiting high heels and heading for the 'What Was She Thinking?' pages of a trashy magazine. Otherwise, what's the point of them?

I wait in a holding area for ten minutes before the people carrier draws up with Payton at the wheel. Nicholas sticks his head out the front passenger window.

'You've scrubbed up more than adequately, darling,' he says, eyeballing me.

I eyeball him back, knowing that I have scrubbed up *way*

more than 'adequately' in a clingy, short, charcoal-grey dress (a decent – if you don't come too close – Alexander McQueen rip-off from ASOS for £39) worn with no hosiery (my legs are smothered in that chip-fat style body grease the models in the Versace adverts are always varnished with), smoky eyes, nude lips and just-got-out-of-bed-hair (which took an hour and a half to perfect two hours after I *initially* got out of bed). On my feet I am wearing truffle-coloured Marni shoe boots (Adele's) and in my hand I am holding a flat leather clutch (ditto), which is more of a yellowy beige. Nothing is more damaging than 'matchy-matchy' accessorising – it can make an outfit look very cheap. Especially when it *is*.

'Let's get one thing straight,' I tell Nicholas. 'I'm not here because of your lecture on being some sort of desperate old husk.'

'No?' He smirks at me as the window whirs up. 'Of course, you aren't.'

The back door of the people carrier slides open and Barb lowers herself onto the tarmac. She is wearing a metallic dress that coils down into a twisted fish tail, with stilettos and a feathered head-dress. That's more like it.

She whistles at me. 'Check you out. Cinder-freakin'-ella is certainly going to the ball.'

'Cheers.' I smile. 'Although, I can't afford to lose one of these shoes. They're not mine.'

'Lose? Ha!' Barb cackles. 'Cinderella didn't *lose* that goddamn slipper. Girlfriend clearly had an agenda. Can't blame her though … did what she could to get out of a bad situation. You have to admire that.'

Maximilian gets out of the people carrier next. He jumps down next to Barb.

'And here's Prince Charmless,' I mutter. 'Hi, Maximilian, you look …' I glance casually at him, '… *nice*.'

Make that *dazzling*. His complexion is ultra matte and unblemished, except for the jagged scar, which I have a feeling could have been accentuated with cosmetics. His hair is artfully tousled and gelled to give the appearance of being ever so slightly wet, as if he could either have just leapt out of the shower or out of some dangerous rapids after rescuing a baby deer from drowning. His pectoral and stomach muscles are conspicuously nudging the fabric of a precisely washed-out grey T-shirt with the sleeves casually rolled up so that the full curve of each bicep is on display. The indigo-blue jeans he is wearing are also exquisitely distressed and tucked half in/half out of his scuffed hiking boots. Barb must employ a crack team of men with a similar physique to Maximilian to wear his brand-new clothes until they are sufficiently worn-looking for him to pop on.

'Hi, Vivian. You look *nice* too.' He gives me a pointed look and pauses as Barb goes over to the wing mirror to redo her lipstick. Then he lowers his voice. 'About what happened at my house … I should have said something when Nicholas spoke to you like that, but I'm …'

'An arsehole. As well as a pretentious wanker.'

'No, well …' He gives me one of his very slight smiles. 'Sometimes. But not on that occasion. Look, this is going to make me sound like a tool, but before you arrived I was in a shitty mood about the stuff Parks printed … and then I got some bad news about the sequel for *The Simple Truth*. The producers are looking to cast someone else as Jack Chase.'

'Yeah, I overheard. Your publicist doesn't have the quietest voice.'

'I was gutted. I still am … and before you have a pop at me, I am *fully* aware that there are worse things going on in the world than my inability to re-secure the lead role in an action franchise.'

'Yeah? Name one …'

He ignores me and continues. 'The thing is, I don't want to lose the part. I can't. That character means so much to me. I made him. I am him. I *believe* in him.'

I laugh. 'I bet you had an imaginary friend as a child.'

'Forget it,' he says, shaking his head. 'You clearly can't give the back chat a rest for five minutes, can you? I was only trying to be honest with you.'

I allow myself to stare at him again. The sincerity written over his face makes me uncomfortable. It's not just Jack Chase he believes in … he believes in himself. I don't let myself consider if that look has ever been written on *my* face.

'Okay, okay … so, who might nick your role, then?' I ask.

'We're hearing rumours that JP Goldstein wants Orlando Bloom.'

'Ha! It's not 2006 … since then it has been proven that Bloom only works well as part of an ensemble cast in a fantastical location with some form of historical weaponry at hand; bow and arrow, sword, sickle – delete as applicable.

If he ever plays the lead in a modern setting the film flops.'

Maximilian thinks for a second. 'I don't think I've ever seen him in one.'

'Exactly, neither has the rest of the developed world. If you wanted to feel really confident, though, I suggest you take a look at *Elizabethtown*, which Orly stars in with Kirsten Dunst. There's a scene in it where they speak to each other on the phone till dawn. It's excruciating. They should have used it on a loop as one of the torture devices in a *Saw* movie.'

Amusement flickers across Maximilian's face. 'Thanks for coming, Vivian, I appreciate it.'

'That's okay, but I haven't come here because of you.'

And that wasn't more back chatting. I genuinely have not. Nor have I come – as Nicholas has assumed – because he goaded me into it. Nor have I come – as Barb has assumed – hoping that the event will serve as the defibrillator for my flat-lining career. Nor have I come because I'm not exactly thrilled with Luke's plans for this evening. The reason I came is because it's my birthday and therefore *essential* I distract myself as much as possible, to stop me thinking about my other birthday, *that* one, when *it* …the *darkness* … descended …

Barb totters over and slaps Maximilian on the back. 'Shake out the tension, Maxy. Shake it out, shake it out, shake it *out* …'

'Calm down, Barb,' he replies, as he hunches his shoulders up then releases them, in quick succession. 'It's not as if I haven't done this sort of thing before. I'll be fine.'

'I know, but it's been a while. You're bound to be feeling the pressure. After the torture and isolation you suffered last year …' She drifts off – a pained expression on her face, as if it wasn't that long ago her client was unzipping an orange boiler suit after a stretch in Guantanamo Bay, not packing his jim-jams after a two-thousand-euro-per-night stay at a leading Swiss clinic.

Nicholas opens the passenger door and nods at Maximilian. 'Remember what I said, Fry. I want you looking suitably *moved* during the awards – some mild welling-up will suffice – and keep yourself in check if you bump into Parks. Oh, and get some decent shots with the kids. Go for the ones who have *obviously* been through the mill. Wheelchairs, braces, not quite complete re- constructive surgery … make every shot count.' I choke and even Barb looks disapproving. 'Lighten up, ladies,' he snorts. 'Isn't that why he's here?'

A blonde woman from the events team dashes over to us. She is talking nineteen to the dozen into a mouthpiece hooked round her head.

'Yup … currently in docking area. Yup, yup, yup … *really?* Already in. Great … yup. Great … yup. Yup! Yup, yup, *no* … not them. Cancelled. *Pricks!* No, no … she's here. God, yes. Div-*ine!* Yup, collecting Maximilian Fry now. ETA meet and greet with charity reps approx. three minutes. Yup. *Totally.*' She swings her mouthpiece to the side. 'Hi, hi, *hi*. I'm Gabriella, Gabby, Gabs – *whatever!* – senior production coordinator and executive head of celebrity liaison.' She beams manically at us, eyes popping out of her skull; high as a kite on pure un-cut *organisation.* 'Are we ready, Mr F …' She stops mid-flow as Maximilian turns to fix his eyes on her. '… ry?' This comes out as a squeak.

'Ready,' he replies. 'Do what you want with me.'

As they stride off, the rest of us head into the foyer for drinks where staff in pale-grey uniforms are on hand with canapés and champagne. There is no vodka. Barb zaps round the room greeting contacts, whilst I hang around in the background like an aide on *The Apprentice.* I'd prefer to do this than engage in any small talk. I find it excruciating. I once read somewhere that your basic social skills are learnt *before* the age of ten, but it is *after* this age you develop the ones you will rely on in adulthood because you are more likely to find yourself in a wider variety of places and situations. But for me, the opposite was true. I hit ten and my world reduced.

I am knocking back a third drink when my mobile rings from inside Adele's bag. It's Luke. I am pleased for the distraction.

'Is that the birthday girl?'

'It is.' I clip-clop across the foyer to get some privacy behind a pillar.

'Where are you? It sounds all echoey.'

'I'm in a Roman amphitheatre.'

'Yeah, right …'

'Not really. I'm, er,' I hesitate. 'in Topshop.'

Granted this is a lie, but it's a white lie. Not brilliant white, more in the same area as the deceptively muted Farrow & Ball off-white Burn's is painted in.

'Bought anything nice?'

'Jusht looking …'

He laughs. '*Jusht?* Have you been on the grog already?'

'Grog? *Luke!* It's booze or alcohol … and no, I haven't. I'm, er … knackered. Warren got back in full on "party mega-twat" mode at seven. I don't know when he's more annoying, like *that* or how he is the rest of the week: entirely resistant to any human interaction and on the brink of suicide.'

'Ha! Jeez, sorry. Listen, reason I'm calling; you know Kevvo from the building site?'

'Mmm …'

'His flatmate is going travelling for a couple of months and said we can have his room for *free* while he's away. Before you ask, it's got a garden for Monday and it's in a quiet street. The place is on the outskirts of Streatham. Apparently, Streatham is the new Balham.'

'Which still needs a decent bar and a rocket up its backside before it's even the new Clapham, and that's *still* south of the river.'

'Oh, I thought you would be pleased about not having to stay at Wozza's,' he says lightly, but I can sense minor deflation in his voice. 'Kevvo's girlfriend lives there too …'

He says this as if it is a plus point. I've met Kevin's other half before. She is not irritating, she is fingernails-down-the-blackboard *excruciating*. Whenever she laughs she *always* says, 'Oh, that's really funny!' mid-laugh, as if the sight and sound of her chortling away hadn't given the game away.

'… so it's really tidy and there's always loo-roll.'

'In that case, it sounds *great,*' I say, rolling my eyes.

He laughs again. 'I am picturing your face, right now ... are you rolling your eyes?'

I laugh too. 'Maybe ...' I look out into the foyer as the guests mingle, chinking their champagne flutes with one hand and throwing the other around animatedly as they effervesce with delight at being in such well-connected company. This is what hell looks like for Luke. 'Listen, I found your note on the kettle—'

'And you didn't freak out?' he interrupts me.

'Don't panic, it's all good,' I tell him. 'I had a think about what you said while I was on my way into town and realised I should just go with it. I'm thirty-five, for God's sake. It's time to take that step ...' It's true, the thought of spending a couple of hours in a tapas restaurant dodging side plates of sizzling chorizo and other oily Spanish delicacies should *not* scare a grown adult. (I'll pop a Nurofen and take some cigarettes.) 'I'm going to try really hard, anyway.'

'Really?' He sounds thrilled.

'Absolutely.'

'You have *no* idea how awes—'

'Stop! You've already sneaked in an "awesome" today.'

'"Awesome" doesn't count as Aussie slang. It's a generic term used by extreme sports enthusiasts ...'

'The only people more annoying en masse than Australians. I'll see you later.'

He laughs and hangs up.

As I do too, I feel a light tap on my shoulder. It makes me jump. I manage to hold on to my champagne flute but I drop my bag and phone. The latter lands with a crunch on the marble. I bend down and check the screen. It has cracked.

I look up to see a good-looking blond guy in a hotel uniform grimacing apologetically at me. I think he could be a porter or something.

'I'm *so* sorry. I didn't mean to give you a fright,' he says, in a Midlands accent. 'I came to say that all the guests are being ushered upstairs to the dining room. I should've gone round the other way. Has your mobile bust?'

'Yeah, the screen's cracked.' I wave it at him. 'But don't worry. I've been due an upgrade since the turn of the century. I'll sort it out next week.' I'm not trying to make him feel better, either. I can easily go for a few days without a phone. I like being incommunicado. In fact, it's the *only* thing I miss about 'back then' … the sense of calmness that came with enforced solitude. 'Maybe I'll go crazy and get one with an inbuilt camera and emoticon facility. Apparently, that's all possible now.'

The porter smiles as he examines the archaic Nokia technology in my hand, then picks up the back panel and the battery, which have spun across the floor. 'You should get an iPhone,' he says.

'Christ,' I laugh, 'I wish there was an App that iPhone users could download that stops them telling people to get one.'

He laughs too and passes me the remnants of my mobile. 'Thanks for being understanding. The majority of that lot,' he indicates towards the lifts in the foyer, 'would have gone mental at me. Good karma will come your way.'

'Will it?'

'Yeah, your aura will attract it. Call it my inbuilt spiritual App. I can tell you're a decent person.'

CHAPTER THIRTEEN

As if I needed further proof that the porter was prone to misjudgement, when I take the lift upstairs, I don't walk out into a 'dining room' (as he had described it) but more of a *banqueting pitch.* Vast windows boast 360-degree views around London, an ornate painted ceiling depicting crazy biblical shenanigans is hung with row after row of heavy crystal chandeliers and a central podium boasts a full jazz orchestra. They are currently belting out a scat version of One Direction's biggest single. I examine the tables. They are laid out with solid silver cutlery, heavy crystal glasses and starched-linen cloths with a centrepiece of white lilies. Thick cream cards by each placemat describe the *six* courses that await us. The first one is already waiting: squid with samphire and a purple blob of purée – possibly beetroot. I can navigate my way around that.

'Looking very tasty …'

I spin round to see Clint wearing the gold variation of his 'Parksie' bomber jacket, which he wore with matching trousers when he presented a Brit Award last year.

'Absolutely,' I agree, smiling at him. 'On my way here, I was hoping we were in for at least *some* form of pulped root vegetable. It isn't offered enough.'

He laughs. 'Not the food, Vivian, you doughnut. I meant *you*. You're looking tasty. Not that you don't usually, of course.'

I shoot him a look. Whenever I see Clint outside of work, he flirts with me. He flirts with *every*one. 'Yeah, yeah, Clint. So, how's your wife? All going well with the pregnancy, I hope.'

'The biological bump is just dandy, but the missus has got another 'ump … with me. I missed 'er scan at the 'ospital yesterday. I was interviewing Rihanna at the Ritz, then I bumped into a few of the gang and we ended up at some gig Sophs was putting on, so,' he grimaces guiltily, 'it all went a bit crazy bongos.'

'Tut tut. I'd be careful, Clint. *Apparently*, pregnant women get a teensy bit tetchy around the whole subject of needing-their-partner-to-be-present-when-being-told-important-news-about-their-child's-development. Just something I've heard …'

'Oh, she'll come round with a bit of the ol' Parksie charm. She knows I don't do these things on purpose, they just seem to 'appen,' he adds, more to himself, and wipes his nose. 'So, I gather from my editor you're 'ere with Fry and 'is posse.'

'Mmm … I've got the whole day off, so I thought I may as well get tanked up for free. It was either this or old episodes of *The Hills*. But I don't think even *I* could handle Audrina and Justin Bobby's stagnant exchanges for a second time.'

Clint laughs but then leans in close to me. I can detect a stale chemical mustiness permeating through the Envy by

Gucci and excitement. 'Be careful with Fry's lot … 'ave fun this afternoon but don't get too involved. Know what I mean?'

'No, what do you mean, Clint?'

'They're all a bit, well … *unpredictable*,' he explains. 'Fry's one can short of a six-pack, Silver's a ball breaker and that Van Smythe … 'e's ruthless. One of my juniors on the paper got smacked when he was sniffing round Maximilian after the whole Zoe Dano break-up palava. 'E thought 'e 'ad something else on my original story. Van Smythe never did nothing to get 'im*self* stitched up, but I knew 'e was behind it.'

'Oh, don't worry about me, Clint. I doubt if I'll be seeing any of them again after today. It's not as if Maximilian and I are going to be bagging one another seats at the Olivier Awards. I'm not that deluded.'

'I know you've got your 'ead screwed on, Vivian, but we look out for each other, don't we?'

'We do.'

'So I felt I should warn you.'

'Warn her about what?' asks Nicholas, sidling up next to us. He fixes Clint with a smile that feels about as heartfelt as Teri Hatcher's whenever she posed next to the other cast members of *Desperate Housewives*. 'Come along now, Parks, let's not start all that playground nonsense. Today is all about the poor kiddies … that's what we are here for.'

'*They* are *'oo* we are 'ere for, I think you mean.' Clint smiles. 'But I get your drift and it warms my 'eart, really it does. Oh, and can I remind you it's not me that started things last time, Van Smythe, it was your lunatic client. If 'e can control himself, so will I.'

'He will … and that's appreciated,' Nicholas says curtly, before turning to me. 'Time to sit down, darling, the ceremony is about to start. That rather foxy classically trained piano player is hosting. You're over there somewhere …' He nods at the centre of the room. 'And I'm at the front with Silver.'

'Where's Maximilian?' I ask.

'Top table by the stage,' replies Nicholas. 'Now, chop chop.' He gives Clint the briefest of handshakes and slithers off through the guests.

Clint nudges me. '*Where's Maximilian?*' he repeats. 'I'd say someone 'as got a bit of a crush.'

'Bore off, Clint. I was only asking so I know where to find him later to do this pathetic picture.' I look over his shoulder to locate the whereabouts of the top table. 'Trust me, Maximilian is not my type at *all* …' I see Maximilian being guided to his seat by *Gabriella, Gabby, Gabs – whatever!* She positions him between an up-and-coming offbeat female singer songwriter – that's offbeat as in folky as well as in literally *without rhythm* from what I could gather at last year's Wireless Festival – and a top soap star, who is wearing far too much foundation even by my grouting-style standards of application. 'I don't even *like* him,' I add.

Clint laughs and nudges me again. 'But that's the most exciting way to fancy someone, isn't it?'

'What is?'

'When you *don't*.'

'Don't what?'

'Like them.'

*

My table is a mixed bag: a breakfast show business reporter, her representative, a hairdresser to the stars, his handsome Brazilian boyfriend, a blokey lads' mag journalist who is always on those talking-head shows enthusing about trends from past decades and three twenty-somethings who are the current faces of Saturday-morning hangover telly. The two guys are wearing ultra tight-fitting blazers with T-shirts underneath bearing iconic prints from a decade before they were even born. (Al Pacino waving a gun from *Scarface* and The Rolling Stones' *Forty Licks* album cover.) They therefore score highly on the twat-ometer. I have no idea what their names are, but the girl is called Noelle Bamford. She is managed by Sophie Carnegie-Hunt. I know this because Sophie brought Noelle to Burn's for cocktails, to celebrate her becoming a hot new trend icon with a spread in *InStyle* magazine. Noelle's look is made up of two components. 1.) Clothes that look ultra old-fashioned but are actually by designers so astonishingly *fresh* they haven't yet been captured on a sonogram; 2.) Brogues. Today's are tan with white laces.

At least I haven't been shoved to the edge of the hall – where by rights, I *should* be – with the Z list: the willing desperados who have only been invited to pad out the room and make the proper stars feel safe. They are human bubble wrap. I am sat between the male writer and someone who hasn't turned up. As everyone begins to tuck in to their starter – and I toy with a samphire stalk – the missing person appears.

'Viv*ian!* Twice in one week! *Coincidence*. I tried to find you to say goodbye the other day …'

She's got the part. I could tell on the 'ian' of Vivian. 'Hello, Harriet.'

'Or you could call me "Debbie". Yes indeedy, I got the good news late last night,' she beams, then coughs and plonks down a glittery purse and twenty Silk Cut next to her starter.

I tap the packet. 'I thought you were worried about wrinkles?'

'I was, but I'm going to go for a bit of cosmetic landscaping. The fabulous bastards are shelling out a lot more money for *Surf Shack* than I thought so I'm treating myself. You've met my boyfriend, Stephen?' She swings her arm round the men's magazine writer next to me.

'Yeah, hi.'

I smile at him in acknowledgement but still don't bother to congratulate Harriet about getting the part, which she doesn't make a point of. She would expect the same reaction from any of the other actresses on the circuit. We may be highly trained performers but generosity of spirit is one thing we can't fake.

Harriet twitters on. 'Good news about Adele getting hitched … I got a group email from her last night. So, what are you doing here, Vivian?' She asks this extra loudly. 'I never bump into you at industry shin-digs. You're usually on your *shift*.'

At this point the three *yoof* TV personalities all turn to hear my reply.

'Maximilian Fry asked me.'

'You mean his management team?' corrects Harriet. 'Publicity stunt after the other night, I assume.' She has a sip of wine and turns to the others. 'Vivian's the one who got caught up in that brawl with Fry. She's in hospitality, works at Burn's in West London …'

I have to give it to her, this is a fair comeback for my seaweed wrap and Yoda digs at the audition.

'No way!' simpers Noelle, in her signature soul-sapping West-Country-with-a-dash-of-LA accent. I had hoped this was just her TV voice. 'I thought I recognised your face. My agent is a member there. I used to work in a bar once, you know …' She says this as if she was admitting to once being involved in the fur trade. 'It was only for a few weeks after I left college, but then I auditioned for *The T Zone* and got the job. Before I knew it, the press were saying I was going to be the new Alexa Chung.' Everyone nods rapturously, evidently forgetting that – as with Pol Pot – the world really does not need another one.

'Maybe Mulberry will christen a handbag after you too, like they did with Alexa,' gushes Harriet. '*The Noelle*. Perfect for the festive market …'

'You know my *actual* birthday is *actually* Christmas Eve …' Noelle informs everyone. 'It *is!*'

I chew my samphire stalk fifteen times and glance over at Maximilian. He is sipping on a glass of water. The singer-songwriter is leaning across the table to reach for a bottle of wine whilst clearly thrusting her breasts in his face. Rather hypocritical of her considering all her songs have a strong feminist bent.

'You always look like you're having such a lush time on *The T Zone*, Noelle ...' comments Stephen.

'I do, but I'm leaving next month,' she replies. Her two fellow presenters look suitably devastated. 'I've signed up for this sort of fashion-dating-confidence-reality-makeover-sclf-cstccm thing for ugly kids who could look like a celebrity with the right – well, a *lot* of – help. I'm hoping it will lead to some more serious projects for me as a presenter, you know? Ideally, I'd like to become a spokesperson for my *entire* generation ... but still be able to hang out in the cordoned-off bit at Glastonbury with my friendies without any fuss, *you know?*' She looks back over at me. 'So, what's he like, then, Veronica?'

I don't give her the satisfaction of correcting my name. 'What's *who* like?'

'Maximilian Fry. He's so damn sexy. I'm sure he gave me the eye when we were having our photo-call, but then, maybe not ... I mean, I'm not a supermodel goddess like Zoe Dano,' she says, by this stage not merely fishing for compliments but literally sending out a deep-sea trawler to net them in. 'I'm just a skinny goofball who d ...'

I zone out. It is either that or drive a steak knife through my left eyeball so I can't see that side of the table. I can also feel my energy levels slumping as the adrenalin that has been soaring round my body since I received Barb's text this morning starts dwindling and the woozy effects of the alcohol kick in. I can drink vodka for days on end, but with champagne I go from 0 to 100 mph after the first few glasses ... and then my engine stalls. I'm not going near the white wine – Lady Petrol, as Roger calls it. A.) it's liquid sugar; b.) it turns *all* women *mad*.

'Anyway, I'm going to introduce myself later.' Noelle is still rattling away. 'I felt something, you know? It's nothing to do with him being *the* Maximilian Fry. Okay, so my last three boyfs have been famous, but I *never* specifically aim to date people that are, you know? I'd go out with the pizza delivery guy if we had a connection, but I'm more likely to be at some sort of *event* than ordering take-out. Like, this year, backstage at …'

I drift off again, imagining a scenario where I *do* plunge a serrated piece of cutlery into my eye, but no one at the table notices the horrific, bloody damage because they are too entranced by Noelle's faux-bashful retelling of how *everyone* at Coachella fancied her. But then I am forced to refocus. A waitress brings over three fresh ice buckets of wine. After putting them down she shifts other paraphernalia around the table. I sense her deliberating whether to shove the lily centrepiece to one side, but then she thinks better of it and picks up a crystal glass plate of sliced artisan bread which was sitting directly in front of the hairdresser. She puts it down again. In front of me. I stare at the rows of doughy, yeasty, seed sprinkled slices. For fifteen seconds? Maybe more.

Then I place my napkin over the plate. I mean, no one wants or needs to look at that, do they? It's not *just* me. My eyes dart around the room. Maximilian has left his seat. Barb is yacking to Nicholas. The musician presenter wafts past en route to the stage. She is in a pale-green strapless flowing gown – she isn't anyway *near* as bony as she was post-divorce. Gone are the days she would lean over the piano and you'd see her spine protruding out of her evening gown like a prehistoric exhibit at the Natural History Museum. Harriet's boyfriend lifts up my napkin, helps himself to the chunkiest slice of bread and reaches for the butter.

Nurofen? *Cigarette.*

I slip out of my seat, manoeuvre my way through the tables, leave the dining room, take the lift down to the foyer, loiter in the car park, open the packet of Marlboro Lights that I bought months ago, have a few puffs on one, then on another, loiter some more, go to the loo, redo my make-up, floss my teeth, brush them, gargle with a handbag-sized bottle of Listerine … and get the lift back up to the dining room. When I walk back in most of the guests are up; roaming round and re-chinking their glasses during what appears to be a break in proceedings.

'I've been looking for you, kiddo,' says Barb, trotting over to me. 'You missed Maxy present his award. I have to admit, even by my Herod-like enthusiasm for family life the rug-rat who won it was kind of deserving.' Suddenly, she spots someone and springs up on her tiptoes like a meerkat. 'Ah, he's here …'

'Who?'

'Charles Benson. His chat show starts again soon …' She narrows her eyes. 'Oooooh, that's his wife. Sheesh, terrible surgery. She's got that wacko expression on her face that looks like she's thinking, *Have I left the freakin' the iron on?*'

'What should she look like she's thinking?'

'I'm gonna sack that lazy bitch maid if she doesn't press

the next batch of my two-thousand-thread-count Egyptian cotton bedsheets properly …' Ha! Back in a sec, kiddo. I need to schmooze.'

Barb shimmies off in time to something by Kelly Clarkson set to a ragtime beat and I sit down in my original seat at the table, which has been abandoned by everybody except the breakfast show business reporter. She is yacking on the phone. I look over at the top table to see Maximilian in conversation with Noelle. I lipread her saying the word 'spokesperson' repeatedly.

I smile, then find myself laughing as I imagine trying – but failing – to find the right words to sum up her almost admirable vacuousness to Luke. In that moment, I decide I *will* tell him where I've been to today. I should have done in the first place. It's not as if he would read anything in to it … not when I have always made sure there are no other words on that particular page that could reveal the whole story. I check my watch and finish my champagne. It's nearly four. I can't be arsed to do that 'matey' shot with Maximilian. I should go home, have a power nap, then limber up for the big match later; Mediterranean finger food *versus* me.

I slink back through the tables towards the lift. I call it, get in, press the button for the foyer and rummage around for some change in my bag to get a cab. I count out *just* enough to get home without stopping at a cashpoint. It's not often this happens.

'Sssssssssstop!' a male voice hisses. 'Hold the lift …'

Suddenly, the doors judder and halt. I glance down, a perfectly scuffed hiking boot has been jammed into the gap.

The doors open again. Maximilian jumps in and slams his hand frenziedly against the buttons on the control panel.

'What *are* you doing?'

'You need to help me,' he says, his eyes darting about. 'I need to get out of here. Take me somewhere. *Anywhere*. I've got no money.'

'Ha!' I laugh, as the doors close for the second time. 'I'd like to check that statement with the team at *Forbes* magazine.'

'As in I don't *carry* any cash. Or cards.'

'Sorry, I'm going home.' The lift begins to descend. 'Go back up and get Barb or Nicholas.'

'You're not listening. I *can't* go back up.'

'Ring one of them to come down, then.'

'I don't own a mobile.'

'Christ, your life is *ridiculous*,' I tell him. 'What's happening upstairs, anyway?'

'I've seen someone.' The lift stops on the ground floor. 'Someone I didn't want to.'

'Clint? Oh, he'll be all right. He's more interested in flirt—'

'No,' interrupts Maximilian. His voice is strained as he stares down at his hiking boots. I haven't seen his face from this angle before. The perfect symmetry of his features is even clearer. 'Someone else.'

'Your ex?' I guess.

His voice cracks as the lift doors open. 'Yeah, my ex …'

'Zoe?'

'Mmm …'

'Did she see you?'

'No. Back was to me … I recognised her from … from her hair … I left the room before she … oh look, I know I don't exactly deserve your help. I admit it, I *was* a fucking arsehole …'

'*And* a pretentious wanker.'

He gives me that hint of a smile. 'But get me out of here. *Please*.'

CHAPTER FOURTEEN

I take him to The Red Lion pub, not too far from Adele's flat. It was where I first met Luke and is about as low key as it gets. Anyone wanting to while away a Sunday afternoon with a complimentary copy of the *Observer* and a jug of fennel-infused Bloody Mary can pick any other pub in the neighbourhood as every single one has been converted into a bar/eatery, complete with leather banquettes and a guy called Jimmy in low-slung Deisel jeans and a portable credit card reader poking out of his back pocket. The Red Lion has an orange swirly carpet, a cash-only policy, a clientele made up of locals from the nearby estate and a landlord who calls his punters 'squire' because he always has, not because he once saw someone do it in a Guy Ritchie film. The usual handful of pale regulars are slumped around the bar, supping pints and watching horse racing on telly. They have no idea that the man once described by *GQ* as 'forging solo into a whole new territory of cool …' has just walked in.

Maximilian waits for me at the most private table in the corner whilst I get our drinks. Vodka on the rocks for me, but not Grey Goose; it will be a '*moins de sept euro*' dubiously labelled brand picked up by the landlord on a recent *supermarché*-sweep across the Channel in Calais. But I don't care. After all that champagne it will help level me out. It's amazing how vodka does that. It's as close to water as alcohol gets. I place the Jack Daniel's and Coke Maximilian requested in front of him.

'Thanks,' he says, clearly much less tense than he was when we were leaving the hotel. 'For the drink … and for bringing me here. It's a good place. Real. *Gritty*.'

'I'm surprised you like it,' I reply. 'Celebrities always profess how much they loathe glitz and glamour and are much happier communing with bog-standard civilians, when in reality they are weeping tears of joy when an invite to Elton John's annual White Tie Ball slips through the letter box.' I take a sip of my vodka and nod at his whiskey. 'I thought you were teetotal?'

'Why did you think that?'

'The fridge full of branded H2O, your well-publicised trip to *rehab* …' I don't add, 'and you weren't drinking at the awards' because then he will know I was staring at him.

He shrugs at me. 'I like to keep rehydrated and for your information, I didn't go into therapy because of alcohol. I like a drink, occasionally – but only in private and never that heavily. Not very cool, I know …'

Exactly like when he pointed out how 'unattractive' his lack of hosting skills were, it is difficult to sum up *how* 'cool' he appears as he says this. *GQ* was right. Sitting hunched over the table, head lolled in one hand, eyes squinting into the hazy late-afternoon rays of sun that are pushing through the mottled window … I force myself to look away and shift in my seat to the left.

'And before you ask, I don't touch recreational drugs,' he continues.

'Me neither.' I don't consider this a lie as I don't use them for recreation. I use them for recovery. 'Why don't you?'

'My parcnts' fault. Long story.' He doesn't pause to ask if I want to hear it. I guess when you've been asked to appear on the *Late Show with David Letterman* (twice) you can be confident that people are pretty keen to hear your anecdotes. 'Basically, they were party animals. Our house was insane; I'd come home from school and find rock stars, socialites, artists, models and TV stars fuck*ed* and fuck*ing* all over the place … it was a freak show, and it went on for years. Then one day – I was twelve – the shit hit the proverbial. I opened the fridge and found a massive homemade chocolate cake, so I helped myself to a slice. Then another. Half an hour later, I lost the plot. Turned out the cake was meant for my parents' party guests and was packed full of LSD and magic mushrooms. I was in hospital for a week. When I regained consciousness neither my mother nor my father were at my bedside. Just the au pair. I can't even begin to tell you how fucking angry I was. I saw red …'

'And gold and blue and green all coming together in these really crazy, swirly patterns …' I laugh.

He gives me a semi smile. 'Anyway, I asked to go to boarding school after that and most of the time I didn't even bother going home on exeats.'

'What's an exeat?'

'Traditionally, an enforced weekend break in the term at a private centre of study used to show the institutionalised, homesick minors their parents are getting on just *fine* without them,' he explains drily, and takes a hefty slug of his drink. 'But I used it to show mine how much I wasn't missing *them*.'

His half-shut eyes flicker over me and I can tell he is about to steer the focus one of two ways: *my* school days or *my* family. Before he can pursue either, I grab the conversational wheel and point at the 'Z' tattoo in black ink on the inside of his wrist.

'So, your, er ... *that* ... why have you never had it lasered? Or had it covered up with something else? Johnny Depp turned WINONA RYDER into WINO FOREVER. You've only got one letter.'

'Because that would be too much of a public statement,' he replies, 'about a private matter. To do that would invite people to make some bullshit judgement on what I'm thinking. They'd assume it was a calculated move to show I was over the relationship.'

'When you're not ...'

'Sometimes I am, somctimes I'm not.'

'What is it you miss the most?'

He appears to zone out for a few seconds.

'Maximilian?'

'Mmm?'

'What is it you miss the most?'

'About who?'

'Zoe.'

He gazes into his glass for a few seconds, as if searching for words among the ice. In the hazy light his skin appears to have a nap to it, like velvet. Or a really expensive suede.

How could Zoe have given that up for Rick Piper's blotchy and pitted bacteria fun park of a face?

He looks up. 'Just … *her*, I suppose. Obviously, she's pretty …'

'Stunning.' We're talking Christy Turlington *circa* 1990 levels of doe-eyed, long-limbed, baby-fawn style exquisiteness …

'Stunning …' he repeats.

'With *incredible* hair,' I add, to make it look as if I am one of those easy, grounded women who isn't affected by another woman's looks. (Not that such a thing actually exists, because *all* women are affected by other women's looks, no matter how good-looking they may be themselves. Everyone except Gisele, of course.)

He nods and looks back into his glass. 'Yeah, she does have in*credible* hair …'

'And face. And body. She's the whole package, really.'

'Exactly, the *whole* thing. But I saw something else over and above her beauty,' says Maximilian. 'I saw my best mate …'

But not *soul* mate? Interesting. But also rather satisfying that the supermodel failed to achieve this ultimate hallowed status.

'And I miss not having that,' he continues. 'Or maybe I simply miss loving someone. Fucking corny, I admit … but it's just, well, it makes *everything* worthwhile …' His eyes are still half shut, even though he is not in direct sunlight any more. 'Anyway, what about you?'

'What about me?'

'Tell me about *you*.'

'But we were talking about you.'

'Fuck, I'm always talking about me. Sometimes it's nice to have a day off.' He drains his whiskey. 'So, d'you fall in love easily, Vivian? Like that …' He clicks his fingers. 'Or do you take your time … more of a slow burner?'

I stop myself from rolling my eyes. I find it so *pedestrian* how men assume that as women our whole *raison d'être* is to *plod* around looking for love. I have never done that. I thought I had found it once … with Ziggy Dunhill, the most popular boy at school. He went out with Kate Summers. He was the worst possible person I could have fallen for, but in a round-about way he taught me the most valuable lesson I could have learnt: that there is no point looking for someone to love you when you don't love yourself. *You* need to be the first discovery. But that journey can take time – a *long* time – so as you travel, you may as well arrange some stop-offs. I did exactly that; my first was with Screw-it Stuart (mine and Adele's good-looking but badly behaved housemate at college), so called because he would screw women, then treat them with a huge lack of respect the next day, hence the 'it'. But really, I was no better. The next morning, I got up and left without saying goodbye, and not *just* because I had a busy day ahead …

I take a casual sip of vodka and prepare to give one of my standard depersonalised answers.

'Actually, Maximilian, like many emotional responses, I find the whole subject of …' I don't actually repeat the key word, '… unquantifiable. How do you identify it, for sure? It could be no more than a chemical reaction: the result of adding "like" to "lust" in an enclosed space, and th—'

Suddenly, he interrupts. 'Forget it, Vivian. You don't need to give me any more waffle. I was right, wasn't I? About what I said to you at my house … you can't do it.'

'Can't do what?'

'You can't reach inside and *pull out a truth.* I can see it in your eyes.' Which is surprising given that he is now looking at me through a three-millimetre gap under his heavy eyelids. 'Or is it just that you choose not to?'

'Christ,' I laugh, nervously diffusing the atmosphere. 'Enough with the heavy-duty questioning, Maximilian. We're in a pub, not a shrink's office. Wow. You really are so … *intense.*'

'Yes, I suppose I am,' he concedes. 'In fact, I'd go as far as to say, I'm,' he beckons at me to lean across the table, then he cups his hand millimetres away from my right ear and whispers softly, '*fucking* screwed up.' I feel his lips brush against my cheek and earlobe, then he leans back again. 'Not very sexy, is it?'

Yes, I think. But in the silence that follows I realise I've said it out loud. 'Yes, it *is*.'

That's when he does it. Maximilian Fry smiles at me. He smiles properly … and it's *that* smile: the mega-watt dazzler that earned him *Sexiest Screen Smile* at the MTV Movie Awards. It's the one Jack Chase uses to first seduce the Arabian princess in one of the most memorable – albeit corny – scenes from *The Simple Truth*. In it, the two characters (who have only met that day) have escaped the insurgents and are hiding in a bunker under the town walls as bombs and landmines explode all around them. Despite her own secret agent training, the princess is shaking with fear and sadness at the annihilation of her beloved city. So Jack takes her in his arms and promises that he won't just make her feel better, he'll 'make the earth move…'. *But the ground beneath them is already shaking thanks to the bombs and landmines!* It's a lame joke and the princess is initially unimpressed, but then Jack gives her *that smile* and she starts tearing off her hijab.

But the grin on Maximilian's face doesn't last for long. Suddenly, the skin surrounding his scar sort of twitches, then his eyes glaze over and close. I manage to swipe both our glasses off the table before he slumps forward.

CHAPTER FIFTEEN

'Vivian! You *have* to wake up. I'll combust if I don't show someone. Look at this! James's brother has done the initial layout for our wedding website. It's so professional. Eek, everything feels *very* official now that we are *www.adeleandjames.com.*'

I force my eyes open. Monday is asleep next to me, stretched out down the length of my body but not quite touching. I find it faintly unsettling when he does this. Luke told me this is how pythons size up whether they will be able to digest their prey. As my room comes back into focus, so do the *unfortunate* events of last night. I lean over and grab a bottle of Volvic from my bedside table. Adele flops down on the bed the opposite side to Monday and flips open her laptop.

'I need your opinion,' she says. 'D'you think this picture of me wearing my engagement ring on the homepage says, "I'm looking forward to a happy future with James …" or, "Na na na na naaa! No one's leaving ME on the shelf"?'

I down some water and look at the photo. 'No offence, but it does look a bit staged. Listen, I need to use your internet for a minute. It's really important.' I go to grab the computer.

She pulls it out of my reach. 'Hang on … *staged?* In what sense?'

'In the sense that no one walks around with their left arm stretched out in front of them with their hand at a rigid ninety-degree angle to their wrist, whilst staring at the piece of jewellery on their fourth finger …' I mutter. 'Why on earth have you got a website, anyway?'

Adele bops me on the head with the copy of *Brides* magazine she has also brought in with her. 'You don't get married in this day and age without having your own website, Vivian. Actually, I was going to ask y—'

'In a minute, Dels, I need to see if Luke has emailed me. I was meant to go out for dinner with him last night, but I broke my phone and couldn't get hold of him. Log on to Hotmail, would you?'

She ignores me and examines the screen from a different angle. 'D'you think James should be in the photo too?'

'Nah, not really. Why would you need the groom in there? It's *your* wedding, not *his*.' I raise an eyebrow at her and she giggles. 'Please. Hotmail. Now.'

'All right, all right …' She taps at the keyboard. 'Had you arranged to meet that Roger as well?' she asks idly. (Adele has never warmed to Roger. For no good reason than the fact he is my *other* best friend.)

'When?'

'Last night.'

'Nope, why?'

'Oh. I got a text from him whilst I was over at Mops and Pops for supper. He was wondering if I was with you or knew where you were. Maybe he was short staffed. Anyway, I told him you'd gone to some 'do' earlier but I didn't know your plans after that. Here you go.' Adele passes me the laptop.

I enter my log-in details and press return. My inbox is full of the usual crap; ASOS sale alerts, Net-A-Porter bulletins on the latest high-end designer fashions (purely for inspirational purposes), property lists from Ibiza real estate companies (ditto), some YouTube footage of a squirrel playing with a baby fox in a park from Tabitha, twenty-odd e-flyers to scuzzy club nights and some motivational messages from God – sent via my mother (due to the troublesome broadband in Heaven, presumably). There is nothing from Luke. I click on 'SENT' and check the message I wrote him last night at 10.06 p.m.

You're not going to BELIEVE what happened today. Will tell you everything when I see you, but basically, my mobile went kaput … and you KNOW I don't remember any numbers off the top off my head. I tried ringing the tapas place from a pay phone but they said you weren't there, and there wasn't even a booking under your name. I've been to your flat and you're not there either. Anyway, when you get this, come over to Adele's. I'll be back there in a bit. SORRY I screwed up our dinner.

'No reply,' I tell Adele. 'I'll have to go round to his flat again after work. I've got no other way of getting hold of him.'

'Don't you back up your mobile phone numbers?' asks Adele, as if this was a perfectly normal thing that people do. 'You really *should* get an i—'

'iPhone? Mmm … intriguing suggestion. I have heard

they're *quite* useful.' I bury my face in the pillow and exhale loudly like a horse. 'He's clearly pissed off with me.'

Adele sniffs semi-disinterestedly. 'It was only dinner. He'll get over it. Listen, are you going to be working the day after tomorrow? James and I were thinking of getting a few of our work buddies down to Burn's for a bit of a knees-up. A sort of precursor to our official engagement drinks. I really want you to catch up with Toby.'

'Christ, Dels, why do I need to do that?' Toby is a posh prat. The traditional type that you didn't think could possibly exist in this day and age any more. He is the Surrey-born, Fulham-living, rugby-obsessed, plummy-voiced, prone-to-getting-his-cock-out-in-public proof that spending fifteen grand a year on your child's education from the age of eight to eighteen can back fire horribly. 'I've got nothing in common with him.'

'You have now. You're going to be my bridesmaid and *he* is going to be James's best man.'

'*Best* man? Ha! Well, that's a case for Trade Descriptions if ever I heard one.'

She tuts at me. 'He's not that bad, Vivian. Anyway, I want you and him to contribute to the website ... with your own blog.'

'My *what*?' I peer out from the pillow.

'Blog. You don't have to add to it daily, just a little something now and then to keep everyone in the loop about the big day.' I stuff the corner of the pillow into my mouth to stop myself from saying something that could decimate our friendship forever. She swivels her engagement ring round on her finger a couple of times. 'Anyway, what was the big deal about having to meet Luke last night?'

'It was my birthday.'

'It wasn't!' She gasps loudly. 'No! *Was it?* Oh crap. Of course, it was. *Crap.* I am CRAP! In all the excitement with telling everyone about the...' She waves the magazine at me. 'I totally forgot. I can't believe I did that. I've *never* forgotten your birthd—'

'It really doesn't matter; you know I never make a big deal out of it,' I sense an opportunity to ask a favour. 'Listen, can you drive me into work?'

'Not *reeeeeally.* I'm meeting Melz for brunch. I want to pick her brains about venues. She's still got her wedding file with all of her old notes in it, so I'd like t—' She clocks the expression on my face and stops. 'I'll, er, get my keys. Tell me when you're ready to leave.'

Adele drives me to work in her convertible BMW. With the roof *off*, a fresh vest and a new pair of skinny-leg trousers *on*, I am feeling better. Still guilty but less hungover and ready to sort things out. Tabitha is behind reception when I arrive. She doesn't give me her usual breezy smile. She appears slightly bewildered.

'Hi, Tabs. Yes, yes, I know I'm early for *once.*' This is an actual fact. 'Has Luke called in?'

'Where were you last night?' she asks, as she tightens her sequined scrunchie.

'That's not an answer, that's another question. I asked you if Luke had called ...'

'We were at Shoreditch House.'

'So?'

'So *everything*.'

'Eh?' I shake my head. 'Tabitha, this isn't a scene out of a surrealist French film. Can you give me a straight answer, please?'

'*You* were meant to be at Shoreditch House too,' she says dolefully, and comes out from behind reception to give me a hug.

'No, I wasn't. We had no plans to meet last night. It was my birthday, remember? I was meant to meet Luke at some Spanish place for tapas. Not that I got there …' I distractedly hug her back and try to read the size on the label that is sticking out of her skirt. 'What was happening at Shoreditch House?'

'Your party!' she squeals, jumping back.

'What party?'

'Your *surprise* party.'

'My surprise party?' I feel nauseous.

'Mmm … the whole tapas thing was a smoke screen,' she explains. 'Luke had organised a dinner for you; in a private room, with a DJ, loads of Grey Goose … he'd even got the chef to make a Skinny Cow ice-cream-flavoured cake.'

Now I feel sick. 'Please, tell me you are joking.'

Tabitha solemnly shakes her head. 'I'm afraid not. He put a tab behind the bar too.'

'He *what?* How did he aff—' *Christ*. The overtime.

'Who was there?'

'About fifteen of us: me, Dane, Roger, Pete, another Australian called Kevin and his girlfriend who was *such* a cutie-pie – we swapped numbers – plus a few others who I didn't know, people you go out on the town with apparently.

Even more turned up after we'd eaten too. It's been organised for weeks. Luke popped in when you were shooting that sofa advert to ask us all. That's why I gave you your prezzie early, so you didn't smell a rat. We all tried calling you but your phone kept going through to voicemail. I even popped round to your flat but there was no reply. In the end, Roger got your flatmate's number off the computer and sent her a text to see if she knew where you were. She told him you'd gone to some party thing in the afternoon, as you'd borrowed a bag from h—'

'You didn't repeat that to Luke, though, did you?'

'Repeat what?'

'That I was at some party *thing*.'

'Ummm, yes … I did.'

'You said I was at a *party*?' I snap. 'Tabitha!'

She shrugs, innocently. 'He was worried so I *had* to tell him what I knew about your movements earlier that day. Was that the wrong thing to do?'

'I told him I'd gone shopping … oh, Christ. *Christ.* He's going to think I got off my head and couldn't be bothered to turn up. CHRIST. I was *fully* intending to meet him.' I say this more to myself than to Tabitha. 'I was looking forward to it.'

'Where did you end up, then?' she asks, her eyes wide with confusion.

'Someone was ill. I had to look after them, get a doctor, then contact their … Oh look, it doesn't matter. Can you do me a favour, please? Ring that girlfriend of Kevin's you swapped contact details with and get Luke's numbers for me … mobile and landline. Thanks.' I hang my head for a few seconds, the guilt and stress churning in my stomach. Maybe I should have a few puffs of a cigarette, brush my teeth and gargle. Or a Nurofen? I glance back up at Tabitha. 'Was he *really* upset?'

She squashes her face up and nods at me as Roger walks in to the foyer.

'It's all right,' I tell him. 'Tabitha has told me everything. I'm *so* sorry about last night. I know you tried to track me down, but it wasn't my fault and I am going to sort it out. But first, I'm going to nip outside for a quick cig—'

'In a minute,' he interrupts me, and puts his hand on my shoulder in an unexpectedly comforting way. 'My office ... *now*.' I examine his face. The look of vague amusement that fills it whenever the two of us are usually talking is not there. 'Something has happened.'

'Something *else*?' asks Tabitha, tightening her scrunchie again, eyes now like saucers.

Roger doesn't faff about. He sits me down at his desk and double clicks his mouse. An image appears on his computer screen. It is on the website of notoriously lowbrow but highly popular newspaper *The First*. It shows Maximilian and I walking away from a cashpoint machine; the one round the corner from The Red Lion. He is looking ahead but I am staring at him in the manner I imagine Monday would gaze at his food bowl if he ambled into the kitchen for his tea and unbeknownst to him I had prepared a King Henry VIII style feast of roast pheasant, devilled kidneys and wild boar. I scroll down to find two more pictures. I am continuing to stare at Maximilian in both of them. Granted, this will not be the best end to Luke's weekend – the cherry on top of the Skinny-Cow-ice-cream cake, in fact – *if* he sees it. But he doesn't read the tabloids.

I flop back in the leather study chair. 'I know it all looks a bit dodgy, Rog, but it was entirely innocent,' I explain. 'Maximilian's agent invited me to an award ceremony as an apology for him punching me, and I ended up going for *one* drink with him afterwards. He had a funny turn in the pub so I had to get the landlord to find a private doctor, then obviously I had to stay with Maximilian until I could get his people to collect him. But I had to track them down first. So whilst Maximilian was passed out I called his publicist's office in the States, then *they* had to call *her* – because my phone had broken so …' I pause. 'Listen, I *know* I've cocked up so there's no need for you to look at me like that. Oh, and I'm guessing you helped Luke arrange everything at Shoreditch House using your membership, thank you …'

'I did. But, Vivian, you really need to s—'

'Speak to Luke – I know, I know. That's what I was about to do before you dragged me in here. Tabitha is getting his number for me. D'you mind if I do it now before I start my shift?' I get up.

'Hang on, *sit down!*' says Roger, in an overly agitated voice. 'You need to scroll down a bit more.'

I sit back down and I scroll. There is another photograph at the bottom of the feature. It's only me in this one: sat on the doorstep at my parents' house. I am wearing a pair of dungarees, a black T-shirt, a denim jacket and espadrilles. All purchased for me from a 'special' catalogue by my mother because I refused to go into a high-street clothes shop. It is the middle of summer and I am sixteen. I know this because my face is red. It was at this age I learnt how to hurl up my guts after a food binge. (The sheer force of expulsion made the capillaries in my cheeks dilate and burst.) But I am also puce from the sheer embarrassment of being alive. It is hard to tell from the picture what in the exact moment it was taken *without my consent* is weighing me down more: the mental weight I am carrying or the physical one. Because …

… I was fat.

FAT.

Not just pre-menstrually bloated or post-festively plump … *FAT*. Okay, I wasn't quite as alarming as those *Honey-I-Blew-Up-The-Kid* lumps you see these days, waddling around American theme parks clutching metre-long hot dogs and forty-litre vessels of Pepsi, but throughout secondary school I was big. Big enough to get pushed and shoved *every* day. Big enough to accept it. Big enough to come home each afternoon feeling like less of a person. Big enough never to get excited about any kind of forthcoming social event. (The words 'end of term disco' were almost as terrifying as 'compulsory double swimming'. I would constantly wish for power cuts and water shortages.) Big enough to know I would never get a decent part in our annual production of *The Wizard of Oz*. By decent I mean a role that was technically a *character* as opposed to a piece of scenery. Not that I hold a grudge against my drama teacher. Who exactly would the poor woman have been able to cast me as? I couldn't have played Dorothy without looking suspiciously as if I hadn't really lost my way out of

Kansas but had actually *eaten the entire city*, and my size would have been far too distracting to play the Tin Man, Scarecrow or Lion. There is no way I would have been able to convey to the audience the effect of having no heart, brain or courage. They would have just been sitting there thinking, *There's only one thing you haven't got, Chubster ... and that's will power.*

I wasn't like this because I had the obligatory lazy thyroid or had inherited some rare cake-guzzling gene from my parents. No, I had turned myself into this blubbery monster because on the day of my tenth birthday I started stuffing my face ... and I didn't stop.

Roger walks round to the other side of his desk and crouches down next to me. 'If you want the day off, take it. Dane can cover for you. It's no problem.'

'Don't be ridiculous,' I find myself saying, but I can't actually feel the words come out of my mouth. 'I ... I ...'

'You?' Roger rubs my back.

'I ...'

'You're in shock, Vivian, I knew you would be. I'll be honest, it gave me a bit of a surprise too but now I've *almost* forgotten *all* about it. You have to remember that is how everyone will react. That's the joy of the internet, isn't it? You're only one click away from an even *more* offensive story about someone else's weight.'

And on he goes, trying to make me look on the positive side, which feels strange. Not just because Roger usually can't wait to rib me. But also because when I was fat, I don't remember any positivity from anyone. Some people – specifically Kate Summers and her gang – made a point of making me see the negativity in what I was doing to myself with their consistent abuse. It was me who sugar coated everything, both literally and metaphorically. Each time I spooned – no, *ladled* – another mound of food into my mouth, I told myself that I deserved it. That it wasn't my fault I was getting fatter and fatter … it was my father's.

'Besides,' continues Roger, gently, 'we've all got a past, haven't we? Now we all know that yours was spent free-diving in trans-saturated fats. So *what!* You should have seen me as a teenager. I went the other way … I had less meat on me than a leftover chicken wing at Jessica Simpson's baby shower.' He manoeuvres my chair round so we are face to face. 'It will be okay, Vivian.'

But I turn away – to face him means facing up to who else may *have* seen, *is* seeing or *will* see the picture – and get up. I vaguely hear Roger trying to coax me back into my seat, but I wave away his concern and walk through to the restaurant. It's packed full of our regular customers nursing hangovers with a cheeky hair-of-the-dog but the usual noisy self-congratulatory braying is interspersed with ear-piercing squeals: Sunday is the only day of the week we let in children. I spot a family in the foyer waiting to sit down and switch onto autopilot.

'Welcome to Burn's,' I say. 'Let me take your coats and get you signed in. Table *for* ..?'

'Three,' says the exasperated mother, juggling a small child in one of those all-in-one furry romper suits with teddy bear ears, a pink Kindle, Marc Jacobs leather bag, Smythson day planner and canvas Tote. 'As close to the bar as poss., somewhere we can link up to Wi-Fi … and can we get some crayons? We'll be eating too. Please, tell me you're still serving that honey granola with soya yogurt or Minty will scream her ruddy head off.'

Too late. The kid starts crying. The woman shoots her husband a look that says, *If the fucking au pair isn't going to work on a Sunday you'd better find someone who will.*

'Yes, yes and yes – follow me,' I say, taking her computer and bags, then helping to remove her lightweight military-style jacket.

The father folds up his Micro Scooter. (We get a lot of dads arriving on novelty transport at the weekends.) 'Before we even sit or look at a menu can you tell the barman we'll start with a couple of Kir Royales and a, er …' He looks blank. 'A milkshake for my daughter. Mango or pineapple or *something*.'

'For crying out loud, sweetheart, she's been funny with cow's milk since she was born and hates tropical fruit,' says the mother flatly, and then asks me in a much friendlier voice, 'Can we have a smoothie made with some mixed berries and rice milk, and scrap my Kir Royale – I'll have a hit of methadone instead.'

'No problem.' I smile, or at least I think I am making the shape of a smile with my mouth. 'I can do the heroin substitute for you on the rocks with a twist of lime. Blueberries and strawberries okay for your little one?'

The mother laughs and puts her hand on my forearm. 'You're a life-saver. Nice trousers, by the way. Where are they from? They look fab. Mind you, you'd look good in a sack. You're so skinny.'

Then she gives me *that* look. The one I've *never* got used to and which no one who ever gives it has any idea how much work it took to qualify for. It's a look that assumes this is simply who I am. Who I was. Who I will be. *Skinny.* Slim. Slender. Svelte. Scrawny, on a good day. There is nothing else behind it. I feel a prickling sensation in my eyes and my throat tightens. I try not to *ever* let myself think about what it took to become this version of me.

Laughably, I deluded myself that it would be easy to lose weight once I made the decision to do something about it. When I was lying in my bed/coffin I'd even imagine how my transformation would be portrayed in a movie: in one of those speeded-up watch-the-seasons-pass montages with a backing track that relied heavily on a stirring string section. The montage would start in the height of summer with me walking past some builders digging up a road. Too ashamed to wear a flimsy frock, I'd be sweating in a Puffa jacket so *puffed* up it could double up as sea rescue aid. I wouldn't get a single wolf whistle, but one of the builders would ask if I could stand on a pavement slab to help it set. Realising I had hit rock bottom, I'd waddle home and frenziedly throw out all the bad food from my kitchen. Next stop would be my local sports shop, where I would buy a pair of high-performance training shoes – in gold – that glowed like a gift from the gods as I took them out of the box. Then, I'd sign up to every high-cardio class at the gym and hold my head high at the front of the class as thin girls in cropped tops made faces behind my back. As autumn arrived I would be filmed jogging (wearing *Flashdance*-style faded sweats and my celestial trainers) through fallen leaves in the park, then down the high street past all the fast food shops – without stopping. Soon winter would fall. Cut to me doing star jumps in the snow and refusing anything more than a slice of turkey for Christmas lunch. On New Year's Eve – with the clock ticking towards midnight – I would try on a pair of my old trousers. As they fell round my ankles, fireworks would simultaneously explode outside the window. The final scene would be me skipping out of a hairdressing salon in glorious sunshine with a brand-new choppy'n'layered cut to show off my razor-sharp cheekbones. Spring had arrived … *and so had I.*

The reality wasn't like that. It was a hard, lonely, painful slog. The most painful section being the *two and a half years* of initial weight loss. It took that long because I wanted to avoid getting droopy skin. I wasn't going to all that effort to resemble a cuttlefish when I took my clothes off. I cried each night for those nine hundred and twelve days, but it worked. I am an entirely jiggle-free zone. In fact, the only evidence you would find to prove I was once tipping the scales at 'Jesus wept!' are some faint stretch marks – which have been pummelled with pregnancy oil daily for fifteen years, and are *always* coated in fake tan. Oh, and obviously my chest suffered along the way. Boobs are to dieting what house prices are to the credit crunch. If you have to start tightening your belt they will be the first thing to drop. I rectified this situation with two student loans and an overnight visit to a surgeon based in Harley Street. Then finally, I was ready to look at myself in the mirror … and I saw the body *I* wanted, a body that *any* girl would want. But I didn't feel elated. I felt nothing. *Nothing* was what I had longed for.

That's because I couldn't feel *nothing* when I was fat. Fat people can't look at themselves without feeling *something*. It's compounded by the fact others can't either. Especially, women. There is always an emotional agenda behind a simple look. As a fat girl, other fat girls would look at me in relief – as I did with them – because we took the spotlight off each other. You'd go from being (no pun intended) the elephant in the room to the *two* or *three* elephants in the room; less of a circus act and more of an *enclosure*. Thin girls were more complex. On the outset, they examined you in the ways you would expect: with a hint of superiority, smugness and arrogance – maybe some pity. But there was a weird mix of fear and appreciation behind their eyes too. I could sense it. Deep down underneath the bravado, they were terrified that one day they could end up looking like me, and to that end, they were grateful to me for being fat. I was the visual stimulus they needed to put down their knife and fork when they were satisfactorily replenished … not when they needed to undo the top two buttons on their jeans and release the catch on their bra. No one ever *just* looked at me when I was fat. Not like this woman is doing right now. But then I look back at her and realise there *is* something behind her eyes. *Respect*. Because I am thin, i.e., *I am in control.* She wouldn't feel that way if she knew who I really was … And in about five minutes' time when she sits down with her Kir Royale and goes online, she'll meet *that* person. I bat my eyelids to get rid of the prickles and swallow hard. I am not going to cry. I haven't cried since that day I felt nothing … and those were happy tears.

What Maximilian said at his house pings back into my

head. *Until you know your truth … who you really are, you can't pretend to be someone else.* He's wrong. I do know who I really am, that's why I can pretend to be someone else. I've been doing exactly that for years. The truth? The truth is it hurts.

I carry on. I check in the family's coats, get their drinks from the bar, give them menus, tell Dane to take their order … But then I see the woman remove a Sony tablet from her Tote and I need to get out. *Fast.* I get Luke's number from Tabitha and call his mobile from the phone at reception. It goes straight through to voicemail. I try the landline at Warren's.

'Oi oiiiiiiiii! You are through to the oooooh-ahhhhhh; ultimate rave star … the self-appointed party tsar. Get your mitts outta his cookie jar … that's right, it's the one and only … Wozz-aaaaaaaaaa!'

I hear bass booming and people laughing in the background. I wonder if Warren has been to bed at *all* this weekend and feel a flicker of relief that I didn't make my party at Shoreditch House, if he was there drifting in and out of a K hole babbling nonsensically about 'wikkid' hi-hats and cowbells. How *not* to bump myself up the membership waiting list.

'Warren, it's Vivian. Is Luke there?'

'Nah, he's not. Pass us that blunt, matey …' he adds to someone in the room.

'Where is he?' I ask.

'Don't know, but I know where *you* are … in the Snoop Doggy dog house.'

'I know, I know …'

The bassline gets louder again and Warren inhales. 'Woooooooooh! Head russsssssssh.'

'Warren? Hello? *Warren? WARREN!*' My voice stiffens. 'Seriously, do you have any idea where Luke could be?'

'Not at the moment, no.'

'What about later?'

'That would be telling …' he says, exhaling.

'Warren!'

'All right, all right … I got him a gig later through my matey at SundaySoundz. Last-minute thing, one of the guest DJs couldn't sort their visa. The Lukazoid is doing the warm-up so he'll probably be on in about, ooooooooooh, I'd say an hour or so.'

I rummage in my bag for my cashpoint card but I know I've left it in Adele's clutch. 'Is it too late for you to put me on the guest-list?'

'Why should I after your no-show? Not impressed, Vivian. How could you do that? The Lukazoid went to so much troub—'

'It wasn't my fault.'

'Yeah, *right*. 'Parently you got rinsed earlier in the day and couldn't be arsed to turn up.'

'That is not what happ— I didn't. I promise.' I feel the prickling and tightening return. 'Please, Warren … I'm … *please*.'

He inhales and exhales dreamily again. 'Okay, you can say you're my matey, Chrissy …'

'Chrissy what?'

'Crackers,' he says, in monotone, as if he had just said 'Jones'. 'His name is *definitely* down and he *certainly* won't be leaving here today. He's zonked out in front of me, munted off his tiny little head. I might see you down there – depends how messy it gets here.' Everyone in the room cheers. 'Laters, Vivian. Oh, and good luck.'

'Luck?'

'Yeah, you're going to need it. Ooooh, tuuuuuuuuuune! Oi *oiiiiiiiii!*'

CHAPTER SIXTEEN

I borrow a pair of mirrored aviator Ray-Bans from Dane and go straight to the venue – a disused warehouse next to an old paper factory in East London. The SundaySoundz parties are always in places like this: all very back-to-the-spirit-of-rave if you overlook the £17 entry passes available to purchase online or more-on-the-door, where they also have a merchandising kiosk to flog their mix CDs and branded T-shirts.

When I arrive the party is revving up. Outside, people are mooching up to the entrance and standing in line or chatting on their mobiles trying to arrange last-minute hook-ups, drug orders and guest-list favours. They are typical Sunday clubbers. Half of them have been out partying since Friday and although outwardly excited, inwardly they are visualising the dark come-down that lies ahead the following week. The other half have stayed at home for the rest of the weekend in preparation for this event. Either way, they are all desperate to get inside and get dancing. The door girl knows this.

'Yes?' she says, arching an over-plucked eyebrow at me as I get to the front of the guest-list queue. She is the usual Zelda-from-the-*Terrahawks*, hatchet-faced crone in experimental make-up and battered Vivienne Westwood pirate boots. I know I have already pissed her off simply by daring to exist in the same stratosphere as her.

'Hello, I should be on the list.'

'Name?'

'Chrissy.'

'Chrissy who?' she asks half-heartedly, whilst staring into the lenses of my sunglasses to check her hair.

'Er, *Crackers*. My name is Chrissy Crackers.'

Face set in a world-weary frown she scans through some pieces of paper attached to a clipboard, clicking her tongue. 'Crackers, Crackers, Crackers ... *Chrissy Crackers.* Nope, you're not down. You'll have to join the paying queue.' She gesticulates to the left with her Biro without looking up. 'Next!'

'Hang on a second.'

'What?'

'But my name should be down.'

'Well, it isn't.'

'Can you check again?'

'No, I *can't*!' She sighs, totally exasperated – as if she was distributing food in a war-zone on behalf of the Red Cross, and not just *intermittently* lifting up a piece of rope for the odd pie-eyed raver to step past.

'But I, er, know Warren.' It's not often I would admit to that, but needs must. 'He's got a whole load of names on the list. He arranged them with one of the promoters. *Dave*?' A calculated stab in the dark, there's always *some-one* involved called Dave.

'Dave? But I've just checked his list ... anyone he'd have on there, *I* would know. Who do you work for?'

'Eh?'

More tongue clicking. 'Are you involved with the industry in some way?'

'No.' I regret this as soon as I say it. It is a general rule of thumb that everyone who is employed in 'Clubland' has absolutely *no* desire or inclination to help anyone who exists outside of it. It's like a Masonic Order with strobe lights.

'In that case, you'll have to wait until I can talk to Dave. Go and stand over there.' She does a shrugging-nodding-pointing hybrid gesture in no particular direction.

By 'over there' she means that Bermuda Triangle of nightclubs: the area between the guest-list queue, the paying queue and the ticket-holders queue. I have no hope of getting in now … I have slipped off the radar altogether. I know that the door girl is doing nothing to try to contact Dave because I can hear her yacking away to the bouncer about how the crowd isn't like it used to be, that she's *majorly* considering getting out of the whole game, possibly moving abroad … blah blah *blah.*

I move to 'over there' and the uneasiness sets in. I hate standing on any sort of periphery. It is where I spent so much of my youth. Even after I lost weight it took me ages to feel as if I didn't still belong there – *looking in.* Socialising at all the normal sort of places where people went to 'pull' felt alien. (I had only ever imagined being welcome in a bar like the one in *Star Wars.*) It took even longer for me to realise that once I was in those places I could get tipsy without being labelled a hapless saddo, because suddenly I was 'minxy' and 'up for it' … and I had *options.*

I reckoned I'd be lucky to attract the attention of a few desperate dregs blinded by beer goggles at the end of the night, but I was wrong. Before they'd even ordered a drink, top-quality specimens with 20:20 vision were eager to get their hands on me. Let me tell you, if you've spent a decade of your life thinking that the only way you'll ever be touched is with a cattle prod, this feels incredible. It's the ultimate proof that you are thin, and the ultimate sign that it's about time you loved your body. *They* do, so you should too. It's a thrill. But it's also addictive. I think about *all* the 'Men I've Been With' since Screw-it Stuart ... how they knew nothing – about each other *or* about me. But now they will. I visualize the picture in the newspaper. *Everyone* is going to know *everything*. They will know I used them as stop-offs on the journey to love myself. My heart races. My hands go clammy. *And they will know why I never got to that final destination ... or ever will.*

I see Luke, pulling up on the side of the road in his Ford Escort. An olive-skinned girl with dark hair is sitting in the passenger seat. I vaguely recognise her as a friend of Warren's. Luke gets out of the car and goes round to the boot, which he has to open by untying the length of rope that keeps it shut. I shout his name and run over to the car. As he looks up and sees me, something shocking happens. I feel better. Only a tiny bit, but definitely better. The only person who I have *ever* relied upon or given permission to make things better is *me*. I never look to other people as a portal for emotional assistance. Dizzily, I lurch towards Luke.

'Before you say anything, I am *so* sorry about last night. Tabitha told me what you did and I ... *I* ... well, it's no surprise you didn't bother replying to my email. Clearly, you thought I'd gone out partying but that is not the case … at *all*. There is a reason why I didn't tell you where I was going, it's all to do with stuff that's happened … stuff that I didn't think I could tell you about, but now, literally the moment I saw *you* see *me* … I have realised I can. I think I may have had a Road-to-Damascus moment on a no-through street in Dalston.' I smile at Luke, but as I do I become aware that his face is expressionless.

'Don't stress about it,' he says in a very even voice. 'It's no big deal.'

I take off Dane's sunglasses. 'Come on, Luke, I'm *allowing* you – no, *encouraging* you – to give me a hard time. Please, give me a bollocking and then I can make it up to you. Because, I want to. We need to talk. Like I was saying, I've realised something … Well, actually I think I may have realised it a while ago … there were definitely a few signs. I should have read more into them, but my life isn't a film starring Rachel McAdams. I don't *reflect*. If you knew who I used to be, then you'd underst—'

He interrupts me in the same flat tone. 'I better get inside, I'm on soon.'

'Don't panic, Lukey,' trills the girl, as she gets out of the car. 'You've got about half an hour.'

I notice she is *holding a sunflower*, the visual equivalent of slapping everyone you meet in the face and screaming, '*Hey people, I'm kooky!*' I have definitely met her before. She's some sort of fashion student. I think her name is Georgie. Or Joey. Something you would call a hamster before you knew its sex.

'Can I see you in there in a couple of minutes?' he says to her. 'Tell Dave I'm on my way. Cheers, Sammy.'

Sammy.

As she *skips* off, I watch Luke lug his record bag out of the boot. I sense this is not the right time to make a dig about him still insisting on playing vinyl at gigs. I put my arms around his neck and give him a kiss. He doesn't reciprocate.

'Tell you what …' I kiss him again. 'Why don't we celebrate my birthday *now*? I'll watch you play your whole set – not get remotely wasted – and then, we could go for a drink. Like I said, I want to talk to you. It's important.'

He extracts himself from my arms. 'I'd rather you didn't come in to the club. I need to concentrate.'

'O-*kay.* Well, why don't you come over to Adele's afterwards and stay the night? She'll be over at James's place.'

'No.' He grabs a pair of headphones from the car and hoists his record bag up onto his shoulder. 'I can't. We'll end up doing *it*.'

'And on a scale of one to ten that's bad *because*?'

'Because … this is *over*.'

'What did you say?'

'This is over.'

'As in?'

'We are finished,' he mumbles, staring down at the pavement but I can tell there is an expression on his face now – it's that crumpled one. 'It's time to knock it, this, *us*, on the head. Take care of yourself. Say goodbye to Monday for me.'

I laugh nervously and use one of our in-jokes. '*And the*

award for extreme over-sensitivity whilst loitering outside a stinking East End warehouse goes to … Come on, Luke, we can sort this out. Stop being so dramatic.'

'Vivian! *We are splitting up.* I think this is actually the one time I am more than within my rights to be dramatic, thanks.' He kicks his foot rhythmically against the kerb. 'I've made up my mind. I can't be with someone like you.'

'What's that supposed to mean?'

'Exactly what I said. We can't be together. You're a mind-fuck, and you're grinding me down.'

'This is about me not wanting to get up the duff, isn't it?'

'No, it's *not* … but again, nice choice of words. Actually, while we're on the subject, I'm glad you said "no"… because if you hadn't, you may have well been allowed to influence the development of another human being. Something I wouldn't wish on anyone.' I think he surprises himself at how horrible this sounds, but he carries on. 'How on earth would you teach a child what's right and wrong? You haven't even mastered the basics yourself.'

'Excuse me?'

'You heard what I said.'

I did. So I try yet another tack. 'Luke, listen to me, we can sort this out. Once I explain everything to you, you'll see that there are various reasons why I am the way I …' But his face indicates that this tack will fail too. I try another. 'You said I never turn to you in a crisis; well, now I *am*. A crisis has occurred and I … need … you.' I surprise myself at how weirdly elating it feels to say this. 'Honestly, I—'

'Honestly, you *WHAT*?' He shouts this. I have never heard him raise his voice before. 'Let's look at an example of you being honest, shall we?'

He unzips his record bag, pulls out a copy of *The First* and waves it in my face. I freeze. I wanted to be the one to show him.

'But you don't read any tabloids …' I say. But as when I was in Roger's office, I can't feel the words coming out of my mouth.

'Kevvo's girlfriend texted me this morning. She said you were in it.'

'This is why I've come here, to talk to you about what you might have s—'

He cuts me off. 'Now? You thought *now* would be a good time to *chat*?' He shakes the paper at again. 'We've been together for over a year. Why weren't any of those three hundred and seventy-eight days of any use to tell me you were once so …'

'*Fat*?' The word that I *never* say out loud leaves my mouth in a violent and anguished scream, as if I were being exorcised of some vile, Satanic plasma.

'No, unhappy.' He stares at me. There is a very disconcerting mixture of pity and bewilderment in his eyes. I look away and it is still there when I turn back. I reach for his arm, but he snatches it away from me. 'You lied.'

'I *never* lied to you, Luke. I just didn't …' I decide to borrow Maximilian's line. 'I didn't reach inside and pull out the *whole* truth.'

'Really?' Luke opens the paper and with his index finger scans down the copy accompanying the picture of me.

A nervous heat tingles across my chest. I hadn't read the words.

'*According to Stuart Hayes,*' reads Luke, he looks up to see me flinching at the mention of Screw-it Stuart '… *a fellow student at the drama college she attended, Vivian lost a substantial amount of weight whilst studying for her degree. "It was hard for anyone to see her shrinking, though, as she covered herself up in baggy T-shirts and jogging bottoms," says Stuart, currently appearing in a European tour of* Les Miserables. *"I didn't fully appreciate how thin she had got until the day she wore a* suit … *"*'

My only suit. I'd just bought it. I wore it the morning after I had slept with Stuart. He must have watched me leave from his window.

'"… *for her* …"' I thought he was still asleep. He must have watched me leave the house from his bedroom window. '"… *father's funeral.*"'

I stare at Luke. Then I find myself shrugging.

'That's it? That's all the explanation I deserve? A *shrug*!' He shakes the paper at me. 'You told me your dad wasn't in your life any more.'

'He isn't.'

'Because he *passed* away, Vivian. You told me you had lost contact.'

'We have.'

'Because he is *dead!*'

'So, he's not in my life any more. He's not living. I am. Hence, no contact. Simple.'

Luke doesn't say anything back to that. He chucks the

paper in the boot of the car on top of a load of looped-up cables then slams the lid shut. But immediately it bounces back open, so he crouches down to re-tie the rope. I crouch down next to him.

'Okay, I fucked up, Luke. I should have told you he died, but I didn't because …well, because you would have expected me to show how sad that made me. But it didn't make me sad back then and it doesn't now. Not exactly the nicest of things to admit, is it? You want to know why I don't see my mother that much? It's because it's hard having to pretend I miss my father as much as she does, when I don't. I already put her through enough when I was so f…' I trail off. I can't say the word again. 'My brother and sister can sense exactly how I feel … and they despise me for it. Especially my sister. She hates me. My own sister! If she can manage to feel this way about me, I'm sure if I went round telling other people how I feel – especially people like you who love their parents unconditionally – I know they would hate me too.'

Luke turns to me. 'Not…' he begins, his voice much softer again. 'Not if they already love you.'

The heat intensifies across my chest. 'And you do, *do* you?' I retort back almost angrily, because it's easier then acknowledging his sincerity. 'It's not as if you've ever said…'

'I love you?' He jumps up.

I jump up too. 'Yeah. You've *never* s—'

'Yes, I have,' he interrupts. 'I told you yesterday morning, on your birthday. I've wanted to tell you for ages but I knew you'd freak out. D'you have any idea how insane it is to be with someone for over a *year* knowing you can't tell them how you feel? For that to be *normal*?'

He looks directly into my eyes, and for some reason all I can think about is the day I got home from school to find Mum had installed that second mirror in my bedroom.

'I don't remember you saying it,' I tell him.

'I wrote it at the end of the note I left you by the kettle. I said, *I love you, Vivian.* You *know* I did. When we spoke on the phone you said you could handle it … that you were ready to take that step.'

I drop my head. 'I thought you were talking about going out for dinner at that Spanish restaurant. Christ, Luke, I didn't read the whole note … I only got as far as "tapas".'

With that he picks up his record bag and CD wallets, then barges past me. I call after him.

'Luke, come back! The final word we say to one another cannot be "tapas".' But he ignores me so I go into attack mode. It feels a lot more comfortable. 'Fine, go. Go and be with Sammy. I'm sure *she* wasn't baptised at Sea World or the first time *she* wore heels she struck oil … and when she goes to a restaurant I bet she gets a menu not an estimate.' I stop, even though I have hundreds more of Kate Summers' put downs to choose from.

Luke replies without turning round. 'I picked her up half an hour ago, Vivian, she needed a lift. Jesus, won't you *ever* grow up?'

'Grow up?' I shout after him, slapping Dane's sunglasses back on. 'Grow up! Ha! That's rich coming from someone who … *who* … *who* …' I struggle to find an area where Luke behaves less maturely than me, and apparently to

prove my point that I am *way* ahead in the puerile stakes I throw one more childish comment at him. 'Actually, hang on a second. I've suddenly realised something else … you're *jealous.* It's that picture of me with Maximilian Fry that's really got you, isn't it?'

This time he does turn round. 'No, Vivian. It isn't. I didn't think for one minute you were having an affair with a film star.'

With that, he crosses the road and goes up to the entrance. A swarm of clubbers who don't appear to be in any specific queue are now buzzing around the door girl. But as soon as Luke lugs his record bags towards them and swings his headphones round his neck they divide for him to walk through, as if he was some sort of electro apostle. Elbowing my way through the crowd after him, I hear him introduce himself to the door girl.

'Ah Luke, Dave said to look out for you.' She snaps a neon green band round his wrist. 'He's expecting you. You'll find him in the VIP area to the left of the DJ booth. Welcome to the SundaySoundz family.'

I push my way to the front. 'It's me …' I tell her.

'God, not again … Have you got hold of Warren?'

'I don't need to.' I glance at Luke. 'I'm with him.'

She sighs, and twists back to him. 'Is she with you, *Luke*?'

He doesn't skip a beat. 'No, she is not *with me* …' he says, slowly and succinctly, not even bothering to face me because both of us know he is right.

'Right, glad we got that sorted,' replies the door girl smugly. 'Have a good set, Luke. Oh, and can I suggest that if you spin here again you email me your guest-list in advance, then we don't get issues on the door. That's the thing about *chancers* … they, er, always think they're in with a *chance*.'

With that, she lifts up the rope for him then peers over at me and raises that eyebrow again, as if she has just come out with a philosophy of Nietzschean significance.

CHAPTER SEVENTEEN

The Terry Ward Film and Theatre Agency on Berwick Street, W1, is a chaotic homage to the last fifty years in British entertainment. Every shelf is piled high with old scripts, show reels and theatre programmes, whilst the walls are completely masked by yellowing signed photos and original movie posters. The last tiny section of blank space disappeared years ago, under a framed cartoon I bought Terry shortly after I moved to London. He helped me find a bedsit and enrol on my drama course, so I had it drawn for him as a thank-you. In the picture, Alfie (Terry's fox terrier), is depicted as an eccentric theatre impresario. He is sprawled across the ancient velvet chaise longue in the study waving a cigarette around in his paw, and he is saying to Terry, *My dear, I'm sick to the back teeth of playing man's best friend. Can't you find me something with a bit more grit?*.

'Chin up, Vivian,' says Terry, tapping a copy of *The First* from yesterday with a pencil. 'At least you got some coverage in a national newspaper. That picture is over half a page.'

I roll my eyes at him. 'Because I wouldn't fit on any less. The only service that article has provided to my career is demonstrating to casting agents that I have the ability to carry extra weight …' I shoot Terry a look because I know what he is thinking. 'And I am telling you now, don't even *think* about it. You know the rules.'

Terry sighs then smiles. As always I can't help but notice that when he is smiling at me it's when he looks least like his brother: my father.

'So, the question remains, where did the picture come from?'

'My sister,' I say emphatically. 'She must have taken it without me knowing. The only other person who'd want to rattle me like that is my brother, but I doubt he'd go this far. He'd still find it funny, though.'

'So Tracey would have been the instigator?'

'Of course. You know the drill, Uncle Terry. She was Daddy's little girl, She still blames me for stressing out the family when I left home and didn't contact them for years – etc., etc., etc. – and that led to *Dad* …' I force myself to use the fonder way of referring to my father in front of Terry. 'Having a heart attack.'

'He had a hereditary congenital defect.'

'As if an intensively researched medical fact would hold any bearing with her,' I mutter, as I rub my head – it still hasn't stopped aching from yesterday despite the fact I've taken six Nurofen – and sink back into the threadbare sofa. It is properly knackered, not just artfully tired like the furniture at Burn's. I want a cigarette.

'Have you called your mother?' asks Terry.

'No. She reads the *Express*, so she won't have seen it. I'm not going to tell her because it would only cause upset.'

Would she be upset? I rephrase. 'Irritation. Raking up all those memories … she was permanently exasperated back then.'

'What about either of your siblings … will you phone them?'

'Definitely not. They'd only say it was a joke and they didn't mean it.' Just like they used to say to Mum it was, 'only a joke and we didn't mean it' when they used to jog round the cul-de-sac in my tracksuit bottoms, one of them in each leg.

The doorbell chimes.

'Ah, that must be her!' says Terry excitedly.

He straightens his tie and leaves the room – stumbling over a pile of old VHS videos en route. I twist round in my seat and stare out of the window into the street below. As a kid I stayed with Terry whenever I could. He was more like my best friend than my uncle, and I don't mean that in an 'Alert the relevant authorities!' kind of way. He figured out I wasn't too happy at home so he took me to see his clients in plays and musicals to cheer me up. He couldn't have been more different to my father. Put it this way, Terry was a huge fan of *Cats.* My father preferred pussy. I really liked Soho too. It was full of oddballs: drag queens, punks, rubber fetishists, exotic dancers, crack-heads … So no one stared at me, the porky kid. Terry and I would go to this brasserie on Old Compton Street and I'd quite happily chomp my way through a golden syrup sponge pudding with custard knowing everyone in the restaurant was more likely to be looking at the pissed Eastern European hooker in the PVC basque at the table next to me.

That restaurant is still there – it doubles up as an internet café, but the menu is pretty much the same. I know this because I went in there before I walked up to Terry's to see if Luke had emailed me. He hadn't. Then I checked Sammy's Twitter. I *knew* she'd have an account. She wore friendship bands on her wrist, for Christ's sake, there was no way she would be able to resist a more advanced and far-reaching way for showing off how well liked she was. Anyway, I found the account easily. Her Twitter name is @SammySparkles. She has 567 followers. Her profile picture is a hand holding a pile of coloured M&Ms with a different shade of nail varnish on each finger. (Filtered, obviously.) Anyway, there it was … posted a few minutes after midnight on Sunday; the 122-character Tweet that told me everything I needed to know.

OODLES OF FUN AT SS! BEZZIE NIGHT OUT IN AGES + NOT OVER YET, YAY! LUKEY, U ROCKED IT! BIG LUV *#couldbethestartofsomething*

Could be the start of something? It was obvious what had happened over the evening. I pictured it immediately. Luke stepping back from the decks after executing the perfect warm-up set for the headliner; the promoter, Dave (I visualised him having some kind of ironically styled facial hair), slapping him on the back, telling him he 'killed it *pwoper*' and insisting he join the 'soundz team' on a regular basis. Luke finding Sammy by the bar, telling her the good news, her squealing, offering him her congratulations … and an E. Luke defying his usual anti-drug stance and necking it to spite me. Forty minutes later, they are entwined round each other in the back of the roped-off VIP section, which Dave has personally invited them into. Their eyes lock onto each other's as the hypnotic minimal beats envelop them …

'Freakin' hell!' exclaims Barb Silver, as she steps into the office and takes in all of Terry's paraphernalia. 'You Brits can never throw anything in the trash, can you?'

'On the contrary, Ms Silver.' Terry grins, going pink, this time because he is blushing. 'We merely have a sense of history.'

'It's Barb … and you can still have a sense of history *and* a key to a storage facility,' she replies, and then turns to me. 'Still alive, then, kiddo? Woah! I know actresses who'd have climbed into a warm bath with a freakin' sharp razor blade if a picture like that got out. How many of them are there out there?'

'Overweight people?'

Barb cackles. 'No, *photos* …'

'I didn't even know there was that one.'

'Well, no need to get down … every cloud has a silver lining. But you're even luckier, kiddo. *Your* cloud has a *Barb Silver* lining.'

She winks at me. I'm surprised by how upbeat she is. When Terry had called to let me know Barb wanted to meet up I was expecting her to be fuming that her precious Maxy had been associated with the *anti*-skeleton in my closet.

The intercom buzzes on Terry's desk and a woman's voice with a Suffolk burr says, 'We're back, Mr Ward, anything I can be getting you?'

'Oooooh …' Terry nods at Barb. 'Tea? Slice of sponge cake, Ms Silver? Sorry, *Barb*?'

She grimaces as if he has just offered her a witchetty grub.

Terry leans into the intercom again. 'Just send the furry chap in, please, Carol. Thank you …'

A moment later, the door opens a few inches and Terry's fox terrier bursts through, chewing on his lead, thrilled at having been on *exactly* the same walk round the block that he has been doing at four o'clock every day since he was a puppy. He does a quick circuit of the room taking in any new smells, dunks his head into his water bowl, then clambers onto the chaise longue where he collapses with his back paws inelegantly splayed apart like a spatchcock chicken.

'And I thought *I* had some moves,' mutters Barb, appalled but amused at the same time.

'That's Alfie,' explains Terry. 'Named after the lead character in the original Michael Caine film, I hasten to add, and not that awful remake.' He leans back in his chair and smiles suavely at his guest. I can tell he is taken with her contemporary shtick. 'So, tell me, what can I do for you, *Barb*?'

'Well, first let me say, I wouldn't be here if I didn't think that Vivian could be trusted, but …' She nods at me. 'I was impressed by what you did the other afternoon when Maxy spun out.'

'What exactly was wrong with him?' I ask.

'That's not important.' She shrugs. 'What *is* is that you did the right thing: getting a private doctor, giving a false name and *keeping your mouth shut*. You know how to play the game, kiddo, and I like that. Anyway, I got an interesting call last night from JP Goldstein. His studio financed and produced *The Simple Truth.* He – and only he – has the option to do the sequel. I'll be honest with you, prior to our conversation last night he wasn't so much having second thoughts about Maxy making a comeback as filing him in the drawer marked "J". That's *"J"* for "Just isn't going to have the career we all thought…" or "J" for "JOSH HARTNETT". Ha! Anyway, JP had seen the shot online of Vivian with Maxy and he wanted to know if they were dating … So, I said it was early days.'

Terry splutters. 'You said *what*?'

'I said they were seeing how things developed – but that yeah, they had a *connection*,' Barb says, clasping her hands together to underline this. 'I wanted to see how JP would react, and he thought it was ad*orable.* These big cheeses are all the same. The more dysfunctional their own lives – JP is on his fourth wife – the cosier they like their stars. But there's another angle I like. Up until now, Nicholas Van Smythe has always insisted I market his client in an ultra high-brow manner and shroud him in privacy, but those days are over. Actors can't simply pose for Annie Leibovitz in an air-conditioned studio every twelve months and gabble on about their *craft* … they have to open up, let the public in, appear *available*; especially if their popularity has taken a hit. They find a hook to make themselves seem more real, and use it.' She swings round on her shiny boots and points at me. 'Kiddo, *you* are going to be our hook.'

I glance over at Terry. He is looking rattled. Alfie notices his expression too and gets into air-raid position – head buried underneath his front paws as if a grenade was about to be thrown in through the window.

'Exactly *what* are you suggesting?' asks Terry.

Barb rolls her eyes at him. 'Isn't it obvious? Vivian and Maxy are going to become a couple. We'll fabricate a relationship between the two of them for media gain. It's like a freakin' movie already. Hell, the script is writing itself. The public has already witnessed their "meet cute" *and* their first date. It would be rude not give them the next instalment.'

I stare blankly at my uncle. His face is rigid. Barb misreads our lack of reactions.

'I knew you would both dig the idea.' She grins. 'Trust me, the public will dig it even more. After all, famous men tend to go out with other famous women. Failing that, they might begrudgingly still be with their childhood sweetheart, who they'd actually much rather *not* be with so that they *could* bang someone famous, but can't leave for fear of the bad press they'll get. In general, male heart-throbs only have *affairs* with *civilians.* They might pump the childminder or a random lap dancer, but they rarely parade them around in front of the cameras and they certainly wouldn't date someone who used to be … how do I put this delicately?' She gives up trying to think of a way and shrugs. 'Freakin' *Titanic.*'

Terry manages to speak. 'Excuse me? My niece is a real person, you know …'

Barb pulls up the sleeves of her black silk shirt and wags a finger at him. 'Ah, but she is so much *more* than that now. She's a living, breathing "look at me then and look at me now!" feature in a celebrity magazine. She's the beacon of hope for every chubby-chops in the land that there's life beyond lonely Saturday nights on the sofa in front of the latest lousy Reece Witherspoon flick, digging out the doughy bits from a family-sized tub of Ben and Jerry's.'

Terry emits a negative growl and Alfie follows suit. But Barb continues.

'Lighten up, *sugar*,' she says, as coquettishly as she can whilst chewing hard on her gum. 'It'll only be for the summer – three months tops. By then, Maxy will be considered a man of the people, Goldstein will have green-lighted *Truth 2* and your Vivian could possibly have a career. *Job done on all fronts.* After that we'll split them up. It'll be touchingly amicable. Usual bull: work commitments.' She reaches inside her Birkin, pulls out a stapled set of documents and places them on Terry's desk. 'I've made some notes for you to look through – including details of the allowance she'll get each week. She'll also get a cut of the staged paparazzi shots at the end if she keeps her side of the deal. But I need to know one way or another by tomorrow morning, so we can get the ball rolling. These set-ups are always about momentum.' Her eyes dart from Terry to me and back to Terry again. 'Are we all in?'

He bangs his hands down on the desk and Alfie winces. '*Are we all in?*' he booms. 'Are you out of your mind? Suffragettes did not throw themselves under horses for Vivian to prostitute herself in this manner.'

'Relax,' says Barb, waving her hand. 'They'll only engage in some light petting for the cameras. It's going to be so neat. Even their names are similar.' She sits down next to me and squeezes my arm. 'I bet the press call you "Maximivian".'

Terry snorts at her. 'Or you could combine their surnames, Fry and Ward. Then they can be known as "Fraud". Rather more appropriate, don't you think? Vivian doesn't need to get caught up in your lies. They'll be other opportunities for her d—'

'Down the line?' interrupts Barb. 'No, there won't. Not like this. You and I both know she is on limited time. Don't let her be one of those performers who turn down their greatest chance to make it. The history of entertainment is littered with them. Like that forgotten stage school kid who left the Spice Girls training camp to go back to college and was replaced by Emma Bunton. Okay, so living alongside chronic bulimia, crazed ambition and crackpot Girl Power – and that was just Geri, ha! – can't have been easy, but sheesh, what a boz—'

Terry interrupts her back. 'Don't make out this would feed Vivian's career as an actress. She would be chewed up and spat out the other side as reality-TV mulch. Neither of us needs to hear any more, Ms Silver. You've given us both ample time to think. Hasn't she, Vivian?'

Yes, she has. But I haven't been thinking about her offer. I'm thinking about Sammy and Luke sprinting hand-in-hand out of the club, Sammy quickly rushing back in to grab her sunflower, the pair of them zooming back to her flat (she'd own it outright – a gift from her minted art dealer parents for getting a First in her textiles degree) … Luke frenziedly ripping off Sammy's clothes in the corridor, then shagging her in the lounge – although she'd probably call it 'The Den'. It would be just like he and I used to do it … but with one crucial difference. As Luke collapsed onto her Hello Kitty bean bag after coming, he would realise that what we used to do was *have sex*. He and Sammy had just *made love*.

'Vivian?' repeats Terry.

'I … I … my head hurts.' I get up from the sofa. 'The answer is "no", Barb. Sorry. Bye, Terry. I've got to get to the tube. I'm working at Burn's in a bit …'

I run out the room, past Carol at her desk and down the stairs onto the road. I stand on the pavement for a few seconds, thinking about how black the darkness seemed. But you know what, I always had one recurring positive thought that beamed like a bright light through the negativity: that my state of mind would heal and recover completely when I grew up. But as it turned out, this was as naïve as Justin Bieber thinking he could take his pet monkey on a world tour without any quarantine issues. Little did I know that the way you function back then stays with you. *Growing up* is simply learning how to *cover up*. The essence of becoming – and continuing to be – a convincingly normal adult is tricking people into thinking you must have been a normal child.

I make my way to the tube station, Soho life bustling around me … but I can't seem to hear a thing.

CHAPTER EIGHTEEN

But that night, I hear the whispering. As soon as I walk into the restaurant a table of three women (all long-term members who work for a glossy weekly fashion magazine) stop dead in their tracks, forks loaded with seared tuna en route to their mouths. They wait until I have passed and then clack their heads together. I can just about make out the editor – an ambitious hag in a Chanel neckerchief – say, 'Must have had lipo, at the very LEAST…' Her tone of voice isn't merely snide, she also sounds unsettled. Which I suppose is not unexpected. After all, I have been exposed as having a *past*. The whole point of places like Burn's is that everyone acknowledges each other in the *present*. Everyonc is defined by who they are *right now*; their dynamic jobs, their cutting-edge clothes, their well-connected friends … not who they may have once been. At Burn's no one is fat, lonely, shy or slothful; no one has frizzy hair, goofy teeth, acne, cheap plimsolls or glasses with thick lenses. That's why people join places like this – to be seen as the person they always wanted to be.

Everyone except Adele, that is, who loves it here for one reason only: the possibility she will get free alcohol. Oh yes, my flatmate may earn a fortune but she is tighter than a ferret's poo shoot. At seven o'clock, she pitches up with a group of colleagues, including Melanie, her unfathomably close friend. I can tell they have both already been drinking.

'Hiy*aaa*!' Adele gives me a massive hug, two kisses and one of those giddy cock of thc hcads combined with a shoulder shrug. She smells of cigarettes. (I can be more specific now; she has been drinking *white wine*. Adele goes from militant non-smoker to lab beagle within two glasses of Lady Petrol.) She passes me a bunch of flowers. 'Can you put these in some water? The girls got them for me. It's just us for the moment. James will be down later.'

'With Toby?'

'Of course. He's the *best man*, Vivian.' She says this as if I have suggested James has a conjoined twin who won't be accompanying him.

'Well, he better not try to bring his Labrador in here, *again*.'

'Ha! I'll text him. Now, any chance of a few bottles of *vino blanco* on the house? Special occasion and all that …'

Melanie unwinds a cream pashmina from around her shoulders and removes a pair of Jackie O style sunglasses. She has permanent panda tan marks around her eyes from the year-round skiing trips she goes on.

'Hi, Vivian, you well? I almost *died* when I saw that picture of you in the Sunday rag. I never *knew* you used to be … anyway, curveball. Literally! More importantly, tell me you're *not* boffing that Maximilian Fry? Adele told me you weren't,' she adds.

'Well, you're *not*. Are you?' Adele says quickly, and

with no emphasis on the 'are' to imply that she is asking for my confirmation.

Melanie also doesn't give me time to reply. 'Ah well, shame. He is effing fit.' She hooks her arms round two of the other girls. 'Right, ladies, let's get sozzled.'

She tosses her wrap over the flowers I am holding, mutters something about possibly ordering 'some charcuterie' and saunters up the stairs with the other successful women; all three of them solid Burberry-suited, Lanvin-heeled evidence of what can be achieved when you don't loll around the flat all day watching dubiously staged American telly waiting for your fake tan to dry. Adele hangs back.

'Ignore Melz. Between you and me, she's boozing a bit too much at the mo; got a few issues going on with her hubby. Anyway, are you okay?' She grimaces at me and squeezes my shoulder supportively. 'Listen … *that* photog—'

I cut her off. 'We'll discuss it later.' I have no intention.

She sees my expression and doesn't push me. 'What did Luke say about it?'

'Not a lot.' I shrug. 'We've split up.'

'Sorry?'

'We're not together any more.'

Adele gives me another hug, shoulder shrug and cock of the head combo. 'Ah. You dumped him …'

'You say that as if I was always going to.'

'Well, you *were*, weren't you?' she says, matter-of-factly, 'At some point. It's what you always do.'

My head throbs even harder. 'He dumped me.'

Adele jumps back. 'You are joking? Luke dumped you? You got *dumped*?'

'Yes.'

'Shit!' Her mouth drops. 'I never saw that coming … God, he was *obsessed* with you. Anyone could see that. I thought he was going to end up on your relationship scrap heap like *all* the others. But *he* dumped *you*? I can't bel*ieve* it. Come here.' She lunges back at me for another hug and exhales deeply into my hair extensions. 'Dumped? What a bastard. I never thought you'd get to know what it feels like …'

I don't need to see her face as she says this to detect a glimmer of satisfaction, because I can hear it through the tipsy-ness. She would be mortified if she knew I had identified it, but I have. Because here's the thing: when we first started at drama college I was only a few months in to my diet. Yes, I had lost a number of pounds but I was still very much in 'Stand back from the strappy vest!' territory. For Adele, I was the perfect side-kick – overly loyal but under confident. I could tell she saw me as the Barbara Hershey character in *Beaches*, always content to 'walk a step behind'. But everything changed after my one-night stand with Screw-it Stuart. Despite Adele flirting with him relentlessly, he'd never got round to sleeping with her. When she found out I had nailed him, it was official … I was no longer 'the wind beneath her wings', but the dark storm cloud that had rained all over her parade.

She pulls back and shakes her head at me. 'You'll be fine, Vivian, I know you will be. Your ego is probably a bit bruised right now, because you're not used to getting rejected by men. It's always *you* giving *them* the boot. At least, this way you are free to look for Mr Right. Luke wasn't exactly husband material, was he? Good guy; funny, sexy, kind … James *really* liked him. But was he what you need going forward? Maybe you should take this as a sign it's time for you to stop getting about – you *know* I don't mean that in a bitchy way – and look for that one special person. It will happen. Look how many times I've been dumped and now I'm planning a wedding.' She pauses. 'Oooh, there's a thought … will you be able to find another one for The Big Day?'

'Boyfriend?'

'No, DJ. If Luke isn't coming we'll need someone else.'

I grit my teeth. 'Yeah, I'm sure …'

'Great. Now, shall we get those drinks? I'm *gasping*.'

There really is no such thing as sisterhood, is there? However, the brotherhood appears to be alive and well. It never ceases to amaze me how someone like James (introvert, went to grammar school, family all civil servants) could be friends with Toby (extrovert, private education, family *has* servants). When they both arrive an hour later I am seating the three crones from the fashion magazine for after-dinner drinks in the upstairs bar.

'Awooogaaahhh! Awooogaaahhh! Awooogaaahhh!' shouts Toby, launching into his trademark Maori-style greeting dance at the arched entrance. He sticks his tongue out, slaps his ruddy cheeks, jiggles his moobs, then leaps over to where Adele is sitting and pretends to honk her breasts like a car horn. It is a sequence of moves that I am sure the dignified elder statesman of the ancient New Zealand tribe would be thrilled by. 'Delsie Pritchard! Getting my Jimbo under the thumb like that … in six months? Splendid work, you *harlot!*'

James comes over and gives me a kiss on the cheek. 'Thanks for organising everything tonight, Vivian. I really hope you haven't been too upset about that stuff in the paper … not nice at *all*. Still, I expect Luke is looking after you. How is he?'

'Pretty good, from what I can tell.'

Typically for someone as mild mannered as James, he doesn't read anything negative into my reply. 'It goes without saying Luke is invited to the wedding,' he says. 'Tell him I won't let Adele strong arm him behind the decks if he doesn't fancy playing. You've got a decent guy there, Vivian. When we were on holiday, Adele said she'd noticed good changes in you during the time you've been together with him … that you seem to be on a more even keel.'

'Only because I gave up coke …' I reply flatly, and walk off.

It gets messy later. Upstairs becomes packed so Roger tells me to stay behind the bar. Adele and her City-girl pals demolish seven bottles of Chablis and Melanie harangues our resident DJ to play something by … *get this* … Jessie J. *Jessie J!* Who actually *asks* to listen to her records? Shortly after being rewarded with the join-the-dot lyrics of 'Price Tag', Adele shrieks at everyone to be quiet so she can make a drunken toast to *herself* on getting engaged. As everyone claps she raises her glass to James and thanks him 'for saving me', which makes Melanie burst into tears. Toby lumbers over and attempts to cheer her up by rubbing his face in her chest and awoooaaagggh-ing.

'Keep the volume down,' I snap at him.

'Killjoy,' he mutters. 'You know Vivian barred my Truffles,' he adds sulkily to Melanie. 'Can't see why, there are plenty of hounds in here … ha!'

She wipes the corners of her eyes. 'Oh, don't worry about her,' she says, quite audibly. 'It's not as if she runs the place.'

I bite the inside of my cheek and shoot Adele a look. She leans across the bar. I can sense the white wine coursing round her blood stream.

'Try to be a bit understanding, Vivian. I told you Melz is having some *issues* at the moment. Her husband has asked for some space.'

'Space, eh?' I fire back. 'The recession's answer to divorce.'

Melanie squints back over at Adele. 'What did she say? Was she making a fool of me?'

'No,' I reply. 'There's no need. You always do a marvellous job of that all by yourself.'

Adele gasps and tries to placate her colleague. 'She didn't mean it. Vivian can get a bit shirty at work.' She glares at me. 'Aren't you going to say sorry?'

'No,' I retort calmly, but at this point I know I will not be keeping calm for long. I wasn't like this when I was younger. When Kate Summers and her gang wound me up I would accept it. I'd never retaliate because I knew how stupid and ugly I would look. All wobbly and pink faced. 'I have a rule, you see, Melanie …' I turn to her. 'Not to ever apologise to *anyone* who wears a *fucking* pashmina.'

'Vivian!' Adele gasps and slithers off her bar stool. 'You're out of order.'

'*I* am? Ha!'

James mouths, 'Sorry!' at me, then swings his arm round his fiancée. 'Hon, I don't think you meant that,' he says diplomatically. 'I also think it's time we went home.'

Adele stamps her foot. 'I'm not leaving *my* engagement drinks.'

'Ah, but it's not your *actual* "engagement drinks"', is it, Dels?' I tell her. The throbbing in my head now so acute I wonder if people can see my temples vibrating. 'It's an initial congratulatory "get-together". In a few days' time you've got a cocktail party to celebrate your news, which – when I logged on to adeleandjames.com earlier – I understand is now the precursor to an official dinner you have booked in for next month. Then, after all of that – just in case any of us have forgotten you're getting hitched – we've got the hen do, for which, according to the schedule, I will need to take a week off work and have an up-to-date passport.'

She scowls at me. 'So? We're obviously going *away*.'

'Where?'

'Egypt.' She shrugs defensively, as if she had said, *That salsa bar just off Tottenham Court Road …*

'Egypt?'

'Yes, Egypt. I've never been. Stop moaning, Vivian. Everyone else is more than willing to get behind my special day.'

'Of course, we are,' sniffs Melanie. 'I, for one, couldn't be happier for you.'

Adele smiles at her. 'Thank you, my lovely. Clearly, Vivian is finding it a little more difficult.' She shoots James a look before he attempts to intervene again. Then she pauses, waits until most of the bar is listening, shakes her hair to one side and squares up to me. 'Obviously, I understand it can't be easy for you having to think about my wedding, Vivian, what with your relationship going tits-up … the day after your birthday. I feel for you, really, I do. *We all do.*' She sways and grabs the bar for support.

'Right, that's it.' James gives me an apologetic grimace and picks up Adele's handbag off the floor. 'Hon, you're pissed,' he tells her. 'We are leaving. *Now.*'

'What's the problem?' she trills innocently. 'I was simply saying it must be hard becoming thirty-five *then single* on consecutive days.'

Sometimes I forget that Adele almost completed her course at acting college. Despite being smashed, that was a great delivery, especially accompanied by that Herbal Essences toss of her bracken curls. Everyone is now staring at either me or Adele. I can tell the majority of them are on her side because she is the bride-to-be, which automatically guarantees her blameless status. Interestingly, though, given her earlier behaviour, the style magazine editor appears to be looking at me more softly. I reckon it's because she isn't married either – or even in a relationship. She has the demeanour of a woman who has hit forty-five and found her walk-in wardrobe full of the hottest designer labels but her hand-carved Nordic sleigh bed decidedly empty and cold.

Adele and I stand in silence, glaring at each other. I am thinking: *Shot of vodka, Nurofen, cigarette.* But then the silence is broken.

'Vivian …'

My eyes dart to the arched doorway that leads into the bar. Maximilian Fry is standing there, a vision in distressed fabrics; off-white cords, faded grey cotton vest and an almost threadbare navy woollen beanie.

'We need to talk,' he adds.

Not moving, he gazes languidly at all the drinkers in the bar. They stare back … entranced. I am not surprised. Maximilian looks extraordinarily handsome – even more so than at his house or the hotel, almost inhumanly so – as if he had been developed in a Petri dish at a laboratory. I glance back at Adele and across at Melanie. I don't think either of them would have looked more shocked if Jessie J had clomped into the bar in her ill-advised footwear instead.

Maximilian doesn't say anything else. As a BAFTA-winning actor he understands the concept of leaving an audience wanting more. He simply strolls over, loops his arm round my shoulder and guides me out of the room, down the stairs and past a bug-eyed Tabitha – clearly still in raptures from his arrival. We leave the club through the fire exit at the back.

'What do you want?' I ask, angrily jabbing one of the recycling bins with my foot. I can't face him. My whole body is shuddering with embarrassment knowing he has seen that picture. 'I've already made it clear I'm not interested in Barb's plan.'

'She told me,' says Maximilian. 'I didn't come here to persuade you. She and Nicholas don't even know I'm here. I came to see if you were okay and to say sorry. That story in *The First* was my fault. It's happened to me before … dragging someone into my world … them suffering the consequences. If I hadn't asked you to leave the hotel with me, we would never have been papped, and they never would have printed that phot—'

'I'm over it and I need to finish my shift, so …' I still can't look at him. '… you can go. Really, *go*.'

He doesn't. He perches on a stack of empty bottle crates. 'Listen, Vivian—' his voice is softer '—I understand about having secrets. I can't remember a time in my life where I haven't been trying to keep *some*thing under wraps. My parents, my dyslexia … my depression.' He talks with the same chat-show ease as when we were in The Red Lion. 'That was why I went to rehab, by the way. Of course, Barb stuck to the party line – "party" being the operative word – and told the press I had simply been out on the town too much after my break-up. No action hero wants the words "anxiety", "reliance" or "barbiturates" to be among the first in their Wikipedia entry. It's not a good look.'

I don't bother glancing across at him again to see *how* good-looking he appears as he says this but carry on staring at the ground.

'So yeah,' he continues, 'that's why I whacked out in the pub; prescription meds. I hadn't taken anything for a while, but when I saw my ex, I got spooked; double dropped a

Xanax, it hit me like a brick. When I need to, I take other stuff too: Codeine, Ambien, Lunesta, Adderall, Vicodin …'

'Sounds like a list of Tara Reid's top baby names,' I mutter, and sit down on a stack of empty bottle crates opposite him.

He carries on talking, but I lose concentration. Further images of what Luke and Sammy have been up to in the past forty-eight hours flap mockingly through my mind, faster and more graphically. Luke skiving off work, more 'making love' followed by Velcro-style spooning, Sammy suggesting they call for a Dominos, Luke looking on fondly as she orders a myriad of brightly coloured toppings and side dishes without flinching, DVDs, cuddling, giggling, more 'making love', Sammy photographing their pile of empty take-out boxes and putting the shots up on Pinterest …

'Anyway.' Maximilian kicks my foot gently with his scuffed boot. 'I didn't come here to bore you with any more of my shit. I know you don't want to talk about that photo, but for what it's worth I didn't think you looked *that* bad. I, er, liked your denim jacket.'

'Liar. It was *far* too small for me and *stone-washed.*'

'Exactly. If you hadn't noticed I like clothes to look a bit worn, so stone-washing is all right with me. Speaking of which, do you like my new beanie?'

I glance up at him again as he points at the bedraggled woollen mesh on his head. 'Is that *new*?'

Nodding, he smiles and removes it from his head. Unlike any normal person who wears a hat on a muggy summer evening, his hair has not been forced into a damp, sweaty helmet. As soon as he whips off the beanie each dark, lustrous tendril of hair springs perfectly back into place. I attempt to smile at him but can't.

'Okay, Vivian, I'm going to say something that I know will make you want to punch me in the face and I'd appreciate it if you didn't, what with the whole Orlando issue we have right now – the one plus I've *always* had over him is bone structure.' He raises an eyebrow at me. 'I'm joking.'

'You're not.'

He laughs and clears his throat. 'I think you should see what has happened as a *good* thing. If people finding out that you were once a little on the, er, heavy side was the *one* thing that you've been scared of, now that they know, it'll never be able to hurt you again. Will it? Okay, so you feel bad now, but you won't ever feel as bad again. You've been given your freedom. I wish I had the luxury of being free.'

'Why? Because being famous you're trapped in some way? Christ, Maximilian, you're *such* a cliché.'

'Maybe.' He rubs his head and the tendrils fall back into their correct alignment once more. 'But I'm not expecting you to feel sorry for me, Vivian, I made my bed a long time ago …'

'I imagine you have a housekeeper to do that now.'

'Six days a week. She has Sunday off.' He smiles. 'Look, all I'm trying to do is explain something to you about, well … *hiding*. Years back I had to make a decision. Be "me", or be the "me" my audience wanted. I went for the latter because I'd already worked too hard, made too many sacrifices and come too far to risk anything – or anyone – damaging what I had achieved. Besides, fame and success were the most constant elements in my life – they were *real*. For most people they are the dream, but that was my reality … and I wasn't about to give them up for a life that had no guarantees of ever providing me with any sort of happiness. But then … something happened and I *did* get a fleeting glimpse into whether another life would make me happy, but I wasn't strong enough to take that ch …'

I've stopped listening altogether now. I am watching Maximilian's mouth moving but I am not listening to the words coming out of it, because I am envisioning what will happen next with Luke, Sammy … and my sanity. I see myself investing in the latest fucking iPhone so I can access Sammy's internet presence wher*ever* I am … witnessing the engagement announcement *live* on Twitter (*#wejustknew)* a year to the day since they met, the Instagram album of the beach ceremony (with a laidback registrar-come-local poet in dreads and guests in bare feet), and not long after … the baby sonogram as Luke's profile picture on Facebook and tons of 'likes' from his gushing friends and 'Aussie rellies'. Then Sammy writing a pregnancy blog. She would glow on a nuclear level right up to her due date …

Meanwhile, I would be *feeling*. I would be eating those feelings … and getting fat. Getting fatter. Being fat. I would be 'me' again. In the pit of my (empty) stomach I had always feared it would happen. That no matter how many tricks I performed, the illusion was never going to last. I may have duped my audience, but not me. I knew that eventually the smoke would fade and the mirrors would reflect the truth.

Or would they? Suddenly, my head stops pounding.

Maybe I simply need to find another stage to perform a brand-new show on.

'I'll do it, Maximilian.' The words sound shaky. 'I'll do it.'

'Do what?' he asks. 'Have you heard anything I've been say—'

'It doesn't matter. I'll do it.'

'You'll do what?

'Barb's plan …'

'You'll do it?'

'I'll do it.' This time my voice doesn't waver.

CHAPTER NINETEEN

I don't complete my shift. I return to the flat and start packing. As Barb said, PR 'set-ups' are about momentum. I can now see the reasons behind this are twofold: so that the public's interest stays piqued and so that no one involved has time to consider the implications of what they are doing. I fill two bin-liners with clothes, a holdall with shoes and a supermarket carrier bag with tanning equipment. Monday sits on the bed watching me as I pack, so I make sure not to give him any more hints that I could be about to get his cat carrier from the top of the cupboard. I will do this seconds before we leave. Even if he sees me put a chair in place ready to climb up and reach it, he will disappear and hide somewhere he has never ventured before. I'm sure terrorist leaders have been captured with the use of less surveillance and decoy techniques than it has sometimes taken to secure Monday for a visit to the vet.

I hear the front door slam, then a set of keys jangling against the inner door to the flat and seconds later Adele staggers into my room. Mascara is smudged round her eyes, she's got someone else's foundation on her shirt collar and random flower petals in her hair. Under her right arm she is carrying one of her shoes. It could be from either foot as both her feet are shoeless. On the left one, a piece of bloody loo-roll is trailing from the big toe. She *reeks* of fags. Clearly, she kept up on the Lady Petrol after I left. I shoot her a curt smile.

'I've often wondered what the rushes would have looked like if the director on the advertisement for Blossom Hill had kept the cameras rolling,' I mutter, unsure of which way she is about to turn. It's hard to tell with Adele at this stage in the night, but she usually goes one of three ways: a.) tears, b.) tantrums, c.) toast. I don't welcome any of these options. Particularly, the latter.

'Don't jusht pretend what jusht happened didn't happen jusht then,' she slurs at me. 'You owe me an apology.' She's gone for b.)

'*I* owe *you* an apology? That's an interesting slant you've put on things.'

She throws her shoe onto the floor. 'Itsh true. You were sho rude about my plansh for the wedding. The way you shpo-shpo-spoke to me in front of … I-I-I- …' Then she stops, sways a bit and slowly begins to focus on what I am doing. 'Are you going shomewhere?'

At which point, James appears holding Adele's other shoe, her handbag and what was the bunch of flowers – now a bunch of stalks. He grimaces at me. 'Fortunately, the cab driver was very understanding when she started pulling off the heads and firing them out of the window at passing traffic.' He looks at his future wife. 'I think it's time we got you to bed.'

'No!' she snaps. 'I'm not going to shleep. Not until

Vivian has apologished.' She pushes James away. 'Leave ush alone, we need to shpeak.'

'Not the best idea, hon,' he says gently.

She kisses him. 'Jamesh, I love you very, very, *very* much … but shtop talking now. I need to shpeak to Vivian. I won't shay anything I don't need to shay.'

'Okay, okay …' he backs down. 'I'll go and make you some toast.'

'I don't want any toasht.'

'Sure?'

'Yesh!'

'You should have something to sober you up.'

'I'm not pished and I don't want any toa—' She stops and grips onto the door frame. 'Actually, a slishe with marmalade, pleash … wholemeal, no crushts. Oh, and a pitta … with cherry jam. Not the one that'sh already opened. There'sh a nisher one I bought the other day … with a *few* shcrapes of butter.'

Great, now the toaster will stink out the flat.

James shakes his head at Adele. 'Please, don't become any more low maintenance, hon, or I may have to reconsider our engagement.' Then he gives me a kind but awkward look of concern. 'Vivian, I'm sorry about Luke.'

I itch my neck. 'You better get a plaster for your fiancée's foot … drawer under the cabinet in the bathroom.' As he pads off, I click my tongue at Adele. 'Wow, he is *officially* the world's most understanding man. And before you say anything, that doesn't make me jealous. I'm pleased for you.'

Adele yanks her shirt out of her waistband. 'Pleashed for

me, *maybe*. But really you think I'm *deshperate* to get married after only knowing shumone shix monthsh.'

'No, I don't,' I retort indignantly. But I realise I am looking into a bin-bag, not at her.

'Yesh, you do. It wash written all over your fashe when I told you. Well, not everyone ish as ash *hard* ash you, Vivian. Shum people *need* to be with shumone else. *One* pershon. I don't want to jusht shag around like you. I want it to *mean* shumthing and I want to shelebrate it …' She lurches forward and has to hold onto the door frame again. 'And that doeshn't make me shome short of *shaddo*, it makesh me human. You've alwaysh looked down at me for wanting to find my Mr Right. Don't deny it – you *have*. Back at college when I shaid that I thought Shcrew-it Shtewart could be hushband mat—'

I hold up my hand. 'I'm not listening, Dels. You're tanked up. If you need to discuss something that happened fifteen years ago, a few more hours won't make a difference, so we'll speak in the morning … *before I go*.'

'Go *where* exshactly?'

'Primrose Hill,' I say to the bin-bag again.. But then I force myself to look up. 'I'm going to be staying there for a while.'

'With who?'

'Maximilian Fry.'

'You *what?*' Her eyes spring open. Suddenly, she doesn't seem so pissed.

'I said, I'm moving into Maximilian's place for a bit.'

'*Why* would you do that?'

'Because I've got to move out of here, remember? And,

well, he invited me. We …' I pause for effect as well as to build myself up for lying. 'We *get on.*'

Her face constricts awkwardly. 'Vivian, are you saying you've *slept* with Maximilian Fry?' This time she doesn't slur on a single 's'.

'No, I haven't.'

'Oh.'

'However, if I *did* sleep with him, Dels,' I tuck my pro hair straighteners into the holdall full of shoes, 'you'd be happy for me. *Right?*'

The next morning, I hear Adele get up, but she doesn't go into work. She goes to the bathroom, is sick and then goes back to bed. She is still in bed when Payton arrives to pick me up. He helps me load up the people carrier, and as I go back inside to lure Monday into his own mode of transport with some strips of organic turkey, I consider knocking on Adele's bedroom door. But then I decide that maintaining momentum is more important, so I leave without talking to her. Within half an hour I am at Maximilian's house. Payton takes my luggage, then his wife, Mrs P – Maximilian's housekeeper – gives me a bottle of Fiji water and shows me into the vast drawing room (it's definitely *not* a lounge). I scan the elegant blend of pale silver and very light grey soft furnishings and think it would be safe to assume no one has ever attempted to slob out in here with a TV supper of spaghetti bolognese and red wine … which is okay by me. I like being in rooms that don't encourage food to be brought into them. Barb is waiting for me on a suede corner sofa.

'Well, look at you, Ginger Snap,' she says, peering into

Monday's cat carrier. 'You really could do with a week at a decent spa to lose a few freakin' kilos. I can't fault the fur coat, though. Good colour … very pre-millennium Dries Van Noten.' Then she peers at me. 'You all right, kiddo? You look a little peaky.'

'I'm fine.' Third 'fine' today. Mr and Mrs Payton each got one each too.

'Take a seat.' Barb points at a mist-coloured silk-covered armchair and eyes me suspiciously. 'You're good to move forward? Because you need to be *absolutely* sure …'

'I'm ready,' I reply, sitting down. 'The sooner everyone sees that Maximilian and I are together, the better for us all.' By 'everyone' I obviously mean *Luke* and by 'us all' I obviously mean *me*. 'When will you announce it in the press?'

Barb raises her hand. 'Woah! Easy, kiddo. I won't be making an announcement. Are you crazy? That's so tacky. Remember, I am ingratiating you and Maxy into a media that has become tired and cynical of celebrity relationships being blatantly used for promotional purposes. *Silver's Golden Rule Number Twenty-two: If you can smell PR the publicist stinks.*'

'But I thought you wanted to keep up momentum?'

'I do,' she nods, 'and we will. Or rather, *you* will. Once you've dropped a few hints to your pal Parks, there won't be any need for me to say a word. He'll do it all for us. The rest is down to the visuals: intimate papping – *i.e., private moments in public places* for the press – and then for the fans: uploading cute-but-cryptic shots of you both to Maxy's new Twitter account. There'll be no official appearances yet – that's too in-your-face. For now, I want the world to see you, Vivian Ward, as …' She launches into an impression of a movie trailer voice-over artist. '… *the gutsy waitress who lost the weight but never her spirit*, and I want them to see Maxy as … *the broken blockbuster star who only ever wanted to be a regular guy*.' She claps her hands together excitedly. 'You hear me, kiddo?'

'I heard you, and you said, "waitress". You know I am not a waitress, I'm a *hostess*. Of course, there's nothing wrong with being a waitress but I am *thirty-five*. Do you have to make me look as if I am still at an entry-level position of employment?'

Barb grins at me and leans back against a mound of shimmery pastel scatter cushions. 'Listen, a hostess doesn't have the right ring to it. People freakin' love a waitress, kiddo … *especially* a perky one. Look at Jennifer Aniston. That woman could have gone on a violent murder spree through the Bible Belt whilst she was playing Rachel in *Friends* and she'd still have walked free. Not a single American would have wanted to see the flustered cutey-pop who couldn't handle the froth valve on the cappuccino machine at Central Perk on Death Row.'

I want to laugh, but I can't even manage a smile. I undo the buckle on Monday's cat carrier. He sticks his head out, blinks a few times at me and raises his eyebrows so that I am aware of his displeasure over the sudden and non-negotiated venue change, then he walks across the carpet to the sofa. He nudges the material with his face, then – clearly impressed by the texture – jumps up and pads towards the corner section where he does a series of stretches, as if establishing the 'give' in the foam.

Apparently content with the standard of this, too, he flops down and shuts his eyes.

Barb cackles. 'At least someone round here knows how to relax.'

'I *am* relaxed,' I tell her, but my jaw is stiff. I need to get things moving. The longer things around me are *normal*, the more likely I am to slip back into normal*ity*. 'It's just the, er, "perky" thing … I've never come across as perky.'

'I'll make sure you do. You'll be photographed at *max* perkiness in the first throws of romance with Maxy. I'll have you walking hand in hand through parks, gazing through real estate agency windows, admiring wrought-iron antiques in reclamation yards, trying on hats in bustling street markets …' She pauses to place an imaginary hat on her head. 'Maybe even leaving Whole Foods laden with big brown paper bags.'

'*Really*, Barb? I certainly don't think the words "Fair Trade" or "quinoa" should crop up in a relationship within the first year, let alone the first three weeks. It doesn't sound very sexy.'

'Yeah, I know. But we need you to appear wholesome and human; because you're a stick insect. When she was skinny, look at the flack LeAnn Rimes got every time she was pictured at a five-star resort in Cabo gripping on to Eddie Cibrian with the determination and intensity of a praying mantis on a swaying branch. You need the likeability factor.'

'Not that we don't like the person you are now, Vivian,' says Maximilian, walking into the room in a holey white T-shirt (the holes are too symmetrical not be professionally punctured) and a pair of blue tracksuit bottoms, as faded as the grey ones I met him in. He smiles at me. 'You're a bit fucking sarcastic from time to time, but I guess that's all part of your charm. No last-minute change of mind, then?'

'She says she's "fine",' replies Barb, dubiously. 'So she better be. Anyway, I'm going to leave you kids now. I've got a meeting with the producer on *Benson*, Maxy. The new season returns soon, not long after JP flies back to town. I'll hustle you a slot on the show and get him a front-row seat. You'll be ready in a few weeks for a studio interview.'

'Pre-recorded?' he asks her.

''Course. It'll be a walk in the park. Charles Benson won't give you a hard time. He retires after this summer and for the last few years he's been about as confrontational as a Subway side salad. Right, kiddo.' She turns back to me. 'Any issues call me using this …'

She extracts a phone from her red Hermès bag and tosses it across the room to me. It's a Nokia, thankfully. I turn it on.

'Mine and Nicholas' digits are in the contacts list. So are Payton's – he'll ferry you to work and back from now on …' She places a sheaf of stapled paper on the sofa. 'And here's a copy of your contract. Your agent has got another one. The only pressing business for today is for you both to sign and get Parks primed, but remember: *subtlety is key.*'

'That's *it*, Barb?' I organise a Saturday night out with more attention to detail.

'I don't want you to over-think things so neither will I,' she says with a shrug. 'Trust me, I've orchestrated much more complex freak shows. This is just a simple media circus.' She jumps up. 'So yeah, that's it. Oh, except no smoking any freakin' death sticks anywhere you could be papped and no liquor, period. In the meantime, chill out, get unpacked and settle in …'

'Shall I take you to your bedroom?' suggests Maximilian.

I jolt slightly as he says the word: 'bedroom'. This may be an illusory world I am entering but the reality is I will be inhabiting it with *the* Maximilian Fry … day and night. Obviously, he will *never* see me without make-up or with wet hair. I don't do 'fresh' for anyone. Actually, scrap that – I *do*, but it takes twenty-five minutes using a combination of skin primer, illuminating foundation, liquid cover-up, highlighter stick and iridescent bronzing pearls. Followed by a blob of heavy-duty serum in my hair, an untangling mission with a wide-toothed comb and a carefully positioned non-snag ponytail tie. A dab of tinted moisturiser and a towel in turban formation will *never* do. The thought of having to up the ante on my already intensive beauty regime is exhausting.

… and is made more exhausting as we pass the five-foot-high photographic portrait of Zoe Dano at the base of the staircase. I get a much better look at it this time. She is reclining on a Bedouin-style pouf in front of a colourful mosaicked wall. The Missoni patterned towel that's draped across her matches the North African décor. I examine her face. No, she is definitely not wearing any slap … not even any under-eye concealer. I peer closer, zoning in on her scalp. I can't see any bonds. *Glamour* magazine was correct: no extensions.

'This is your room,' says Maximilian, stopping outside a door on the first floor. 'If you don't like anything, we can change it.' He turns the handle.

I go in. Like the rest of the rooms I have seen so far in Maximilian's house it isn't exactly a treasure trove of knick-knacks and personal touches. Bar a king-size double bed, built-in cupboard, an armchair and spotlights, it is empty. It is also *very* white. White walls, white wooden floor, white linen, white blinds, white upholstery. I walk into the ensuite bathroom. White towels, white tiles, white egg-shaped bath … making the entire suite the worst possible environment to apply, aerate and dry fake tan.

Maximilian sticks his head round the bathroom door. 'I thought it best to leave it as a blank canvas, then you could do what you liked …'

'Who had the room before, then?'

'What do you mean?'

'You said it was "best to leave it".'

He clears his throat. 'Zoe had this room. Yet another one of my screwed-up habits, which I'm sure you will be quick to label more of an arrogant celebrity affectation; I find it difficult to share a bed …'

Actually, I don't think this is so strange. I've always had an issue with that. When I was fat, I assumed no one would want/be able to share my bed. After I lost weight the block was more mental. The fluctuating and clashing changes in body temperatures, the sudden movements and the *constant* noise … snoring, sleep-talking, even the sound of breathing would grate. I also used to hate sleeping in any bed other than my own. Whenever I pulled a guy, I never went back to his place. On waking, I wanted instant access to my supersonic styling equipment and Adele's sloppy but expensive beige lounge wear. Even if the *relationship* went somewhere, *I* rarely did. In fact, out of all the 'Men I've Been With' Luke is the only one who managed to get me to stay at his place regularly. The first night I did was after he had completed the initial stage of his renovation work. Squashed up next to him, his active airways operating millimetres away from my left ear … I thought it would be a miracle if I hadn't smothered him with a pillow by 2 a.m. I slept right through till morning.

'… impossible, in fact,' continues Maximilian. 'If I don't get eight hours of solid, uninterrupted sleep I can be a bit of a fucking nightmare the next day: moody, intense, pessimistic, stressed out, cranky … it's all right, I'll let you say it.'

'Say what?'

'That it would be hard to tell the difference.' He pauses and peers at me. 'Listen, Vivian, if you've changed your mind and want out, tell me. It would be annoying, but not half as infuriating if you do it in a few weeks and I'm made to look like a mug.' He rubs his head and a second later his hair automatically re-styles itself. 'I don't mean to make this all about me, but …' He smiles at me. 'It kind of *is* … so, you need to let me know now bef—'

'Maximilian, can I ask you something?' I don't wait for a reply. 'How can you keep so many reminders of Zoe near you? This room, that tattoo, the picture in the hallway … doesn't it all do your head in?'

'Not really.' He shrugs. 'I've got four other floors of living space, so it's not as if I ever need to be in this room. You know why I still have the tattoo. As for that photograph, I haven't taken it down because it serves a purpose.' He pauses and leans against the door frame. 'It was taken at my villa, it was the first day I said …' He trails off. 'A *year* to the day I found out about …'

'Rick Piper?'

'*Prick* Piper more like. Anyway, the point is I keep her picture in that particular place to remind myself on a constant basis that at least I am capable of it.'

'Of what?'

'Falling in love. Even if it ends in hate …'

We both stand in silence for a few seconds. Then Maximilian sighs deeply and goes back out into the bedroom. I follow and find him staring out of the window, his features just as impressive and precise from the side as from the front. I look down into the neighbouring gardens. They are all intricately designed. The standard outside area grass/flowerbed/paving set-up has been replaced with complex urban architecture, dynamic water features and exotic planting. Monday will like it here. These are the sort of people who put only the best (providence-assured) meat on their (gas-fired) outdoor grills. They'll fall for his, 'It's hard being ginger…' shtick.

'Vivian?'

I turn back to Maximilian and find his eyes searching my face.

'You are all right, aren't you?'

'Yeah, I told you … I'm fine.'

But after Maximilian has left for a meeting with his

money broker, I am unpacking my hair straighteners when I find myself wondering what Luke has done with the pink ones he gave me. *I bet Sammy doesn't straighten her hair. Probably lets it dry naturally … doesn't even use a fucking hairdryer.* The next moment I am hunting the house for a computer to check her Twitter feed. Adele once said that in today's world, it is impossible to 'let go' after a relationship finishes, not when social networking wizardry means you are, in her words, only ever one click of a mouse from finding out who the rat is sleeping with… I laughed and called her a stalker. That now makes me a hypocrite. I find an aluminium Apple Macbook Pro on the desk in the study – it probably belongs to Barb or Nicholas. Given Maximilian's lofty attitude to technology, I doubt it is his.

I find a half-composed email on the screen: to a biggsyknowsbest@hotmail.com, hoping that he will enjoy staying in Miami again and to *Help yourself to anything at the Delano: spa treatments, room service, dressing gowns, etc. And check out the King of Diamonds Strip Club. You'll find the sights particularly arresting!* I minimise the window and log onto @SammySparkles. There is one new Tweet: no words, just a smiley fucking face; and her profile picture has changed. She has replaced the original headshot with an artsy snap of a yellow sunflower. *That* sunflower … wrapped round the stalk are two SundaySoundz green wristbands. Although the flower doesn't look as bright or the bands as neon because she has *obviously* digitally manipulated the shot. Christ, has the kooky dullard got some sort of sight sensitivity that everything in her world needs to be filtered through a sepia-tinged lens?

'Exactly *what* do you think you are doing?'

I jump and nearly topple the chair over. Nicholas is leaning against the door watching me.

'Christ, you nearly gave me a heart attack.'

'I repeat, *what* are you doing?'

'Using the internet. Maximilian said I should make myself at home, s—'

'That's my Mac,' he interrupts.

'Sorry, I thought it was his,' I fib.

'Fry hasn't got a clue about technology. Never used a computer in his life as far as I'm aware … probably thinks Firefox is something Ray Mears would do on a barbecue. For future reference, this room is out of bounds. It's *my* office.' He walks over to check what I have been doing. 'Twitter? Hasn't Barb told you we're only setting up an account for Fry?'

'Yeah, it's not my account. I was looking at someone else's.'

'Good. Because women in the public eye have to be very careful with Twitter. Nothing more unattractive than *assuming* people are interested in you. Of course, *some* of them are interesting. But for every Lady Gaga commenting insightfully on the psychology behind global pop stardom, there is a Cat Deeley droning on about the behind-the-scenes atmosphere at *So You Think You Can* sodding *Dance.*' He leans across me and switches off the screen. It bleeps then zaps to darkness. 'Don't get me started on the appalling grammar the majority of them use. Have you ever read Cheryl Cole's Twitter? Personally, I can't see why her management don't write it for her, like I will be doing with Fry. It's what you have you do with dyslexics.'

'Cheryl Cole isn't dyslexic,' I tell him. 'At least, I don't think she is.'

Nicholas smirks at me. 'No? Well, someone needs to tell her that an exclamation mark is not the same as a full stop.'

'Maybe she's easily surprised.'

'Ha! Maybe.' He slams the laptop shut and checks his chunky gold Tag Heuer diving watch. 'It's one o'clock … time for a spot of sustenance, I think, darling. My treat. I'll take you to my favourite restaurant. You won't have to eat anything if you don't want to … just *listen*.'

CHAPTER TWENTY

We go to The Ivy in the West End. I've been here twice before. Once reluctantly, when Terry insisted we commemorate what would have been my father's fiftieth birthday. The next time quite happily, for Roger and Pete's wedding meal after their civil partnership ceremony. It's impossibly classy yct cffortlcssly understated.

'I've got a little anecdote for you, darling,' says Nicholas, lightly caressing the rim of his wine glass as we wait for our order to arrive. "A struggling actor returns to his neighbourhood one evening and is shocked to find police and fire engines surrounding the smouldering remains of his home. "What happened here?" enquires the actor. "Well," replies one of the officers, "it seems that your agent came by your house earlier today, and while he was here he assaulted your wife, beat your children, shot your dog and burned your house to the ground." The actor is struck speechless; his jaw hangs open, he shakes his head from side to side in disbelief and tumbles to the ground in shock. Then, in a quivering voice he looks up and asks the officer, "My agent came to my house?" Ha!' Nicholas clicks his teeth and shrugs his shirtsleeves up his arms. 'Do you get it?'

I nod, but I am having difficulty concentrating. The

smiley face on Sammy's page is beaming out from the centre of my brain like the mega-watt light bulb that once dangled from the ceiling in Luke's room. A waiter puts down our food on the table. Lobster for Nicholas and seared scallops for me – fortunately my dish is only accompanied by some sort of green herb. Nicholas tucks his napkin into his collar, takes a slug of wine and expertly cracks open the red exoskeleton on his plate.

'Now,' he continues, 'I want you to know that I am *not* – and never have been – that agent in the anecdote. I have lived every single second of Fry's career right by his side. Without me he would be nothing … and he would readily admit that.'

'When did you start working together?' Gingerly, I prod a scallop.

'At our school … Sturrow. It was his first year and my last. He'd been cast in some dull Shakespearean tragedy the school was putting on. I don't think I'd ever heard Fry talk up until that point, I'd only ever seen him snivelling. He used to get teased rather a lot about his dyslexia. Not nice, but that's boarding school for you, all personal afflictions are fair game. Still, I think *anyone* would have found it amusing to see him turn up to a dormitory *toga* party dressed as a *goat*. Hi*lar*ious.' He pauses to laugh and then spears a piece of succulent white lobster flesh with a fork. 'But the moment I heard Fry quote Shakespeare was a revelation. It felt like that oppressive Victorian hall on a ball-numbingly cold December afternoon was suddenly filled with the joy and warmth of early spring … and that, darling,' he raises his eyebrows at me, 'is the *absolute last* time you will ever hear me say anything remotely poetic. Within a week, I'd organised for a superbly edited showreel to be made then viewed by the producer of *A Son and a Lover* – an old Sturrow boy. Fry was called to audition and that was that; his life changed forever. At eighteen I brokered his multi-million-dollar deal to star in *The Orc's Progress* and since then I have accompanied him to every film set he has ever worked on, making sure all he has to do is act. I deal with *everything* else. It has not always been easy – I had to live in Tasmania on-and-off for nearly five years when he was shooting the *Orc* trilogy.' He balks at the memory as he chews his seafood. 'It's the kind of place where a bag of Doritos and a jar of salsa are considered the height of cocktail party sophistication. But I dealt with it, just like I deal with his daily dramas, affectations and demands … because of all *this*.' He waves his fork around the room.

'The Ivy?'

I nibble the scallop and take a large gulp of my double vodka on the rocks with freshly squeezed grapefruit. Fish = high protein and low fat. Alcohol = energy. Citrus = metabolic booster. This is fine. I am *fine*.

Nicholas wipes the corners of his mouth with his napkin. 'Not just The Ivy, darling. Success and domination, *period*. Failure and *getting by* … ugh. I can't be around it. All my pals are business moguls: hotel giants, entertainment heavyweights, property magnates – we're at the top of our game. People work for *us*. We're nobody's bitch. Goldstein has been on at me for years to join his company – to spread my acumen – but why would I? The thought of anyone else calling the shots other than myself makes me feel … *ill.*' He leans forward and whispers, 'Tell me, have you ever been to Hull, darling?'

'Not as far as I can remember.'

'I doubt anyone would remember if they had,' he snorts. 'It's the most wrist-slashingly bland town in Britain. I was born there. As a child I was dying to get out of there, so I studied like a maniac and won a full scholarship to Sturrow. None of the other boys knew I'd got in without paying. I ditched my Humber accent, changed my name from Smith to Van Smythe and pretended my parents lived in Hong Kong. They still live in Hull, by the way; their mundane, repetitive drip-dry existence has not changed in forty years.' He shudders and sips his wine. 'Tell me, how do you see yourself getting old, darling?'

'Old?'

'Yes … because it will happen. It *is* happening. How do you see your twilight years panning out?'

The answer is I have no idea because I don't think about it … *ever.* I never have done, either. When I was fat, it was too depressing to look ahead, because I could only see myself in exactly the same position: in bed … but with some sort of hoist system in place. When I became thin, I only ever wanted to think as far as the weekend, because I had been denied weekends when I was fat. I spent them in my room, eating. I was always fatter by Monday. But when I lost weight, I revelled in Friday through to Sunday. Even better, all the activities I filled those days with (working, exercising, shopping, clubbing, sex), were top-notch calorie burners so I would be even thinner at the end of them.

Suddenly, I looked forward to seeing Monday. It was why I called my cat exactly that.

'It's not something I've thought about too much,' I tell Nicholas. 'The future …'

He leans back, staring at me as he swirls his wine round the bulb of his glass. 'That's what I predicted you would say. I get it. You're too busy enjoying the present … and why not? You've worked hard to get here.' He pauses. 'Actually, I think you and I are very similar creatures, darling; we both reinvented ourselves to escape who we once were and continue to do so. I think we would also agree on another thing.'

'What's that?'

'Neither of us ever wants to be recaptured.' He leans forward again, his voice thickening. 'I want you to know that Fry is not the only one relying on Silver's plan to work – I am too. Of course, I'm pretty sure you will rinse this opportunity for your own worth, I wouldn't expect anything less, it's what I would do. But screw me around, darling, and I will make your life, quite literally…' He yanks off a prickly pink leg from his lobster and sucks the flesh from its interior. '… *Hull.*'

CHAPTER TWENTY-ONE

I use the fire exit to slip through the back entrance of Burn's but Roger sees me creep past his office.

'Not so fast, Vivian!' he shouts. 'Get your behind in here, *immediately.*'

As soon as I step into the room, my eyes zone in on the jar of truffles. They are now almost depleted. You see? That's the kind of bad behaviour that one can submit to if based in a private office. I'm glad I didn't take the managerial post; subservience doesn't bother me as long as I am expending kilojoules. Roger clicks his fingers to get my attention and I look up. His eyes are wide behind his Joe 90 spectacles.

'Tabitha told me all about the drama last night with you, Maximilian Fry and his *Officer and A Gentlemen* routine, so I need to know the details. Firstly, as your boss, given that you left before the end of your shift. Secondly, as a pink-blooded male who is currently being *consumed* by jealousy at the thought of you seeing *that* body in the buff. But thirdly, and most importantly, as your pal. Why didn't you tell me you'd split up with Luke?'

I shrug. 'I'll stay late tonight. I haven't seen him naked, but I do plan on it. It's not a big deal.'

'Yes, you *will*. *Full* details when you do. And it *is* … you liked Luke. A lot. Are you okay?'

'Fine.' Number seven.

Roger sighs and leans back in his chair. 'That's the thing I admire most about you, Vivian – your ability to open up, share your vulnerabilities and let people in to help you. Your raw emotion moves me.'

'Your sarcasm moves *me*, Rog.'

'Nicely swerved. Well, if you won't talk about you, how's Luke?'

'I haven't spoken to him, but I know for a fact he is also okay.'

'I very much doubt that,' says Roger, more gently. 'He would have dropped off your stuff *himself* if he was. Obviously, he didn't want to bump into y—'

I interrupt him. 'What stuff?'

'Your stuff from his place. His flatmate dropped it off at recept—'

But I am already pelting down the corridor, through the restaurant and out into the foyer. I jump behind the reception barrier. Next to the large antique chest of drawers where Tabitha keeps any lost property is a cardboard box. I recognise it immediately. It's the one Luke used to store his old vinyl in, which also doubled up as a bedside table. There is a splodge of wax on the top of it. He has gaffer taped the sides to prevent it splitting open.

I yank at the tape, but then I stop. I stand up and back away from the box. Tabitha approaches me. She is sipping an unacceptably frothy iced beverage with real whipped cream on top.

'Do you need a pair of scissors?' she asks.

'No, I'm going to chuck it.'

'Don't be silly.'

'I don't need anything in there.' I stare at Tabitha's drink … suddenly, I am seeing Ally McBeal. Remember her? In my head, she is arriving at her law offices in the morning … a mere spinal cord in a boxy power suit clutching a Styrofoam coffee cup.

'How do you know?'

'Because I *do.* Is Clint here?'

'No, why?'

'Tell me if he comes in.' I shove the box back into the corner with my foot. 'Leave it there; I'll dump it in the recycling bin on my break.'

She taps my arm and the row of plastic neon bangles on her arm jangle. 'But you don't even know what's in there.'

'Tabs, don't start …'

'I'm not *starting* anything,' she says. 'I'll put the box in the staff-room cupboard. That way you can have a look through it later and decide what you want to hang on to. It's healthy to have a few keepsakes of the good times you've shared with people, no matter how the relationship has ended or even if you've moved on with someone else. I read that in a magazine once.'

'Ha!' This actually makes me laugh. 'Probably written by some kooky airhead' – like *Sammy* – 'who also believes that the twelve signs of the zodiac are applicable to the six billion people living on earth and Zooey Deschanel is, oh my God, the *best!* Honestly, Tabs, sometimes …'

She taps my arm again.

'Tabs, you're *jangling.*'

'Sorry, I was only going to say I'm here if you want to talk about what happ—'

'There is nothing to talk about,' I snap. 'Christ, why do you all want to dissect things like Nobel Prize-winning entomologists?'

Tabitha looks away, hurt. I knew being 'perky' would be a struggle. *Perky needs sugar.* It gets even harder as the afternoon progresses, so I lock myself in a toilet cubicle in an attempt to 'perk up'. But the red mist continues to descend. I am angry at myself for letting Luke get in my head. In my entire 'relationship' career I have never let that happen. With all the other 'Men I've Been With' I've only let them in my bedroom.

Adele once suggested I see a therapist about this attitude I had cultivated towards men. She thought it was 'dysfunctional'. I didn't go for three reasons. Firstly, I didn't want to waste the money. Sunlounger in Ibiza versus the psychiatrist's couch? In decision-making terms not exactly up there with the one Meryl Streep has to make in *Sophie's Choice*. Secondly, given her own monumentally disastrous dating history, Adele giving advice about guys seemed about as misplaced as Britney Spears recommending a hair-extension technician. Thirdly, I *knew* why I behaved like that. It was genetic. My father was the same. I could tell that Luke could see I was 'dysfunctional' from the moment we first met. He suggested as much, but not in an accusatory way. I remember the exact look of *non*-judgement in his face. It made me feel uncomfortable ... *not* being judged. Because then it was up to me to judge myself.

I stop. *Keep up the momentum.* I leave the toilet. Where the *fuck* is Clint?

He doesn't turn up until shortly before closing. I am smoking/ignoring sugar cravings/texting people my new number – forcing myself to make the illusion more real – when Tabitha pops her head round the door. She says Clint has stumbled in for last orders. I don't even bother to brush my teeth or gargle before rushing up the stairs to the first floor, knowing Clint will be going straight to the loo. I make sure I am loitering in the corridor as he leaves the bar area. He isn't wearing one of his usual flamboyant jackets, just a baggy promotional T-shirt emblazoned with the words: MEL GIBSON 'WHAT WOMEN WANT'.

'Wow, what a difference a few years make, eh, Clint?' I deadpan, knowing I must stick to the normal banter I usually have with him.

He chuckles. 'Yeah, it was a freebie we 'ad kicking round the office. The missus slung me out when I didn't come 'ome after that awards do at the weekend. She still 'asn't let me back in to get any of my clobber.' He leans across to give me a kiss. I can't smell any Gucci Envy *or* excitement … just drug-induced sweat, booze and fags.

'Mmm …' I pretend to swoon. 'Eau de tabloid journalist.'

'Yeah, I know, I know … bit off my nut, sweet'eart. I needed it, though … was interviewing that Noelle Bamford for a big feature – favour for Sophs. Fuck me, what a contrived little madam. My gak dealer's got more gravity and intuition. Speaking of which …'

'Of what? Your escalating cocaine bill?'

He rolls his bloodshot eyes at me. 'No, lacking discernment. I'm aware you went to The Ivy earlier with that Van Smythe.'

This is going to be easier than I thought.

'Don't ask me '*ow* I know,' Clint chatters on. 'It's swarming with paps and 'acks round there. 'E took you there for a reason, Vivian: to show people you're now 'is territory. Think of it like a dog pissin' on a lamppost. Out with it, then ...' He looks up at me. 'What's going on between you and Maximilian Fry?'

Much easier than I thought.

'Not a lot,' I reply casually. 'I like Maximilian. He likes me. We'll see. But what may or may not happen between us is nothing to do with Nich—'

Clint coughs in my face. 'Bleedin' 'eck, sweet'eart. Wise up ... men like Maximilian Fry don't come as a single unit. They're part of a team, and 'is ain't a team that play fair. I told you, don't get involved with 'em, they're not like us. We're on different sides of the fence.'

I shrug at him. 'Maybe I want to see if the grass is greener on the other side.'

'If it is, it will be fake. Astro turf.' He waits for a couple of members to walk past us and down the stairs. 'Look, you know I told you one of my boys got a slap sniffing around Van Smythe? We've got a lead now, from this old girl ... she phoned me at the paper, said Van Smythe ruined 'er son's life, smashed 'im to pieces ... 'e was 'is personal trainer.'

'Maximilian doesn't have one.'

'But 'e *did* ... and therein lies the rub.'

'Oooh, stop the press! Major movie star parts ways with member of physical support staff.' I feign a yawn. 'Cheers, Clint, your concern is appreciated, but really I will be fi—'

But he interrupts. 'Will you? Don't be so confident. When this relationship blows up in your face, which it will, you'll b—'

'How can you be so sure it will go wrong?'

'Leave it out, Vivian, you and Maximilian Fry as a couple is not a workable dynamic. You're about as ill suited as Kim Kardashian and that doofus basketball player she married for five minutes.'

'I hope I am the doofus basketball player in this scenario … he's got the smaller arse.'

Clint smiles and sniffs gutturally. 'Look, you and I both know that celebrities need to date their *exact* equivalent. Kim Kardashian needs someone as 'umourless, vain, stunted, delusional and publicity 'ungry as she is. She needs …'

'Kanye West.'

'Exactly! Joking aside, though, sweet'eart, you've also got to remember this …' His voice becomes more serious. 'Fame is only worth 'aving if you don't mind losing it. Yeah, you might 'ave a nice couple of months in the spotlight, but when that spotlight is taken away I guarantee one thing: you'll still be shining it on yourself, and the longer you look at yourself in that light … you may not like what you'll see.'

I squeeze his arm. 'Thanks, Clint, but I'll be fine.' I get it out this time. The ninth. 'More to the point, can you start looking after *your*self? Carry on the way you are and your septum has got far less chance of survival than my relationship. I'll see you later. I need to finish up here…' Then I add, casually, '…then ring Maximilian's driver. He's picking me up.'

'Is that on or off the record?'

'It's whatever you want it to be, Clint.'

But I don't leave. Not even when all the members have departed, the cleaning staff have been and gone, and the only other person in the building is our overnight security guard. I do two shots of green-chilli-infused vodka – everyone knows hot spices zap sugar cravings, right? – and go to the staff room, drag the box that Warren left for me into the middle of the floor and cut through the masking tape. And at that moment the momentum is lost.

This is what I find inside.

1. Three V-neck T-shirts from America Apparel I had given to Luke as presents. He said they were too tight and the V was too deep. They *weren't.* They were *fitted* and the V merely gave a *hint* of man cleavage.

2. A bottle of Grey Goose vodka he had bought me that I was only allowed to open if I ever got a mention in *Empire* film magazine.

3. The new do-gooding hair straighteners. (Told you *she* wouldn't need them.)

4. My – *our* – video camera.

5. Luke's hooded grey sweatshirt. It's at the bottom of the box. I pull it over my head. I can smell the fresh air and the concrete. It was brand new the day I met him properly. It still had the protective plastic on the toggles.

I flip the box shut and put it in the cupboard at the back of the staff changing room, so it is hidden away, neatly; like everything else I have had to compartmentalise in my mind since my tenth birthday …

We had moved house three weeks previously. My mother wasn't thrilled with our new cul-de-sac, but I wasn't fussed because the house was bigger. This meant I got my own room and didn't have to share a bunk with my younger brother. I wasn't bothered about having a party as I didn't know anyone at my new school well enough to guarantee a decent attendance, and besides, a girl in my class called Kate Summers – who appeared to be the most popular – was having her own bash on the same day in the comparatively glamorous location of the local swimming baths. But Mum insisted on asking over her new friends from the Born Again church up the road for tea. At 3.15 p.m. she told me to go and get my father from the garage he was now running. He had taken it over after losing his job (or, as Mum had worded it to us, 'losing his enthusiasm') at the car dealership he was running previously. She wanted him to set up the trestle table and chairs on the porch. So I went to get him. When I got to the garage the gate was shut so I slithered easily through the bars into the forecourt, wandered round the back to the office … and that's where I saw my father. With a woman. He saw me. Then she did. I sprinted home and straight into the kitchen where I splashed water all over my face. As I turned round from the sink, I saw the party food Mum had prepared. One particular plate – a large engraved crystal glass one she had given my father as an anniversary gift – was covered with silver foil. I can't remember what went through my head at this point. All I recall is that the next moment I was on my bed peeling off the protective aluminium sheet. Underneath were forty sandwich triangles made with sliced bread, margarine and a selection of fillings. I ate every single one.

I look at the box once more, then slam the cupboard door shut. That's when the momentum speeds up again ... *in reverse.*

Twenty-seven minutes later I am in Shepherd's Bush, pressing hard on the door bell with my index finger. It is 4.17 a.m. but Warren answers. I knew he would be up. I don't think Warren has ever intentionally *gone to bed* – he simply waits until he passes out in a Class A, B or C induced stupor. He unlocks the door but leaves the chain on the latch.

'What do *you* want?' he asks, in a sullen tone (it's his comedown voice). Through the two-inch aperture I can see he is holding a large spliff and wearing a *DangerMouse* T-shirt. The rodent super hero is in his classic pose: grinning with one arm raised in victory, knowing he is the greatest secret agent of them all.

'I need to see Luke.'

'You *need* to see *Luke*?'

'Yes.'

'I *very* much doubt Luke will *want* to see *you*.'

'He will.'

'He *won't*. He *wouldn't*.'

'Warren, can you please stop over-emphasising words for dramatic effect and let me in.'

He unhooks the chain. I rush past him, through the kitchen and into the living room. No one is in there. On the table is a set of scales and a pile of white powder. Probably mephedrone. After all, I am in Warren's scabby den in Shepherd's Bush, not a drug lord's mansion in the hills on the outskirts of Bogota so it's not likely to be premium-quality blow. I go up the corridor to Luke's bedroom. The door is open and the room is in darkness. None of the usual green and red LED lighting is beaming out from his music equipment and the fridge he bought me isn't buzzing either. I flick the light switch. The room is empty. No decks, no cables, no records and no clothes, bar an old snowboarding jacket and the combat trousers I hated, which are lying on the bed.

'I've got his music gear in my room,' says Warren tightly, as he walks up behind me. 'He said I could have them. Mind you, I haven't played them yet. It doesn't seem right somehow. Sort of seems disloyal to my …' he searches for the word, '… *clubland brother*. Crackers is moving in next week. Maybe we'll have a bit of a session then.' This is the longest I have ever heard Warren speak without oi-oiiiing.

I turn round. 'Make sure you look after Luke's stuff, he'll be annoyed if any of it's damaged when he returns from his break.'

Warren sucks on his joint and shakes his head at me. 'You're not listening, he hasn't *leant* them to me. They are mine to *keep*. He's not on holiday. He's left. He's not coming back.'

'Ever?'

He nods and exhales smoke. It's hard to tell who looks more defiant: him or DangerMouse. '*Exactly* that.'

'But he's on his mobile?'

'Nope. Dumped it. He's changed his email address too, in case you were wondering. He wanted a completely fresh start.'

I look over at the shelf and notice that my casting card, which Luke kept there, has also disappeared. I get a temporary jolt of hope thinking he may have packed it in his rucksack and taken it with him. But then Warren follows my line of vision and points at the small metal bin in the corner of the room. The torn-up pieces of glossy black-and-white card are clearly visible through the wire mesh.

'I think that tells you everything you need to know,' says Warren.

I stare at my torn-up self. The only time I have ever destroyed a photo, it was of my father. It was *that* afternoon. After eating the sandwiches, I came down from my bedroom – hands clammy, heart racing – and did it. It takes a lot to rip through someone's face. Hatred, in fact. I walked into the lounge, selected a family shot and did it. Mum caught me mid-tear and went bonkers. I don't know how long I am staring at Luke's bin for, but long enough to know Warren is right. It does tell me everything I need to know. I take my time to assimilate this information.

'Vivian?' Warren prods me with reluctant concern. '*Oi!* Here, have some of this.'

He offers me his spliff. I stare at the glowing roll-up in his hand and almost retch. Marijuana is the most dangerous drug of all. It induces hunger.

'No, thanks.' I start walking back down the corridor.

'You okay?' Warren shouts after me.

'Mmm … I'm fine.'

It's the tenth time today I've said that. But it's the first time I've meant it.

PART TWO

CHAPTER TWENTY-TWO

'Anything I would have liked?'

'The Seventh Seal,' mutters Maximilian, staring ahead at the crackly monochrome credits rolling on the screen.

Even from the doorway I can sense his low mood.

'Never heard of it …'

'You've *never* heard of *The Seventh Seal*? It's the most famous Swedish film ever made, Vivian. Completely ahead of its time …'

He turns to me as he says this, and as he does, my face tingles. Not because I am embarrassed about my poor knowledge of early world cinema but because this is the effect Maximilian still has on me, even after a month. It's not a reaction I am surprised by. I was like this at school with Ziggy. He was also perfect looking, and his looks were given an extra blast of cool by an ever changing directional haircut, the jangling army dogtags round his neck and a yellow Sony Walkman that was permanently clipped to his trousers.

I shrug at Maximilian. 'Was it?'

'Yes.' He nods. 'Directed by Ingmar Bergman; it's set during the medieval plague. The plot revolves around a soldier's last battle: a haunting game of chess with Death.'

'Not exactly a laugh-a-minute ...'

I slide down into the black sofa. It's a squishy one; the only couch in the house that you feel *wants* you to utilise it for reasons of comfort. Equally, the screening room is the only space in Maximilian's home that is home*ly*. I had feared that it would be one of those naff personal cinemas you see on MTV *Cribs* that the celebrity has had designed to resemble a real-life movie multiplex; with rows of chairs with cup holders in the arm rest, a glass popcorn dispenser and a proper kiosk where a papier mâché cashier checks your ticket stub. But it's a simple room with a flat telly on the wall and stacks of DVDs and Blu-ray discs on the floor.

'To be honest, Maximilian,' I continue, '*generally* speaking, I don't really like black-and-white films.'

'Shut *up*.'

'It's true, I don't. Except *In Bed With Madonna* ... that was seminal. You must have seen that?'

'No, I haven't had the pleasure.'

He rolls his eyes at me but I can tell I am cheering him up. I like it when I do this. I get the opportunity fairly often. Maximilian always seems to have stuff he is 'dwelling' on. It is important for me to dwell on *nothing* ... so the dynamic works.

'Well, it's all shot in black and white except for the scenes where Madge is performing on stage during her Blonde Ambition tour – that's in colour.' I pause to rearrange my new Joseph leather leggings around the knee area to limit any wrinkling, cracking or bagging. 'Is the whole of *The Seventh Seal* in black and white?'

This time Maximilian smiles and playfully swats my leg. 'The film is about decay, disillusionment and damnation, Vivian. Sudden bursts of Technicolor wouldn't really fit the mood.'

'No conical bras, either, then?' I smile back.

If our banter sounds easy, it's because it is. It's all been easy. My transition from Vivian Ward to the alien consonant in 'Maximivian' has not been hard on a public *or* personal level. As far as the former is concerned, from the first story in *Clint's Big Column*, the idea of the once massive actor (in terms of box office receipts) falling for the once massive waitress (in terms of Body Mass Index) has been lapped up by everyone who counts, i.e., the press, its consumers and JP Goldstein. As for me … I've merely had to take a mental *leap*. Which believe you me, is not even comparable to the physical *haul* I made previously. That reinvention took sweat and tears. This one has simply taken a shift in my own focus to *see* the new me … which I can do: in newspapers, magazines and online. And the new me is looking fine, thanks to my thrice-weekly visits to the Net-A-Porter website. During my ASOS addiction, I only ever let myself (computer) window shop at Net-A-Porter, but with my new allowance I can actually buy stuff there. I've gone for an edgy look – it evens out the 'perkiness' – with men's accessories. I like this touch of androgyny. (Also, the sturdier the accessory the more fragile your bones appear.)

'So, speaking of moods,' I kick Maximilian, 'are you going to tell me what's up? My guess would be that your dinner last night with JP at Nobu didn't go to plan.'

'Is it that obvious?' he asks.

'Yes, you look like you've been slapped in the face with a wet fish – black cod, presumably. Don't tell me the Orlando rumours are circulating again?'

'No, no ... he wasn't mentioned. There have been mutterings of the two Ryans: Gosling *and* Reynolds, but JP pretty much made out that I am now the frontrunner.'

'What's the issue, then?' I stretch out my legs. As I do, I notice that my leather leggings automatically spring back into shape around the knee. Not surprising really, given that they cost £695. It makes me wonder what the three-thousand-pound quilted Balmain ones – I also spotted on Net-A-Porter – would do. Know when they need to visit the specialist dry cleaner's? Get a round in at the pub? *Cat sit?*

'The issue is with the movie, Vivian,' explains Maximilian. 'It's not going to be like the original *Truth*, it's being ramped up on every level. The budget has quadrupled, the stunts are outrageous, huge names are being lined up to do cameos and JP wants Jack Chase to become as iconic as Indiana Jones, Rambo or John McClane.' He puts on a cigar-chomping Yank movie-executive accent. '*Max, my boy, we're talking blockbuster with a capital goddamn B and phenomenon with a capital goddamn F...*'

'It was probably a P ...' I advise him gently.

'Either way,' he says, not quite convinced, 'Barb was over the moon. You should have heard her in the car as she considered all the promotional tie-ins. It was like she had global youth brand Tourette's.' This time Maximilian impersonates his publicist perfectly with a growly New York tone. '*Nike! Apple! Diesel! Uniqlo! Virgin! Sony!*

Sure! Budweiser! Pepsi! McDonald's! Freakin' hell, Maxy, I've freakin' died and gone to contra deal heaven!'

'What about Nicholas?'

Maximilian doesn't bother with an impression this time. Worry floods his face. 'He thinks this is *it*. Time to join the stellar league … If this movie does the business on both sides of the Atlantic, I'll become one of the most bankable actors in British film history.'

'Hmmm …' I rub my chin and pretend to think hard. 'Let me get this straight, then, Maximilian. You've been told the role you love is yours for the taking, but this time it will make you even richer and more powerful within the industry than you were before. Shit happens, eh?'

'You think I'm being an ungrateful arsehole …'

'It makes a change from being a pretentious one.' I smile. 'I still don't understand what the panic is over.'

'The thing is, Vivian, if things get all … all encompassing … all I'll ever be to anyone is *the* Maximilian Fry – and yeah, yeah, *yeah* …' He shoots me a look. 'You'll have to overlook the italic "the" and imaginary parenthe – things on this occasion because I need them to state my case. Look, once an actor takes on a movie like this, there's no going back to anything resembling normality … *especially* if they had trouble accessing that before.'

I nod as if I am being empathetic, but isn't being given the opportunity for people to only *ever* see you as the person you've invented, not who you really are, something to celebrate? But I don't even consider starting a debate. Besides – I glance down at my huge Micheal Kors men's diving watch (it makes my wrist look like that of a seven-year-old)

– it's three o'clock. I haven't got time. I've just got back from my shift at Burn's and in five and a half hours Maximilian and I are making our first official appearance together at an art exhibition. That means I've got one hour and fifteen minutes in the gym, three hours to get *almost* ready, an hour to make sure I am *actually* ready and fifteen minutes for an *absolute* final edit … and therefore zero minutes to be faffing around chatting. This needs to be tied up.

'Okay, Maximilian,' I begin, 'I understand you're feeling apprehensive, but the idea of any sort of change is bound to have that effect. You're a control freak and everything in your life has a specific place and order …' I raise my hand before he can argue. 'But look, *you* don't have to change too. It's only a movie. It's not real … but *you* are; and only *you* can decide who you want to be. Not JP, not Barb, not Nicholas, not your fans, not the papers … *you*.'

'But—'

'No buts …' I interrupt him. I don't even know what I am going to wear tonight yet, and whatever I choose, I need my tan to be Sahara dry before I get dressed. '… or I will have to agree with the "ungrateful arsehole" tag. I don't think you have any idea how fortunate you *are* or how fortunate you have *been*. You hit the jackpot at your very *first* audition.'

He grimaces guiltily. Even when he is pulling a face, his features seem exquisitely positioned. 'Am I allowed to ask what happened at yours?'

'I'd rather you didn't, but since you could do with some

perspective on things … it was for the *Wizard of Oz* at school. I was fifteen. I went for the role of Dorothy.'

'You didn't get it?'

'Obviously not, and I will never forget the afternoon that cast list went up outside the assembly hall. I ran my finger down the list; past all the best-loved characters, half a dozen Munchkins with reasonable speaking parts and a succession of winged monkeys … before I found my name: VIVIAN WARD: METEOROLOGICAL SUPPORT.'

Maximilian looks confused. 'Meteorological support?'

'Yep. I was to improvise changes in the weather,' I explain. 'I was a tornado in the first act on the farm in Kansas, the sun in the second during the yellow brick road scenes, and a thunder storm in the third at the witch's castle.'

Maximilian bursts out laughing. 'Fuck. Sorry, that's not funny …'

No, it wasn't. Not when Kate Summers had won the role of Dorothy. That afternoon after school, I binged and purged so violently on refined carbohydrates, I passed out. But today I join in with Maximilian and laugh too, as I have been doing since I moved in whenever the subject of weight arises. Although, much of the evidence that showed my secret past may have been dug up and exposed already, there is a lot more beneath that could be. Humour is an excellent tool to prevent further excavation from Maximilian, or anyone.

'So, *seriously*, try to relax about JP's plans. I can't see any downside. Oh, except possibly one thing …'

As I am talking, Maximilian gets up from the sofa and

stretches his arms above his head. His T-shirt shoots up and I get a flash of that exquisitely defined 'V' of lean muscle that leads down to his pelv—

'What's that?' he asks.

'What's what?'

'The downside.'

I refocus. 'You may let your inner child come to the fore. Because that's what happens with a lot of male stars when they get *really* famous, isn't it? Like John Travolta turning his drive into an aeroplane runway and that guy out of the Backstreet Boys paying NASA millions of dollars to train him for a moon flight.' I give Maximilian a sincere look. 'Promise me you won't have a skateboard park installed in your bathroom.'

'I promise.' He smiles. 'Although, I may lay a BMX track on the roof. Cheers for the talk, I appreciate it. When you're not taking the piss, you make sense. Not a lot, but some.' He leans down and rubs my shoulder. 'Now, you can stop indulging my ungrateful arsehole-ness to go and do whatever it is that you are clearly itching to go and do.'

'Gym,' I tell him. But I wait until he has removed his hand from my clavicle before I move.

Obviously, my workout routine has intensified since I moved in with Maximilian. Partly because I am sharing a house with someone whose bum, stomach and thighs have all at one time topped a *Britain's Most Sexy* poll. Partly because his gym is so luxurious; with top-of-the-range electronic machinery and a massive open cupboard that is hung with an assortment of pulleys, padded harnesses and metal contraptions to rival Christian Gray's Room of Pain in *Fifty*

Shades. But moreover because I am being photographed daily. Fame – even a tiny bit of it – is like having your own Marine Sergeant Major perched on your shoulder shouting instructions into your ear to work harder. (There is a reason why Cameron Diaz can drag HGV tyres across baseball pitches.) I like this external voice. It's a welcome relief from mine. Every time it shouts louder, mine is drowned out a little more.

I stare down at the time gauge on the running machine. I've done seventy-five minutes; split into twenty-five sections of two minutes sprinting, followed by one minute walking on a slight hill. Then, I *literally* ramped things up: grabbed an old fleece that I found in the back of the torture cupboard, zipped myself in and altered the incline setting from *vain cow* to *crazy bitch*. I wasn't planning on doing this intense extra portion, but I needed to stop my mind wandering. Because I have to admit, a few nerves are starting to set in about tonight. Will Maximilian and I be convincing enough? It's one thing acting out a well-rehearsed pap shoot at the end of a zoom lens, but this will be unscripted live theatre. Will the other celebrities and assembled journalists – our audience – watch us *close up* and *really* believe that we go at it hammer and tongs on Maximilian's Japanese-style futon … and afterwards I potter about the feng-shuied bedroom in my box-fresh Calvin Klein pants and one of his faded V-neck T-shirts whilst we debate which is the best coming-of-age movie made in the eighties? I reckon Maximilian would go high brow and try to convince me it's *The Outsiders* (black and white) but I would resolutely stand by *St Elmo's Fire* – with a nod to

The Breakfast Club. We'd start squabbling, there would be a pillow fight, the Egyptian-cotton cases would slip off, duck feathers would shower down on us, he'd grab the edge of my T-shirt and pull me back—

Maximilian walks into the gym. He is holding a black box tied with a ribbon.

I slow down the treadmill, switch off my MP3 player and dab at my face with a towel, safe in the knowledge that I won't remove too much of my make-up from earlier. That's the beauty of MAC – it has staying power. You could wear it scuba diving and still emerge from the sea red-carpet ready.

'There had better not be a cake in there,' I joke/tell Maximilian. '*No one* does *flour* pre a major event.'

'Nope, it's not anything edible, but it *is* something for tonight. I completely forgot to mention it earlier; you distracted me by banging on about your problems … *again*.' He groans sarcastically. 'Sometimes I wonder when you'll actually take an interest in *me* and m—' Suddenly he stops. 'Where did you get that?'

'What?' I take a swig of Fiji water.

'That …' He points at me.

'From the fridge.'

'Not the water … *that*.' He pulls at his own T-shirt.

I gesture at the top I am wearing. 'This fleece? Oh, I found it in your gym cupboard. It looked like an old one so I didn't think you'd m—'

'I'd like you to take it off.'

'Now?'

'Yes.'

'Because you're embarrassed I've busted you as a secret

fleece owner? Ha! As long as you're not harbouring any deck shoes or Oakley sunglasses too, I think I can let this go. Goes to show, though, you can take the boy out of posh private school but you can't take the posh private school out of the b—'

'Just get it off,' he repeats, his voice firm but a little quieter.

'All right, all right. Christ, I thought you of all people wouldn't mind someone making an item of your clothing look even more used.' I smile at him.

But he doesn't reciprocate. I press the stop button on the running machine and wriggle myself out of the fleece. As I hand it to Maximilian I notice a logo on the back: PUMP PERSONAL TRAINING.

'I thought you didn't see the point in personal train—'

'I don't,' he interrupts.

'But you used to have one…?'

'Temporarily.'

'He wasn't good enough?'

'No,' says Maximilian, folding up the top. 'He just fucked off.'

'Why?'

'No idea … it's not a big deal.'

'That's what I said to Cli—' Shit. *Well done, Vivian.*

Maximilian takes a step closer to me. 'Clint? Clint *Parks?* Why are you talking to him about my business?' His voice is now a little sharp. 'I thought he was meant to be on our side now. More to the point, I thought *you* were.'

'He is. I am.'

'Why were you discussing this subject together, then?'

'It wasn't a *discussion.* Clint made a very brief comment a while back that I wasn't interested in, and that was it.' We both stare at one another for a few seconds. I continue to ramble. 'I'd forgotten all about it until now … but anyway, I really don't care one way or the other who was once monitoring your exercise regime so there's no need for us to have an argum—' Good … a diversion. 'Hi, Monday!'

My cat strolls into the gym, pausing to sharpen his claws on a padded bench and do a victory roll on Maximilian's yoga mat. He has settled into this house very quickly. So much so I have been wondering if maybe his original owners were super wealthy, but due to a few turns of fate he ended up slumming it with me; a feline Oliver Twist.

He meows loudly and plaintively.

'Looks like someone wants their tea,' I say quickly. 'I better feed him before he drops in next door for hors d'oeuvres.' I grab my towel and iPod, then jump off the machine.

'Hang on a second, you haven't opened this.' Maximilian – apparently pleased with the diversion too – passes me the black box. 'It's something to wear tonight.'

'Really? Thank you. That's so, *er*, thoughtful of you. I appreciate it.'

But my chest is clenching. I think of the scene in the last season of *Sex and the City* when Alexsandr Petrovsky presents Carrie with that Oscar de la Renta pink puffball prom dress. I stare at the box in my hands. If the contents are pink, puffball shaped or prom inspired, *I am not even trying it on.* Gingerly, I untie the ribbon and lift the lid. Inside, wrapped in silver tissue paper, is a tight, short, dazzling-white

Alexander Wang tunic with gold foil inserts and a pair of Camilla Skovgaard chain-mail high-heeled sandals. It's a look that goes beyond edgy into hovering-on-the-precipice territory. It is everything I could want in an outfit.

I gasp. 'Wow, did you choose this, Maximilian?'

'No,' he replies. 'Barb did. Although, I did tell her what I wanted for you.'

'What was that?'

'Something in a colour that would put you off wearing so much fake tan or make-up. You really don't need it, Vivian …' He squeezes my shoulder again, like he did in the screening room. But this time his palm rests there a few seconds longer. 'You're beautiful.'

An hour later, as I am setting a fresh, rich application of St Tropez bronzing mousse with the cold setting on my hairdryer and waiting for my first layer of foundation to settle, I consider that most people in my position would probably have pushed Maximilian for a few more details over any mysteries regarding ex-employees (or their agitated mothers), but frankly, why should I? I don't need to be in control of everything … only me. That was why I signed up. Besides, as a fat kid, whenever I used to watch *Scooby Doo*, as soon as the ghost-busting gang arrived at a haunted house and split up into two groups to hunt for the ghoul, I never wanted to be with Velma, Fred and Daphne, actively seeking clues. I always thought Scooby and Shaggy had the best idea: avoid any potentially scary confrontation and head for the kitchen to find some decent snacks.

CHAPTER TWENTY-THREE

At eight o'clock, Barb calls to say that she is waiting in the people carrier outside the iron gate. As Maximilian and I wait for the car door to whir open fully, a heavy herb-and-musk-noted fragrance – possibly Joop! – hits us.

'Guys, this is Achilles,' says Barb, indicating to a man in a white shirt sat next to her.

'Hello,' I say, climbing in behind them to the back row of seats. 'I've been wondering … Achilles *what?*'

'Just Achilles,' he replies, in a confident Thames Estuary accent. 'Barb said one word would be sufficient.'

Barb laughs. 'I told him that his jawline can do the talking.'

She has a point. It appears to have been crafted with a spirit level it is so impressively square. Maximilian gets in the car next to me – his Issey Miyake instantly clashing with Achilles' fragrance.

'It's really cool to finally meet you, Maximilian,' enthuses Achilles, over his shoulder. 'I'm a massive fan. Interestingly, I always get photographers commenting on how I bring a similar intensity to my modelling work that you do to the big screen. I guess that's how you practised when you started out.'

Maximilian flops back into the seat next to me. Clearly, not having found this statement in the ballpark of 'mildly diverting', let alone 'interesting', he rolls his eyes and doesn't bother to reply.

'Maxy was *never* a model,' Barb explains.

'Oh right,' says Achilles. 'But you do some modelling now, don't you? For Dior Homme …?'

Maximilian uses his thumb and forefinger to motion firing a gun at the back of Achilles' head. 'That's Jude Law,' he corrects him. Then he whispers in my ear, 'I thought we were meant to be letting that fucking jawline do the talking.'

I smile at this. I don't laugh because I'm quite tired – getting ready took it out of me – but also it will look as if I am flirting. Maximilian will think I took him calling me 'beautiful' *literally*, which I didn't. I certainly won't be saying anything too complimentary back. That would be embarrassing for us both. Look, of course, Clint was right … I've got a crush on Maximilian. But who wouldn't have one? Even Monday goes a bit funny around him. But I know my limit. I've pulled some hot men over the years, but one whose name rests comfortably between parentheses and has an italic 'the' preceding it? No. I learnt my lesson on that front back at school, appropriately enough, *during a lesson*: Biology. I found a note in my pencil case 'From Ziggy xox', telling me he thought I was 'beautiful' and asking me to meet him at break-time in the shed used to store the sports equipment. At 11.03 I found myself hovering excitedly outside. I kicked open the door and walked in. Ziggy wasn't in there. But on the wall – in Kate Summer's cutesy, arty bubble handwriting (with hearts in place of the dot above each 'i') – there was a message: VIVIAN WARD IS A BIG, FAT IDIOT!

Achilles is still wittering on. '… funny to think that it won't be long before they'll be talking about the *new* Jude and the new …' He twists round in his seat to nod at Maximilian. '… *you* from the next generation of young talent.'

'Yes, Achilles,' mutters Maximilian, 'fucking *hilarious* to think that.'

Achilles turns back to Barb. 'I wonder who I'll be *the new* …'

'Good question,' replies Barb. 'Let me think.'

Maximilian cocks his imaginary weapon and refills it with some make-believe ammo. 'Chris O'Donnell?' he suggests.

On arrival at the gallery, Barb and Achilles get out of the car first. Barb shows Achilles how to make the most of the assembled photographers by walking very slowly up the black-carpeted walkway as if he has landed on the moon. Maximilian and I hang back, wait until the entrance is clear and then wander up to the venue ultra casually. The paparazzi shout his name and a cheer goes up amongst the crowd who have stopped to watch. Maximilian narrows his eyes at them and smoulders. When the paps shout my name too, he spins me round to show off my dress and then theatrically yanks me in close to him so our lips are millimetres away from each other's. We stay locked in this position as the screams get louder and the camera flashes shower down upon us. In the fading evening light I have never seen

Maximilian look more like a star. He knows it too. When we finally step foot in the gallery he shoots Achilles his MTV Award-winning smile, although he may as well have said, *Watch and learn, Ken doll…*

Inside, we're offered flutes of Bollinger Rosé and bulbous glasses of Merlot or Sancerre. Barb has said I can have a drink tonight. But given that the first two options are not on my allowed colour spectrum I am forced to drink the white wine. *Lady Petrol.* Initially, the taste makes me wretch, but after a glass, it seems to slip down quite easily. I feel myself getting 'perky'. I've sunk two more by the time Maximilian and I have done a circuit of the artist's work to appear suitably interested. He and I appear to be convincing people we are together. He is focused, barely even glancing at any other women in the room, despite there being some very attractive, famous faces milling about. Models, pop singers, It-girls, fashionistas, television presenters … including Noelle Bamford. She has just arrived. I can see her waiting to be photographed in front of the official sponsor wall.

A member of the catering staff in a fitted white shirt approaches us. I examine the tray he is holding. On offer is a selection of miniature servings of 'honest British grub': single nuggets of fried fish each with their own chip on sticks, ten-pence sized steak and kidney pies or squares of toad-in-the-hole made with cocktail sausages. I stare at them. The portion sizes may be meant as ironic but I don't find it funny.

Maximilian shakes his head at the waiter. 'We're fine, thank you.' As the waiter walks off he turns back to me. 'Sorry, I'm assuming you didn't want to …'

'... *try one?* Christ, no way,' I tell him, forcing a laugh. 'Everyone with eating issues knows there is no such thing as trying "one" when it comes to nibbles. It's the equivalent of an alcoholic saying they are off to the pub for a "swift half" only to find themselves waking up the next morning slumped in a shop doorway hugging a traffic cone and missing a shoe ... then heading to an off-license for breakfast. Ha!' Another forced laugh.

Maximilian smiles, then shoots a disparaging glance in the direction of Achilles. '*Fuck* knows what Barb is thinking with *him.* She's backed a total dud. He's got about as much chance of an acting career as you have of being a spokesperson for sensible eating.' He turns back to me. 'I mean, seriously, Vivian ... how can you be *frightened* of a fucking canapé?'

'A canapé is a lot more complex than that bit of beefcake,' I nod back in the direction of Achilles, 'and you're wary of *him.*'

'You get a "touché" for that ...'

'It's been a long while since you gave me one of those.'

'Yeah, I know. I've been waiting for the right moment ... and that was definitely it.'

He drops the subject and I smile to myself. This is the best thing about hanging out with Maximilian – or I imagine any celebrity. They're never likely to dig deep into the under-soil of your issues because they're always too busy turfing over their own.

'Vivian! What a lovely ickle surprise ...'

Christ. It's Sophie Carnegie-Hunt. She rearranges her Charlie Chaplin-esque bowler hat at a more dapper angle, swoops in and plants two air kisses either side of my cheeks, then repeats the process with Maximilian.

'Maximilian Fry, *hi* … Sophie Carnegie-Hunt – *Get On It!* public relations. Vivian and I have been pals for-*ever*. Don't you a-*dore* this artist? He's making such a bloody *amazing* statement about … *stuff*. Are you going to Stella's drink-a-links later in Bond Street?'

'Stella who?' asks Maximilian, genuinely.

Sophie hoots with laughter. 'Good one! Stella *who*? Ha! You're an *angel*. Bloody amazing. I don't know how long I'll be able to stay there – probably an in-and-out job – I've got to show my face at some breast cancer bash and then onto Bungalow 8 for Kimberley Stewart's birthday do. Rock heritage does not come more authentic than her …' She opens her sequined blazer to expose a vintage Rod Stewart *Body Wishes* tour T-shirt. 'I a-*dore* Kimbo.'

'Paris Hilton without the small dogs, charisma or international appeal,' I mutter to Maximilian, thoroughly enjoying the buzz I am getting from my Lady Petrol. I see why Adele is addicted to it – you get an instant *wooomph*.

'Any-hoo …' says Sophie, pushing the boundaries of *jaunty* by tipping her hat even further forward. 'Bloody *amazing* to meet you, Maximilian. You must come and have a chatski with my Noo-Noo … Noelle Bamford. She said you met at that bash for the *bwave kiddiwinkles* …' She puts on her baby voice.

'We did,' says Maximilian. 'Pass on my regards.'

'Oh, you *must* do that yourself. She'd adore to catch up. Ooooooooooh, while I'm here … sneaky heads-up for a do I'm putting togeths … new artist … Da Goblin MC …

bloody *amazing* kid … blew up on YouTube … buzzing on BBM … *serious* urban flavour.'

'Where's he from?' I ask.

Sophie laughs and casually throws a gang sign. 'Esher, Surrey. Not exactly the mean streets, but trust me, those kids are so much easier to work with when the parents are *nice* … anyway, showcase is Friday, eight till late at Koko … you'll both come?'

Maximilian shakes his head. 'I'm recording the *Benson* show that night. What a shame.'

'A *real* shame …' I add.

'*Such* a bloody wuddy shame,' confirms Sophie.

As Maximilian and I attempt to stifle smiles, Barb whizzes over and grabs him. He leans down so that she can whisper something in his ear. I have no chance of hearing whatever it is because Sophie has yanked me over towards her and is hissing in mine.

'Listen, Vivian … have you heard about Clint?'

'What about him?'

'He's been suspended from *News Today.*'

'*Eh?* Since when?'

She emits an irritated snort. 'Since about three hours ago. The editor found lines of stardust on his desk. I'm livid. I was expecting him to cover Gobzy's gig in his *Big Column* but that's up in the air now. What was he thinking? It's nose to the *grindstone* during the day, nose to the *cistern* at night. He should know the bloody rules!'

I am shocked. I knew that Clint's cocaine intake had escalated from blasé to Belushi over the years, but to put his job in jeopardy? In all the time I have known him, he's never minded putting his health, safety and personal relationships at risk, but he would *never* have risked his title on the newspaper.

'Worse still, that sherbet wasn't even his to waste,' continues Sophie. 'I gave him the bloody cash to get some and now he's left me not high and *very* dry when I've got a long evening ahead.' Suddenly her eyes dart across the room and she cheers up. 'Oooh, there's Jade Jagger. Bloody *amazing* woman – heart her. Another rock 'n' roll baby and a true survivor.'

This time, I can't help laughing. 'What's Jade Jagger had to *survive*?'

Sophie looks *stunned*. 'People severely underestimate how hard life can be growing up in the shadow of rich and famous parents. It's not *all* vast cash deposits and holidays in Mustique, you know. Well, maybe some of the time, but you can't take away JJ's talent. That jewellery she designs is bloody amazing. It's so … so … *shiny*.' She envelops me in another painfully insincere hug. 'Ciao wow, Vivian.'

'Yeah … *ciao wow*, Sophie.' I deadpan, and try to catch Maximilian's attention, but Barb is still in his ear.

Nicholas arrives looking immaculate in a sharp steel-grey suit and black silk shirt.

'Evening, everyone.' He breathes in the atmosphere. 'Excellent turn-out, don't you think?'

Barb stops whispering to Maximilian. 'Sure is, and it's only going to get better …' I notice she's making that face she sometimes does, which implies she would be raising her eyebrows if they weren't paralysed by botulism. 'Isn't it, Maxy?'

But he doesn't reply. He is looking over at the arched gallery doorway even though there is no one standing in it. I quickly check the whereabouts of 'Noo-Noo' Bamford to see if she is in the vicinity, but she is by the bar boring an actor from *Downton Abbey*. Her brogues are fucking *patent* today.

Barb smiles at me. 'Okay there, kiddo?'

'Yeah, except I've just heard Clint has been suspended from *News Today*.'

'Really? *Sheesh …*'

Nicholas shrugs. 'Well, that's what happens when your leisure activities effect your working life. A habit should remain a *hobby*.'

'How do you know that's what he got into trouble for?' I stare back at him.

'Just assumed …' replies Nicholas, without skipping a beat. 'It's the most likely scenario, isn't it? What with him being a filthy, dirty chang monster.' He nods at Barb and his voice drops. 'The cretin gave Eden's mother my new number. Doesn't he know I've got better things to do with my time than fend off calls from menopausal old crones? I already receive enough from you, Silver …' He winks at her.

Barb laughs and tuts at Nicholas. 'FYI, I'm a *long* way from The Change.'

'Mmmm … happened back in eighteen seventy-six for you, didn't it?' Nicholas smiles, and goes back to scanning the room. 'Catering is a bit slack. Where's the sodding booze?'

With perfect timing Achilles strolls over holding two

flutes of champagne for him and Barb. Before he can pass her a glass, Nicholas swoops in and snatches one from him.

'At last, I'm parched. Make sure you keep them coming, there's a good fellow … and can you bring over a tray of food too. Something meaty, I only had a very light lunch …'

Achilles gasps and his impressive jaw clenches. 'You think I'm a waiter? Tell him, Barb. Tell him I'll never wait tables … *ever again*.'

I laugh and look across at Maximilian, wondering which one of us will be the first to make the obvious joke about Nicholas finding Achilles' heel. I think I ought to leave it to Maximilian – he'll get more pleasure from it. But he doesn't seem aware of what has happened. He still isn't listening. Neither is Barb. They are both staring towards the arched doorway. Now, a woman is standing there. She is wearing jeans with a white T-shirt and is posing for the paparazzi. She has her back to us, with one hand on her hip and her legs crossed. Outside, the photographers are shouting at her to give them more poses. Then she spins round, smiling.

It's Zoe Dano. She has short hair.

I am *agog*. It is an unwritten rule in modelling that no one who has *ever* had long hair looks better when it is suddenly cut short. You only have to witness makeover week in all those *search-for-a-new-face* telly shows, where the host drags a model wannabe (always the prettiest – er, jealous?) by the ponytail to a hair salon and orders a stylist to lop it off in a bid to make the girl more *high* fashion. The resulting hardcore fascist buzz cut is such a *low* blow to the contestant's confidence, she doesn't stop crying or comfort eating until the fifth episode, whereupon she will be eliminated for not 'working with' the host's creativity (read: bitterness). Incredibly, though, Zoe's new cut only goes to show that she wasn't hiding behind her hair before. As an awkward hush descends onto the room I hear someone swear, and then realise it's me.

Barb prods Maximilian. 'Go on, Maxy. Remember what I said. Be *cool*. Work it. Freakin' *own it*.'

'Stay in view of the paps by the entrance, Fry,' hisses Nicholas.

'Okay, okay … I know what to do,' he replies, sounding reasonably upbeat, and reaches for my hand.

But I don't take it. Why would I want to meet a supermodel? So Maximilian strolls over on his own – everyone in the room following his each step. Well, almost everyone. In the background I can hear Sophie Carnegie-Hunt talking about an international pilates retreat she's doing the press for. 'Do it. Bloody relax and unwind – you deserve it, Jade.' When Zoe sees Maximilian, her smile contorts into a nervous grimace. But then, as he gets closer, the smile returns. I can only assume Maximilian is smiling at her too. Cautiously, she steps forward and gives him a kiss on the cheek. He pecks her back. As the photographers go crazy, I slip outside, grabbing another glass of wine en route.

At the back of the decked smoking area, I find a lump of dark marble (which is either a seat or a Surrealist statue), and sit down. I pull a month-old packet of Marlboro Lights out of my bag, select one, light it and inhale. After a month of no smoking, I'll be honest, it tastes utterly *vile* but I smoke it anyway. Not how I usually would have done – with a few light inhalations and not bothering with the remaining two-thirds – I drag on this one down to the butt.

I drain my drink, drop my zapped cigarette onto the floor and grind it into the decking with my heel. I am deliberating lighting another when I feel a hand on my shoulder. I twist round.

It's her.

In *close-up*: Zoe Dano. I fail to react because all I am thinking is how can she *not* be wearing foundation, cover-up or concealer yet *not* have a single visible pore on her face?

'Hey, you're Vivian, right?' She has a Deep South American accent. 'I'm Zoe. You probably know that I was, er, engaged to Max, a while back.'

I manage to nod. *She must use some sort of mineral make-up, or possibly one of the latest blemish balm creams, or at least a base primer …*

'It's sure good to meet you,' she continues, 'I've been reading online in the States about you and Max. It's real nice to see him looking happy after, well, *everything* …'

No, nothing. Not a dab of cosmetic camouflage.

'Anyway, I'd like to talk to you, if that's okay.'

She has the complexion of a baby. Not a real-life blotchy baby, but the ones who are clearly wearing make-up in those soft-focus advertisements for post-weaning milk substitutes. I manage another nod.

'Thanks …' She plonks herself on the seat next to me and digs out a packet of full-strength Camel cigarettes from her T-shirt pocket. 'Yeah, I know I should try a lower tar brand but I'm a model. Chain smoking is what we do. Well, *that* and pretend we like other models when we want to scalp each other. No wonder most people think we're so annoying.' She giggles. 'Have you got a flame, dude?'

I flick my lighter and now I move from assessing her face to her figure. She is skinny, obviously, but *effortlessly* so in the way *only* models are, i.e., genetically. There is a difference between a thin model and a thin celebrity. You look at a picture of Alessandra Ambrosio and you get the impression she doesn't even bother weighing herself. You look at a picture of a certain girl band star-turned-WAG-turned-fashionista and you *know* she is one steamed edamame bean away from a calorie-counting meltdown.

'So, I kind of want to apologise for pitching up here,' says Zoe, sucking hard on her cigarette. 'I knew you guys were going to be here – I got my agent to find out – but I've not come to cause trouble. I've moved on from Max, *genuinely*, I have … and I'm real pleased he has too, with *you*, but I needed closure. He's never let me explain why I—'

'Slept with a rock star?' I interrupt haughtily. That must be down to the white wine. I am never *haughty*. I'm turning into Adele.

Zoe sighs again and taps her ash on the ground. 'Look, I know you're only going on the picture of me drawn by the media, but I'm no hussy. I was brought up in Alabama, we're talking full-on Bible Belt. My family weren't simply God-fearing Christians they were goddam *terrified*. When I left home at nineteen I hadn't even been in front of a boy in my bathing suit let alone my birthday one. The British press made me out to be some ho who'd always put herself around, but Max was my first boyfriend. Believe me, that night I spent with Rick Piper *was* and *will always be* the biggest mistake of my life.'

'Why are you telling me this?'

'Bccause I care.'

'About?'

'Max.' She nudges me. 'I love your dress, by the way. I should get dolled up more often, but I can never be bothered. Agh! Sorry, another annoying model trait – that whole, "I live in tees 'n' jeans" thing,' she groans, then becomes serious again. 'Hand on my heart, I feel *real bad* about what I did, but when I met Rick my relationship with Max was in a *real bad* place. I didn't think he was committed. He never wanted to spend his spare time with me; he was either working or working out. I felt … what's the word? Sidelined. Yeah, *sidelined* … But I guess that still doesn't make up for my behaviour. You must think I'm gross, huh?'

'Not really, if you hadn't been such a shameless slut then I never would have ended up with him.'

I smile as I say this, so she knows I am joking. Not because I suddenly *like* her. I don't think it is possible for anyone to *like* a supermodel, not unless they were one of those freakishly ugly ones who work on the edgier side of the market. But I appreciate that she has a certain level of self-awareness and I empathise with a childhood put in the shade by the crazy parasol of religion.

She hangs her head. 'You think I'm a *shameless slut*?'

'*No!* Who am I to judge you, Zoe? It's not as if the

security code on my chastity belt hasn't been cracked a fair few times over the years.'

'But that's the thing, dude.' She sighs. 'Mine hasn't. No one's cracked mine, except Rick. My cooter *was* and *is* strictly off limits.'

I raise an eyebrow at her. 'Your *cooter*?'

'Sorry, that's a Southern thing. A cooter is what us ladies call … ahem, you *know* … our honey pot. That's when we're not calling it our pink taco, passion fruit or cherry pop.'

'All of which make "beaver" sound like a sophisticated physiological term.' I laugh. But then I stop, suddenly realising what she has implied. 'Hang on a second, you've only ever …'

'Slept with Rick? Yep. Once.'

'*What?* You never went all …'

'… the way with M—'

'Maximilian?'

'No,' she replies plainly. 'He knew about my upbringing from the moment we met and totally respected that I wanted to wait till our wedding day. The whole chastity pledge thing is kind of weird to you Brits, isn't it?'

'Only because it gets in the way of having sex,' I say. Although, at school there was one person who made that vow. 'So, Maximilian never, *er* …?'

'Pressured me? Not once. I guess that was why he was so pissed when he found out about Rick. The fact he had been so patient and all.'

I shake my head, almost too bewildered to talk. *They never did it?* What *else* do you do in the initial phase of a relationship? When I first met – it doesn't matter who – I spent an entire *two weeks* in bed with him … I didn't even go into work. I told Roger I had suspected bird flu. More to the point, Zoe could have lost her virginity to *the* 'Maximilian Fry'. Yet she chose to do it with a man who regularly Keeks himself on the toilet in his tour bus. One thing is for sure, to cheat on Maximilian, Zoe must have felt more than *sidelined.* Kicked off the team, I reckon.

Zoe takes a last long drag on her Camel and chucks away the end. 'Anyway, I don't want to take over your night. You better get back inside, Max was looking for you. Are we cool?'

'We never weren't,' I say magnanimously, and make myself cringe at the same time. 'Let's go and get a drink.'

She gets up from the bench. 'I need some food, too. I'm starving. I only had a burger, fries and cheesecake for dinner and I get real hungry when I'm anxious. I eat *all* day and *all* night …'

I roll my eyes at her as I stand up. 'You know you said people find models annoying? *That's* why.'

'Agh! I'm such a pain in the butt sometimes, I actually annoy *myself.*' She giggles. But then suddenly, she clasps my arm. 'Dude, can I ask you something? I know I shouldn't because *you* are with *him* now and you're *both* so into each other, but I need to…' She takes a deep breath. 'D'you think Max ever *truly* loved me?'

I stare into her delicately boned face with its wide, almost extra-terrestrial-like features. She looks very sad. I consider telling her about the picture that Maximilian still keeps at the foot of the stairs, but then I decide against it. I don't think that makes me a bitch. Would *any* woman want to make a supermodel feel better about herself?

'Your silence speaks volumes, dude,' she says dolefully. 'He didn't, did he?' Her big, aquamarine eyes look even more oceanic as they brim with tears.

Christ, I have to say something, don't I? There is something almost endearingly vulnerable about her. I find this interesting. I grew up thinking supermodels couldn't have weaknesses. They certainly didn't show any in George Michael videos.

'Of course, he loved you, Zoe.'

'Why did you pause, then?'

'Because I was trying to think of an example as proof … and now I've thought of one.' It's not quite as much of an ego boost as the photographic evidence. 'Personally, I think you can always tell how much someone was into someone else by how uncomfortable they are being in the same room as that someone after they've split up.'

A tear tips over her right lower lid and slides down her face. 'In that case, Max *definitely* didn't love me,' she says. 'He was fine when we saw one another a few moments ago. *More* than fine …'

'Only because the cameras were on him. Trust me, when he saw you at The Rexingham he couldn't get out of the place fast enough.'

Zoe dabs her eye. 'The Rexingham Hotel?'

'Mmmm …'

'But I've never stayed there. My agent always books me in at Blakes when I'm in town.'

'You've *been* there, though,' I remind her. 'Just over a

month ago. For that awards thing. Maximilian saw the back of your head – your long *tresses* – across the room and before you turned round, he bolted.'

This confuses Zoe further. 'But I haven't been in London since February and I'd already cut my hair by then. It must have been someone who looked like me … I guess I've got a pretty common face.'

I burst out laughing. 'Aghhhhhhhhhh!'

She laughs too. 'The second most annoying thing a model can say, right?' She claps her hand to her forehead. 'I'm boring myself now, as well as you … Let's go in.'

As we step back inside the gallery, I see Maximilian on the other side of the room. Noelle Bamford is yacking away excitedly in his ear, her body arched towards him in a configuration that is definitely not a natural resting posture unless you are a professional gymnast at the end of a floor routine. I grab another drink, but as soon as I take a sip, my head judders and feels heavy. I take another sip and the same thing happens but my head feels even heavier. Like a boulder.

I know what this is. I've witnessed it so many times. Roger and I call it The Crash. It's what happens to women in Burn's when they've put too much Lady Petrol in the tank. One moment they are whizzing along in the outside lane, the next – boom! –they're strewn across the central reservation. One of two things could happen next: a.) I'll go on the attack about something. Anything. But as with the Iraq war, there will not be a shred of incontrovertible evidence on which to base my actions; or b.) I'll be overcome with hunger verging on starvation. I've seen Adele toast an entire loaf of bread after a night out on white wine. *Bread.* BREAD. DEAD. Before I can locate a tray of those ironic canapés, I stumble back out of the fire exit, past the smokers and hail a cab back to Primrose Hill.

CHAPTER TWENTY-FOUR

As soon as I am in the door, I cram five rice crackers in my mouth – dry, to prevent over-indulgence. Still chewing, I grab a bottle of Fiji water and lurch upstairs to remove my make-up; the prospect of which feels like a Herculean task. But I think of Zoe Dano's blemish-free face and refuse to be defeated. I use a foaming facial wash and sponge to begin with, then I give my T zone the once over with a handheld electrical exfoliating brush and a grainy scrub. This should shift everything. Well, almost. It's the best I can do without industrial blasting equipment. After cleansing, I smear a thick layer of Crème de la Mer over the top. I've always wondered if the hype of this cream (10/10 in *every* broadsheet Sunday supplement beauty poll *ever*) versus the price (£660 for 250ml) could be justified, but I can tell you, it is. You get a *brand-new face* by the following day. Seriously, some mornings Monday has woken up next to me on the pillow and done a double take.

Currently, he is lying diagonally across the bed, fast asleep. I gently push him to one side to get in and he shoots me a look of vague annoyance, then blinks … and blinks again, and nods off again. But I can't sleep. I wish I had a sleeping pill. This is the first aperture I have had to well, *think* … since I got here. So, I don't. I return to the bathroom and apply further unguents. There is a knock at my bedroom door. I freeze. I can't see Maximilian without anything on my face except for a scoop of moisturising marine derivatives, so I keep quiet.

'I know you're not asleep, kiddo.' It's Barb. 'Your light is on.'

'Hang on.' I let her in. 'Did you get my text?'

'Yeah. I said you could have "a" drink.'

'Sorry …'

She tuts at me. 'You have to be careful.'

'I know, so I left. Look, I was tired before I got there … that's probably why I drank so much. Can't I do less hours at Burn's? My schedule is killing me.'

'I told you, kiddo, we need the public to see you as the perky waitress.'

'But they wouldn't find out about a reduction in my working hours,' I moan, as I climb back into bed. 'I mean, when Meg Matthews was married to Noel Gallagher from Oasis everyone said how impressive it was she kept herself in full-time employment as a party planner, but I bet she didn't continue being so hands-on at each event; hanging glitter curtains and blowing up balloons.'

'Possibly not …' Barb smiles. 'But Nicholas would say "no". It's best for you and Maxy …'

I humph at her. 'So, where are they?'

'Gone to meet JP at a casino in Mayfair. I put Achilles in a cab back to his. He overdid it on the liquor too. I was about to introduce him to this up-and-coming British director who blew up on the festival circuit last season

… told him we'd hit PR paydirt if I can get him seen at next year's Sundance. Get this, he looked at me and said, "Why would I want to be photographed at a rave, Barb?" Ha! Sheesh, I hope he was drunk. No one can be that stupid, can they? He makes Zac Efron look like a CIA tactician.'

I laugh too and plump up my pillows. I think Barb is about to leave but then she gives me *that* look. The one where her eyebrows are struggling against an injected toxin to levitate.

'What?' I stare back at her.

'Tonight …' she says.

'What about it?'

'You and Maxy …'

'What about us?'

'That was about to be my point.'

'I don't understand.'

'You said "us".'

'That's the correct pronoun.'

'Ah, but it's not, is it? Not *really* …'

'Barb, either I'm still wasted or you're talking absolute gibber—'

She taps the bed. 'You want it to be *correct*. You want *him* and *you* to be an "us". A *real* "us".'

I yank the covers from underneath her so I can pull them around me. 'That's ridiculous.'

'Why did you storm out of the gallery when Zoe rocked up, then?'

'I didn't *storm* anywhere. I wanted a cigarette.'

'You haven't smoked for a month.'

'I was drinking *white wine*. It's what happens. I defy the leader of the anti-smoking lobby to neck the best part of a bottle of Chablis and not want a fag.'

'Hmmm … sounds like you're trying to convince *yourself* as well as *me*. But relax, kiddo, I'm not pissed at you …' Barb waves her hand. 'It was to be expected. All chicks fall for the leading man when they're cooped up with them twenty-four/seven. It happens on set the whole time. You living with Maxy is no different to shooting a film with him … it's intense. You're forced to look at this freakin' flawless specimen *all* day so you're naturally going to spend *all* night thinking, well, *you* know what you've been thinking … I don't need to tell you.'

'You're wrong, Barb. Obviously, Maximilian is very, very, *very* attractive.' I confirm this woozily. 'There is no point me arguing that he isn't. But that doesn't mean I have any intention of attempting to sed—'

She laughs and interrupts me. 'Ha! Back in the day when I was a director, there was this actor – Flynn Daniels – who I never had any intention of seducing either. By that I mean I spent every waking minute on set working out how I could bang his goddam brains out. He knew it too … used to play me like a freakin' Stradivarius. His wife was one of the first *Sports Illustrated* covergirls – your textbook free spirit-*slash*-Amazonian goddess who acted as a spokesperson for PETA. I used to dread her coming to visit us on location: zooming up in her convertible Mustang with all these flea-ridden rescued mutts in the back seat, unfolding twenty fucking metres of leg from the driver's seat and diving into Flynn's pumped-up arms.'

I watch Monday flex his paws in his sleep. 'So, what happened?'

'Well, one day she was driving away from the set, lost control of the wheel and crashed into a truck on the highway. She snuffed it on impact. Freakin' tragic. Turned out someone had drained the brake fluid from her car.'

'Barb!' I gasp. 'You *didn't*?'

'Nah, I didn't,' she cackles. 'But I found myself hovering over that bonnet once or twice. He made me go loony tunes. You know what, though? As soon as we wrapped the movie and I got back to New York, I felt nothing for Flynn. Zero emotion. It was a fantasy. Anyway, my point is this, kiddo. *Silver's Golden Rule Number Twenty-five: There's only one thing you make if you believe in the make believe, and that's a mistake.*'

'Wow, Barb … that sounds like something Miley Cyrus would Tweet,' I deadpan, leaning back against the pillows. 'Look, we don't need to be having this conversation. I know *exactly* where I stand. This is business. Believe me, I know I am not the next Zoe Dano. Clearly, Maximilian likes a certain *type* of girl, and I am not that type.'

'What type would that be?' Barb attempts to move her eyebrows north again.

I raise mine back with no problem. '*Virginal.* Zoe told me … about the chastity pledge.'

'*What?* She *did*? Don't freakin' repeat that to Maxy. You know how private he is. Seriously, that would wind him up. You won't w—'

'No, I won't. As long as *you* stop winding *me* up.'

'I was only looking out for you, kiddo. I wouldn't want you to get …'

'Hurt? As if.'

Only the *truth* hurts … and that night it haunts my dreams. Then, I wake up to a nightmare.

CHAPTER TWENTY-FIVE

It's my own fault. On the way to Burn's in the people carrier I can't resist checking the papers for coverage from last night. That's when I find another picture. One that was taken when I was f—

Again, it's in *The First* … but this time it's laid over a double-page spread in their 'FEMALE First' section; a weekly pullout that is supposedly a serious forum for debating women's issues, but actually just baits women into having serious issues *with each other*. There are three photographs in the feature. One of me and Zoe at the gallery. The other two are of us in our teens. Zoe – already cute despite metal train tracks on her teeth – is standing on a podium wearing a bikini with a silver tiara and is draped with the Stars and Stripes flag, presumably having won some sort of beauty pageant.

I am standing on a beach – I can tell it's Brighton – which means Carl must have taken the picture, because Tracey was on holiday in Greece the year we went there. I am wearing a floral swimming costume, which *by law* should *not* have been allowed to be sold to a plus-size customer. It was from a shop on the local high street, not a catalogue. Mum had refused to risk wasting the money on one from the latter in case it didn't fit: *They won't let you return intimate goods, Vivian …* Safe to say, when I die I don't fear being sent to Hell to live out the rest of my days. I know it will be far less sweaty and stressful than the ninety minutes I spent in a packed communal changing room the day before we left, trapping my rolls of flesh into obscenely patterned Lycra-infused polyester. On our first morning at the seaside, as I waddled past his deckchair, my father made a joke about Pamela Anderson's job on *Baywatch* probably being safe for the moment.

There is no way I'm going to Burn's. This time the female members won't even *try* to disguise their delight at me being taken down a peg so publicly. I've clocked their jealous expressions over the last few weeks as mine and Maximilian's 'relationship' has become public knowledge. I can feel their eyes tracking me as I swan round the club in my new edgy threads. It was to be expected, though. After all, it's another one of the unspoken rules about working in hospitality – you are there to make the customer's life better. At no point must they think *you* are leading a better life than *them*. Thinking about it, maybe that's why Meg Matthews stopped running her events firm. It wasn't because she was tired. It was because her clients quickly realised that no matter how marvellous a bash she organised for them at a glitzy venue, she was having a far better time in her *own* home, Supernova Heights, partying with the cream of Brit Pop.

I ask Payton to drive me over to Bayswater. The builders let me in to Adele's flat. They have nearly finished putting in the new bathroom next to my old room. I find Adele in her bedroom transferring the contents of her wardrobe into storage boxes. She is wearing a smock dress decorated with tiny appliquéd daisies and a yellow silk scarf that isn't so much restraining her red curls as emphasising how wildly abundant they are. Even by her own rather twee style standards, she looks astonishingly winsome. I half expect Bambi and Thumper to bounce through the window and help with her packing. On the bedside table, steam is rising off a pungent herbal brew. It has the usual stench of cinnamon and wee … but this time I can smell ginger too. She jumps when she sees me.

'Vivian! Er, *hi* … I, er, how did you know I was here?'

'I phoned your office and got put through to Melanie. She said you weren't feeling well so were staying at home today. What's the matter?'

'Nothing really, I'm just feeling queasy,' she says, folding up a light caramel-coloured sweater and placing it on a pile of similarly muted shades of cashmere.

'Me too. I was drinking white wine last night. I don't know how you do it. That stuff is completely unpredictable … you can't see the tipping point coming.'

'Oooh, the not knowing is the best bit.' She giggles tentatively, clearly testing to see whether it is okay to lighten the mood. 'Listen, Vivian, before you have a pop at me, I *was* going to return that text you sent – with your new number – and arrange to meet up. I shouldn't have let the *situation* between us drag on unnecessarily, but you were obviously fine so I thought that I'd leave it until … well, and then I … anyway … I've had quite a bit going on…' She grimaces at me. 'You of all people know what I'm like. I can be … testy.'

'You? *Testy?*' I smile. As much I was planning on giving her a hard time – at least, initially – seeing her and being back in my old home is instantly comforting; a bit like when I used to pull on my old UGG boots after being out all night in a pair of Adele's brand-new stilettos. 'Well, I *suppose* I should have said "goodbye" in person.'

'Yes, you *should* have done. After nearly a decade and a half of flat-sharing … you didn't exactly put the *moving* into *moving out*,' she tuts. 'So, have you seen the new ensuite?'

'Yep, it looks great. Very user-friendly, what with the whole *shower, basin, loo* set-up. But then again I'm only involved in a service industry so I'm not your target market. I imagine if I were looking at it through the eyes of a "young professional", I wouldn't merely be seeing simple ceramic shapes but a sexier and more stream-lined work-life balance.' I flop down on the bed next to a row of neatly balled-up socks.

Adele rolls her eyes at me. 'All right, smart arse … Oh, and since you're here I may as well give you some news that will make you even more smug. I've decided to scale down the celebrations for the hen.'

'We're staying in Europe and won't need jabs?'

'No, we're not flying anywhere. Contrary to the recent more positive reports coming out of the financial capitals across the globe, things in the City are still perilous. Despite government intervention recovery will still take some time …' She explains this to me very slowly, as if outlining the credit crunch to a gerbil. 'Once again our bonuses aren't going to be a patch on what we used to get. My wedding planner is costing me more than a new kidney. When Melz used her she was almost unknown, but now she's done a couple of celebs and a minor royal …'

I roll my eyes at the mention of Melanie.

'Stop it,' chides Adele. 'She's not *that* bad.'

'Dels, she wears a *pashmina.* You've clearly forgotten the rule we made at college – it is never okay to make friends with girls *swathed* in anything. *Swathing* is wrong.'

Adele giggles and further previously unchartered curls spill out of her scarf and down her shoulder. 'You are terrible, Vivian, but as much as it pains me to say it I think that's what I have missed the most about living with you; the constant low level buzz of toxicity. James is so nice about everyone, he refuses to backbite, *ever*. He genuinely only likes to see the good in people … and yes, before you say it, I *will*. Thank God for that, or I'd probably still be single.' She pauses. 'So, come on then, tell me all about your *fabulous* new life.'

'My fabulous new life? Well, yeah … it's pretty much that, except …' For a second, I consider telling Adele how I am really feeling. But it's only a split one. *I remember Mum smiling at my father's joke.* '… except that *The First* have run another picture of me. This one is even worse. I'm by the sea … in *beachwear*. Or rather, *beached* wear. Put it this way, it is quite clear that the only waves I was going to catch that day were SONAR ones. Ha!' My laughter is tinny and canned. I sense that prickling behind my eyes and blink hard like Monday does.

'What did Maximilian say?'

'He hasn't seen it yet, but I'm sure he'll be really sweet like he was when it happened last time and tell me it doesn't matter in the slightest.'

'Sounds like he's a keeper,' she says.

'Mmm …' I agree. 'That's the *best* thing about Luke. He loves me for *me*.'

Adele cocks her head. 'Luke?'

The name punches me in the stomach. I feel winded. 'What's *he* got to do with anything?'

'You said the best thing about *Luke* was that he loved you for *you*.'

Now it kicks me in the face. I feel disorientated. 'I said *Maximilian* did.'

'You didn't.'

'I did.'

'You *didn't*, but so what. I know you meant Maximilian. It's not as if you would be missing that spatially challenged backpacker, is it?' She reaches for a beige mohair shrug and peers at me. '*Is* it?'

I force myself not to pause. 'No! Anyway, stop showing a vague interest in something other than your wedding, Dels …' I throw a balled-up pair of socks at her head. 'You're weirding me out. So, what are we doing for the hen?'

'Weekend trip to a spa,' she says, happily resuming the conversation. 'Someone at work recommended this place in Surrey. It's famous for holistic treatments and therapies for the mind, body and soul.'

I groan. Spiritual pampering is pretty pointless as far as I am concerned – especially those two-day packages. It is going to take more than forty-eight hours of background whale music and a couple of rub-downs with some organic herbs to penetrate my outer layer of fake tan, let alone have an effect on my inner core.

'Is it licensed?' I ask.

'I don't know.' She pauses and gives me an odd look. Her face sort of squirms. '*Act*-ually, I won't be drinking.'

I burst out laughing. 'Ha! As if you'll get through your hen night without a drip of Pinot Grigio.'

'I've got through the past *fourteen* nights,' she retorts.

'Impressive. Are you detoxing for the wedding already?'

'Oh no, I haven't done it for me. Or James. I'm doing it for someone else. The thing is, you know I said I wasn't going to allow children to the service or reception?' She gets up and looks down proudly at her floral-covered abdomen. 'I'm going to have to bend the rules a bit …'

I jump off the bed. 'Shit! Dels, are you *pregnant*?'

'I am.'

'And you're keeping it?'

'*Vivian!* Of course!'

'Shiiiiiiiiit, you're having a *baby*!'

'Yes! A baby. I'm having a *BABY*!'

I shake my head. 'Jesus *Christ*!'

'Well, maybe,' she laughs. But I don't want to *absolutely* guarantee the Second Coming before the twelve-week scan.'

'Ha! I gave you that one.' I climb over the bed and give her a hug. 'Congratulations, I'm so … *happy* for you.' That's what you're meant to say, right?

She untangles herself from my arms. 'Thank you. Oh,

and I've got even *more* good news for you. I've decided to do a mother-to-be blog on jamesandadele.com, so you don't have to carry on with your bridesmaid's one. It makes sense as I'll have so much to report over the next few months. Everyone can watch my bump growing,' she beams, as if this would be something 'everyone' would want to do.

'Wow, Dels…' I squeeze her hand. 'Remember those times we did pregnancy tests when we were younger …' Neither of us were on the pill. Adele because it made her moody and hormonal. Me because I was concerned about weight gain. 'We used to *pray* that second blue line wasn't going to appear.'

She wrinkles her nose. 'Did we?'

'Er, *yes*. Don't you remember being *really* late after that one-night stand you had with that bloke when I dragged you all the way to Gatecrasher? The one who wore that skintight neon tank top covered in fridge magnets …'

'That was fifteen years ago, Vivian,' she retorts, placing her hands protectively over her stomach as if to prevent her unborn child from hearing about unsavoury subjects such as what young men wore to techno nights in the Midlands at the back end of the nineties. 'We've all moved on, thank goodness.'

Thank goodness? 'Come on, Dels.' I shrug. 'You can't deny we didn't have fun back then?' I worked hard at it … relentlessly trying out every major night-time trend as soon as I heard about it. Having the confidence to go *clubbing* – as opposed to living in fear like a defenceless blubbery creature on the seashore in danger of being *clubbed* – was a highlight of being skinny. 'Don't you remember how excited we'd be by the middle of the week, planning in minute detail how we'd spend the rest of it?'

'Vaguely.'

'It was our generation that made Thursday the new Friday.'

'What a legacy ...' she mutters, uninterestedly, whilst taking a sip of her tea. 'Anyway, what colour Bugaboo do you think I should get? Navy or chocolate brown?'

'Eh? What the *hell* is a Bugaboo?'

She tuts. 'One of those tough three-wheel prams you can use on pretty much any kind of surface – Melz says they are the, "Land Rovers of tot travel..." Honestly, you ought to brush up on your parenting know-how or you are going to be a bit stuck when it comes to becoming a mum yourself.'

'You know I'm not up for motherhood, Dels.'

'Shut *up*! You do come out with rubbish sometimes, Vivian.' She puts one hand on her hip and rubs her lower back with the other, as if she was in her third trimester with triplets. 'Of course, you'll give birth one day. It's what we're all here for. It's the *whole point*.'

CHAPTER TWENTY-SIX

'That is such *bull*!' says Barb, when I tell her what Adele said about having children. 'Whenever women get knocked up they *have* to say that because it makes them feel better about the unavoidable horror in store for them: mood swings, incontinence, varicose veins … and their other half watching on in total shock as the woman he has committed his life to stops shaving or putting out in the sack, then eats her way through the kitchen cupboards and morphs into John freakin' Candy.'

'Isn't he dead?'

'Ex*actly*!' she cackles.

It's Friday night. Barb, Nicholas and I are at the television studio in the private Green Room we have been allocated for Maximilian's appearance on *Benson*. On the television monitor in front of us a comedian is warming up the audience who are so geed up already they are dissolving into hysterics before he even hits his punchlines. I'm sucking Smints and doing my best to appear upbeat but I've felt anxious all week, panicking about what other pictures may emerge. I feel as if the past month of paparazzi shots are now meaningless. The thin me is firefighting the fat me … and the blaze is spreading. I am being choked by the smoke.

The comedian takes a bow and some guy with a beard introduces himself as the producer of the show.

'Looks like they've had a change at the top,' says Nicholas, leaning against the as yet untouched bar. 'Isn't that the chap who was in charge of the BBC's political debate show? Let's hope Benson remembers this is a chat not an interrogation.'

'He will.' Barb shrugs. 'Last season, he was over every guest like a cheap suit … he told Will.i.am that he would leave a legacy of hit singles to rival Michael Jackson's. Ha!' The camera does a loop of the audience. Barb jumps up and points at the screen. 'There's JP, first row on the left …'

Nicholas peers closer. 'With his legal flunkies, too. Good. We need to be at least *talking* contracts tonight. He's off to Paris in the morning to see a couple of French actors who won at the Césars. I don't think I'd recover if Fry lost the part to a frog.'

The lights in the studio dim to signify that recording is about to begin. As the three of us settle into the sofa, Nicholas's mobile beeps. He shows Barb the caller ID.

'Sheesh …' She noticeably flinches. 'Not her again. She's giving me the willies.'

'Oh relax, Silver.' Nicholas drops the call and chucks his phone on the coffee table in front of us. Immediately, it rings again. The name 'Eden' appears in the window. 'I'll switch it off. You know I've dealt with everything. The mad old bint will get bored eventually.'

The lights in the studio come up again.

'Here we go …' Nicholas stares directly at the screen. 'You had better make us proud, Fry.'

'I'm proud of him already,' mutters Barb, more to herself.

'… all of which leads me to the first guest of my final series. He is an actor who many critics consider the most gifted of his generation. Having shot to stardom in his teens, he went on to capture the hearts of movie fans as a very convincing wolf, then won a BAFTA for his only marginally more clean-shaven role as action hero Jack Chase in *The Simple Truth...*' Charles Benson pauses for the audience to titter at his joke. 'Having taken a break from public life, he's back. Ladies and gentleman, Maximilian Fry.'

Everyone claps vigorously and the in-house orchestra launch into an instrumental version of 'Glad You Came' by The Wanted. Maximilian appears at the top of the studio stairs wearing an assortment of distressed fabrics that don't look so much *worn* as passed through an entire lineage; teamed with his favourite navy beanie hat and scuffed hiking boots. He smiles gratefully for the applause and jogs down to the interview platform to greet the host with one of those classic matey celebrity handshakes that builds into a hug. As the clapping dies down a few whistles and giddy shrieks from female audience members linger in the air.

'That's quite a reception, Maximilian. One which must mean a lot to you,' says Benson, the warmth of his introductory welcome cooling off slightly.

'Absolutely, it does …' replies Maximilian. 'I've been on quite a journey.'

'Indeed, one that has been well documented for everyone to see and hear … and at times it has not been pretty.' Benson pauses to rub his chin. 'Was there a point where you thought your reputation may have been damaged beyond repair?'

Maximilian shrugs regretfully. 'Well, the honest and I suppose somewhat shameful truth is that at the time I didn't really give a f—' He stops himself. 'I didn't care what people were saying about me. Obviously, my management told me what was being written, but I didn't read it myself. One of the perks of being severely dyslexic,' the audience laughs, but Benson doesn't, 'I guess, sometimes you have to fall a long way down before you can get back up and walk again, even then it is one step at a time.'

'Twelve steps in total, hmmm?' snipes Benson, looking pleased with himself. 'Whilst it is admirable that you were proactive in wanting to overcome your problems I can't help but feel that when celebrities announce these trips to rehab so publicly it gives youngsters the impression that a stay in such a centre is a normal career trajectory – or indeed, a means to an actual career *boost*.'

I glance over at Nicholas. He is glaring at Barb, that vein in his right temple throbbing. 'So much for being all over him like a cheap suit …'

Barb looks uncharacteristically rattled as she replenishes her gum. 'The new producer must have told him to switch things up and go in hard.'

'*Clearly*,' replies Nicholas. 'This is going to end in tears. Fry will blow his top and lash out.'

He could be right. We all turn back to the screen to see Maximilian tightening his grip on the arm of his leather chair.

'Believe me, Charles, I tried to keep a veil of privacy

over my recovery but when I was *photographed* at Geneva airport accompanied by a team of doctors there was not a lot I could do but admit to where I was heading.'

'Ah yes.' The host nods, with another smirk. 'That famous shot of you walking through customs carrying an audio copy of *The Power of Now*.'

For a few seconds, Maximilian sits in silence. Barb stops chewing her gum and clasps her hands together. Maximilian looks up and stares into the camera – eyes dilated – as if he could be about to snap. But then he clears his throat and turns back to Benson.

'With all due respect, Charles, I was about to embark on a voyage into the depths of my being.' His voice is hard and precise. 'Exactly how were you expecting me to pass the time … with the latest Penny Vincenzi?' The studio audience erupts with laughter. 'And as for going into rehab as a publicity stunt, rest assured if I had wanted to draw attention to myself I think I might have found a less mentally gruelling way to do it. Having a team of the world's leading psychotherapists digging relentlessly into the darkest recesses of your psyche is not exactly fun …' He raises an eyebrow. 'I suspect Will.i.am felt the same during your interview with him last series, Charles.'

Barb cackles delightedly. 'Way to go, Maxy!'

'But as a public fig—' begins Benson.

Maximilian interrupts him. 'As a public figure, I am well aware that I have a responsibility to live an exemplary lifestyle, but my heart had been broken …' He looks around the studio and a sympathetic hum buzzes through the audience.

Nicholas gets up and walks closer to the monitor, muttering, 'This is it, Fry, this is *it*.'

Maximilian waits for silence. 'And when that happens, when your heart *breaks*, suddenly you're not an actor, or a celebrity, or a *brand* …'

'Less of that, Maxy!' shrieks Barb. 'You're *always* a brand!'

'… you're just a *man*.' The audience break into applause and Maximilian looks over gratefully. His eyes are now watery with emotion. 'You're just a man who goes to bed at night staring at an empty pillow and wakes up to find that nothing has changed.'

Nicholas manages a half-smile. 'Look at Benson *squirming*. He knows he's losing.'

Maximilian relaxes back into his chair too. 'So, Charles, as much as I understand you need to ask me about what happened, it would be great if we could move on because,' he pauses and rubs the jagged scar on his cheek, 'I have.'

Benson nods and smiles, graciously conceding defeat, and asks Maximilian about his recovery. I drift off at this point, staring down at my leather-clad lap. I am wearing new leather leggings – these ones are Acne. They were delivered this morning along with a pile of Agent Provocateur underwear and a pair of Christian Louboutin knee-high gladiator sandals. I am not going to say *exactly* how much the latter cost, but they will work out at £10 a wear … if I wear them one hundred and sixty-five times. It is safe to say, I have been spending my feelings on Net-A-Porter. Clearly this is much better than *eating* them, but I need to be more careful with my allowance. Earlier, I called Terry to see if he had been contacted by any casting directors for potential acting work, but – as he predicted – he has only been sounded out by talent negotiators for a couple of reality TV shows. This is not a route that I would go down … *ever*. The ones shown at primetime on terrestrial stations might offer good money but it's a slippery slope. One year, you're *mentally* crapping yourself over the creepy crawlies in the jungle on *I'm A Celebrity Get Me Out of Here!* … five years later, you're *literally* crapping yourself; being filmed having an enema at an Indian ashram alongside Speidi and a bankrupt R 'n' B star on an obscure satellite channel for *Detoxing With The Stars*. Insert 'full of shit' based tagline here.

Barb nudges me. 'Look, kiddo … it's … *you!*'

'What?'

She motions towards the television monitor. It is showing a scene from an old episode of *Prime Suspect* where I – a prostitute – am walking down a side street wearing a skintight lace boob-tube with a pleather miniskirt. I stop when I get to a parked green hatchback and lean in through the passenger window to ask the driver what service he requires.

I jump up. 'What the *f*—'

'Awww, you look so *cute!*' Barb grins.

The camera swoops back onto Maximilian. 'At first, I simply wanted to get her off the streets,' he jokes, 'but then it blossomed into something else.'

Benson chortles and turns to the audience. 'Of course, for any of you who have been living on a desert island for the past month or so, that VT featured Maximilian's new …

well, *partner* …' He faces his guest again. 'I can call her your partner, can't I?'

'If you want,' says Maximilian. 'Although I've always thought that sounds as if you are involved in playing some sort of racquet-based sport together once a week as opposed to being in …' He pauses and coyly looks down at the floor. 'Er, you know.'

I glance back at Barb. She clasps her hands together tighter, her jaw is going like the clappers. The camera zones in closer to Maximilian's face as his eyes (no longer moist) start to smoulder sexily. Benson leans forward and taps his guest on the knee.

'In *what*?' he says.

'Love …' says Maximilian, flashing his award-winning grin round the entire audience as if his head were a camera on a tracking dolly. He acknowledges their whimpers of delight and excited whoops by grinning again.

Benson smiles back. 'And is that somewhere we would find, er, …'

'Vivian.'

'… too?'

'Well, you'd have to ask her that,' says Maximilian, self-consciously scratching his pumped left bicep. Then suddenly his expression changes – a cartoon light bulb may as well have appeared above his head. 'So, why don't we? Can I borrow a phone, please?' he asks.

A member of the floor crew rushes forward and hands him a mobile. Maximilian makes a goofy face as if confused by the technology. The crew member switches on the phone, then Maximilian whispers in his ear whilst he taps in a number. Nicholas nods at me. I know what to do. I grab the Nokia Barb gave me from my bag.

I look up, an audio device is being placed on the crew member's phone. Charles Benson takes it with one hand and uses his other to try to calm the shrieking audience. He is beaming from ear to ear, clearly already imagining this will be the footage they play when reading out the nominations for *Most Popular Entertainment Programme* at the National Television Awards. My mobile bleeps … I press receive.

'Hello?' I hear my voice – on a slight delay – coming out of the telly.

'Vivian? This is Charles Benson… I'm sitting here having a bit of a chinwag with a certain M. Fry, Esq.'

'I know. I'm watching. Watching whilst slowly *dying* of embarrassment.' But I am not, quite the reverse actually. The bigger the lie I weave, the less of the truth I unravel; the more *alive* I will become. 'What can I do for you?'

'Well,' says Benson, 'I was wondering if you had something you'd like to add to the conversation I was having with Maximilian a few moments ago.'

I attempt to giggle coquettishly. 'I do actually. Could you please tell him that this is the last time he is allowed to use that gag about the hooker. I think everyone in the civilised world has heard it now.'

Benson titters along with the audience and nods knowingly at Maximilian. 'Feisty, isn't she?'

'She is …' agrees Maximilian, and he nods at Benson to give him the phone.

Barb grins at me and makes the shape of an 'O' between her thumb and forefinger to indicate I am doing well.

'Vivian?' Maximilian looks directly down the camera lens.

'Yes …'

'Are you cross with me?'

'Why would I be cross with you? The only way this situation could be made more uncomfortable is if you made me join you in the studio … which, by the way, if you do, I will confiscate your entire collection of perfectly scuffed hiking boots and polish them to perfection.'

Maximilian laughs softly and looks even more deeply into the camera. Utter sincerity emanates from him. He truly is a brilliant actor.

'I know that thing I said earlier might have shocked you, Vivian …' he says.

'The bit about the "empty pillow"? Yeah, that was unforgivably schmaltzy.'

'No, not that …' Maximilian smiles but doesn't lose his focus down the lens for a moment. 'The bit about me loving you. Because I do. *I love you.*'

Nicholas pokes me on the shoulder. 'Say it back!'

I stare at the television monitor and think about all the times I have avoided saying those three words to anyone. The endless side-stepping using 'ditto', 'me too' or a pathetic 'backatcha', or simply muffling the words into their neck or another part of their anatomy as part of a decoy display of affection. Then I think about that *one* person I almost said them to because I thought I *could* mean it, the difficulty that involved …

But this time it's easy, because it is all part of the lie. My lie. I feel the smoke that was choking me begin to dissipate. Only the truth fuels the flames.

'I love you too.'

'You do?'

'It's only ever been you.'

The rest of the programme is a chat show master class by Maximilian. Benson can't get enough of him. Even when Maximilian is shunted up two seats to make way for the other interviewees, the host continues to draw him into conversation or gives him the floor to relay another anecdote. Halfway through a purposefully self-deprecating story about being mistaken for the pool boy at Chateau Marmont, I leave to find somewhere I can have a cigarette.

As I walk through a warren of corridors I look at the framed pictures that line every wall of the stars who have fronted programmes produced at the television studio. The order descends through the years: the fashions, haircuts and make-up getting more ridiculous. Every so often, there is a gap where a photo has been taken down and I try to figure out which famous personality may have once filled that space and why they are no longer there. A simple case of re-framing? More likely, they are 'disgraced'. Exposed as an adulterer, tax evader, alcoholic, junkie, wife batterer, paedophile … all of them able to live a lie during their heyday simply because they were 'in showbiz'. Ironically, the brighter their limelight … the more they could hide. Not that I would want to take any lessons from the above, but they prove one thing: if you're going to create a persona; you need to do it well. Not just to convince everyone else of who you are, but to convince yourself. That's how it works … and right now, I can feel it working. After only one puff of my Marlboro Light, I stub it out.

I go back inside to brush my teeth and gargle, then head back to the Green Room. Approaching the door, I can hear that Barb and Nicholas have been joined by other people.

'Barbie, I got to hand it to you,' shouts an American guy, 'that was TV gold. D'you have any idea how many hits that's gonna get on YouTube? Freddie Prinze Junior could not fist himself for that kind of comeback publicity.'

'I'm guessing my Maxy is back in favour, then, JP?' she replies.

'Back in favour? Ha! Right now, I love him like a son. Obviously, not the ones from my first two marriages who don't talk to me, but hey, family shamily … ha!'

'Drink, JP?' asks Nicholas. 'I've chilled a bottle of nineteen-ninety Dom Perignon rosé …'

'Pop that cork, buddy.'

'Vivian …'

I spin round. Maximilian is striding down the corridor with a member of the production staff by his side. She is staring up at him proudly like a groom escorting the triumphant Grand National entry into the winner's enclosure.

'Thanks, I'll be fine from here,' says Maximilian, planting a kiss on her cheek. She blushes and backs off up the corridor. He smiles at me. 'So, what did you think of my interview?'

'It was cheesy. *Really* cheesy. The breakdown of your actual *breakdown* was cloying enough, but you really did give it the full fondue by the end.'

'The bit about believing that children are our future?'

'I missed that. Please tell me you did *not* steal a line from Whitney Houston?'

'I did. I thought you'd find it funny. I was only trying to cheer you up. You've been down – and don't pretend you haven't – about that picture.'

I look away as he says this. Suddenly, his naturally photo-shopped perfection and the beyond-all-computerised-help image of me are juxtaposed in my head: Beauty and the Beast.

I cut the conversation and point to the door of the Green Room. 'You need to get in there. JP has arrived.'

Maximilian swallows. 'And …?'

'From the sound of it, you're back.'

'Back?'

'As Jack Chase,' I say nonchalantly. 'I very much doubt JP will be bothering with his trip to Paris because it sounds as if you've got the part *dans le sac.* As we speak, they're toasting you with a six-hundred-pound bottle of vintage champagne. Congratulations, Maximilian.'

But his smile dissipates to a … I can't figure out exactly *what* the expression is. He turns away from me and walks back up the corridor.

'I'll get that runner to call a cab,' he says, without looking back.

'Why? Where are you going?'

'Out.'

'Now? Don't be in*sane*, you can't leave.'

'*I* fucking can.' He twists round. 'And *you* are coming with me.'

CHAPTER TWENTY-SEVEN

We walk straight back to Primrose Hill from Da Goblin MC's showcase at Koko in Camden. Or rather, I walk straight … and Maximilian zigzags. As soon as we get through the metal gate he trips over his own feet and lands in a flowerbed of purple hibiscus. I yank him up with one hand, in the other I am holding a hot polystyrene box. Inside is the lamb kebab Maximilian was bought by a fan who spotted us leaving the gig. I wish he would eat it. After necking neat double vodkas on only a packet of Smints, the waft of dubiously reared meat and curry sauce is playing with my mind.

'Cheers, Vivian,' he says, staggering to his feet. 'For tonight. It meant a lot for you to come with me and celebrate my last few hours. You made me feel … *safe*.'

I roll my eyes at him. '*Safe?* You make it sound like you're about to embark on a perilous tour of duty. Can I remind you that the closest you will be getting to danger on location for this sequel is the possibility of a light bulb popping in your Winnebago.'

'You don't understand. No one does. It could be dangerous for me.'

'Now, I know why you don't drink. The paranoia sets in …'

'I'm not being paranoid.'

'Is that what the voices in your head are saying?' I laugh. 'Come on, let's go insi—'

He interrupts me. 'Seriously, am I *really* ready to join the action hero elite?' He does his impression of Barb. '*Stallone, Willis, Schwarzenegger, Gibson, Chan, McQueen, Ford, Lee, Norris, Eastwood … Fry*. Being *that* famous will make me,' he rubs his eyes, '*vulnerable*.'

'To what? The horror of travelling by Learjet? The pain of extending your property portfolio? Or the sheer abuse of having goody bags stuffed with a hundred thousand dollars' worth of gifts hurled at you as you leave award ceremonies?'

'Very funny.' He pulls his arm away from me and weaves off up the decking, muttering at me over his shoulder. 'I only wanted someone to hear what I have to say, but fuck it, it doesn't matter …'

'I am hearing what you have to say – I *always* listen to you, you know I do.'

He turns round and shouts back, 'Do you, though? How can you really know what it is to *listen* to someone else when you don't want anyone listening to *you*. Tell me, Vivian, is it because no one is special enough for you to let down your guard?'

'What?'

'You never talk to me – not properly. I am not getting to know you, I am only getting to know the you that you *want* me to know. Don't think it hasn't gone unnoticed. To the outside world we maybe faking it, but in *our* world we are real, so why can't you be real with me?'

I swallow hard. 'Oh, shut up, Maximilian, don't get all intense on me. It's three a.m. and you're pissed. You'd better eat your kebab before it gets cold. *Catch!*'

I don't put quite enough welly behind my throw. Maximilian jumps onto the paved area surrounding the pond to try to grab the takeaway box, but the stone slab he lands on is loose and tilts forward. He wobbles on the edge long enough to accept he is going to fall in and quickly rips off his precious beanie hat. He manages to throw it into the lap of the Buddha statue before he goes head first into the pond, soaking me from the waist down in stinky water.

'Noooooooooo! Not my leather leggings, they were *so* expensive.' I try to wipe them dry with my hand. 'Seriously, I've gone on a week's holiday for less – that's including flights, hotel, spending money, duty free and transit costs. You are *such* a pain, Maximilian.'

But he doesn't reply. I look down at the pond. It is lit up by the moon. The water is still. Slices of pitta bread and shreds of lettuce are floating on the surface of the water. So is Maximilian. I watch in horror as his body drifts quietly into the middle of the pond. He must have hit his head on the bottom.

'Shit! *Maximilian!*'

I run over to the pond, jump in, and wade through the water to where he is, sending exotically coloured fish darting off in a mad panic. I roll his body towards me so that he can get some oxygen into his airways. His eyes are shut. Cradling his head in the crook of my arm I check for a gash on his head but can't find anything … which must mean that something is wrong inside it. *Brain damage*. There is no point me trying to recall the initial emergency procedures taught during our water safety classes at school because I never attended them. Presumably, 'Stay calm!' would have been up there. I scream and give Maximilian a very sharp slap.

'Wake up, *pleeeeeeeeeease.* Wake *up*!' I hit him even harder. Nothing. 'Oh my God, I am so sorry, I didn't mean to hurt your face. Your perfect face. Because it is perfect, *you* are perfect … now, please … *wake the fuck up*!'

I try to think – again, a presumption – but 'Call for an ambulance!' would have been a front runner too. Shit. I haven't got my mobile … I left it in the Green Room. Maximilian doesn't own a phone. I drag him to the bank of the pond but there is no way I can lift his body out.

'Shit. *Shit!* SHIT!' I gaze drunkenly up into the dark sky and babble. 'Please God, I know I am a heinously shallow atheist who only contacts you when I take Monday to the vet, but my mother has put in *major* legwork with you over the years, so *please*, help me. Now. You have to help me. Look at him. That's *the* "Maximilian Fry". Look at him, how could you not want to save that face. *That perfect face* …' I wallop it again. 'HEEEEEEEEEELP *me*!' I can barely hear myself, my voice is thin and raspy with fear. I glance down at him. 'Wake up, *please* … you're so … *special* … to me.'

I am still looking down at him when suddenly his eyes open. They are glassy, exactly as they were when he stared straight into the camera on *Benson.*

'Maximilian? Hello? *Hello?* Christ! Oh my God, can you hear me? Please, say you can see me. Can you feel your toes? Wiggle them! Your head – does it hurt? Are you thinking? You know what happened, right? You were trying to catch your takeaway, you lost your balance, then I couldn't g—'

Finally, he speaks. 'Vivian?'

'Yes, yes! It's me, *Vivian* … you're in the pond. I think you hit your head, but everything is going to be fine. I'm going to go inside and ring 999, then we can get you ch—' His chin starts to wobble. 'Maximilian?'

'Mmmm …'

'Can you focus?'

His chin wobbles again. 'Mmmm …'

'Maximilian?'

He bursts out laughing. 'Got you!' He wriggles out of my arms, stands and shakes the water from his hair and ears. 'I fucking *got you.* Stitched up like a kipper … or should that be a koi carp? Ha!'

I stare at him in stunned silence for a few seconds, as I slowly click what he has done.

'You *wanker*! You WANKER! How could you do that to me? I thought you were dead!"

He is now bent over in hysterics. 'Oh, Vivian, that was a fucking *classic*. I can't tell you how hard it was to keep a straight face and that's saying something given that I'm a BAFTA Award-winning actor and Oscar nominee. You were *brilliant*. Talk about a stirring performance. You made Cate Blanchett look like Ashley Tisdale.' He sobs dramatically. '*Help me. Help meeeeeeeee*!'

'WANKER!' I reiterate. 'These leggings cost more than a foreign excursion. I hate you.'

'No, you don't. You think I'm special. Special with a *perfect* face,' he laughs, wiping water out of his eyes.

'Wankerwankerwanker …' I mutter, splashing him. 'I only said that because I knew it would make you come round. You're so vain and needy you'd regain consciousness to hear a compliment.'

'Bullshit, you *meant* it.'

He retaliates with an even bigger splash. It drenches me and I shudder with cold and *fear*. I know my make-up won't have wiped off, but Maximilian has never seen me with wet hair. I slosh over to the other side of the pond, scramble up onto the statue podium, grab his beanie hat from the Buddha's lap and dangle it over the water to distract him.

'*No*, doooooooooon't!' he shouts. 'Not my beanie. *Not my beanie!* Come on, Vivian. Play fair.'

For a second, I forget what I am doing as the exact point in the pond where he is standing starts to shimmer. The moon is shining directly down on him. The droplets over his face sparkle as if he has been dipped in sequins. *Typical*, I think … only Maximilian could manage to find a spotlight in the middle of the night. Then I plunge his hat into the water.

'That was bang out of order, Vivian! I've spent *weeks* trying to get that beanie looking as if I've had it for *years*.' He fishes it out – some sort of green sticky reed and a bit of tomato from the kebab are attached to it.

Leaving him swearing in the pond, I slosh up to the house in my wet clothes. As soon as I reach the porch, security lights flood the garden, so I hold my jacket over my head until I can get inside and do an emergency makeover. In the kitchen, I find Monday sitting on the counter, utterly miffed at not getting his dinner on time. I weigh up what is more important: his hunger or my appearance. Monday wins, by a whisker.

I am putting a dish of organic grouse chunks on the floor, when I hear shouting. I go over to the window and look down towards the pond. Maximilian is now standing – sopping wet – by the Buddha statue. Nicholas is there too. His shirtsleeves are rolled up and he is circling Maximilian, every so often jabbing him in the back with his forefinger. Maximilian's head is bowed down onto his chest but then finally he looks up to say something. This seems to appease Nicholas; he stops shouting and lays a brotherly hand on Maximilian's shoulder and they shake hands. But then Nicholas takes a step back and thumps Maximilian hard in the centre of stomach. He steps back again and plants another punch in the same spot – this time with far more force. Maximilian doubles over and drops to his knees. Nicholas calmly strides away down the decking and lets himself out of the metal gate. I run out of the kitchen.

When I get to Maximilian he is curled up in a ball on the stone paving. I hear the sound of Nicholas' car engine starting, grinding against some grit in the road and whizzing off.

'Are you all right?' I crouch down next to Maximilian. Weirdly, although he is grimacing with pain, he doesn't look shocked. 'We should get you to hospital. You might have internal bleeding that could result in organ failure …'

Maximilian winces as he uncurls his body, and then sits down with his head in his hands. 'Thanks for the encouraging diagnosis. I'll be fine … really, don't worry. It was nothing.'

'Don't be ridiculous; Nicholas floored you. I should be calling the police.'

'He didn't mean to hurt me.'

'From where I was standing it looked like that was *exactly* what he meant to do.'

'Stop fussing, Vivian, it's not a big deal …' He shuts his eyes and breathes deeply for a few seconds before he speaks again. 'I deserved that tonight … if one of those kids outside the kebab shop had videoed me – drunk – after everything I said on the show about rehab, moving on, being a role model … It was my own fault. Look, you don't know Nicholas. He can get het up, but he's a good guy.'

'Ha! Spoken like a textbook victim of abuse. Christ, Maximilian, if you were taxed on emotional intelligence you'd be getting a rebate. Nicholas is merciless. He definitely d—'

I consider telling him what I know: that Clint had warned me about Nicholas from the off, that Clint had been investigating accusations of Nicholas assaulting Maximilian's trainer, that Maximilian thought he had 'just fucked off' but clearly there was more to it, that the guy's mother was going bonkers about it and harassing Nicholas with phone calls, that one had even come through in the Green Room earlier …

But I stop myself, remembering Maximilian's reaction the last time I even *hinted* at Clint's name.

'What?' asks Maximilian.

'Er …'

'He definitely *what*, Vivian?'

I study his face. 'He did *that.*' I say randomly, pointing at his scar. 'Didn't he?'

Maximilian looks away and gazes into the distance, the floodlights by the house giving his face a dreamily lit lustre, much like the one Kylie Minogue uses in her music videos to soften her face. (Which has absolutely, definitely 100 per cent not had *any* cosmetic work done *at all.*) He is silent for a few seconds then turns back to me.

'Yeah, you're right. It was ages ago. He flicked a belt at me when we were boarding at Sturrow. He didn't mean to catch my face. All the prefects used to whack the juniors ...'

'And you didn't report them to whoever it is that's supposed to look after your welfare at those backward institutions?'

'Our house master? No, you couldn't, it was tradition. Besides, Nicholas was the first person to look out for me there, so if I'd grassed him up he would have almost certainly been expelled. Then I would have had *no one.* The cut needed stitches, though, so I told Matron I tripped head first onto some cricket stumps trying to take an important wicket.'

'Is that the boys' private school equivalent of saying you walked into a door?'

'Something like that.' He rubs my shoulder. 'Look, don't worry about me ... I'm a big boy. Besides, if I ever want out of all this – which I don't – I've got an exit plan ... investments and stuff. But thanks.'

'For what?'

'Caring.'

'I'm being paid to.'

'Charming. You do really, though, don't you? Care about me …?'

I am about to make another joke but the look in his eyes tells me he really doesn't need to hear one. Temporarily, *the* Maximilian Fry has left the garden. He *is* vulnerable.

'Okay, I suppose I do a bit … maybe more than a bit.' But immediately I say this, I feel vulnerable too, so I play my Joker. 'Although, we both know there is someone who *did* care and *does* care for you *far* more … and they always will do.'

Maximilian shivers and removes his hand from my shoulder. It's taken a while for his wet clothes to affect him. 'Who?'

'Zoe, of course.'

'Oh, right.'

'She told me at the gallery. I reckon if you wanted to get back with her you could,' I add emphatically. 'That's what you want, isn't it?'

He sighs. 'No, it's not. I don't act rationally around her. *Sometimes* I can – like at the gallery – but other times, I lose the plot. Look what happened when I saw her at that awards thing.'

I sit back onto the rough stone paving and sigh too. But not for the same reason as Maximilian. (In the moonlight I can see that my leather leggings have clearly puckered.) 'Do you want to know something funny? It wasn't even Zoe you saw. She wasn't there.'

'Really?'

'*Really*. She was in America and she'd cut her hair by

then. I wonder who it was … maybe *they* could be the one for you. You should ask Barb to get the guest-list.'

Maximilian's eyes narrow. 'Why are you so intent on hooking me up with someone?'

'Because it's clear you want to be with someone. I think you're lonely …'

'Aren't you?'

I shrug. Then he leans forward and kisses me.

CHAPTER TWENTY-EIGHT

I kissed him back. *Obviously.*

But Maximilian's face is not the first I see the next morning. Monday's is … a centimetre from my nose. I wonder if he realises that it isn't the magical power of his feline gaze that forces me to open my eyes, but a violent blast of his gamey cat breath. Not that I have slept. I spent what was the rest of the night thinking about what happened after the kiss.

ME (pulling away so as not to look keen): Sorry, the earth's not moving.

MAXIMILIAN (opening his eyes): What?

ME: In *The Simple Truth*, you promise the princess that the earth will move when you kiss h—

MAXIMILIAN: No, *I* don't. That's Jack Chase.

ME: So, you weren't acting?

MAXIMILIAN (drunkenly irritated): Did it feel like I was acting?

ME (realising I should have shut up and carried on): I wouldn't know. I've never kissed an actor before.

MAXIMILIAN: And I've never kissed someone who felt like I was acting. Maybe next time you'll feel *me*. (He picks up his wet beanie, gets to his feet and stares at me.) Think of that as a rehearsal.

ME (as annoyed at myself as he is): Rehearsal? So, you *were* acting?

MAXIMILIAN (shrugging): No, I wasn't. But you were right to cut the scene. I need to stick to the script. Nicholas will not allow any sort of edit. But one day, I'm going to rewrite the whole fucking movie … just watch me. (He weaves his way back to the house.)

Rewind. Play. *Repeat.* Rewind. Play. *Repeat.* Rewind. Play. *Repeat* … No matter how many times I watch the scene, I still can't confirm *exactly* what it displays – other than that Maximilian and I (embarrassingly) overuse movie references when pissed. I always used to tell Adele that over-analysing every single word said to her by a man she fancied was pointless. The only way you could tell if he fancied you back was if there was a *lunge*. Okay, so he didn't attack me … but technically, a pass was made. Which, let's face it, is *pretty fucking exciting*.

So, despite no shut-eye, I am feeling exhilarated. I am showered, tanned, made-up, dressed and out of the house to begin the breakfast shift at Burn's with thirty-five minutes to spare. It is the second time in over a decade of employment at the venue I have turned up early. It is also the day I get sacked.

'Stop mucking around, Dane.'

He shrugs at me semi-apologetically from behind Roger's old desk. I notice he has already given the room a mini-makeover to make it more his own by putting up black-and-white prints of legendary singer-songwriters on the wall. His guitar is propped up against it.

'No, I'm afraid it's true,' he says. 'I've got to let you go.'

'You can't *fire* me ...' I smile semi-nervously, imagining how Nicholas will react to this 'edit'. I nod at the largest portrait by the window. 'It's not in keeping with the spirit of folk. I'm sure Joni Mitchell would have only given me a written warning. I was here *early* this morning and I was on time at least two days last week.'

He laughs but I can tell it is not exactly *with* me. 'Oh, man! Because, of course, the majority of the however many million people that make up the British work force don't manage to do that two hundred and sixty days a year.' He picks up a pen and starts tapping his palm with it.

'God, that was *such* a Roger-ism.' I try a different tack. 'Look, I hear what you're saying but give me one more chance, Dane. I'll even *waitress* at some private functions, if you want ... anything except parties over Fashion Week where self-consciously hip TV presenters play ironic lounge music. I've got to have *some* self-respect, right?'

'Ha!' Now, he laughs properly and the expression on his face mellows. 'Listen, man, you know this is tough for me. You and I are mates, Vivian, I hope we always will be ... but Roger is insistent I let you go and that I do it before he gets back from holiday. He's already found a replacement. Trust me, I tried to change his mind but he really freaked out when you didn't turn up the other day.'

'You mean, when that picture of me in my swimm ... on the b—' I can't go there. It will ruin my buzz. 'Come on, Dane, as if I was going to come in after that. Every single one of our members would have seen it.'

He chews the end of his pen. 'I'm sure it must have got you down, man, but you could have called to let the team know you weren't on your way. Besides, it's not purely down to that particular incident …' He peels off a yellow Post-it note from a pad. 'According to Roger's staff log, in the last twelve months you haven't turned up for work *sixteen* times … and I remember you having a couple weeks off sick before that.'

'Excuse me, I had suspected bird flu.' Well, that's what I told Roger, and I *was* in bed, but not with a potentially life-threatening virus. It was the first two weeks after I met … Oh, it's not relevant. 'It could have been serious.'

'Mmm, you were lucky …' Dane smiles. 'Thing is, man, I guess part of your charm was that you always behaved as if you didn't really want to be here but *really* we all knew you did. Recently, well … it's as if you *really* don't.'

I lean back in the chair and make an indignant harrumphing sound, even though I know he has an iron-clad case for my dismissal.

'So, my services are no longer required?' I force a smile.

''Fraid not. You'll get paid a couple of months' salary but you're free to go now. This isn't a personal thing, man. We'll all still hang out, right?'

'Right.' I wave my bag at him. 'One last cigarette out on the fire escape for old time's sake?'

'Nah,' replies Dane, shaking his head. 'I've got quite a lot of admin to get through. You go for it, stick your head round the door and say goodbye before you leave. It's been a real trip hanging out with you over the years. I mean that.' He pulls a pile of paper-clipped invoices towards him and is already signing the first sheet before I have left the room.

Weirdly, Tabitha is not her usual empathetic self when I tell her what has happened.

'Don't you think that at the very least Roger should have given me the boot himself? We've been mates for *years*.'

'I s'pose so,' she says. 'Although, to be fair, you didn't come to his party last week, which the board threw to wish him well as the new General Manager, which kind of evens things out.'

'Excuse me, Tabs, I was sacked a few minutes ago, I could do without a guilt trip to push me over the edge.'

'I was only saying that y—'

'I *know* what you were saying.' I stare over her shoulder into the busy restaurant. Not that I ever felt essential to the smooth running of the place before but I now feel totally superfluous. It's not a pleasant feeling. 'I wonder what the new hostess will be like?'

Tabitha sheepishly twirls her hair around her index finger. 'Actually, I met her yesterday. Roger wanted to introduce us all to her before he flew to Turkey. She seemed really n—'

'Don't you *dare* say she was "nice".'

'Stop interrupting me,' she squeaks. 'I was going to say she was *nondescript*. I mean, I'm sure she'll turn up on time every day, be thoroughly efficient behind the scenes and make sure that she is personally responsible for the enjoyment of every customer … but she'll never replace you in the areas where it really counts.'

'That's better,' I say, letting her invade my personal space to give me a hug.

I go out onto the fire escape one last time, but I don't

spark up a Marlboro Light. I am not feeling nostalgic, I am focused. I stride up and down outside for a few minutes … thinking. *Play your cards right, Vivian.* I've already done my Joker. Now, it's time for an Ace. I go back inside, neck a Nurofen and get Clint's number off the computer in reception. I ring him.

'You know what's 'appened, don't you?' His voice is raspy, his tone flat. 'I got the elbow from *News Today.*'

'Yeah, Sophie told me. Sorry, I should have phoned you. It's been hectic my end.'

'Whatevs, Vivian. Van Smythe set me up. I know 'e did. Just what the missus needs: a baby Daddy with no disposable income – oo's already disposed of 'is savings on Class-A narcotics. I'm in serious arrears to some well unfunny people. Proper 'orse's 'ead shit. That git has ruined me … I tell you, one day I will get 'im.'

'What about today?'

CHAPTER TWENTY-NINE

We arrange to meet on Platform 6 at Euston station ready to catch the 11.03 to Birmingham New Street. I am wearing a pair of men's Dior sunglasses, the lenses of which have a total surface area of thirteen square inches. No one will recognise me. I know this because I am standing next to a woman reading a full-page article in the *Metro* (under the headline, *Fry grilled by Benson and admits: it's love!*) and she hasn't even done a double take. I am close enough to see the tagline at the bottom of the feature flagging up what time the show airs on Sunday.

Clint arrives in a shiny purple Adidas tracksuit and swigging from a can of beer. The other fivc from the six-pack arc under his arm.

'Hi, Clint. I see the Iron Man training is going great guns.'

He sneezes and winces as he rubs the immediate area under his nose; it is raw and swollen. 'Leave it out, I've 'ad no sleep. Met some posh bird at Burn's … and went home with 'er. She 'ad – I shit you not – a triple-barrelled surname. Those ones always 'ave decent gear, though.'

'Ah, the classic "spending a night with some rich bitch and caning her cocaine" routine … What number would that be in the *Top Ten Ways To Get Your Pregnant Wife Back On Side*?' I hand him a Kleenex.

He honks loudly into the tissue and the woman reading the *Metro* jumps. 'Don't … She won't even talk to me. And 'er mum is staying now. I tried going round there but the old bag won't even let me into *my own* 'ome to talk to *my own* wife. She thinks I'm some womanising chancer 'oo 'as let 'er daughter down.' He manages a weary smile. 'God knows 'ow she came to that conclusion.'

Clint chucks his can on the floor and pulls the ring on another in a smooth motion. The train slides into the station. The doors open with a mechanical hiss and we step in.

When we get to Birmingham I buy Clint a toothbrush, toothpaste, hair wax and a can of deodorant from Boots and tell him to sort himself out in the public toilets. He meets me in the taxi rank fifteen minutes later clearly having utilised none of the grooming products but with a suspicious spring in his step and a forehead glistening with sweat. We find a cab, head to a village on the outskirts of town and drive down a street of small Victorian terraced houses with tidy paved porches. Clint presses the buzzer at number 73. Through the frosted-glass panel in the door I see a blurry figure in blue approach.

'Marjorie?' says Clint.

The door opens. A woman – probably around sixty – nods at Clint, then eyes me suspiciously. 'Mr Parks told me you were coming too. You better not go blabbing back to the mothership, dear.'

She takes us into her lounge. Pride of place above the gas fire place is a framed university certificate outlining the qualifications in sports education and nutritional science attained by 'Nathan Gareth EDEN'.

Bingo.

Next to the certificate is a picture of a young man collecting a ribboned scroll. He is wearing a mortar board – the tassel dangling comically in his eyes – and a red velvet gown. He is smiling but I feel like I can hear him talking. There are more photographs of Nathan on other walls and surfaces. All action shots of him in specialist headgear and goggles, leading the field in swimming or cycling races and sparring in a boxing ring. His mother's pride in him lights up the room. It makes me feel awkward.

Marjorie spots me looking at the pictures. 'And before you think I'm suffering from a bad case of empty nest syndrome, I'm merely proud of what my Nathan has achieved. He knew what he wanted to do even as a kid … always chirping away about the importance of regular cardio-wotsit and balanced meals.'

'Where is he now?' I ask, trying to concentrate on the matter in hand.

'America somewhere. He left a month or so ago – wanting "space to think", he said. He had been working at a hotel in the capital but he was miserable … No matter how long he rested his body, he knew he'd never get back to being a personal trainer.' She pauses. 'Of course, it's all my fault, he would never have moved down south if I hadn't mollycoddled him so much. He needed to spread his wings.'

Clint leans forward. 'So, 'ow did your lad originally get the job with Fry?'

'The concierge at The Dorchester phoned up the gym

in the West End where Nathan worked. He wanted an expert to show a female guest how to use some newfangled piece of machinery she'd had installed in her suite. Gyro-something-or-other …' She clicks her fingers.

'Gyrotonics?' I suggest. 'The guest was Maximilian Fry's publicist, Barb Silver.'

'That's right, dear.' She nods at me. 'Anyway, she was so impressed with Nathan she hired him to get the actor ready for his new film. They took Nathan on location and after shooting finished he stayed on as part of their team. Then suddenly, he was sacked.'

'He didn't just *leave*?' I suggest.

'No, no … he was definitely given the boot.'

'For what?' asks Clint.

Marjorie shrugs. 'He wouldn't tell me. It was so upsetting. He had never kept any secrets from me…' She looks at me as if this is a standard component of a mother/child relationship so I give her a generic 'agreement' expression back. 'But when I tried to probe he clammed up. Something very serious had happened … it was obvious.'

'There was nothing 'e let slip at all? You didn't 'ear 'im on the blower or anything?'

'No, he didn't speak to anyone, Mr Parks. He was depressed; barely left his room. Then, one morning, he came bounding downstairs saying he was off to London and might be reinstated. The next thing I know I've got an Accident and Emergency doctor on the phone detailing his injuries.' She explains them to us. 'Then the police. They'd checked his mobile phone … the last text message – odd spelling, they said – was from Nicholas Van Smythe, asking him to meet. My boy walked straight into his trap.' Her eyes fill with tears.

Clint flops back in the sofa and sighs. 'Why didn't the cops call Van Smythe in for questioning, then?'

'They did. But then they let him go. Sergeant Biggs said the evidence against him was purely circumst—'

I interrupt her. 'Sorry, did you say Biggs? Was he known as Biggsy?'

She dabs her eyes. 'May have been. The other officers called him "sir".'

I turn to Clint, excited. 'I saw an email from Nicholas to a "Biggsy" … promising him a freebie holiday. The way it was written didn't make it sound like the first one he'd paid for either.'

Marjorie gasps. 'He must have given him a sweetener to fizzle out the case. Surely, you can get a story out of this?' She looks to Clint.

''Ardly,' says Clint. 'The lawyers would spike it. They'd smell the defamation of character lawsuit before they'd got to the end of the first paragraph. Like I said to you before, the only way this 'as got legs is if your son was willing to sing.'

'He won't discuss the case any more … said he's already lost enough. I suppose he fears a reprisal.'

'Or,' Clint continues, 'we can 'ack Nicholas's emails.' He turns to me. 'Vivian, can you find out the address he uses for personal mail?'

'Er, yeah, I suppose I could tr—' I begin. But as I talk, Marjorie hangs her head in her hands and this time the tears flow. It is hard to watch. My mother has never let me seen her cry. Revelation Chapter 21 Verse 4: *He will wipe away every tear from their eyes, and death shall be no more, neither shall there be mourning, nor crying, nor pain any more, for the former things have passed away.*

Clint goes over to Marjorie's chair and crouches down next to her.

'Shoosh now, Mrs E. Don't go upsetting yourself any more. I'll 'ave a bit more of a dig, see what I can come up with. So will Vivian. We'll call you as soon as we've got something. Come 'ere.' He gives her a hug. As she embraces him back I can tell by the wired and exhausted expression on his face that right now he needs that cuddle as much as she does.

When the train pulls into Euston later that afternoon, Clint is pale. I take him back to the flat he is renting in a newly converted block behind the Portobello Road, a short walk from Burn's. It is sparsely furnished and any gadgets are still covered in protective plastic. He has at least attempted to use the stove. A frying pan of burnt, congealed baked beans is sitting on the left hob.

'I don't s'pose you fancy staying for a bit, sweet'eart?' he asks, collapsing into the only armchair in the room. 'We could 'ave some fun. I've got a few cans, plenty of that posh bird's nose candy I nicked …'

'You've borrowed that line from one of the *High School Musical* movies, haven't you?' I swing my jacket round my shoulders. 'Sorry, I've got to get back.'

'Fair enough, but if you're goin' to be a party pooper I might go out in a bit … think I've got a second wind.'

'Clint! You must be on your zillionth and second …'

I go into the bedroom to redo my make-up, but the only mirror in there is on the bed; scratched up and dusted in a white frost. I step into the bathroom. It stinks of damp. A dressing gown from a hotel in Tenerife (that has clearly had its duties extended to towel, bath mat and floor cloth) is in the sink. I spray the dregs of some Gucci Envy around the room and steadily apply a series of cosmetics … using the time to imagine how I will relay my findings to Maximilian. I will opt for a simple approach: informing him that his manager is a thug who destroys anyone who gets in his way, and needs to be got rid of before he takes his client down too. The key is this: to make Maximilian think I've got this information to help *him*. Not me. *Or us.* With any luck, the 'us' will be the by-product.

I leave the bathroom to find Clint passed out in the foetal position, his tracksuit zipped up to the chin, cocaine messily racked out on his laptop on the floor. I feel bad for him. Comedowns off heavy coke consumption are brutal. When he wakes up in a few hours he will feel as if his soul has been ripped out and beaten with a medieval mace. I stare at the lines and hear *him* asking me *that* question: *You want to get stuck into the speedo, Vivian?* I shake my head. No, I don't. I want to face what is about to happen in the moment, and enjoy it … in *real* time.

But when I get back to Primrose Hill I can't find Maximilian. He isn't in the kitchen, gym, drawing room, conservatory or screening room. I go upstairs to his bedroom. My stomach starts to sink. On the bed is a monogrammed Louis Vuitton suitcase. It is almost full of clothes; on top is a large matching leather washbag.

I stare at this for a good three – maybe four – seconds before I start rifling through its contents. Arm & Hammer toothpaste, Floris shower gel, Bobbi Brown blemish stick, Dr Sebagh serum, StriVectin moisturiser, Kiehl's sunscreen, Phytologie hair-styling balm, Penhaligon's nail clippers, Taylor of Old Bond Street razor, Viktor & Rolf antiperspirant, Tom Ford Neroli Portofino body scrub, Philip Kingsley shampoo, Acqua di Parma shaving cream, Clinique cleansing foam, Issey Miyake eau de toilette. I zip open the side pocket and find a pair of travel ear-plugs, two silver foiled sheets of Xanax and three packets of – now, my stomach plummets – *condoms*.

Durex. Ribbed, flavoured and 'intense'.

'What are you doing in here?' Barb walks in behind me laden with designer shopping bags. Her voice is angrily staccato.

I jump back from the bed. 'Oh, *hi.* I just got back from work and was looking for Maxim— Is he leav— … is he going abr— …?' I pull myself together. 'Is he jetting off for a bit?'

'Mmm … to his villa,' she says, dropping the bags on the floor.

'The one in the picture of Zoe downstairs.'

'Yep. He's going to host a party for JP there and *Luxury* magazine are going to shoot it.'

'Sounds like fun,' I reply through gritted teeth as I stare at that washbag. Clearly, Maximilian is planning on having a particular type of fun over and above what Barb has scheduled.

'Fun?' She clicks her tongue at me and pulls a pile of

faded grey T-shirts out of one of the bags. 'More like serious damage limitation. Maxy needs to do some major freakin' sucking up to JP after the stunt you two pulled last night. Nicholas is *not* your number-one fan right now. Know this, kiddo, if it weren't for me persuading him otherwise, you'd have been booted out of here last night.'

'Sorry … so, will I … er … see Maximilian before he goes?'

'Nope. He and Nicholas are en route to Paris. JP is already there. They're taking him out this evening to try to claw back the situation. They'll stay overnight and fly out tomorrow.'

I imagine Maximilian reclining against a mound of sequined scatter cushions on his roof terrace as dusk falls. He is slowly and seductively untying a silk scarf from the head of an impossibly mysterious and exotic beauty. The women are stunning in Morocco. Tyra took her girls there during Cycle 16 of *America's Next Top Model*. The locals were *far* more attractive.

'What time do they land in Marrakesh, then?' I ask, in a clipped tone.

'Marrakesh?'

'Yeah. Isn't that the main airport?'

'For Morocco, maybe,' she says, placing the T-shirts into Maximilian's suitcase. 'But Maxy's holiday home isn't in North Africa. It's only decorated like that. Anyway, you can wipe that miserable look off your face because you're coming too.'

'I am?' My chest thumps. *He packed that washbag for me.*

'Yeah.' She glances up. 'But you better freakin' behave.'

'Oh, I will. I will! I *promise*. So, where's the villa then?'

'Ibiza.'

PART THREE

CHAPTER THIRTY

'On behalf of myself, Jean, and the rest of the cabin crew we thank you for travelling with British Airways today and wish you a pleasant stay ... in Ibiza.'

Pleasant. As the plane taxis along the runway, I un-click my seat belt and can't help smiling to myself. As soon as I had lost enough weight to get in a swimming pool and not be mistaken for a sit-on inflatable, I started going to the White Isle, and one word I have *never* associated with time I have spent there is 'pleasant'. The first trip I took was with a bloke I dated after I dumped the owner of that cocktail place. He was a barman, although it was 1998 so he called himself a *mixologist.* The ten days that followed were a relentless rollercoaster ride that left me financially drained and physically empty. I couldn't wait to go back. As soon as we got home, I ditched the 'boyfriend', blagged a loan and persuaded Adele to return with me for a long weekend. We lost each other at an illicit cave rave along the coast from Salinas. The next time I saw her was forty-eight hours later in the departure lounge. She was hallucinating, playing a pair of bongos that didn't exist. It was the last time we would go abroad together.

The following summer I met Roger at Burn's and we

started going to Ibiza for at least a fortnight each year. I loved it. Each trip I came back even thinner. Ibiza was my Utopia: a land where having fun resulted in weight loss. I had always associated being skinny with hard work and secrecy, but here it was easy and no one questioned it. I barely ate. I barely touched any water either, given that the bottles for sale in the clubs were so extortionately priced. Safe to say, I was never in any danger of becoming one of those tabloid statistics who put their life in danger by drinking too much H20 on E. I was far more likely to have died of acute dehydration, but I savoured every parched second.

The aeroplane doors open, a dreamy blast of Mediterranean heat is sucked into the cabin and like every other time I have landed here a flurry of butterflies charge through my stomach. It's what Roger and I used to call The Balearic Whoosh – an involuntary spasm in the body: part excitement, part trepidation, part surrender. *You're in Ibiza now.* This time, though, as we shuffle towards the exit, my 'whoosh' feels different, more serious. Partly because the BA staff waiting to bid us farewell are wearing uniforms. (The airlines I usually use put their cabin crew in sweatshirts.) But mainly because I *know* that's what could happen to me and Maximilian over the next few days. We're going to get *serious.*

B. SILVER says the placard being held up in Arrivals. The girl who is holding it has most of her face hidden behind the board, but as soon as I clock her over arched eyebrows and flamboyantly angled liquid eyeliner I know who it is … I scan down past her mint-green terry-towelling romper suit to her feet. *Christ.* There they are … those

Vivienne Westwood pirate boots. It's that door bitch from SundaySoundz. Clearly, she found the inner strength to leave behind her colleagues in London's Clubland. (I'm surprised I didn't notice any bunting around town.) She cocks her head at Barb.

'Barb Silver?' she enquires, her right eyebrow almost hitting her hairline. 'Welcome to the island. I'm Suki, your fixer from Ultimate Ibiza.' She pronounces Ibiza, 'Ehbeeza', like the locals do. 'Is Mr Fry with you?'

'He's flying in later with his manager …' replies Barb, glancing at me in the same disapproving manner that she has been since last night. 'From Paris. Have a car waiting for them at six.'

That means I'll have around five hours to get ready.

Suki nods at Barb. 'I'll make sure the local paps are all over Mr Fry from the moment he lands.'

'Cool,' says Barb. 'Everywhere except the villa. That's off limits because I've done a deal with *Luxury* to cover the party tomorrow night.' She nudges me. 'Same with Vivian, here. We want as much exposure as possible, please.'

Suki gives me a blankly professional smile. She evidently doesn't recognise me as 'Chrissy Crackers' in the aviator shades from the queue at SundaySoundz. *I* wouldn't recognise me. But that's a good thing.

'Pleasure to meet you, Vivian.'

'Hi, er, Suki.' I pass Barb my passport and bend down to re-buckle my over-the-knee Christian Louboutin gladiator sandals, so Suki doesn't examine my face too hard.

'Have you been to *Ehbeeza* before?' she asks me.

'Mmm …'

'Well, if there is anything *you* don't know about the island, please do ask … because *I* will.'

'Thanks.' As I stand up, I distract her again by pointing at the hideously ugly tattooed lettering she has had drawn all the way up the side of her neck. 'Wow, that really is something.'

'Isn't it? I went to this in*cred*ible artist near the fort. It took eight hours and the pain was excruciating … but so worth it. It spells out my boyfriend's name. I wanted to show him how much he meant to me.'

I think about Maximilian's 'Z' tattoo on his hand and wonder if he will *finally* laser it, or maybe have it re-tattooed into 'VW'. Ha! Although then it might look as if he is a fan of Venus Williams or a Volkswagen Beetle obsessive.

Barb snorts. 'On your neck, though? That's a bit extreme. Couldn't you just buy him some aftershave?' She examines the design. 'Ancient Hebrew … reminds me of bailing out of Sunday School. You're Jewish?'

'No, I like the way they spell, though,' replies Suki. 'It's very … what's the word? *Religious.*' She leans over and takes Barb's leather padded vanity case. 'Let's make tracks. I'm parked outside. We can run through the details for the party on our way to the villa.'

We settle into Suki's electric-blue jeep – branded with the Ultimate Ibiza logo – and crawl out of the airport behind taxis and holidaymakers getting used to their rental cars, but when we hit the main road Suki slams her foot down on the accelerator and we whiz along towards Ibiza town. Barb gets out her BlackBerry and scrolls through her notes.

'Okay, so here's the low-down,' she shouts from the back seat, leaning forward to target Suki's left ear. 'The party tomorrow is in honour of movie executive, JP Goldstein. *Any*one who is *some*one on the island has to be there. I want the food to be executed by a stellar chef, the drinks to flow all night and the music has got to be on the money too. So *don't* get me some drug-addled egotist on the final leg of a five-day bender who wants to take people on a freakin' journey. I want the guests to stay put and not have to shout above nosebleed techno. Nothing too chilled either … I want ambi*ence* not *ambient.*' She disposes of her gum into oncoming traffic. 'Who's the hottest ticket on the island right now DJ-wise?'

'Any of the Chileans or Romanians,' says Suki, as if playing records were an Olympic sport. 'They're packing out Amnesia on a more minimal tip but for a house party I'd suggest a more eclectic vibe. We've got some great spinners on our books who we use for all the celebrity parties. Trust me, they really know how to' – I cringe before she even says it – '*read* the crowd.'

'Good. I'm relying on you so don't f—' But before Barb can finish, her BlackBerry vibrates. She glances down and taps Suki on the shoulder. 'We'll continue this conversation at the villa. I need to take this. It's Achilles,' she adds to me.

'Is he joining us?' I ask.

'If he doesn't get outfoxed by checking in online,' she explains drily – still not quite her usual cackly self with me – then slinks back into her seat to answer the call.

We slow down at a busy roundabout and Suki runs a hand through her tousled mane. She's got that effortless beachy hair look down to a T: presumably because she has *physically* been spending time by the sea as opposed to wrestling with a variety of useless salon-branded hair serums in neon-coloured pots called *Beachy Hair*.

'How long are you out in Ibiza for?' I ask her.

'In *Ehhhbeeezzzaaah*, you mean?' She corrects me by pronouncing the word in an even heavier local dialect than before, as though she pitched up before the Phoenicians. 'Forever, I've got no intention of going back. I was working on the club circuit in London but had really maxed out on that whole scene, so when the guys at Ultimate *Ehhhbeeezzzaaah* offered me a job at the beginning of the summer, I moved straight here. Me and my boyfriend are renovating a small finca ... we're pretty much done, bar the kitchen and hallway. It overlooks Es Vedra, the island off Cala d'Hort. Have you ever been there?'

'Nah, I've never got round to it.'

In fact, I narrowly avoided visiting there last time I was out here – two years ago –shortly after Roger had been promoted. He wanted us to attempt a more grown-up break, so we rented a villa for four in the north of the island. He brought Pete, his future husband, and I brought this guy I was seeing: an overly trendy manager of a retro sneaker shop. It was a rubbish trip; a bore-athon of barbecues and siestas punctuated with a few fully hydrated trips to some upmarket bars. It wasn't what I came away for and it made me anxious; because I knew that this was a perfectly normal way to spend a holiday. But I couldn't enjoy myself. Without getting wasted there was too much time to, well, *think*.

'... you *must* take a boat over ...' Suki is still yakking

away. 'Es Vedra is a magical place. Just make sure you leave an item of your personal belongings in the mouth of the big cave as a gift ... a witch lives there.' She says this emphatically; in the same way a respiratory specialist might say, *Human beings need oxygen to function ...*

Ten minutes later, as we are travelling north-east to Santa Eulalia, Barb hangs up and tells Suki to turn off the main road. We bounce up a twisting, rocky, hillside driveway and arrive at Maximilian's villa. On first impressions I'm a bit disappointed. I knew about the Middle Eastern décor but had been hoping the actual building would be a pimped-up version of his Primrose Hill home – a breathtakingly modern construction made using so much glass it would not be visible to the average naked eye, only the senior editorial team at *Wallpaper** magazine. But *everything* has a Moroccan influence – including the architecture. There are whitewashed walls, gold-plated turrets, a vast swimming pool lined with thousands of multicoloured mosaic tiles and an ornate courtyard that is stuffed full of terracotta pots, coloured sculptures and wrought-iron lanterns. We are welcomed by the housekeeper-come-land manager.

Pedro is at least six foot four with a *very* deep tan – on the DIY wood stain colour chart either a Walnut or a Dark Mahogany. He has a shaved head and the kind of body you don't get from posing and flexing at Body Pump three times a week, but by doing proper physical labour out in the elements involving a range of dangerous vibrating machinery. His eyes are hidden behind an enormous pair of *Terminator*-style shades. He picks up our heavy bags as if they contain polystyrene balls and heads towards the house, trailing a potently masculine smell: base notes of sweat and top notes of lawn cuttings, engine oil, cigars and chorizo.

'And to think of all the times I argued with my mother about there being no God,' I whisper to Barb.

Finally, she cackles. 'You're not his type. Now, *listen*, I can't emphasise enough how important the next few days are – not just for Maxy but me as well. I've got to get JP to sign the contract before he leaves the island or Nicholas will go loony tunes. Bring your A game, kiddo.'

'Don't worry, Barb,' I tell her, as I crunch up the gravel behind Pedro. 'This place *always* brings out the best in me.'

By 5.50 p.m. I have unpacked, showered, St Tropez-ed, ghd-ed, selected some perky/edgy lounge-wear to put on later (white racer-back vest with a pair of yellow men's trunks) … and plastered a selection of caramel-and-brick-coloured cosmetics on my face. I achieve the perfect holiday glow in the first ten minutes, but then I carry on layering until I end up creating more of a not-of-this-planet phosphorescence. Solid base complete, I wrap a towel round me and climb up the iron spiral staircase onto the roof to aerate my fresh tan.

As soon as I step onto the terrace I recognise it as the back-drop to the photo of Zoe Dano in Maximilian's hall-way. The Moroccan theme continues, with ornately carved wooden screens and a plunge pool under a brocaded canopy. I look out over the valley towards the sea – the sun has dipped in the sky and the beaches have almost emptied – and think about what will happen tonight.

Barb will probably want Maximilian and I to be papped looking gooey-eyed at one another in a restaurant, which is fine by me. But I'm hoping she won't book us a table at one of the places on the twisty cobbled streets leading up to the castle in the Old Town. The outside tables are perfect for being *seen*, but most of the establishments are family run and take great pride in their authentic Spanish cooking. The waiting staff do *not* appreciate it if you return a plate of food that has merely been prodded with a fork; not when it's a precious recipe handed down from their '*bisabuela muy muerta*' (very dead great-grandmother). Wherever we go, one thing is for sure, I'll keep the conversation with Maximilian light and flirty. I am not going to bring up the subject of Nathan yet. I'll do the big *reveal* after the party, when JP has signed on the dotted line. Only then will Maximilian feel ready to release Nicholas from his position and turn my temporary one into a full-time post. Job *done* …

'Not a bad view, is it?'

I turn to see Maximilian circling up the stairs in a battered straw hat. The *last* place I wanted him to see me on arrival was where he *first* fell in love with Zoe. Suddenly and annoyingly, I feel nervous.

'Very nice. So, er, you're ahead of schedule … good flight?' I cringe at how dull that sounded. 'How did it go in France?'

'Disastrously. We didn't meet JP. His fourth wife filed for divorce yesterday afternoon … blindsided him. He was fuming. So was Nicholas. He's gone to hire a sports car to cheer himself up.' Maximilian looks out to the sea. 'This party tomorrow is now more important than ever … it's my D Day.'

'Well, it probably doesn't have *quite* the global impact as the original one, but I get what you're saying,' I tell him. 'Relax, it will be fine. Barb has got a special fixer on the case. The bad news is that she is one of the most irritating human beings I have ever met. The good news is that she seems to be as efficient as she is annoying.'

Maximilian smiles and I think he is about to lean in and kiss me properly, but instead he gives me a 'mwah' peck on the cheek as if thanking me for a particularly good quality Easter egg. Then he sits on the hip-height white stone wall that runs round the terrace – not a millimetre of his taut abdominal flesh tips over the waistband of his trousers, only that stupidly defined section of pelvic muscle.

'So, what do you think of the villa?' he asks.

'Incredible ...' I wrap the towel tighter round my body and sit myself on the side of the plunge pool. Down by the garden shed I can see Pedro loading himself up with an assortment of heavy and awkward gardening tools: a horticultural Buckeroo. 'It's almost bazaar like.'

'*Bizarre?* You think it's strange?'

'No, I meant "bazaar", as in a shop selling various Arabic wares. A *bazaar*. B A Z A A R ... get it?'

'Ah. I didn't realise they were spelt differently. Words like that are a dyslexic's worst nightmare. Those and fucking anagrams.'

I think of Nicholas laughing at Maximilian's confusion over the goat/toga party at Sturrow, but I bite my tongue. I'll save that for tomorrow to underline my point about the lack of respect he has for him.

'I'm looking at extending the villa so it's even bigger,'

continues Maximilian. 'You've met Pedro? He's working on plans for a two-storey turreted annexe. I'll give him the go-ahead if I get the movie. All the stone will be imported from Casablanca.'

'Really? Wow, he's really into the Moroccan thing, isn't he?'

'He's got Persian ancestry.'

'So, it's in his tagines?'

Maximilian smiles at me again and I smile back, searching for some sort of elaboration in his eyes to show me how he is feeling about me, but his hat is tipped over them. He clears his throat. I know what's coming. I envisioned it on the flight over.

'Vivian,' he begins. 'About, er …'

'The other night?' I help him out.

'Mmmm … by the pond …'

'We were there for a while; which *exact* part of being by the pond did you want to discuss?'

'You *know* … *that* bit.'

'The bit where you …'

'Acted like a jerk, walking off …'

'Leaving me there … *alone* … in the darkness … soaking wet … and *shivering*.' I chatter my teeth together then stand up and go to sit on the wall next to Maximilian. 'That bit?'

Yeah, *yeah* …' He grins. 'That's the bit. Thanks for the dramatic reconstruction. I should expl— … well, apologise—'

'No need for any explanation or apology, Maximilian,' I say casually. 'You don't need any distractions until you've got that contract signed. For a few seconds, we forgot the real reason why we were *there* … why we are *here*, in fact.'

He is silent for a while. Then he rubs my shoulder. 'Your understanding is appreciated. Cheers, Vivian … you're great.'

'I know. Now, don't get all emosh on me. Let's put our energy into getting the job done and whatever happens after that …'

'… *happens.'* Now he is squeezing my shoulder.

'Exactly.'

He stretches and yawns. 'Not that I've got much energy. I'm fucking knackered. I couldn't sleep last night. Nicholas and I had a row at our hotel. He had another pop at me for losing focus …' He trails off. 'It was pretty intense.'

'How did he get his point across to you this time? Another thump to the spleen or did he smash your head in the mini-bar door until your legs stopped twitching?'

Maximilian tuts at me and flicks a gnat off his arm. 'No, he didn't. I've told you, Nicholas is not some crazed tyrannical figure. He loses his rag occasionally – like we all do – but he would never actively try to hurt me … or anyone.'

'I doubt that's what Nathan Eden said as he lay on a trolley in the Accident and Emergency ward with a punctured lung, broken pelvis and shattered leg.' Shit. This pops out before I even realise I am saying it. I've done it *again*.

Maximilian tips up his hat. Now I can see his eyes. They dart furtively. 'What the fuck has Nathan Eden got to with anything? Hang on, how do you even know that name?'

Shit. 'Does it matter?'

'Yes, it *does*,' he says, his voice tightening. 'Who have you been talking to?'

SHIT! 'Oh, let's not get into this now. We want to have a nice evening. It's our first night in Ib—'

'*Vivian!* Don't dick me around.'

'Okay, okay, I'll tell you. But you have to believe me when I say I haven't been meddling. I didn't *want* to cause problems.' Maximilian doesn't look convinced. 'Stuff just didn't add up about this Nathan; your personal trainer—'

'I know who he *was*,' interrupts Maximilian, his jaw clenched.

'You said he left with no warning, but that's not true. Nicholas sacked him *then* did him over, that's why he never came back. He still hasn't recovered, his mother says h—'

'You've spoken to his *mother*?'

I nod sheepishly. Looking at the expression on Maximilian's face, I can safely say there is more chance of Victoria Beckham getting on stage with the Spice Girls again than Maximilian and I having a nice evening tonight. 'I visited her with Clint …'

'*Clint Parks?*' Maximilian leaps up. (Make that more chance of Posh actually *singing* a line solo *and* loaning Mel B one of her frocks to perform in.) 'Are you out of your fucking mind? Did you not listen to what I said last time?'

'Calm down, Maximilian. Clint is a mate; I needed him to help me.'

'Help you?'

'Yeah, for *him* to help *me* help *you*. I wanted to show you the sort of man your manager really is. At best he is a control freak, at worst a dangerous *criminal*. He shushed over the incident by showering the copper in charge of the case with freebies and gifts. That's the truth.'

Maximilian turns away from me and looks out over the valley. He doesn't say anything for a while. Then he yanks at his hat. When he turns back to me his eyes are hidden in the shadow of the rim once more. 'The truth, Vivian? Take it from me, you can't handle the truth.'

I pretend to hold a telephone to my head and speak into the receiver. 'Yeah, yep ... okay. You can ... I'll arrange that right away.' Then I pretend to put the phone back down.

'What *are* you doing?' asks Maximilian, moodily.

'Oh sorry, that was the nineties calling. They wanted to know if they can have their most famous catchphrase back: *You can't handle the truth!* Ha! Remember? From *A Few Good Men* with Jack Nicholson, Tom Cruise and Demi Moore. Mind you, for me that movie is more memorable for Demi's duck-tail hairdo that swoops to the back of her head and folds in on itself. It defies gravity and geometry at the same time.' I nudge his hard left thigh, desperately trying to lift the atmosphere.

But he doesn't smile back. 'The truth is, Vivian, that I *know* Nathan Eden was fired and I *know* he was assaulted. I also know Nicholas did the former, but frankly, I don't give a shit who did the latter. Nathan,' his jaw clenches again, 'wanted to ruin my career.'

'How? By over-developing your calves?'

Still no smile. 'He wanted to sell a story on me.'

'Revealing what?'

'Revealing what?' repeats Maximilian.

'Yeah, I bet I won't be half as shocked as you think I'll be.'

'Oh, you will,' he says. 'You won't like it, or *me*, afterwards …' He sounds agitated.

'Has it got something to do with Zoe?' I take a guess.

'Zoe?' he repeats. 'Why are you always banging on about her. *Screw* Zoe.'

'Or not, as the case maybe, eh?' I quip, immediately regretting this too.

'What's that supposed to mean?'

'Well, you, er, *didn't*, did you?'

Maximilian stares at me – his eyes now spacey and dilated – when a sudden blast of engine noise makes us both jump. I look over the terrace and watch Suki roar up the driveway in her customised Jeep. She heads full pelt towards the villa, whisking up a tunnel of dust behind her, and jams on the breaks centimetres from the swimming pool. Then she reverses and executes a faultless three-point turn with all the cool and easy confidence of someone with a manageable natural wave in their hair and Luciano's digits on their mobile. I turn back to Maximilian. He is still staring. I think he is about to kiss me. But he doesn't lean in. He gets up from the wall, takes my hand and leads me down the spiral staircase. Approximately, half a minute later, we are in his room. Another three seconds later, my towel hits the floor.

CHAPTER THIRTY-ONE

This time the earth *does* move. Maximilian's fingers are tangled up in my hair as he keeps our skulls clamped together, his lips exploring every part of my face, whilst every so often releasing a soft whimper. It's sexy, heated, cinematic – in a bordering-on-assault Paul Verhoeven-esque erotic-thriller kind of way. It's also flattering. Especially when Maximilian leans back briefly for air and I can see the intense concentration in his eyes. I think to myself, *This is it.* Finally, the head of PE has called in the school caretaker to white-wash off that message from the sports equipment shed wall. Kate Summers was wrong. Vivian Ward is *not* a big, fat idiot. She is kissing *the* Maximilian Fry …

And *he* carries on kissing *her*. Vigorously. In fact, the attack and drama is upped a level every minute until I feel a cluster of extensions on each side of my head coming loose, my skin reddening and my cheekbones potentially bruising. Of course, the whole pleasure/pain thing is enjoyable, but when you have a photo shoot the next day, it's necessary to keep a lid on the latter. So, I pull away, and take matters into my own hands … or rather *mouth*. I know Maximilian won't be disappointed. Why? Well …

Look, there was a reason I turned up to the sport's equipment shed that day at school to see Ziggy. I genuinely thought *he* had written the note, not Kate ... because he had written me others asking me to meet him at various out-of-bounds hidey holes around the school. The first time he summoned me, he was clear and polite as to why had requested my company. He wanted a blowjob. 'Kate won't do it,' he said. 'Some loser rule she has about remaining "pure" until her wedding day... and she doesn't like putting things in her mouth. Do you?' There was no point me arguing that I didn't – my equator of a waistline was evidence enough to show that I'd put *any*thing in that particular orifice – so I got stuck in. It became our regular thing. It wasn't long before Ziggy announced I was a 'champion nosher'. It was nice to receive a compliment. Every time he wrote me a note, I was *there*, like a rat up a drainpipe. (Obviously, a fat rat up a very wide drainpipe – one that other svelte rodents would probably use as an aquatic fun park style water shoot.)

So, two decades of practice later ... I am not exactly surprised by Maximilian's reaction. His soft whimpering soon morphs into a deep moan, then panting, then shallow, uneven breathing. By this point, his legs are wobbling so hard he has to grip onto the Moorish sideboard against the wall. Small silver and wooden artefacts rattle, shuffle to the edge then drop to the floor. Eventually, he is forced to collapse back on the leather day bed by the balcony doors, but I don't stop. He is only lying there for a few seconds before he thumps the cushion next to him and I know he is about to climax ... so I stop. This goes against the number-one policy Ziggy enforced: *An unfinished 'job' is a sackable offence!* But we ought to have sex. Now. It will seal the deal, won't it? It always has done. It always does. I ignore a sudden and unexpected pang of ... *what is that?*

Shyness?

'Go and, er, ... grab one ...' I whack Maximilian on the leg.

'Wh-wha ...' He can't quite speak. 'Wha ... the ... f ...' He attempts to lift his head, but only manages a centimetre of levitation. 'Grab *what*?'

'What do you think I could possibly want, right now, Maximilian? A club sandwich?' I laugh. '*A condom.* Go and get a condom.' I don't add that I would prefer either ribbed or intense over the flavoured (in case it is not on my allowed nutritional colour spectrum) ... then he will know I have been snooping through his belongings. '*Quick!* Nicholas will be here any moment. Let's do it.'

Surely not. Shy was who I was, not who I am ...

Maximilian manages to raise his head a bit higher and gives me what appears to be one of his half-smiles. I haven't seen one of those for a long while. Then he jumps up and pads into the bathroom. Five minutes later he is still in there.

'This is a, er, fucking nightmare,' he shouts, still from behind the door, 'but I haven't got any. Sorry, Vivian, I'll, er, have to go...'

Another pang.

But I am already picking up my towel. I go back to my room, lock my door and sit down on the bed. My whole body shudders. I hear Maximilian calling me, but I don't reply. Then there are a series of knocks on the door, but I don't open it. He tries my name again and says he wants to talk to me. But I don't let him in. The thought of having to look him in the eye as he tries to airily explain away what happened to save either of us any further embarrassment ramps up the shuddering in my body to a rhythmic juddering.

No more shyness. Just shame. I am shameful. Full of shame. Shamed.

Maximilian shouts my name again. I tell him I'm getting in the shower and turn up the taps to full blast, but I don't get in. I use the gushing water for background noise as I redo my face and hair. Then I get dressed into the trunks and vest and slip on some Havaianas. I'm going to have a cigarette, get myself into Ibiza town, find an internet café and book a flight back to London.

As I walk out onto my balcony with a packet of Marlboro Lights, I see Nicholas on the driveway, sipping from a tumbler and admiring the fenders on a bright yellow convertible. He is looking impossibly Euro trash in a pink silk shirt, slim-fit white trousers, camel-coloured leather belt and matching loafers with a cream leather manbag. He sees me and raises his glass.

'You look like you could do with one too, darling,' he observes, accurately. 'Let's bend the rules. Why don't I take you to the Blue Marlin in this *very* naughty Maserati? We can enjoy pumping exhaust fumes at all those loser tourists on mopeds. It'll be a gas.'

'I'm not sure I want to be alone with you.'

'Oh don't be so theatrical, darling,' he laughs, and as he

strolls nearer to the house he pulls a white handkerchief from the pocket of his shirt, and waves it. 'As we used to say at Sturrow, *Trucies!* There'll be no raised voices or intimidating behaviour. Pinky promise.' He wiggles his little finger. 'I'm in a *much* better mood now I know Goldstein is on his way.'

'I'm not.'

'All the more reason for you to have a cheeky drink-a-link, then. Come on, you're joining me whether you like it or not. Barb's gone to taste test the nibbles for tomorrow and Fry's meditating.'

Charming. Was our *moment* that much of head spin? I tell Nicholas I will meet him downstairs. He's right, I could do with a vodka to neck a Nurofen. Then I'll book my ticket.

CHAPTER THIRTY-TWO

The Blue Marlin is splendidly flashy. A beach hang-out and restaurant by day it morphs into more of a bar-come-nightclub as evening falls, and attracts the more mon-eyed locals and holidaymakers. It's the sort of place where the Catch of the Day is not priced on the menu. If you need to ask, you need to go elsewhere. The hostess seats Nicholas and I in one of the heavily branded, cordoned-off VIP sections in the decked open-air lounge that looks out onto the bay. I sink back into the sofa and inhale deeply. The air smells of decadence, of exquisitely prepared seafood, freshly shaken cocktails and richly perfumed after-sun products that would kill even the most precocious mosquito on impact. I scan the clientele, picking out the individual females. They are lithe, svelte, graceful and quite rightly *love* themselves, because this is how they have *always* been. They have a lifetime of self-appreciation behind their eyes. These are the women Maximilian packed those condoms for, not a latecomer like me. They glance over as if I am one of them, but if their eyes rested on me any longer they would see the truth in mine.

'*Delicioso* …' Nicholas smiles, running his tongue over his top lip as a stunning Spanish girl wearing a gold dress and no bra shimmies past in time to the beat. 'I'd quite like to retire on La Isla Blanca. I think the days would slip by rather easily. I'd spend the morning linked up to the necessary medical apparatus at my villa before having a light lunch of squid and gazpacho. Then I'd head here in subtle Maison Martin Margiela separates to loll around on a circular day bed and suck frozen caipirinhas through a straw as fast as my surgery scars will allow. Bliss.'

'Lucky you,' I mumble.

He cocks his head at me. 'I'm not a fan of sulking, darling. As matron at school used to say, *Turn that frown upside down.* We've got a busy few days ahead so I need you on form. Forget Ibiza, if Goldstein doesn't sign on the dotted line tomorrow, I'm more likely to be celebrating seventy in a rickety striped deckchair at Blackpool Pleasure Beach … surely the most inappropriately named stretch of coastline, *ever.*'

'Look, about tomorrow …' I begin, then take a large gulp of my drink: Grey Goose on the rocks infused with green chilli. I used to do this to my vodka when I worked in that wine bar. My old habits are so ingrained they don't 'creep' back in. It takes one knock and there they are at the door. *Hi, honey, we're home!*

'What about it?'

'I won't be here.'

'Excuse me?'

'I want to go home.'

'Home?'

'To London. I'm over all of this …'

Nicholas leans forward to select something from the extensive platter of sushi that is on the low Balinese-style table in front of us. 'What will you do for work? What with you no longer being employed at Burn's …' By way of explanation, he adds, 'I know you've been fired. I called there yesterday to speak to you …' He reaches into his manbag and pulls out my mobile. 'You left this in the Green Room at the television studios. Anyway, that delightful receptionist told me you were no longer with the company.'

I shrug at him. 'I'll get another job. It won't be a problem.'

'Hmmm …' He flops back into the sofa, chewing. 'I beg to differ. As things stand, you're in somewhat of a no man's land, darling. Too well known to go back to being *you* but not well known enough to be accepted as anyone *else*. Besides, you can't leave now. You're part of a team who needs you to play your part. I repeat, a *team.*' He pauses to gaze languidly at the Spanish girl – now seating herself on a stool by the bar – and undoes the top button of his shirt. 'Clearly, but never the less *understandably*, that word doesn't hold much resonance with you. I doubt you have fond memories of team activities during your formative years at school. Always the last to be picked for anyone's side on the sports field … it made you think like an individual. Always out to get what *you* need at the cost of whatever the *team* may need.'

'What's your point, Nicholas?' I ask, although I can tell where this drawn-out metaphor is leading.

'I know about your fun daytrip to see Marjorie Eden.' He waves my phone at me. 'I've listened to some very interesting messages from that low-rent chang fiend, Parks.'

I take a gulp of my drink, but I am not scared. I don't care.

'No need to explain yourself, darling. Initially, *yes* … I was peeved, but then I saw the funny side. The fact that you thought Fry would *ever* get shot of me is amusing. A manager is integral to the star, so is their publicist. Kill *either* of them and you murder the client's career. It is a necessary – but admittedly, a not exactly *holy* – triumvirate. Tell me, do you know who Guy Oseary and Liz Rozenberg are?'

'You're about to tell me …'

'They are Madonna's long-term manager and publicist. Guy was seventeen when he met Madonna. Liz has been in charge of her press since the eighties. They are God and the Holy Spirit to Madonna's Jesus. Her career has been a triple-pronged effort; the three of them working in harmony to turn Madonna Louise Ciccone into *Madonna.* Of course, it hasn't always been an easy job, what with the burning crosses, exposed nipples, Kabbalah water, teeny toyboys and manly upper arms … not to mention the *accusations* of lip-syncing at concerts, ripping off underground dance cultures and self-promotional political activism.' He takes a breath. 'But when you hear her name you don't think about *any* of that. You think: *Madonna – the biggest female star the world has ever known.* Trust me, you don't think that because of Madonna, you think that because of Guy and Liz.' He waves a chopstick at me. 'You might have assumed you know Fry, darling, but you don't. Being *the* Maximilian Fry in parentheses,' he signals the grammatical device with his index fingers, 'is the most important thing to him. Being Maximilian Fry,' his hands drop, '*terrifies* him.'

I shrug again. 'Well, thanks for that astounding insight into the top tier of show business, Nicholas, but I don't actually *care*. I'm off.' I raise my glass. 'So, cheers and goodbye. Oh, and don't worry, Monday and I will have moved out by the time he gets back.'

Nicholas looks only faintly perplexed. 'Now, now, don't be silly. I've welcomed you back into the team, darling. I doubt you'd want to piss me off again, would you?'

Before I can answer, my Nokia rings. Nicholas checks the caller ID and smiles. 'Ah, it's Clark Kent. Shall I answer it?' He switches it onto speakerphone and holds it out of my reach. We both hear Clint's raspy panting.

'Vivian! For crying out loud, I've been trying to get 'old of you all day.' His voice is shaky. ''Ave you got that shady fucker's email yet? We need to 'ack it sharpish. I'm on the verge of getting my nuts chopped off. I sorted the cash I owe with some boys back on my patch but they 'aven't deliv—'

'Lovely to hear your dulcet tones, Parks,' Nicholas interrupts.

'What?' splutters Clint, confused. 'Is *th*—'

Nicholas smiles at the receiver. 'Yes, it's the *shady fucker* ... and I'd appreciate a bit of volume control. You're on loudspeaker and we're – that's Vivian and I – are in a rather high-end restaurant in the Balearics. I'll keep this brief, Parks. This is your final warning to keep that ulcerated snout of yours out of my affairs. You will find no concrete evidence of wrongdoing – not even if you worm your way into my personal correspondence. However, I do have vast quantities of evidence to nail *you*.'

'You've already screwed my career.'

'And I could do exactly the same thing with your personal life.'

'Bastard!' shouts Clint, so loudly that customers on the next table turn round. 'If you lay a finger on my Roxy, I'll …' He trails off and it sounds like he thumps the lavatory door. It is the first time I have heard him mention his wife by name.

Nicholas tuts. 'Oh please, I'm not that sordid. I am rather manipulative, though, and would quite happily tell your wife about the fifteen-year-old you romped with a few months ago.' Clint is silent. 'Ring any bells? The contestant who came second in that beauty contest you judged in the Canaries … the hotel belonged to a pal of mine, and that little tart you squirrelled up into your suite lied about her age on the entry form. I'd say that if your other half found out, it would put your chances of seeing your new tot at below zero. Not to mention how it would go down in the industry. Not exactly what Daddy needs on his curriculum vitae to find a new job, is it?' He stops to laugh. 'Hobbies and interests: cocaine, loan sharks and schoolgirls?'

'Don't get clever with me, you little shit,' rasps Clint. 'We didn't even 'ave nookie, I *swear*. I've *never* cheated on my wife. It's all part of the image.' His voice cracks.

I attempt to grab my mobile again but Nicholas pushes me back in my seat.

'Clint,' I yell, 'I'm so sorry, I didn't realize th—'

'*Leave* it, Vivian,' he chokes. 'I don't want to know.'

I hear a loud sniff followed by that familiar guttural snort. Then he hangs up.

Nicholas hands me my phone. 'Excellent. Glad we got that sorted. Now, I'm going to mingle before we have dinner.' He looks in the direction of the Spanish girl. She has been joined at the bar by an equally fit companion. 'Ah! *Dos para el precio de uno* … two for the price of one. See you in a couple of hours, darling. We're meeting Barb at Amante about nine-ish.' He throws a wedge of euros into my lap. 'Maybe you'd like to take this time to have another drink and consider what I've said. Fry needs me. Fry needs Barb. Without us he is incapable of achieving what he wants to. We pack the punch he needs to fight for his place in the industry. We pack the audiences into those cinemas. We even pack his sodding suitcase. Without us he can't function … on any level. As things stand, he also needs you.'

I am about to drain my vodka, but I stop. 'Sorry, what did you say?'

'Fry needs *you*.'

'Before that …'

'He also needs *us*. Barb *and* I.'

'No, about packing his suitcase …'

Nicholas squints at me. 'Eh?'

'You said you packed his suitcase.'

'I don't. Barb does.'

'Did she pack it to come to Ibiza?'

'Of course, why?'

Whoooooooooosh!

I wait until Nicholas is fully ensconced in conversation with the Spanish girls, and as soon as he is, I slip outside into the dusty car park to grab a taxi. I ask the driver to stop at the family-run guesthouse in Playa d'en Bossa that Roger and I used during our first visits to the White Isle. Jorge the elderly proprietor prided himself on providing his customers with the most important things they would require for a satisfactory stay: a.) clean towels for the beach; b.) bottled water any time of day or night, and c.) decent ecstasy pills. Roger joked that we should give Jorge's place a *rave* review on TripAdvisor when we got back.

I dash into reception. Jorge isn't there but his teenage grandson is. I ask him for *pildoras*, but he says they have stopped producing them in favour of something else *muchas especiale*, and hands me a clear pouch of a brown sugary substance. MDMA. Or, as Roger used to call it, *mud*. I hesitate … but then I sense it again: that immiscible combination of *shyness and shame* layered in my stomach. I need to get rid of it. So I hand over eighty euros of Nicholas's cash – enough for two grams – and run back to the cab.

Halfway up the driveway to Maximilian's villa, I see lights twinkling on the roof terrace. He must be in the hot tub, so I get out of the car and walk the rest of the way. I don't want him to know I am here or see me before I've had time to change. As I dash through the garden towards the house I hear throbbing house music float through the warm, lemon-scented night air. I tiptoe through the courtyard into the house, grab a bottle of Hierbas – the local herbal liqueur – from the kitchen and run up to my room, strip off and slip into a nude silk Agent Provocateur lace two-piece. Contrived? Possibly. But this isn't the time for perky/edgy. Seduction garments on, I grab the booze and one of the pouches of MDMA. Then I leave my bedroom and creep up the wrought-iron spiral staircase. Emerging onto the terrace, I can hear splashing coming from over by the wall. All the lanterns have been lit; the entire space is submerged in a sensual, flickering orange glow. The music has got harder, the beats more aggressive and minimal. I rough up my hair and purposefully readjust one bra strap as if it has casually fallen down my shoulder, like Baby's did in *Dirty Dancing* when she was practising the lift with Johnny in the lake. Before I get a chance to over-think anything else, I scuttle across the roof until I am directly behind the wooden screen. Here, I peek through one of the carved holes …

Maximilian *is* in the hot tub.

But he is not alone. He is with Pedro. And put it this way, they are not looking at plans for a potential annexe.

CHAPTER THIRTY-THREE

I stumble backwards down and round the spiral stairs onto the landing where I hover for a few seconds – listening to the splashing. I tell myself that what is going on in that hot tub is some light-hearted male bonding between two old pals after a few too many glasses of a full-bodied Rioja. We're talking masculine high jinx on a level with the volleyball scene in *Top Gun* at the most. At a push, a spiritual *Point Break*-style bromance between two guys from different walks of life but with the same substance at their core. But when I tiptoe back up the stairs to examine the situation from a different angle – and as I stand there transfixed, the pair of them go on to create a whole *series* of angles you *could* choose to examine it from – all I can think is that Kate Summers was correct. Vivian Ward *is* a big fat idiot … But her words are not painted all cutesy on the wall of the sports equipment shed. They are at the forefront of my mind, lit up, neon bright and ten feet high, as if above a Las Vegas theatre.

I run back to my room, flip open my suitcase and grab the piece of paper that is lying in one of the inner compartments. I punch the phone number that is written on it into my mobile.

'Hi, Marjorie, it's Vivian.' I'm already hurling clothes into my suitcase. 'Sorry to call you so late.'

'Don't worry, dear. Is there any news?'

'Er, well, sort of. I wanted to ask you a few more background questions about Nathan.' I feel a flash of guilt for lying to her but immediately put it to one side as a fresh tune starts pumping down from upstairs. I shut the balcony doors. 'Clint's been chatting to a few people and he said that a certain rumour keeps surfacing.'

'Go on …'

'Apparently problems first arose with Nathan's job when he started getting close to er, Zoe, Maximilian's girlfriend. No one is saying this would have been entirely Nathan's fault as Zoe does have a pretty bad reputation when it comes to getting her kit off but …' I pause, knowing Marjorie is going to interrupt me. She does.

'Oh, I'll stop you right there, dear. My Nathan has only ever had girls as *friends*. It's the way it's always been. Bless him, he – and I – knew very early on that he was always going to be a man's man. His last boyfriend was a while back; before he moved south … a local boy from Brum with his own insulation business. A good egg, but – and this is going to sound mean – he was a *little* dull. I'd always imagined Nathan would attract someone who really … *sparkled*.'

I hook the Nokia between my ear and shoulder so I can carry my toiletries out of the bathroom and deposit them into my case.

'Sparkled?' I repeat. 'A bona fide *star*, you mean?'

'Mmm. I had hoped he would meet a guy with a bit more

razzle-dazzle when he worked in the entertainment world, but that's just me being silly …'

Silently cursing my *own* stupidity, I end the conversation with Marjorie and zip up my suitcase. But as I drag it towards the door, two more realisations hit me: a.) That tattoo on the inside of Maximilian's wrist isn't a 'Z' for Zoe, it's an 'N' for Nathan, and b.) Barb has got my passport. So I leave my suitcase in my room, march across to Maximilian's, go into the ensuite bathroom and rummage in his Louis Vuitton washbag. I ignore a (now open) packet of condoms and remove a silver tray of Xanax. Then I go back to my room, get into bed and neck back one of the tablets with a hefty swig of Hierbas.

But despite the benzodiazepine dissolving into my system I do not fall asleep immediately. I can't get him out of my mind. Not Maximilian. *My father.* I am thinking about the afternoon of my tenth birthday when I discovered him in his garage cheating on my mother. There wasn't a hint of panic in his eyes when he saw *me*, see *him* with *her*. Bent over that woman on his desk in the back office, he even made a joke. 'We're just sorting out the paperwork on a Toyota, Viv…' he laughed. I wondered how he could be so confident that I would keep his secret safe from my mother or siblings. What had he already seen in me to know that this was the sort of person I was? *Weak.*

But he didn't expect me to keep quiet without some sort of payment in return. His currency? Food. Soon the trips started. Fast food outlets, sweet shops, all-you-can-eat carveries, motorway service stations, pub gardens … or sometimes we simply went to the supermarket and I ate in his car, somewhere up the road from the house where his latest fling lived. That was my favourite; when I got to eat alone. Our excursions stopped in my early teens. My father realised he didn't have to put the effort in, because I was doing that all by myself. His secret wasn't simply safe, it was in the *vault*. Because getting fatter had made me even weaker. It makes sense then, that when I finally had lost all the weight, I felt strong. Out of the weakness came strength. This is how I have always liked to assess the last fifteen years of my life; becoming thin I have proved I am not weak. Yes, I know I was not living a normal life. I was not a normal person. But at least I had become one who could not be manipulated, duped or cajoled into a situation simply for a few treats.

But now look at me, I think, as I woozily drift off, *on the outside I might have changed, but on the inside it's business as usual. It never got the memo.*

CHAPTER THIRTY-FOUR

I wake up to the pre-party preparation going on outside: machinery being clanked, lorries beeping as they back up, people shouting at one another in Spanish. I shuffle out onto the balcony. Engineers are up on ladders hanging speakers and lights off a rig that runs round the courtyard. A temporary bridge lined with flowers has been built across the middle of the pool, in the centre of which is a mini stage with mixing decks and a microphone stand. Catering equipment is being offloaded from vans and trailers blocking up the driveway, and a wall of bottle crates has been erected by the entrance to the house. A short burst of thumping bass blasts out round the garden as the sound levels are tested on a PA system, then, almost on cue, the sky rumbles overhead. I spot Maximilian examining a newly erected Bedouin-style tent. He keeps throwing his arms in the air. He turns round and sees me on the balcony.

'Are you okay, Vivian?' he shouts over the background din. 'Nicholas said you didn't show up for dinner last night. What happened?'

'I'm fine, thanks.' Another rupture of bass thunders around the garden. 'I came back here to seduce you but you were already screwing.'

'Pardon?' Maximilian cups hand to his ear and grimaces. 'It's too noisy. Hang on …' He walks towards the villa. 'I didn't hear that. What were you saying?'

'That I could do with a cup of coffee. Is there any brewing?'

'Oh, right. I'll get one for you. By the way *Luxury* magazine have arrived … their stylist has brought a load of stuff for you to try on. Hair and make-up want to start pretty soon too.'

'Really? Well, they're wasting their time because I'm not going to the party.'

Maximilian cups his hand to his ear again. 'Sorry?'

'I was saying I want something suitably Balearic … flowing not *tarty*.'

'Right,' he says again, as he comes to a standstill under my window. 'Have you seen the size of this production? It's fucking ridiculous. I'm starting to get really het up.' He motions in the direction of the garden. 'I thought it was meant to be stylish but intimate.'

I wait for another rumble of bass. 'Well, I thought you were straight, turns out you're gay.'

'Eh?'

'I was agreeing … it's as if they're staging Cirque du Soleil.'

'Mmm. Listen,' he shakes his shoulders as if attempting to release tension, 'about yesterday. I came out of the bathroom and you'd, er …' He waits until two men carrying cases of champagne have walked past. '… disappeared. Were you pissed off with me for not hav—'

I hold up my hand. 'Forget it, Maximilian. Let's not

discuss it …' Another rumble. 'We both know you've made me look like a twat, but it's my own fault.'

'Sorry?'

'I said, why don't you come up for a *chat* … and bring that coffee. I need a jolt.'

But I don't know why I am bothering to joke because I am the only one listening. If I did laugh, I would only be laughing at myself. The joke – as it always used to be – is most definitely on me. The punchline has come full circle. It was only a matter of time … and now it is time for me to go.

I examine my face in the bathroom mirror. It is encased in yesterday's make-up: Death Mask by MAC. I don't bother chiselling it off. I work some moisturiser into the dryer bits, then add fresh foundation on top. As I blend I run through the conversation I will have with Maximilian. I'm not going to tell him what I saw. What would be the point? It wouldn't change anything. I'm leaving anyway. At least if *he* doesn't know that *I* know, it will appear as if I have come to a decision based on what *I* want to do, not because of anything *he* has done. I will appear to have a sliver of self-respect. Such measured responses to a loss of face weren't exactly my forté back when I was fat. When food took a grip, I lost mine. The most extreme example of this was at our final school disco.

Kate and Ziggy looked so happy that night. They drifted round the dance floor cheek-to-cheek, the unofficial but entirely unchallenged prom king and queen. The queen having no idea I had been blowing off her king for three years … desperately and pathetically hoping I would steal her crown. I stood by the catering trestle table consumed *by* jealousy and consum*ing* cheese puffs and Twiglets with a contraband bottle of Thunderbird. Then the music stopped, and the unthinkable happened. Ziggy got down on one knee and asked Kate to m—

There is a knock at my bedroom door.

'You can bung that coffee by the bed,' I yell curtly. 'I'll be with you when I've finished in the bathroom.'

Someone laughs. Not Maximilian.

'On a scale of moderate fame changing you,' the voice continues, 'one being you know what a pint of milk – skimmed, obviously – costs and ten being, "don't look me directly in the eyes unless previously instructed"… I'd say you're heading for an eight. What d'you reckon?'

It's Luke. For the first time in fifteen years, I *want* to cry.

CHAPTER THIRTY-FIVE

But I don't. I blink hard like Monday does and step out into the bedroom.

Luke has shaved off all his hair and his tan has mellowed. (Medium Oak?) He is wearing his 'Cod is a DJ' T-shirt but the logo has faded – the fish looks like a ghostly apparition. On his left wrist is a spiky silver bracelet. It is the first time I have ever seen a piece of jewellery on him. There is something else different about him too, but I can't quite figure out what. I need a second before I can speak.

'I knew you'd be freaked out,' he says. 'I was too when I found out you were here, but I've had a day to get used to it.' He smiles and scans my face. 'I see you're still advocating the natural look.'

'Always.'

'So, how's my little mate?'

'I'm fine.' I smile back, *overwhelmingly* pleased he has used a term of endearment. 'Well, sort of fine. Actually, things are a b—'

'Ha! I didn't mean *you*. I meant Monday.'

'Oh … yeah, he's good. *Busy*.' I swallow and smile again but this time it's forced. 'We're trying to sort out his schedule so he gets a bit more "me" time. You know how up against it he always is.'

Luke laughs. 'It's good to see you, Vivian.'

'Is it?'

'Yeah, of course …'

He looks straight at me and I stare back. Suddenly, I realise what is so different about his face. It appears to have lost its ability to crumple. It doesn't look as if it could crumple any second or in the near future, or has had any reason to crumple recently. Now, I am overwhelmed at how hard it is to be pleased about this.

I clear my throat. 'What *exactly* are you doing here, Luke?'

'Calm down, I'm not stalking you. I live here.'

'In what sense?'

'In the sense that I am an inhabitant.'

'You're not here on holiday?' You can only imagine the envy in my voice. Each time I used to holiday in Ibiza, I would spend the last three days of my stay trying to figure out a way of setting up home on the island without any cash, job prospects or basic Spanish. 'You *live* here …'

'Yeah, have done for pretty much all of the summer, we're definitely not going back …'

The 'we' slices through me as if it were a Samurai sword. We = Luke and Sammy. *Sammy.* Kooky Sammy and her sunflower. I guarantee her @SammySparkles Twitter profile picture is now a fucking sunset.

'It's gone so quickly,' continues Luke, babbling away, but his ultra-casual tone is *too* casual. 'The weather has been ridiculous … a total scorcher, we had a heatwave most of July and August. It reminded me of Sydney. Mid-thirties every day.'

'Really? You must have sweltered doing building work in that heat,' I comment, simply for something to babble back casually.

'*Building?* Nah, I haven't been on a site since I left the UK, not unless you count the house we found. It was in a bit of a wreck when we got it, so I've been doing it up. But as far as work goes … well, you ready for another surprise? I'm deejaying now.' He shrugs his shoulders and half-sighs half-smiles. 'Yep, I actually play records and get rewarded for it with euros. Anyway, that's why I'm here … Suki booked me to play tonight so I thought I'd pop over to check that everything had been set up okay and say g'day to the hostess with the mostest.' He winks at me. 'Didn't want to spring a surprise when you were balancing a large tray of vol-au-vents, did I? I met your man downstairs and he told me I'd find you up here.'

'My man?'

'That Maximus …'

'He's not a gladiator … it's *Maximilian.* What did you say?'

'Not much. Just that you and I used to regularly have the most obscenely awesome no-strings-attached sex.' He gives me a knowing grin. (It takes every kilojoule of energy that I have in my body to reciprocate with a similar expression.) 'Nah, don't panic, I told him I was an old mate of yours from London and then we had a chinwag about this evening. You've got yourself a cool guy there, once you get past that crazy posho accent … but yeah, I liked him. He seems genuine.'

I stand in silence for a few seconds staring at Luke. He stares back at me, his eyes fully centred on mine. They make me feel empty … but not in a good way.

'Listen, Vivia—' he begins.

I interrupt him. 'What happened to your hair?'

'Wozza shaved it off when I fell asleep at my leaving do; thought I might as well keep it short. Makes sense in the heat …' He rubs his head back and forth with his left hand. 'Suki thinks I should bleach it.'

'Suki? Why on earth would you take style advice from that withered husk? You must have seen that hideous tattoo all the way up hcr neck.'

'Course I've seen it, it says "Luke".'

I manage to laugh and mean it. 'No *way*, is that her boy-friend's name too?'

'Yep …'

'How embarrassing. Thank your lucky stars it's written in Jewish, otherwise people might think it's you.'

'Then they would be right,' he explains. His eyes dart away from mine and he sits down on the bed. 'Because, er, Suki and I are together.'

'Ha!' I laugh. 'Yeah, right …'

'I'm not joking, Vivian.' He sort of sighs awkwardly as he says this. 'Suki and I live together as well as work together for Ultimate Ibiza. Well, I do stuff for other clubs too … but whenever the Ultimate team are asked to do a private party Suki gets me the gig.'

'You *and Suki*?'

'Mmm.'

Sammy's Balearic sunset dissipates. Now all I can see is the hallway of Suki and Luke's restoration project finca. It is a DIY chaos of ladders, paint pots, rollers, rags and brushes. But propped up next to each other by the front door are Suki's Westwood boots and Luke's record bag … thoughtfully positioned to ensure the smoothest departure in case of an urgent request to throw a glamorous knees-up at *very* short notice somewhere on the island. I find myself sitting down on the bed next to Luke as my legs appear to have lost their primary function.

'I cannot bel*ieve* you went from a *Sammy* to a *Suki*,' I hiss at him, nonsensically. 'What were you *thinking*? Part of me actually feels sorry for Sammy.'

'Sammy?' repeats Luke, confused.

'Yeah … *Sammy*, @SammySparkles, kooky Sammy and her sunflower …'

'Oh, *that* Sammy. What *are* you going on about, Vivian? Sammy's going out with Wozza. They hooked up when I played at SundaySoundz. You remember that d—'

'Of course, I remember that day. I suppose Suki gave you that …' I thrust my hand at his bracelet and wince as my finger hits one of the spikes. 'Only mildly less bugging than one of Sammy's friendship bands.'

Luke pauses as if to give me a chance to calm myself. 'Look, Vivian, not that you probably care, but I want you to know that nothing went on with Suki the night we split up. Nothing did for ages … because … because I wasn't over you. We moved here together as mates, and then … it sort of *happened.* I hope you didn't get too much of a shock when she met you at the airport.'

I dig deep. 'A bit, but I'm sure it was nothing in comparison to the shock you got when she rocked up home with your name indelibly inked up her neck.'

'I wasn't shocked. It was nice of her … I liked it.'

'Sorry?' I want him to repeat what he said so I can gauge just *how* much he liked it.

'I said, *I liked it...*'

I can't tell. 'But what's going to happen when you go your separate ways? Luke isn't exactly the most pliable of words. She'll only be able to turn it into Fluke … and it certainly would be if she met someone called that. Ha!' My most forced expression of jollity yet.

'It's a good thing we're not planning to split up, then.'

This time the words do not come out of his mouth with the quiet, measured certainty that I know he is capable of. There is also a *very* slight crumple in his face.

'Luke, I …' I take a breath.

'Fucking coffee machine,' swears Maximilian, appearing in the doorway holding a Moroccan-style silver cup and saucer. For a few minutes I had forgotten he even existed. 'Not very good with any sort of gadgetry,' he explains to Luke, as he walks past my suitcase to pass me the drink.

I take the cup from Maximilian without looking at the liquid inside it or at him, but he doesn't notice. He goes straight out onto the balcony and cranes his head towards the sky.

'Sky is looking ominously grey … it's humid too. If the heavens open we'll be fucked … or electrocuted, given the amount of cabling down there.' He steps back inside the room. 'I hope that's drinkable,' he says.

I shrug and mutter something in the affirmative.

Luke's mobile rings. The ring tone is a soppy chill-out track. *Their* song, probably.

'That's Suki,' he says. His face pings back to its original un-crumpled expression. 'I'll see you guys this evening; let's hope the weather holds out. Good to catch up with you, Vivian.' His voice could not be more 'pally'. Overly so. He answers the phone. 'I'm over at the villa,' he says to Suki. 'Yep, sound system is boss … you're coming up the drive? Great … see you in a bit.'

Maximilian nods after him. 'He seems cool. Well, let's hope he is … cut to him opening his set with a Carly Rae Jepsen megamix. God, I need to fucking relax. Anyway, you wanted to talk …'

I take another, even deeper breath. 'No, not really. I've got something to *tell* you.'

'That sounds ominous.'

'You're going to be pissed off, so is Barb.'

'Why? What's the matter?' Suddenly, he peers quizzically round the room. 'Where are all your belongings, Vivian?'

I point to my suitcase by the door. 'In there.'

'Why have you packed?'

Calmly, I get up from the bed and stand squarely in front of him, ready to launch into my planned speech. But I am distracted by the sound of Luke bounding down the spiral staircase still yacking to Suki. Christ, does he need to stay on the phone? He's going to see her in thirty seconds …

clearly, neither of them are bothered about decimating their free minutes.

'...was just chatting to Maximilian Fry and his girlfriend. Yep, really fired up ... you've done a bonzer job. The set-up sounds great. Mmm ... okay, see you by the pool ...'

'The thing is, Maximilian, I'm...' I begin.

'Yeah, literally twenty seconds ... I'm upstairs in the house ... coming down now ... yeah ... er ... of course ...'

'You're ...'

'I'm going.'

'You're *what*?' Maximilian's eyes narrow.

'I'm going. I'm going *now.*'

His face hardens. 'Are you trying to say that you're leav—'

'... of course!' repeats Luke. ' I love you too.'

On the 't' of 'too', I lean forward and kiss Maximilian on the cheek.

'Yeah, leaving.' I interrupt. 'To, er, go into town. I'm going to get my hair and face done by one of the girls who prepare the club dancers and then I'll nip into a boutique to get something to wear. I don't mean to sound like a prima donna, but I really don't want to be dressed and made-up by the *Luxury* team. I'm sure they're professional, but I want a look that's more ... well, edgy. Still perky, obviously. But mainly edgy.'

Maximilian is visibly relieved. 'For a second I thought you wanted to go, as in *leave*.'

'And miss out on all the fun? No *way*!'

He points at my suitcase. 'But why did you pack?'

'I haven't *un*packed.'

'Oh, I jumped to the wrong conclusion.'

'Don't worry, Maximilian.' I kiss him again. 'It happens to the best of us.'

CHAPTER THIRTY-SIX

Four hours later, I am back at the villa, wearing a vintage black slashed and fringed leather Roberto Cavalli bum-skimming strapless mini-dress with a lattice bustier. Luke does not understand fashion. He understands flesh. I have spent the past two hundred and forty minutes thinking about what I need to say to him and now I feel sick. Because I know that this is *it*. I need to face *him*. I need to face *me*. Because if I don't, nothing will ever get better. Because I want things to get better. I want to be better. I slug back some Hierbas. *But what if I cannot be better?*

I tentatively open a pouch of MDMA. The bitter, chemical stench makes me gag. This has never been my drug of choice … it's disconcertingly pure. The high always seemed too unpredictable. The low all too predictable. But I need it. Just for today. The US army are supposed to have experimented successfully with MDMA as a truth serum in the 1950s. Hopefully, it will help me *reach inside and pull out mine.* Grimacing, I lick my finger, plunge it into the crystals, scoop some out and swallow them. I follow this process *immediately* with another swig of Hierbas. It's how Roger used to take it. *The powerfully aromatic alcohol numbs and flavours your mouth as well as burning your throat, removing the before and after taste of the MDMA; usually a combination of human bile and plant stamen ...* I gag even harder and tip the rest of the crystals into a mini bottle of water. There is no way I am boshing them neat again. A few sips of that will see me through to dawn.

By the time I get downstairs, the courtyard is already packed with guests. They are exactly the type Barb wanted: glamorous, loosely recognisable (with no one present more famous than Maximilian) ... and vain enough to drop whatever plans they may have had so they can get their mug in the various international editions of *Luxury*. Luke was right, Suki *has* done a good job and she knows it. I can see her talking animatedly into a walkie-talkie over by the catering tent, making everyone fully aware it is she who has pulled the event together. She is wearing a long peach silk slip that together with her battered Westwood boots quietly whispers island chic. I watch as she clicks off her walkie-talkie and chats to the sushi chef, all the while staring over at the podium above the swimming pool where Luke is. He is crouched over the CDJ unit with his right hand clamped against his right earphone, bobbing up and down in time to the beat. His spiky silver bracelet slips up and down his forearm as he moves. I wonder what Suki engraved on the inside. *Shalom? Mazel Tov?* As if he can sense she is looking over, he lifts his head up and gazes in her direction.

You okay? she mouths at him, ignoring whatever the sushi chef is saying.

I go to the bar, put down my 'Balearic Gatorade' and order a large vodka (no rocks, no mixer). I sense people staring at my outfit and nudging each other. A short, plump man approaches me. He has a bleached mohawk and is wearing one of those *unforgivable* Ed Hardy T-shirts with Swarovski studs splattered over the imprint of an eagle.

'Vivian?'

'Yeah?'

'JP Goldstein.' He kisses my hand and leers at my outfit. 'That's one hell of a dress. There was me thinking you were the "girl next door" … tonight you're more girl next door leasing the bedsit on the top floor with a red glow at the window. Ha! Enjoying Ibiza?'

'Mmm … I love this place. It's the fucking *best*.' The woozy and uninhibited effects of the drugs could be kicking in. 'I was sorry to hear about your wife.'

'Not half as sorry as my accountant. Serves me right for marrying an adult-movie star. Money-grabbing hoes. Actually, make that just money-grabbing. Frigid, the lot of them. Sure, they'll give it their all when faced with a camera crew, a water-tight contract and a line-up of random throbbing cocks. But at home? With the bozo whose paying for their next tit job? *Nothing*.'

Just as I am thinking he couldn't get more odious, he produces an Emporio Armani handkerchief (with visible logo) to wipe sweat off his forehead. Maximilian approaches us. He appears *much* less stressed than earlier. He waves a bottle of Evian.

'Ah, so you've found my Vivian.' Maximilian nods at JP Goldstein.

'Sure have,' replies the movie executive. He taps my glass. 'Nice to see you've got her on the H2O. Trying to kickstart those plans for Junior already, eh?' he says to Maximilian, as if I wasn't standing there.

I snort. *What plans for Junior?* 'This is vodka, JP. Of course, it goes without saying I can't *wait* to have babies with *my* Maximilian, but I'm the traditional sort …'

JP slaps Maximilian on the back. 'In that case, where's the ring, Max, my boy? You can see she's gagging to get one on her finger.'

Maximilian puts his bottle of water on the bar and rubs my shoulder. I let him. Maybe because *I* am now intending on using *him* just as he used me … or maybe because the MDMA has officially clocked in and started to work.

'It'll happen … when the moment is right. Who knows when that will be?'

'Who does, indeed?' says JP. 'But I'll tell you what *I* know and that's this: there's nothing like a wedding in the diary to give a movie's promotional tour that extra edge. Clearly, I'm not the sort of guy who would encourage the use of such a poignant promise between two people to get as many motherfucking butts on seats as possible, but hey …'

'Of course, you're not *that* sort of guy, JP.' Maximilian smiles, his eyes narrowing. 'And besides, I may not be the guy in the film, so this is an entirely hypothetical conversation. After all, it's not as if I've seen a contract yet. It might be *some other guy's* wedding that gets you the press … although, I'd like to remind you at this point, Orlando Bloom hasn't got divorced yet.'

Wow, Maximilian really has managed to relax. JP is also surprised by his reaction.

'Woah!' He slaps him on the back again. 'I like this new

you, Max, my boy. The love of a good woman has put you in a good place … I'm jealous. I only end up in court. Let's make a toast.' He lifts his champagne glass, and nods at the barman. 'Cristal over here.'

'Actually, I'm sticking to water today,' says Maximilian, leaning over and picking up his water bottle from the bar. 'And for the foreseeable future. You want me to focus? I'm focused. To your good health, JP.'

'Health? That ship has sailed,' chortles the film producer. 'I'm diseased to the core. Let's make it wealth.'

I look over towards the swimming pool. Suki is rushing across the bridge towards the podium. She scoots behind the decks and launches herself into Luke's arms as if she has just been released from a long-term hostage situation. A few seconds into the hug, he gently pulls away, hands Suki his headphones and points in the direction of the temporary loos.

'Excuse me, gentlemen,' I tell Maximilian and JP. 'I'm nipping to the Ladies.'

Maximilian smiles. 'Okay, hurry back, though … we need to do some shots for *Luxury*.'

I stride off through the guests. I try to scoot round Barb – she is talking to Achilles – but she grabs me.

'What the freakin' hell are you wearing, kiddo? Didn't you see the dresses *Luxury* brought? Nicholas will go berserk. Get changed into something a little less Christina Aguilera *circa* … well, *circa* whenever. Take your pick.'

'No,' I tell her.

'What did you say?'

'I think you heard.'

Clearly confused, she peers at me then nudges Achilles. 'Hey, sugar … I need a quick chat with Vivian. Go and mingle, will you?'

'Stay here, Achilles,' I reassure him, then turn back to Barb. 'We'll talk when I'm ready.'

'Kiddo, what the freak—'

I hold up my hand. 'I *said*, we'll talk later.' I dash off through the courtyard and past the catering tents to the guest toilets. *'Luke!'*

He waits a few seconds before turning round. 'Yes?'

'Hi …'

'Hi.'

He swigs from a bottle of beer and I wonder when he started enjoying the odd alcoholic drink. I imagine him and Suki in paint-splattered dungarees chinking bottles of Peroni after a long day whitewashing their finca. I bet she wouldn't mind him calling it 'amber nectar'.

'Listen, I wanted to say …' I begin. 'All that stuff about Sammy … I was only mucking about. I honestly didn't give a second thought as to whether … well, that you and she, what*ever*. Deep down I know you would draw the line at trading friendship bands. Hygiene alert! Ugh. Did you know it's an actual *fact* that kooky people trade germs a lot faster than normal people? Their world is like one giant aircraft cabin … ha!'

Luke stares at me blankly. I try again.

'Good night, isn't it? Suki sure does know her *cebollas*. That's Spanish for onions, by the way. All this …' I wave my arms about. 'In such a short time. I'm impressed. So, er, have you got time to talk?'

'No, I've got to get back to the decks,' he mutters. 'Suki can't cover for too long, she's busy.'

'Suki knows how to deejay?' I ask. Although the way I deliver this question, I may as well have said, *I hope she dies vomiting up her own kidneys.* 'Well, she really is the one-stop-party-shop, isn't she?'

Luke glares at me. 'Stop taking the piss.'

'It was a joke, for Christ's sake. Why are you being narky? You were so different earlier. I thought you wanted to be …' I walk closer towards him. Buoyed up by MDMA, I chance an opening. '… *friends*.'

'Now, you really *are* having a laugh. I think you'll find that one of the prerequisites for friendship is respect.'

'I respect you.'

'Ha!' He drains the rest of his beer, chucks the bottle under the lavatory steps and turns, about to walk up. 'Enjoy your party, Vivian.'

I grab the hem of his T-shirt. 'Hang on, don't be like this …' I pause whilst he still has his back to me so that I can wiggle my jaw to pop my ears. They feel a bit blocked. Textbook sign of 'coming up'. 'I thought that we could, er …'

Luke turns round. 'Could, er, *what*? Get back together and pretend that everything that has happened *hasn't*?'

'Why not?' I smile, pleased he is getting thc thrust of the conversation.

'Are you in*sane*?' he snaps, but then he takes a deep breath and calms himself. 'I am happy with someone else …' He does not look at me as he says this.

'Are you?'

'Yes! And so are *you* …'

'But that's the thing, I'm not.'

'Since when?'

'Since *never*. I've never been happy with Maximilian. Not in *that* way.'

'Oh, really? Because it appears you were *very* happy together in *that* way even up to a few days ago.'

'Eh? How do you …' I bend down to itch an imaginary scratch on my leg so I can subtly wiggle my jaw again. '… know?'

'Don't you dare mug me off. I've just seen *it*.'

'Seen what?'

'That show.'

'Which show?'

'On the television. Suki had it on whilst we were getting ready this evening. I listened to every word.'

'You watched the *telly*?' I laugh as I ask this. I always find it hard to get my head round the concept of anyone doing normal things in Ibiza. It's weird when you see the library in town or hardware stores, etc. Travel agencies throw me completely. If you lived *here* why would you ever want to leave? I force my attention back on Luke. 'What did you watch?'

'*Bunson, Benton* … some chat show.'

'Oh, *that!*' I burst out laughing again.

Luke shakes his head at me in disgust. No, *abhorrence*. 'You think it's amusing that you told however many million people that Maximilian was the love of your life and that … and that … the pair of you were planning on having a family *as soon as possible* …'

'I didn't say that.' *Shit.* Maximilian's 'I believe the children are our future' routine after I left the Green Room … no wonder JP thought I was drinking water.

'Believe me, Vivian, I didn't find it too hilarious. I knew you were fucked up, but I never had you down as cruel … or vindictive.'

I give the bottom of Luke's T-shirt another yank. 'Luke, calm down. You've got it all wrong. Maximilian and I are not together. We never were. It was all a publicity stunt. It still is … all conjured up for us to get lots of exposure. But actually, that's not why I signed up in the first place. It was to stop me thinking about what I had lost. Or rather to stop me realising what I had found and thrown away … because if I confronted that, I would have to confront me.' I peer up at Luke, hoping to see a positive change in the way he is looking at me but as yet there is nothing to report. I change tack. 'For your information, Maximilian and I kissed on *one* occasion, well, *two*,' I continue. 'But both times he instigated it and only because he was trying to distract me from, er, stuff that I was about to find out about him. We never slept together. Well, we almost did … *yesterday*, but it went, er, *wrong* … but I'm glad it did because then I saw you and I realised that I'd made a big mistake not trying harder to get you back … because I prefer you to him … well, to anyone, really …' The drugs are giving me the conversational breadth of an eight-year-old, but I'm sure this is a good thing. Kids are sincere, aren't they? 'I've never got you out of my head.' I hang mine. 'I thought I had, but I hadn't. I even said your name by mistake instead of Maximilian's the other day. You've always been in here …' I tap my skull.

My ears feel sludgy again. 'I know this is hard for you to hear … it's not easy for me to say it. The whole situation is complex. But what is simple, is how you looked at me in my room at the villa … just before Maximilian came in and Suki called. You haven't moved on. I *know* you haven't. In fact, you never even wanted us to split up. Otherwise you wouldn't have put your sweatshirt in that box you got Warren to drop off at Burn's. You wanted me to come and find you …' I peer up at Luke again. For the first time since I launched into my monologue he appears to be listening. 'Didn't you?'

'What would you have said if you'd found me?' he asks plainly.

I paw the ground with one of my heels, fully aware that all I need to say is, *I love you.* I open my mouth, but I don't say anything. I end up doing something else.

I yawn.

'Vivia—' Luke stops himself. 'Are you on something? You are, aren't you? *Aren't you?* I *knew* it … I fucking knew it.'

'I'm not!' I shriek, so violently it makes my vision blur. 'Well, maybe … a bit. I needed it … to tell you … because when I saw you … I realised … no, *way* before that … probably from the beginning I … but look, no matter what you have seen … or heard … I haven't ever felt … this … that … I …'

I wait a few seconds for Luke's face to come back into focus … and that's when I see it crumple, exactly like it used to. His forehead creases, then his cheekbones sink and his mouth turns down at the corners. I can see anger, hurt and humiliation emanating from every angle of his face … just like I could on mine when I looked into the inescapable dual mirrors in my old bedroom. I reach round his neck and pull him towards me, but he yanks his head back. I try again. This time his whole body *recoils* and he pushes me away, a look of total contempt added to the crumpled backdrop. Then he jogs up the metal ramp to the toilets. As he is about to enter a cubicle, he twists round.

'Just so we're straight about things, Vivian,' he says calmly, 'I *have* moved on. I'm not living in the past, I'm living in Ibiza … *fulfilling* a career and leading a *fulfilled* personal life; both of which I could never have achieved with you. I'm where I want to be. You're merely the wrong turning I had to make to get here.' He enters the cubicle, slamming the door behind him.

I stand there for a few seconds. I try to sense what I should do next but all I feel is … *fucked*. This MDMA is stronger than any of the pills I used to buy from Jorge. His family must have made serious advances in their production line since my last visit. They used to churn stuff out of their cellar. Now maybe they have a NASA-style laboratory in the hills outside Santa Gertrudis. The music pumping out of the speakers starts to fade. I turn round and stand on my tiptoes to see what's happening. Barb and Maximilian are standing together on the podium. She is holding a microphone. He is swigging from a bottle of water. A distant curiosity suggests I should go over to join them but soon drifts out of my mind. I need to be on my own, in my own head; because that's the one place where, right now, reality is not happening. *Fucking-hell-I-am-fucked.*

As Barb's voice comes over the PA system, I start to walk away, through the garden and beyond the Bedouin tents. Passing the tool shed, I see Pedro at the window in his *Terminator*-style shades making a roll-up. I ignore him and the crack of thunder overhead and rush past. At the edge of the garden, I climb over the fence and make my way down a rough hillside pathway towards the beach. Then I get to another fence looped with barbed wire and climb through that. On the other side the hill is much more overgrown, but I scramble down it until I reach a large flat rock that looks out to sea. I sit down, then lie back and let the drugs continue to do what I have always used them for: to remove me from emotion. I was never one of those girls who went clubbing and hung out by the sinks in the ladies' toilet all night having heart-to-hearts about my life with random strangers. Even with my serotonin receptor gates wide open … I was closed. I was often shocked at how much personal information some women laid bare. Break-ups, abortions, abuse … no personal tragedy was too intense to share as they gurned and sucked on Chupa Chups. Two hours later, I'd return for another pee and they'd *still* be there. *For Christ's sake*, I'd think, *go and fucking dance!*

Another massive crack of thunder shudders through the sky. As it trails off I think I hear something. I sit up, yawn again and this time my ears pop pleasingly. I get to my feet and stand on top of the rock. Someone is standing at the top of the hill, on the edge of the garden, behind the perimeter fence. They are whistling as if searching for someone. They climb over the fence and start walking towards me, then they break into jog, soon they are running and I can see it is

Luke. Halfway down he slips over, loses both his flip-flops and slides down part of the pathway on his backside before getting up and sprinting the rest of the way in barefoot. The whole time he doesn't stop staring straight ahead. I jump off the rock and pelt towards him as fast as I can. The sharp stones cut through thc soles of my feet, but – and I know this sounds a bit *Angelina; the Billy Bob Years* – it is an enjoyable pain. He scrambles through the wire of the second partition, we collide and wrestle each other to the ground. We don't say anything as we rip off each other's clothes. Just as we've got naked a barrage of lightning forks ricochet through the sky and rain starts pouring down. Heavy droplets pound the ground around us splashing up into our eyes. Our behaviour is *feral*. It's the best four minutes of my l—

'Fuck, *Vivian!*'

'I am, I am, *I am* …'

Luke pushes me off him. 'No … your *leg*. Look, *fuck*!'

I look down. A four-centimetre square of skin is hanging off my kneecap; it's swinging like a cat flap, the bone visible beneath it. A thick trail of blood is snaking down my shin. Luke's right arm is also covered in blood. A spike on his bracelet has sliced through my leg. It doesn't hurt. Nothing does … but I can sense that is all about to change.

Luke jumps to his feet and scrambles a few metres back up the hill where his clothes are. He yanks on his jeans, wincing as he zips up the trousers over his still bulging crotch. Then he rips his jockey shorts apart and wipes his arm clean with one section before sliding back down to tie the other bit of material round my knee.

'That should stem the flow,' he says, giving the

makeshift tourniquet one last tug. 'Right, this is the plan. I'll go first, give me at least five minutes before you follow. Go straight to the house, round the back way so no one sees you. Tell one of the caterers you slipped and cut yourself on some glass. They'll find someone to sort out your leg.'

'But what ab—'

'I'll be in touch,' he says, his voice muffled as he pulls on his T-shirt.

He doesn't say anything else. He wipes the rain out of his eyes, then runs back up the path slipping every few steps. Halfway up he finds his flip-flops and I see him briefly assess any damage done to his clothes, then realign his bracelet. I'm not able to see if he turns round to wave goodbye because I am tripping. I am seeing the Olsen twins at New York Fashion Week. Their stick limbs and ginormous lolling heads are poking out of voluminous Gothic gowns like characters in a Tim Burton animation. They are pointing and laughing at me. Then, I am vomiting – violently. The consistency changes from watery and sweet to frothy and sour, and soon I am retching but nothing is coming out of me … except a haunting, strangulated howl.

CHAPTER THIRTY-SEVEN

Pedro finds me. Neither of us says anything. He carries me back to his shed, lays me down on a bed of compost bags and cleans the wound on my leg. As he is bandaging it up, I pass out.

When I come round he is gone. Sunlight is streaming through the dusty windows. It reminds me of the day I took Maximilian to The Red Lion. In a daze, I look round the shed. It is full of garden machinery and work benches with electric saws plugged in above them. On a long shelf at the side are dozens of seed trays full of germinating plants. Each one is carefully marked with a picture of the plant attached to a small stick in the corner. At the end of the shelf is a photo frame. The glass has cracked but you can still make out the subjects in the picture: Pedro and Maximilian. They are both bare chested and laughing, their arms casually draped round each other's shoulders. Maximilian's skin is pale and his hair is long – almost covering his pecs – so the shot must have been taken around the time he was starring in the *Orc* trilogy when he wasn't allowed to get a tan or a cut. Pedro is not wearing his *Terminator*-style shades. I had assumed his eyes would be dark but they are a bluey green; almost aquamarine, and are made even more striking by the intensity with which he is staring at Maximilian. But Maximilian is staring straight ahead … *into the camera.* Typical.

Pedro has left me two full bottles of water. I lever myself up from the compost bags, down about half a litre from one of them and tell myself not to fall into the 'introspection section'. It's pointless over-analysing things the other side of a drugs binge; it negates all the time you've enjoyed not thinking about anything. If you are going to use your mind in some way, everything you imagine must be painted with broad positive brushstrokes. Right now, I need to picture Luke telling Suki what happened; her understanding and resignedly travelling to mainland Spain to get that tattoo lasered. I also need to picture Luke accepting and not judging my arrangement with Maximilian. Then, I need to picture me explaining to Maximilian that despite everything I will honour my side of the deal until the end of the summer. Finally, I need to picture Luke and me using the money to set ourselves up for the future. I need to picture all of this, but at the moment I can only see the gilt framework. The canvas is worryingly blank.

The door of the shed creaks open. I shield my eyes and squint over.

'Pedro?'

'It's me, Barb.' No 'kiddo'. She steps in the room. She is wearing a black velour tracksuit and her bug-eyed Chanel shades.

'So, the, er, rain has stopped,' I mutter, for something to say.

'Yeah, it's stopped … but there's an almighty freakin' shit storm on its way.' Her tone is livid. 'I've been looking for you all night.'

'And now you've found me.' I sit up and examine my knee. Pedro did a good job. The bandage is clean; no red or crusty seepage. 'Barb, I'd drop the attitude if I were you. You're lucky I even stuck around for the party at *all*.'

'Oh, *really*. Why?'

I clear my throat. 'I would prefer to have that conversation with Maximilian first.'

Barb takes off her sunglasses. She appears to still be wearing her party make-up from last night. 'What conversation would that be?'

'You *know* which one.'

'No, I don't. Give it to me straight.'

'Okay, I'll give it to you *straight*. Maximilian *isn't*.'

She snorts at me. 'Sound the lunatic klaxon! Are you *crazy?* Maxy is one hundred per c—'

'Don't even attempt to bullshit your way out of this one, Barb,' I interrupt calmly. 'I saw him with Pedro the other night and I've figured it all out.'

Barb shifts from foot to foot. 'Okay, so he may like to experim—'

'Don't give me that "experimenting" bollocks, either. My mate, Roger – who I hasten to add is *out and proud* – says, "Bi now, gay later …".' I hold up my hand. 'But anyway, it is what it is. I know now. All I need to tell you is that I'm prepared to carry on the pretence, but I, er …' I pause, and attempt to get some initial brushstrokes on that canvas.

'I need an advance on my allowance.' The last of it went on the Roberto Cavalli leather ensemble. Luke might need some cash to help him move back.

But Barb doesn't even acknowledge my request. She sighs, pulls her BlackBerry out of her bag and passes it me. There is a blurry photograph on the screen.

'What's that?' I ask.

She sucks the air in through her teeth. 'I guess you could call it your P45.'

'You can't sack me.'

'I've got no choice,' she mutters.

I zoom in on the picture. It is a couple lying on a hill coiled round each other so tightly it looks like they are some bizarre two-headed mythological creature. It could be anyone, but I know it is me … *and Luke.*

'But we were on private property.'

'No, you weren't. You were quite literally on the wrong side of the freakin' fence,' mutters Barb.

'Who took it?'

'A Spanish pap …'

'You can buy it from him, though, right?'

'Too late. *The First* already have. You're on the home page of the website and front page of the print version. They had the decency to ask me for a statement at midnight, but I may as well have been putting a Mickey Mouse Band Aid on a shark bite.'

'What did you say?'

'That the engagement was off.'

'En … gage … *ment*? Whose engagement?'

Barb flops down on the compost bags next to me. Up

close, I can see how exhausted she is. '*Yours*. To Maxy. It was the climax to his speech. He was acting weird … over-emotional and blurted it out. It was trending on Twitter within half an hour … around the same time you were being papped banging the hired help.'

'Where is Maximilian now?'

'Hospital.'

'Hospital?'

She rubs her eyes. 'Yeah, he's in a mess. After the speeches he was sweating real hard so I told him to go inside and take a shower. But then his breathing went crazy. Before we even got near the villa, he collapsed … about three metres away from JP. Suki called an ambulance … the medics immediately recognised that he was on a freakin' TGI cocktail of uppers that had reacted with the downers he'd taken earlier for his nerves. His heart stopped twice.'

Mine is thumping. 'Oh my God, *no* … please, tell me he is okay.'

'He's regained consciousness but he's not in a great shape. He keeps swearing deliriously that he didn't touch anything and was drinking water all night. But we know he's lying.'

Shit. 'Do the, er, doctors still need to know what he has taken?'

'It would probably help, why?'

'It *could* have been MDMA. Mud. I think you … I think you call it "Molly" in the States.'

Barb cocks her head at me. 'Why do you say that?'

'Because … *because* … well, I, er, had some. He might have, er, had s—'

'Are you freakin' *out of your mind*? You gave Maxy narcotics on the biggest night of his career?'

'It wasn't my fault, Barb. I didn't *give* it to him. He must have picked up my bottle … this bottle of Evian that I'd put *some* … okay, a *lot* of… but it was meant for me … it was sitting on the bar … he must have drunk mine instead of his … it didn't even occur to me that he could have … I am so *so* sorry.' I jump up from the makeshift bed, wincing as I straighten my knee. 'I must go and see him. He's in the hospital in Ibiza town, right?'

'Forget it,' says Barb. 'I'm not letting you anywhere near him.'

'But he's my friend.'

'Friend? Ha!' She snorts again.

'Hang on a second, Barb, you have no right to make me feel guilty. You set me up. You *and* Nicholas … brainwashed me … I could have lost my mind.'

She glares at me. 'And you almost lost Maxy his life! One thing is for sure, he's definitely lost the *Truth* franchise.'

'And I suppose the latter is far more upsetting to you,' I snap back. 'Do you know what? No matter how many lies he has told me from the moment we met, I feel sorry for him. He thinks you and Nicholas care about him.'

'We *do* care. We've created the perfect life for him.'

'Bar the whole reliance on prescription drugs thing to get through any sort of mildly stressful situation, you mean? I'm not surprised he gets depressed. He's disorientated.' I get up. 'He is not who *you* say he is. He is not who *Nicholas* says he is. He is not who *he* says he is. His whole life is a lie.'

In that moment, I realise why Maximilian and I had got on so well from the start. Despite our lifestyles being worlds apart, our actual lives are very similar. They are both prevaricated. We havc both normalised entirely abnormal behaviour. I am the porker telling porkies. He is the actor always acting.

'That's how he wants it,' retorts Barb. 'I am simply there to facilitate that.'

'All you're doing is preventing him from being happy with someone.'

'No, I'm protecting him.'

'Don't be so paranoid. Not all his relationships will end up like his one with Nathan Eden did. There will be some-one who he can trust.' As I say this, Barb's eyes suddenly dart up towards the ceiling and she squeezes her Birkin tighter. The guilt is written all over her face. 'Christ, you made that up, didn't you? Nathan was never going to sell a story on Maximilian … you told him that so he would dump him.'

'I did what I needed to do. For him.'

'Or you, Barb? Was it for you?'

She doesn't answer this question. Instead, she puts her sunglasses back on. I barge past her towards the door.

'Where d'you think you're going?' she asks.

'To get my stuff.'

'You're not going back to the villa, kiddo,' she says firmly. 'Believe me, you don't want to see Nicholas, he doesn't know I've found you. I've organised a car to the airport. You need to make yourself scarce.' She hands me an envelope from her bag. 'There's your passport and a load of cash.'

I snarl indignantly at her. 'You can't tell me what to do any more, Barb. I don't want to leave Ibiza.' But then it occurs to me I don't have any way of contacting Luke or anywhere to go whilst I am waiting for him to try to get in contact with me. Maybe it would be better if I got home to Monday and waited there. 'I need to get changed. I can't fly home like this.'

'You'll have to buy something at the airport.'

'But they only sell tacky club-branded merchandise there.'

'You'll have to make do,' she says.

I follow her out of the shed and through the garden. Bar the Portaloos and one of the catering marquees still in situ, all the equipment from the party has been removed. After last night's rain, the skies are completely blue and it's already hot. I find myself picturing Suki … waking up at the finca, checking her phone, finding her inbox full of texts alerting her to what her boyfriend has done. She doesn't wake Luke immediately. She lies next to him for a few minutes, admiring the top job they made of the bedroom, pretending everything is fine, tears coursing down her cheeks. Then I picture Luke … eyes screwed shut, pretending to be asleep, not wanting to face anyone yet. Finally, I picture Maximilian … in hospital, the zigzag of a cardiac monitor flinching in time to his heartbeat, motionless. This time, all three portraits have been intricately painted and perfected. The oils are dry.

A taxi is waiting at the top of the drive. As I get in, Barb reaches into her bag and passes me a pack of chewing gum and a bottle of water.

'I'm genuinely sorry things had to end this way, kiddo,' she says. 'You were good to have around … and hey, I *was* listening to what you said back there. But in this game you can't trust anyone to play fair. *Silver's Golden Rule Number Three: Always remember, this isn't showfriends, it's showbusiness.* Call me if you need more cash.'

Terry meets me at Stansted. I am clutching two hundred cigarettes, my passport and the envelope Barb gave me. I am decked out from head to toe in Pacha merchandise from Duty Free. Everything I am wearing – flip-flops, baseball cap, hotpants and vest – is emblazoned with cherries. I also sprayed myself liberally with David Guetta aftershave so now as well as nervous perspiration, I also smell of party-starting house music with a commercial pop twist. Officials escort us through the airport, out of the staff exit and down into the car park where Terry's Citroën 2CV is parked. Monday is in the back, the picture of feline reproachfulness. He blinks slowly at me as I get in the passenger seat.

'Where's Alfie?' I ask.

'At Stephanie Beacham's Malibu condo …' replies Terry, in the same withering tone of voice he used when greeting me. 'He's with Carol, of course. I picked up some of your clothes from Maximilian Fry's house but I was in a rush and there wasn't a great deal of room in the car so I only filled one suitcase.'

'Okay, thanks. Probably a good thing you didn't get all of it as that wardrobe in your spare room is tiny.'

'That's not going to be an issue, Vivian.' He sighs heavily. 'I'm sorry but you can't stay with me. You know how territorial Alfie is, he won't tolerate Monday being on his patch. More to the point, the tabloid press are going to be all over you like a rash. I can't have them camped outside the agency, it looks so low rent. I have to consider my other performers.'

'Luke hasn't rung your office, has he?'

'No. But your mother did.' He pulls on his leather driving gloves and twists the key in the ignition. 'She's said you can stay with her for a bit, until all the madness blows over.'

'She did?' This surprises me and cheers me up at the same time. 'Wow, that's generous of her. I don't know whether it's a good idea, though. I really don't want to see Tracey or Carl. They won't hold back fr—'

Suddenly I'm distracted by activity in the wing mirror. At the back of the car park the lift doors judder open and a group of at least ten men tip out … photographers. They charge round, darting in and out of vehicles, shouting my name and letting off random flurries of flashes with their cameras. Monday starts clawing the base of his cat carrier. I fasten my seat belt.

CHAPTER THIRTY-EIGHT

After two and a half hours on the motorway, we turn off and drive through the progressively built-up countryside that borders the small town where my mother still lives. My school looks massive, which may sound weird because when most people revisit places they frequented as a kid they always comment on how Lilliputian the buildings seem. But because of the size I was *then* the environment *now* feels more Brobdingnagian.

We pull into a cul-de-sac that wasn't exactly plush when my family moved there twenty-five years ago. Now it looks knackered. Except for my mum's home at the end, that is. As far as the exterior is concerned, she is still flying the flag for a better Britain with newly pointed brickwork, a neat row of potting tubs camouflaging her swabbed-down dust-bins and a small but tidy flowerbed. The interior she gave up on a long time ago.

Terry hasn't even switched off the engine before my mother is out on the front porch. She gives him a polite wave and taps on the window to get my attention.

I open my door. 'Mum, I know this can't be easy for you so thanks for having me back ho- … here. I'm sorry if I …'

'Shush now. There's no need for us to discuss this, Viv.'

Her face, as usual, is calm, almost expressionless. 'I'm not here to judge, you know that. If anyone has got the right to offer an opinion it's Our Lord upstairs ...'

'In the loft?'

'There and *every*where.'

'Let's hope the Holy Ghost hasn't shown him a copy of the *The First*, then ...' I attempt to joke.

She offers a smile back, then her eyes dart up and down the street. 'Let's get you inside sharpish. Just make sure that cat is kept well away from the baby.'

'What baby?'

'Your new nephew. Tracey gave birth while you were away ... not the most pleasant labour, either, so no bickering with her, she's exhausted and needs all her energy to keep up with feeding times. Tea, Terry?' she offers through the windscreen, half-heartedly, knowing he will not take up her offer.

Terry turns to me. 'Vivian, I'm sorry things didn't turn out better with this whole charade, but—'

'Don't say I told you so.'

'I wasn't going to. I was going to say that it must be a relief that you can go back to being *you* again.'

But I don't need to, do I? I thought I might end up back there, but I won't. Because I'll be moving forward again ... with Luke. The scab on my leg is all the evidence I need of that, isn't it? I take Monday upstairs to my old bedroom. It's now a guest-room-cum-storage space for Mum's clothing catalogues, which date back to when we were kids. She never throws away a single issue. (Except the plus-size ones she used to buy my clothes from. They're long gone.) Safe to say, my mother has never been knowingly undersold on a nautical-style striped Breton sweatshirt or pair of fleece-lined house booties. The last time I slept in this room was the night before I left home.

I let out Monday from his carrier. As he pads around the room doing a series of his essential texture tests, my brother Carl arrives back from work. He steams into my room reading off a customised gold Samsung.

'*In a sensational sequence of events set to stun the world of showbiz, as Fry was announcing his engagement to Ward in front of an elite guestlist at his luxury Ibizan hideaway, she was enjoying a union of a different kind with the DJ hired by the multi-millionaire actor to provide the party tunes at the glamorous bash.*' Carl glances up at me. 'Vivian, you are *such* a dickhead. He's *minted*.'

'Ah, well, you can't force chemistry.' I shrug as breezily as possible. I never show vulnerability in front of my siblings. It was my default setting for survival as a kid. Like cobras, they would sense fear and go in for the kill. 'I don't have any regrets.'

'You're still a dickhead. D.I.K.H.E.D.' He spells it out.

At thirty-three Carl still lives here with Mum. He was a cocky little tyke when we were growing up because he was syphoned off from school to a professional soccer club and told he had the potential to become a star. But his burgeoning career was cut short by injury. Even though he now sells mobile phones, he still attempts to live like a top footballer: buying clothes that have a flammable-looking finish, making faintly sexist remarks and listening to wholly shit R 'n' B pop crossover chart hits.

'How long are you here for?' he asks.

'Don't know.' I shrug again, wondering if he will have the balls to admit flogging that set of pictures he took of me on the beach. 'It'll be fun for us all to spend some together, though, won't it? Tracey, too …'

He laughs. 'Yeah, 'course it will. You can only imagine how much more fun than usual she is since she's only been getting a few hours of sleep every day.'

I get to see exactly *how* fun my sister currently is after I've unpacked and got changed into a T-shirt and my original Joseph leggings. She is downstairs in the kitchen cradling the latest addition to her family and scoffing from a tin of Mum's homemade vegan shortbread. (Having had absolutely no problem feeding her family processed food when we were growing up, in the last decade my mother has become obsessed with the dangers of food additives and allergens. As far as she is now concerned, gluten and refined sugar have blighted the modern world a great deal more than terrorism and ethnic cleansing.)

'Hi, Tracey. Congratulations, on the little chap. He's a, er, *peach*.' He looks like an angry, miniature Winston Churchill.

She half-heartedly accepts my compliment with a nod. 'Look Vivian, I don't want to get into a row with you, I'm far too tired. But let's get a few things out in the open. Ma is not happy about all this drama. She may seem like she's handling it perfectly fine, but she's mortified.'

I know Tracey is right. My mother doesn't simply sweep 'issues' under the carpet, she will also metaphorically vacuum on top then lay down a rug for decorative purposes.

'I'm well aware it can't be easy for her, Tracey, but …' Fleetingly, I am tempted to blame her. None of this would have happened if she hadn't given that picture of me to *The First* at the beginning of the summer. But I don't want to give her the satisfaction of knowing it hurt me. 'I'll try to make things up to her as best I can.'

'And how will you do that? You barely know Ma any more.'

'That's not fair.'

'It's not about being fair, it's a fact. It's all very well you not wanting to be part of *my* life or Carl's. Sometimes even *I* don't want to be part of his life *or mine*. But you should respect Ma. I know she can be closed off, but that doesn't mean you should forget about trying to open her up. I can't remember when you last spent any quality time with her.'

'Come on, Tracey. You know it's always been diffic—'

'It was difficult when you were a *child*, Vivian. I accept that. You're an *adult* now; you should be *and want to be* responsible for other people. It's what defines being a grown-up.' She grabs a sterile wipe to remove some goo from her infant's mouth. 'Look, while you're here, just do us all a favour – but particularly Ma – keep yourself to yourself. Stay in the house and don't make anything worse … yes?'

My sister stares at me, her disapproval so apparent and unwavering she makes Carl's brief and chippy welcome feel like an elaborate UN-style olive branch. It's always been like this. She wasn't just *a* Daddy's girl, she was *our* Daddy's girl. She was the apple of his eye and he was the core of her being. Both saw me as the rotten fruit. When our father had his heart attack I knew Tracey would be looking to blame me, but I didn't realise quite how resolutely she did until years later when she was planning her wedding. She asked Carl to make sure I was sat to the far left of a pew so she didn't see me as she walked up the aisle *without* our father. I decided not to attend. To this day, I've never met her husband.

'I won't make anything worse, Tracey.'

'Good. At least, with you under house arrest, you can't ruin Saturday,' she adds, much more quietly.

'What's happening then?'

'Pa's memorial. He died fifteen years ago this weekend. Don't panic, none of us expected you to remember.'

She is right. I hadn't.

My mother walks out of the old downstairs loo where the freezer is, holding two packets of frozen vegetarian protein mince.

'I'm going to do a traditional bolognese,' she announces, as if Quorn was a staple of Italian cooking.

'Sounds delicious, Ma,' says Tracey. 'I was telling Vivian it's probably better she doesn't join us at the memorial. That's what we agreed on the phone, wasn't it?'

Mum twists round and gives me a weary smile. 'I thought you wouldn't want to, under the circumstances. I'll pass on your best wishes in a prayer. We're having it in the Alpha chapel off the retail park and then a spread afterwards on the chaplain's patio. Tracey is doing the flowers, I'm going to make a cheesecake, Carl is writing something to read at the service…'

'Who needs W. H. Auden …' I mumble.

'I want him to remember some of the lovely things we did,' continues Mum, snapping on a pair of Latex gloves and picking up an onion. '*All* of us together ... as a family.'

'We weren't exactly the Brady Bunch, Mum,' I sigh.

'No,' smirks Tracey, 'but you were the Brady *brunch* ... and lunch ... *and dinner!*'

My mother waves a vegetable peeler at her. 'Now, now ... I've already told Vivian not to bicker with you, so don't be poking her. Ephesians Chapter 4 Verse 31: *Let all bitterness, wrath, anger, clamour and slander be put away from you, along with all malice. Be kind to one another, tenderhearted, forgiving one another, as God in Christ forgave you.*'

When I go back upstairs Monday is asleep on the bed. As I sit down next to him I can see myself in the long mirror with my side profile in the extra mirror my mother had bolted onto the wall. I take a sharp breath. I do not see a thin woman in expensive leatherwear. I see a fat girl in her cheap school uniform, terrified. She is about to leave for school. Her hair is jet black. She started dyeing it when she figured the darker *any* part of her body was, the slimmer she might appear. But the contrast between her dark barnet and ashen – pre-fake tan era – face has simply made her look as if her two favourite things are listening to gothic rock and eating cake, only the latter of which is true. On her lap is a substantially packed lunchbox. The savoury one. The other, which contains all her sweet treats, is hidden in her satchel. She looks down at her watch. It is 8.07 a.m. She needs to start walking to school.

She will walk past her father's garage. He will stare at her as she does, and say nothing. In thirty-seven minutes she will be in the playground and the staring will continue. She will feel the eyes boring into her. But this time they will not be accompanied by silence. There will be horrible words to go with the stares. This doesn't stop until 4.13 p.m. when the bell will go. When she gets home, she will go to the kitchen and eat, then to her bedroom. Here she will sit down on the bed and catch herself reflected in those dual mirrors. Then *she* will do the staring. She'll stare until her eyes swim. Her eyes are swimming now.

I blink hard and repeatedly like Monday does, tell myself that what I am experiencing is a very bad comedown and lie flat. Terry cannot be right. I will *never* go back to being me. The lightning-shaped crack in the ceiling above my bed is still there. My mother has not attempted to have it plastered over. Either she can't be bothered or the damage to the structure is too deep.

CHAPTER THIRTY-NINE

Over the next few days I slip into a routine. After Carl has left for work and my mother has gone to her church group, I get up, make myself a black coffee, put on two of Carl's Kappa tracksuits over the top of each other and go for the burn. I run up and down the stairs, jog on the spot, do star jumps, lunges, press-ups, arm-dips and sit-ups for at least ninety minutes. I stop for another liquid breakfast. Then I repeat the routine for an equal amount of time … or as long as I can tolerate Carl's iPod library.

On the morning of the memorial I am woken by Carl using his electric shaver in the bathroom with the door open. He shouts down the stairs to ask Mum if she can press a shirt for him to wear with his suit. She must have a special low-temperature setting on the iron to deal with the man-made fibres he favours. NYLON / ACRYLICS / CRISTIANO RONALDO. I hear Monday outside my room, clawing on the tired sea grass matting that carpets the whole house. He loves it. To him it is not a dated design statement. It is the world's biggest scratching post.

My mother opens my bedroom door. She is wearing a dusky pink floral coat dress with matching lipstick.

'We're off in a bit, Viv.'

'Ah, okay. I hope everything goes … well, as, er, well as it can.'

'Mmm. Oh, I'm sure it will be fine. Is there anything you'd like me to add into the service?'

I try to figure out what *she* would like me to say, because not a single thought is in my head. 'What do you think?'

'Don't ask me, Viv. That's just silly. Either you know what you want to say or you don't. Oh, not to worry … there'll be more than enough of us rambling on. I'll be back before the reception to pick up the food. I've got the organic veggie man dropping off my weekly box later, so keep an ear out for him …' She goes to leave.

'Mum?'

She twists back round. 'Mmm?'

'It's fine to be sad, today, you know.'

'Mmm …' she says, for the third time.

I stay in bed until I know she and Carl are ready to leave. Then I hear my sister and her husband arrive with the new baby and their other coachload of offspring. From my window, I watch them drive away up the cul-de-sac and wonder what I should add to my exercise regime today. I jump out of bed, pull on my first layer of workout gear and zip into the bathroom. That's when I know I am about to faint. I grip onto the sink to steady myself, then slowly get down onto the bathroom floor and press my left cheek on the cold tiles until the nausea passes. But as soon as it does and I haul myself up, I feel dizzy again. Words and phrases are scrolling through my mind; all in bold Arial black. I recognise them. They are the Google alerts I had set up on my computer when I was addicted to the internet: *Nicole*

Richie, Zoe-bot, liquid only, celebrity fad, rapid loss, exhaustion, Cedars Sinai, crash diet, drop-a-dress-size, low carb, no carb, high protein, skinniest, thinspiration … DOUBLE ZERO.

Putting one hand in front of the other I crawl on my front down the stairs, along the hall, into the kitchen and over to the fridge. I haul myself up on to my knees and open the door … and come face to face with the strawberry cheese-cake Mum has baked for the memorial.

It has been removed from the tin it was baked in and is now sitting on a doily-covered glass plate – the large crystal one my mother had engraved for my father to commemorate a wedding anniversary. When she presented it to him, he gave her a kiss and then pretended he was about to hurl it out the window like a frisbee. My Mum *hooted* with laughter. He laughed too. There was not a trace of guilt on his face. It was almost impressive. Since my father died, the plate has only been used on the most poignant of occasions. The last time I saw it was at his wake. I remember piling it with sandwiches for guests and allowing myself to have a moment of triumph knowing I would not be having *one*. Each time I carried it back into the kitchen for replenishing, I admired my reflection in the hall mirror. It was the first time I had seen my family since leaving home. I was thin. But I looked even thinner on that day because I was wearing black.

A torrent of saliva pours into my mouth as I stare at the dessert. The digestive base is exactly one-fifth of the thickness of the filling, the strawberries have been sliced in half then laid out on the top in ever decreasing circles, with one whole strawberry-green leaves still attached – as the decorative centrepiece. I press for firmness with my index finger. Set perfectly. In one fluid motion I pull the cheesecake out of the fridge, place it down on the kitchen counter and select the pallet knife from the utensils pot intending to scrape off a *sliver* of vanilla cream. But I catch my reflection in the metallic surface of the knife so I throw it to the side, grab a wooden spoon and start eating.

I have no idea how many minutes later I get a moment of clarity, but when I do, the cheesecake is less of a pudding … more an open wound. I lift up the plate and examine the damage. A dollop of creamy filling and some squished fruit is all that remains. As I am staring at it, the doorbell rings. Panicked, I lurch forward. The dish drops onto the laminated concrete floor. The sound of breaking glass is partially muffled by the remaining ingredients. When the doorbell rings again, I am shaking, *terrified* by what I have just done; but I can't decide what is more terrifying: the broken dish or my broken resolve. The doorbell rings again.

I stick my head out of the kitchen door. 'Could you leave the vegetables on the mat, please?' I shout. 'I've just got out of the shower.'

The letterbox flips open, framing a pair of familiar deep brown eyes.

'For fuck's sake open the door, Vivian.'

CHAPTER FORTY

I'd tried to forget how it felt to be caught mid or post-binge. The self-loathing that is consuming your entire body immediately intensifies with the added embarrassment of someone witnessing your behaviour. How acute these feelings are depends on who has caught you. The more perfect that person is on the outside the worse you will feel on the inside. I shout back up the corridor.

'Go away, Maximilian, you're not coming in.' Any relief that he has obviously recovered is entirely overwhelmed by the discomfort I am feeling. 'I don't want to see you.'

'Don't be ridiculous, we need to talk.'

'Please, leave me alone.'

'I know you think I've played you a bit.'

'Played me a *bit?* Ha! I've been your very own human Stradivarius.'

'At least give me the chance to explain.'

'I'm not interested.'

'Stop being silly, Vivian. You are. You're simply afraid to let people tell you what they think in case they make you question yourself. You need to *stop* … and fucking listen.'

I hate that he may have an iota of a point. I scrape my hair back into a ponytail and walk up the corridor. Maximilian flips the letterbox shut and I open the door. He is wearing a boiler suit with a hard hat and carrying a tool box. Across the road I spot Payton sitting in the front of a white Ford Transit wearing a similar uniform. Maximilian rushes in.

'It's a disguise to put off the paps,' he says, slamming the door behind him. 'They're trailing me every time I leave the house. It's a fucking nightmare.'

I don't offer any sympathy. 'Wait here, I need to clean up something.'

But he follows me into the kitchen. As I walk in, I see Monday licking off cheesecake mixture from one of the broken shards of glass on the floor.

'No!' I shout, shocking myself with the volume. 'You'll cut yourself. *Leave it!* MONDAY!'

I have never seen him move so quickly. He actually 'darts' straight under the kitchen table and squishes himself next to the wall behind one of the wooden chairs. There is vanilla cream filling all over his whiskers but he is too confused by my outburst to lick it off. He blinks at me through the rungs of the chair for a few seconds, then scuttles out of the room.

Maximilian removes his hard hat. 'What happened in h—' Then he stops. He scans the open fridge, smashed plate and finally, the disgust written over my face. 'Ah, I see.'

'Go into the lounge,' I mumble.

I clear up the mess and carefully lay out each broken piece of the anniversary plate on a tea towel. I don't use the time to plan what I am going to say to Maximilian, because all I can concentrate on is the sense of compression in my hard distended belly and surrounding organs. This is how I spent so many years; focusing on what I had eaten or was about to eat. I avoided thinking about or being anything … other than *full*.

I find Maximilian in the pea-green corduroy-covered armchair; my father's favourite.

'I'll start, then,' he says. 'I'm sorry. *Really* sorry.' I am expecting him to elaborate but he doesn't. He merely shrugs, then adds, 'Your turn.'

'For what?'

'Apologising.'

'Fine. I'm sorry for what happened at your party. It was an accident, a bad one …' I begin, but the rush of sugar pelting round my system makes me seethe. At both me and him. 'But I think you'll find that the consequences of lying to people are never good, Maximilian.'

'*Vivian*, I did not intentionally try to dupe you. It was more a case of me letting things get out of hand. I developed genuine feelings for you – not in the way I have feelings for a … but … feelings none the less. And there was a part of me that thought we could make our relationship work for longer than originally planned. I swear to you; I was fully intending on explaining my *situation*, but before I was ready you got too close to the truth and I panicked. I thought you were about to figure it all out, and that's when I … well, you know, what I … *we* … did. It got messy and th—'

I cut him off. 'You know what, I'd like to give you the benefit of the doubt and say that you are certifiably nuts, but actually I don't think you are nuts at all – you're perfectly sane. You're merely self-indulgent. Your entire life is dedicated to keeping your name in lights. But I will give you one thing: you're very clever about it. It's always other people that have to suffer so you don't have to. It's *never* you.'

He shakes his head vehemently. 'Rubbish! Do you have *any* idea what I have had to put myself through? I'm a gay man in an industry that requires me to be a Bud-swigging, supermodel-fucking, buddy-hugging, heterosexual cliché if I want to ply my craft without restriction.'

'Don't give me all that craft bollocks, Maximilian. You do it because you're a show-off and an attention-seeker, otherwise you'd be happy doing amateur dramatics at a local village hall. You love the fame. You pretend you don't, but you do.'

'Wrong again. I explained this to you at the beginning – that night when we were outside Burn's, in fact, acting has always been the one constant in my life. It's what I turn to to make me feel alive. I can't have a relationship so I have acting. When there is someone who is *irrefutably* worth giving it up for, then I will. But until then acting remains my passion ... not that you would understand what it is to be passionate about *anything*.'

'What's that supposed to mean?'

He manages to look down his nose at me even though I am standing up and he is sitting down.

'I'll be honest, Vivian, I have *no* idea what it is you have a passion for other than your relentless quest to stay in control of your ridiculous eating habits. It *certainly* wasn't me.

Yeah, you fancied me, but you weren't in love with me. You merely liked the idea of 'us' because it was a fantasy in which you could escape yourself, but it was nothing to do with *me* as a person. Otherwise you would have confronted me at the villa as soon as you saw me with Pedro. You would have got angry, upset, violent even ... but you didn't say a fucking *word*.'

'How did you know I wasn't?' I am still processing what he said a few sentences back.

'Wasn't what?'

'In love with you.'

He doesn't skip a beat. 'Because you don't know how to love anyone, Vivian. You pretty much told me that yourself, so don't deny it. You're emotionally stunted.'

'For your information, I *do* now.'

Maximilian laughs dismissively. 'Oh right, yeah. That DJ guy ...'

'He's called Luke. And yes, *him*.'

'So, where is he, then?' he asks.

'Ibiza, probably ... or maybe, London. I don't know ...' I rub my knee where Luke's bracelet cut it open and knock the scab. It makes me wince. 'I'm waiting for him to get in contact with me.'

Maximilian throws his hands up in the air. 'You see! This is exactly my point. For fuck's sake, Vivian. If you want him, tell him. What you are afraid of? *Reach inside and pull out that truth.* Or maybe you're too shallow to store anything real.'

'Ha!' Now, I laugh. 'Here we go again. Christ, Maximilian, you have absolutely no self-awareness, whatsoever, do you? You accusing me of having no depth is like Anne Hathaway telling Katherine Heigl she's a little bland. At least I don't pretend to be anything other than what I am. Actually, I've just realised something: you're not a good actor because of something so honourable as having passion. You're simply an excellent liar.'

As I am thinking how appropriate it is that Maximilian should be sitting in the chair my father – suburbia's all time greatest liar – used, he jumps out of it. We are standing a foot away from each other now. He looks tired. I feel a flash of something other than rage and indignation, but just as quickly put it to one side.

'You lie to everyone, Maximilian,' I continue. 'Your fans, the press, me, Zoe, Pedro—'

'Pedro? He knows where we stand. It's a physical thing.'

'Not to him it's not. Can't you see he's crazy about you? He always has been. He's dedicated the last decade of his life turning your villa into a mini Marrakesh. Surely after the first batch of hand-dyed silk cushions were scattered it must have occurred to you he was erring on the side of *homemaker*?'

Maximilian wanders away from me up to the window, and stares out. 'I made Zoe a household name. She got what she wanted; and besides, she's over me now.'

'No, she isn't. She still feels bad about what she did. Not only did you let her feel guilty, you even let her get annihilated in the media for cheating on you, when you were with Nathan the whole time. Then, when *he* became surplus to requirement you let your manager beat him up. You're a coward who never fights their own battles.'

Maximilian turns round. I think he is about to say something else but then he walks past me towards the door and reaches down into his tool box. He pulls out a large brown envelope and clears his throat.

'Right,' he says calmly, 'we've established that neither of us are particularly functional human beings, so I think it's best that we don't make our individual conditions any worse by being in each other's lives from this point. Take this.' He throws an envelope onto the pile of newspapers on the coffee table.

'What's in there?'

'Amongst other things … a substantial cheque – I obviously don't do online banking – it's a form of encouragement for you to keep quiet. I wish I didn't have to give it to you, but I prefer to err on the side of caution. I think you'll find the amount more than persuasive.'

I laugh again. 'Are you taking the piss? You're worried I would *out* you? Is that the sort of person you think I am?'

He sniffs at me. 'I'm simply making sure you aren't tempted to. Barb assured me it wasn't your style, but personally, I think you can never be too fucking sure with *civilians*. Look at Nathan. He was easily bought at the right price. I'm sure you would be too.'

I stare at him. I don't know whether I am more irate at his assumption or at myself for giving him the grounds on which to make it. Shock and fury are searing through me. It's time to tell him Barb set up Nathan. Not because I want to do the right thing, but because I want to make him feel as wronged as I do.

'Actually, for your information, Maximilian, Nathan was n—'

But he interrupts me. 'While we're on the subject of *him*, it was me who put him in hospital, not Nicholas, I simply used Nicholas's phone. Nathan got what he deserved. So, as for me being a coward who can't fight his own battles, you got that wrong too. Goodbye, Vivian … best of luck in finding some semblance of integrity one day.'

Now, I choose to say nothing. I watch as Maximilian picks up the tool box, puts on his hard hat and walks out. As soon as I hear the front door slam, I go upstairs to the bathroom where I take four Nurofen out of my washbag and swill them down with water from the tap. Then I rifle through my mother's toiletries. In amongst the endless bottles of Bach Rescue Remedy and homeopathic oils I find some herbal laxative pills. I take four of these too. I feel better knowing that the cheesecake will be on its way out in approximately… I check the side of the packet: 'overnight' results are promised. So, one pill = eight hours. Therefore, four pills = one hundred and twenty minutes. Then I go into my room and pull out my clothes from the wardrobe ready to pack. I need to get back up to London. Maybe go and see Warren. Or Kevin on the building site. They will know where Luke is. Maximilian could not have been more wrong about me. I am not *that* person he said I was. *Am I?*

As I unzip my suitcase, I hear my mother arriving back from the memorial service.

'Hi, I'm upstairs. With you in a second …' I shout. 'I hope it went okay.'

She doesn't reply.

'Mum?'

When she still doesn't respond, I go downstairs. I find her sitting on the sofa in the lounge, her body rigid. The expression on her face is similar to how I imagine it would be if she had been on the receiving end of an air-gun pellet. She has Carl's silver Chromebook on her lap.

'Are you all right?' I ask.

She doesn't respond but clears her throat, all the while still staring at the computer screen. I go over and sit down next to her. She is looking at a piece of video footage with the volume off. I don't need more than a glance at the moving image to know what it is. It's me and Luke … in his room on the evening I went round there after my failed audition for *Surf Shack.* I leap forward and click the red 'X' in the top right-hand corner of the page. The monitor reverts to Carl's screen saver of a blonde glamour girl wearing a Manchester United strip with red over-the-knee socks. My mother and I are silent for a while. Her, no doubt wondering how in God's name she will hold her head high in church ever again. Me, wondering how much Luke must have hated me – *back then* – to have taken the tape out of my video camera before giving it back to me … in case it might be of use some day. But moreover, how much he hates me *now* to have actually sold it.

'Mum, I'm sorry…'

Gently, she places the Chromebook onto the coffee table.

'Shush. Like I've always said, Viv, I am not here to judge. I merely wanted to check if it was true. I was aware of people gossiping while we were waiting to have the service. Tracey and Carl had hoped I wouldn't find out. Did the organic vegetable man c—' She stops. 'I'm going to freshen up, and then you can help me get the party food ready.'

'Mum, please, listen for a second. You need to let me apologise. I did *not* put that on the internet, I swear. Someone that I thought I could trust has let me down.' I swallow hard. 'I had no idea he was capable of doing something as bad as this.' But now I know I am capable of bringing out the absolute worst in someone.

'Viv, enough. Romans Chapter Four: *Blessed are those whose lawless deeds are forgiven, and whose sins are covered; blessed is the man against whom the Lord will not count his sin.'*

'Mum! Quit with the biblical gobbledygook. It's a work of fucking fiction. Not real life … can't you see I'm upset? You must be upset too. We can't just ignore it …' Out of frustration I add, '…like you do with everything else that happens in this family.'

'What's that supposed to mean?'

'We never talk about anything.'

'And you want me to start by chatting about this?' She almost laughs as she jumps up. 'I'd rather not, thank you, Viv. It really isn't any of my business, nor do I want to make it as such. Now, the wheat-free vol-au-vents are in the pantry and the cheesecake is in the fridge. It's already on a plate.'

Christ. 'Mum, listen … about the cheesecake … I had an accident … seriously, can we *not* talk about the food right now, I need t—'

'What sort of accident?'

'I ate some of it.'

She gives me one of her weary smiles, the same one she used to offer me as a teenager whenever an awkward situation arose that was somehow related to my fatness. She meant it to make everything okay, but without fail it made everything worse.

'Not to worry, we've got more than en—'

I interrupt. 'And I dropped the plate.'

'The plate?'

Immediately, she marches into the kitchen. I find her standing with her hands clasped to her cheeks staring at the pieces of broken glass on the kitchen table.

'*Our* plate ...' she mutters to herself.

'I know it looks beyond hope, Mum, but I'm pretty sure I could fix it with some Super Glue,' I reassure her. 'The pieces are fairly big.'

She glances sideways at me. 'Get me some newspaper from the lounge. I'll wrap it up and put it out for the bin men.'

'Don't do that. At least, let me tr—'

'Viv! I said, *get me some newspaper!*' Her voice rises and cracks.

When I don't move, she barges past me. I follow her back into the lounge. She grabs a few copies of the *Express* from the coffee table. As she does, the envelope Maximilian gave me falls to the floor. His cheque and a sheaf of photos slide out. The first ones I see are those that have already been in *The First* and the rest are more of the same – each capturing me at my biggest and saddest. I am wondering how Maximilian got them back for me, when I realise something. My siblings couldn't have been present when all of them were taken. Only one person was.

'*Mum?* These pictures …' I wave them at her. 'They're all yours, aren't they? How did they end up in the newspaper?'

'I didn't sell them if that's what you're thinking,' she snaps, but then grimaces. 'However, I *may* have been a *little* bit naive. That nice girl you went to school with nipped round at the beginning of the summer asking if I had any snaps of you.'

'*Who?*'

'Katherine … or Kate as she was back then.'

'*Kate?* Kate Summers?'

'Mmm, that's her.' Suddenly my mother's tone changes and she reverts to her standard plateau of phlegmatic calm. 'Would you believe she's *still* Summers? I'd have thought she'd be married by now – surely, she would have been inundated with offers. Didn't some boy at your school propose to her? Such a pretty thing in those days, wasn't she? Lovely hair. Anyway, she said the snaps were for a collage to mark the school's centenary – she's an artist now, doing quite well in local circles, by all accounts. She was tracking down pictures of everyone in your year.'

'And you believed her? Mum, she hated me … bullied me for years.'

'How would I have known that?'

You could have *asked!* An inner voice screams this but the outer one stays mute.

'Look, it was a mistake, Viv.'

'A mistake?'

'Oh, go on then …' My mother sighs and walks back over to the sofa where she sits herself down again. 'Get it over and done with and call me a bad mother like you usually do.'

'I've never done that.'

'It's what you think, though, isn't it? That's why we barely see one another. It's fine, though. You obviously still need someone to blame.'

'I have never blamed you for anything.'

'I beg to differ. Other people blamed me too. They saw the size of *you* and saw *me* as a bad mother. I tried to be a good one, to treat you all equally. That's why I took those pictures even when you asked me not to. I needed to collate my own evidence that I had *three* children, not *two* … proof that I loved all of you. But I'll admit something. That day you ran away, I'll never forget looking in your wardrobe and seeing it empty. For a moment I was pleased that you weren't in the house. You cast such a large, dark shadow over it for such a long time. See? Not only am I bad mother but I'm a bad Christian too.'

'I understand you needed a break,' I say.

'Your father didn't,' she replies plainly. 'For some absurd reason he blamed himself for your departure, Viv, when all he had ever done was try to provide for your future. You made him very sad …'

I stare at her, desperate to explain how *he* made *me* feel – but the tears in her eyes show me how sad she *still* is, so I don't.

But then her expression changes. She becomes focused. 'Well, you made him sad*der*,' she rephrases. 'He was sad *before* you left. He was sad with me. He must have been,' a pause, 'to have had so many affairs with so many different women.'

I step back. 'Oh my God, Mum … you *knew*? I didn't think you had any idea that he was chea—' I can't say the word to her face.

She looks away from me. I watch her eyes shoot around the room, taking in all the framed photographs of her and my father: on their wedding day, on honeymoon, in hospital with Tracey, Carl and I as newborns, and finally us all sitting on packing boxes just hours before we moved to this house. My father is slightly blurred as he missed taking his place before the 'stand by' light went off.

My mother gets up from the sofa. She takes a couple of pinched breaths and re-tucks her shirt into her skirt even though it hasn't come out.

'I'm popping back to the chaplain's house now,' she says.

'Mum, *really* … we can*not* leave this conversation.'

'We can, Viv. There is nothing you could say to me that I don't know already.' She walks out of thc room. But then she sticks her head back round the door. 'And there is nothing you could say to me that would soften the *hard* fact that, clearly, you have always known about your father's liaisons but were too weak to tell me the truth. But I'm not upset with you. It is clear who your weakness was inherited from.' No pause this time. *'Me.'*

She heads to the kitchen. I go to my room to continue packing. But I don't rush this time. I want to soak up the last few moments I will ever have in this house because I know I won't be coming back … and I will need to remember why this is the best for everyone. When I get downstairs she is loading trays of food into the boot of her Peugeot. The shirt she is wearing is now patchy with sweat. I stand at the open kitchen window, my whole body numb, bar the satisfactory twinge in my stomach where the laxatives are beginning to kick in. My mother gets into the car, yanks the seat belt over her chest and turns the key in the engine. She never plays music in the car, but as soon as she spots me at the window, she bends down to press play on the stereo. Some deplorable vocoder-driven number one blasts out where Carl has been using the car before her. Then she peers in the mirror, smooths back her hair and releases the handbrake. It is only then that I notice Monday on the pathway behind the porch, pottering back home from the next-door neighbours'. No doubt he was badgering them for a sympathy snack after I shouted at him. I guess he's decided to forgive me because it's time for lunch. Head held high, tail at a perfect perpendicular angle to his back, tummy swinging from side to side, if he could whistle he would be. He pauses briefly to rub his head on a wooden plant tub.

I smack my hand against the window. '*Wait!* Don't move the car! Stop! *Mum!*'

But she can't hear me. I see her lips moving as she mutters something to herself and she turns up the music, drowning me out even more. I run out of the kitchen down the hallway and onto the porch.

'No! *Stop! PLEASE.* Mum! DON'T!'

I hurl myself towards the bonnet of the car but she backs up at full speed. I stumble to the ground, smashing my knees into the concrete and watch as Mum's car crashes into next door's wheelie bin and a row of her wooden plant tubs; scattering earth, geraniums and rubbish all over the pavement. She crunches the gears, then pulls out onto the cul-de-sac and accelerates up the street, the *booosht boomsh boomst* of urban pop making the car vibrate. I crawl over to the pathway. That's when I feel it: an emptiness in my heart that is far more painful than any fullness I have ever experienced in my stomach. Monday is lying on his side with his white paws neatly tucked under his chin amongst the contents of the bin. I immediately pick up an empty packet of fish fingers and a used can of tuna into the road, knowing he will hate the smell, and crouch down next to him. A tiny trail of blood is trickling out of his nose and down the crevice in the path but his eyes are glassy and wide. It's as if he is giving me one of his silent lectures. He only needs to blink.

But he doesn't, and I start to cry.

PART FOUR

CHAPTER FORTY-ONE

'I don't know what I'm doing, Vivian.'

'Don't be silly. You're Adele Pritchard. Of course you know what you're doing. *It's what you do.* You invented the concept.'

'That's what you think. It's what my parents think. It's what my fiancé thinks. It's what everyone at work thinks, it's what he or she probably thinks …' She rubs her ivory-silk-covered stomach. The bump is obvious now. 'And I've done a fine job so far of making sure you all do. But what happens if I get exposed as to who I really am? *Someone who doesn't have a fucking clue.* Because I can see her. *Me.* Taking four hours to leave the house; one minute to get my clothes on, one minute to consider applying make-up but not bothering … and three hours fifty-eight minutes packing one of those gigantic infant travel bags, panicking that I might forget some essential bit of plastic or cloth to keep my child alive. I'll be *that* neurotic mother, and *then* … I'll be *that* neurotic wife who won't let James turn on the car engine before I've spent twenty-seven minutes re-clicking, then un-clicking, then re-clicking the belt on the baby seat to ensure our first born isn't going to fly through the windscreen as soon as we brake at a traffic light.' She gasps for breath. 'James *knows* this is what I am going to become. It's obvious. That's why he booked this …'

Adele grabs the horseshoe-shaped card sitting on the dressing table in our hotel suite, which was delivered by the concierge last night. It's from James. Inside are two tickets to a purpose-built resort in the Seychelles for them to use after the baby is born. (It's six star so there is no *Kidz Klub!*, but an 'interactive and educational daily child care service'.)

'He thinks I am going to be *so* neurotic that the only overseas trip I will be able to handle from now on is an *all-inclusive* one … that I won't even be able to handle the stress of more than one location or more than one twatting bill!'

I rub her shoulder. 'Shush, Dels. You will be a *wonderful* wife and a *wonderful* mother … and today will be the most *wonderful* day.' I learnt from the hair and make-up people who were with us earlier that 'wonderful' is *le mot du jour* at a wedding. It must be used whenever anyone engages the bride in conversation.

Adele shakes her head at the reflection of us both in the long gilt-edged mirror.

'Stop it, Vivian, you've never used a platitude in the entire time we've known each other, so don't start now. For just *one* minute I need you to be *you* … not my bridesmaid.' She dabs at the classic bride up-do (soft tendrils round face and loose chignon at the back as standard) and then her eyes. 'Tell me what you really think.'

'I think you've got what you always wanted.'

'But maybe I only wanted that because I was worried about what would happen to me if I didn't,' she shrieks. 'It's safe, *normal* to want what I am about to get. It sounds corny, but that's why I left drama school. It was all about believing in something outside of normality … something dangerous; your dreams.' She turns to me and clasps my hand. 'I wish I had been more like you and ended up taking …'

'A substantial amount of recreational drugs and never really applying myself?' I smile.

She tuts at me. 'No, *chances!* Come on, Vivian. You'd have hated my life … working silly hours, mortgaged up to the hilt, diving into one relationship after another. Don't get me wrong, I love James so much it makes me feel sick to think I may not have found him … but, flipping hell, look at my track record. I'm so … *needy*. Do you realise that since the age of nineteen there has not been *one* day where I haven't been obsessing over a man. Screw-it Stuart, that Gatecrasher kid, the compulsive liar whose real name I never found out, Rex who fell asleep in the dog basket, Johann from upstairs …'

'The German architect? You *didn't*?'

'I did.'

'But he's m—'

'Married. I know. I was out of order. He was a prick. All of my exes have been. But I would have stayed with *any* of them if they hadn't dumped me. The thought of not being with someone – it doesn't terrify me, it terr*orises* me. Last night, I cried myself to sleep thinking about something bad happening to James. I'm *so* scared of being … *alone*.'

I smooth a loose tendril back behind her ear. 'Shush now,

Dels. You're getting yourself into a tizz … or rather, today we have to call it "jitters", don't we? Look, everyone is scar—' I stop, jolted.

Adele squints at me with watery eyes, waiting for me to continue or elaborate, but I can't be bothered. The past few months have shown me that trying to address *why* you are *who* you are is pointless. By that I mean, if you are fucked up … *you're fucked up.* Don't bother trying to be normal or normalise your behaviour, because you will always be abnormal. Don't fight it. You won't win the battle; you may well lose your mind.

I look away from her and scan the huge, sumptuous suite we are in, taking in all the wedding paraphernalia. Protective zip bags draped over the four-poster bed, presents stacked in the throne-style armchair (none from me until I get some money), cardboard hat box on the coffee table, a velvet jewellery case (containing a locket belonging to Adele's mother, which used to be *her* mother's as well as *her* mother's before that), and the vast vase of flowers delivered by her father this morning. Through the open double doors at the back of the suite, I can see the room where I attempted to sleep last night. On the floor next to the single bed is a bowl of half-eaten plain yogurt, various sticky tubes and un-lidded pots of make-up, my Nokia with a flat battery, a depleted foil tray of Nurofen, plus a screwed-up latex glove that I used to get rid of a few streaks this morning.

Adele touches my arm softly. '*Every*one is scared? Including y—' This time *she* stops. 'You've covered up that pretty well.'

I turn to face her square on. 'That would be thanks to St Tropez Whipped Bronzing Mousse. It gives the thickest, most even coverage. The original formula, though, not the Every Day range where you build up the colour. Life's too short for a gradual tan, Dels. Understand?'

She smiles at me as she pulls the lace veil down over her face. 'I do.'

And then she says it again. At 1.49 p.m. in Marylebone Town Hall. By which time Adele is back *in the zone*. There are more tears, but these ones don't mess up her make-up. Very Naomi Watts. As James and Adele are pronounced 'man and wife', I am staring at the bottom of the leg on the chunky wooden table in front of them, which has been subtly wedged with a folded-up piece of paper to stop it from wobbling. I wonder how many other bridesmaids have used this bit of faulty woodwork as a focal point to distract them from the registrar's address and/or their dress. In my case, a thick – almost matted – silk (the type with those bobbled bits) in a fecal shade of brown; with a bow above the bustle. I don't simply look like shit. I look like gift-wrapped shit.

The wedding party leaves the ceremony room to a steel band playing Mariah Carey's 'All I Want for Christmas Is You', then we all shiver on the stone steps outside for photographs in the falling snow. I engage in lots of small talk with people I have never met before. I keep the conversation strictly focused on the ceremony and/or Adele. 'Wasn't it? Really quite wonderful …'/ 'Doesn't she? Absolutely wonderful…' repeat to fade. I try to avoid people who know who I am, or rather anyone who knows who I might have *been*. The ones who do catch me, ask after my well-being in the same way: head cocked to one side on the 'how', a heavy emphasis on the 'are', a strained smile after the 'you' and a slightly uncomfortable pause before my name. Those with a bit of social sensitivity, that is.

'Filthy whore!' chortles the best man, crawling his fingers round my shoulder and huddling in closer, even though the photographer hasn't asked him too. I can smell brandy and damp dog. 'I thoroughly enjoyed your little foray into the adult entertainment market, Vivian. Any plans for a sequel?'

'Piss off, Toby.'

'Now, *now* ... be nice. Remember today is not about us, it's about Jimbo and Delsie. That said, who knows what may happen after a few cheeky glasses of champers. They say the best man always gets his pick of the bridesmaids ... and since you're the only one, it could be your lucky day.'

I glance down at Toby's hand. His digits are purple and plump like the sausages that Roger and Pete buy from their local artisan butcher. Round his wrist is an antique gold watch with a very tattered leather strap – clearly a family heirloom that has fallen victim to successive generations of over-excited chocolate Labrador puppies. The Roman numerals read two thirty. I visualise the corner of the thick cream wedding invitation I received way back in the summer. *Carriages at 1 a.m.* Ten and a half hours to go. I feel guilty ... wishing away the day. But wanting to speed up time is part of being abnormal ... the sooner 'things' are over, the quicker you get back to being on your own; the less normality there is to compare yourself against.

I gasp faux-delightedly at Toby. 'Oooh, you and me?

Wow! There was me thinking that Christmas wishes don't come true. Looks like Santa Claus got my letter.'

'That's the spirit, Vivian. I know we've had our differences in the past, but pastures new and all that. Let's face it, I've got enough of them. Six hundred and twenty acres on the Kent/Sussex border at the last count. Ha!' He winks at me. As he walks off he adds, 'I've got some delish hokey-cokey for later. You should have a toot. It'll perk you up.'

Melanie swoops in. She is swathed in multiple pashminas. I bet she was thoroughly giddy as she dressed this morning. For the pashmina fan, a winter calendar packed with smart social events must hold the same level as excitement as the annual development and spread of new ice in the Antarctic for a polar bear.

She cocks her head at me. 'How *are* you …' She adds a strained smile and pauses slightly. '…Vivian?'

'Enjoying the day,' I tell her emphatically.

'Oh, that's *great*,' she says. 'It's only that we *all* heard on the grapevine that you haven't been too good since, well … all that … *exposure*. Not that you should be paranoid. I mean, *no one* has been gossiping, just the odd *very* concerned *group* email has winged its way round us girls. When you didn't show up for the hen weekend – given that you're Adele's only bridesmaid – we were worried you might not c—'

'I'm here now.' I sense her building up for one of her usual digs, and clench my jaw.

'Yes, you *are*. So, let's hope you continue to enjoy the day.'

'Why wouldn't I, Melanie?'

The photographer approaches and indicates for us both to pose. Melanie smiles for the camera, baring her teeth as if about to floss.

'Well,' she replies, 'it's just that sometimes other people's happiness can push one over the edge.'

The camera flashes. The photographer makes a flapping gesture with his hand to indicate he wants another couple of shots. I use the time to conjure up some sort of disparaging and defensive remark to make back at Melanie. But as the camera flashes for a third time, I notice Melanie isn't staring into the lens, she's staring into the distance. I also notice her husband isn't here.

CHAPTER FORTY-TWO

The ground-floor restaurant at Burn's has been transformed into the winter wonderland that Adele had dreamt of. There is fairy-light-encrusted holly crawling up the walls, candles twinkling on the tables, deep 'snow' on the floor, bracken laurel wreaths on the back of each chair, crystal pendants hanging from the ceiling and ice sculptures of mythical creatures in the centre of each table. The wedding planner (C. S. Lewis?) may have cost her 'more than a new kidney', but when Adele walks in and sees the decoration she does actually gasp with the gratitude of a long-term organ-transplant patient being told a donor has finally become available, so maybe the price was fair. Roger isn't quite as chuffed.

'Dane should have reined her in a bit,' he mutters to me, as he receives guests in the foyer. 'Burn's is meant to be a *sophisticated* private members' club, not some tacky theme park. I've never seen this space look so grotty.'

'I think you mean *grotto*.' I sip from my glass of water. 'Where is he?'

'Setting up the first-floor bar for a private do. Sophie Carnegie-Hunt has booked it. Birthday bash for one of her clients.'

'Ugh, really?' The thought of facing Sophie, high on bullshit, Christmas cheer and eggnog … 'What about Tabs?'

'In later. She's going to love all this.' He gestures at the whimsical decoration.

'Yeah, it's probably what the inside of her head looks like.'

'So …' He peers at me. 'What's the inside of yours like today? You're okay being back out in the real world?'

'It's all good,' I tell him, uncomfortable with the amount of concern he has given me already.

I've been staying with Roger for the last few months. He had only landed from Turkey when I called to tell him about Monday. Immediately, he drove down to my mother's, equipped with a cream cashmere blanket and a big wooden box lined with packing straw. I put Monday in the box and tucked the blanket around him. After that I didn't touch him because I knew how much he hated being disturbed whilst asleep. Roger and I made the return journey to London in silence, but every time we stopped at a set of traffic lights he sighed empathetically. Whenever I tried to apologise for being such a mess over the summer he smiled and told me I always have been. By the time we got to his house in Islington, Pete had already dug a deep grave at the back of the garden, next to the willow tree he planted when he and Roger got married. He told me he would plant something for Monday over the top of the grave. 'Something orange,' he said.

'Listen, Rog,' I continue, 'you know I really apprec—'

'Stop. You've already thanked me enough. Now, quit

being so stoic and amenable … it doesn't suit you. Speaking of which …' He points at my dress and raises his eyebrows, before turning to welcome more guests.

'Bastard!' Someone coughs loudly behind me. 'How dare someone be so rude about your frock? Now we've got nothing to look forward to doing when we get drunk later. Ha!'

'Hi, Harriet … how's things?'

'Fab!' she gushes, and gives me a surprisingly warm hug. 'I could have put money on Adele putting you in brown, the crafty witch. It wouldn't be a wedding without a pigment war between two bezzie friends!' She nods at her lad-mag journalist boyfriend. 'You remember Vivian, don't you, Stephen? She's Adele's bridesmaid today.'

He smiles at me sympathetically and taps my glass. 'I'd better get you something to take the edge off, then.'

'I'm fine with water, thanks,' I tell him.

The doctor said that consuming alcohol wasn't the best idea whilst I was getting used to the antidepressants he has given me. At first, I wavered about taking 'happy pills' because of the possible side effects I'd read about. But I discussed it with Roger and he quite rightly pointed out that I have spent half my adult life enthusiastically necking most sorts of drug when passed to me in a not-quite-converted-abattoir by some sweating, hollow-eyed raver, so it was a bit rich that I was suddenly introducing a quality control filter with something prescribed at a surgery by a medical professional. Besides, I didn't want to be Adele's 'something blue'.

Harriet bursts out laughing again. 'Don't be ridiculous,

Vivian. You can't get through today without alcohol. It is a proven fact that every hour spent at a wedding when you're not boozing is the equivalent to seven hours of real time. Let's start with a voddy on the rocks.' She shoos her boyfriend over to the bar and shouts after him, 'Make them doubles!' Then she turns back to me. 'So, I've got exciting news … we're *leaving*.'

'Where to?'

'LA.'

'On holiday?'

'Nope, moving out there. Stephen got headhunted for a job with some mobile phone company download provider. They supply the usual aspirational blokey lifestyle crap: sexy women, hip hotels, sharp suits, decent kitchen knives, cool beards … blah blah blah. He got flown out for an interview last month. It's all happened pretty quick.'

'But what about *Surf Shack*? Aren't you going to shoot a second series?'

'Yeah, they are. Without me, though.' She shrugs breezily. 'I'm sure they'll come up with a totally plausible reason as to why "Debbie" has abandoned her only child. Nice excuse for a controversial social services plot line that might get its own late-night spin-off. Anyway, it's over. *I'm* over.'

I shake my head at her. 'I can't believe you're giving up the role.'

'Oh, I'm not only giving up the part, Vivian. I'm giving up acting. I'm sick of the whole bastardy thing. Do you realise I went to my first audition aged ten? That's twenty-six years ago. For most of that time I've been in a pretty vile mood; constantly worrying about my complexion – first acne, then sun damage, now wrinkles … and the rest of thc time all I've been doing is carping about Sienna Miller. I mean, what has she ever done to me? Secretly, I *adored* her when she did the whole boho thing. Outside of castings, I *always* wore a fur gilet and a low-slung studded belt. The truth is, I can't be doing with the competition any more. It would be even worse in La La Land. All the older actresses over there are on a constant conveyor belt of surgical procedures to keep them looking like teenagers. You know Selena Gomez is actually forty-three? Ha! Anyway, what about you? No issues with all that drama that happened this sum—'

I don't let her finish. 'Nope.'

'What are your plans now, then?'

I scratch my neck. 'You know what I'm like, Harriet, scheduling stuff is not for me. That's what is so *exciting* about the future, isn't it? You don't know what it holds. The fact that anything could happen is … *exciting*. Personally, I'm …' I stop. My temples feel tight. The sound of my enthusiasm is giving me a headache. I haven't got any Nurofen.

'*… excited?'* suggests Harriet. She yanks my hand away from my neck. 'Stop scratching, you'll make it sore.'

'It's not hurting me. So, er, where are you sitting for lunch? Are we together?'

'Don't be silly,' she replies. 'You'll be on the top table.'

I hadn't thought about that. If there was ever a more exposed set-up to be served a meal, it is the top table at a social function: facing a room full of people and a flamboyant four-course menu. I go onto autopilot. As soon as we are called to sit down, I arrange crockery, condiments, fizzy water, glassware and a flower arrangement in front of my place mat to obscure the other guests from witnessing my lack of cutlery-to-mouth action. Adele's father – who I am next to at the far end of the table – doesn't notice either. He is too busy being proud of his daughter.

After dessert – a pot of white chocolate soufflé served under a sugar cage with a blob of cranberry coulis and a heart-shaped vanilla shortbread – has been served, James stands up and tings his champagne flute to signify the start of speeches. I glance at Mr Pritchard's Longines watch. The time is seventeen minutes past six. Six hours, three minutes to go.

'I never used to be a fan of Christmas,' begins James, his nerves are tangible. 'It is the, er, Nicole Scherzinger of seasonal holidays: unavoidable, over-hyped and we have been fed the idea that is a whole lot more appealing than it actually is.' Everyone laughs and he adds as an aside, 'I would like to thank Vivian for that opening line.' He smiles at me. 'But of course, my attitude to the festive season will now change, as my wedding anniversary will be Christmas Eve. Actually, the rest of the year will be pretty great too … because I will get to spend every day with Adele.' He chokes emotionally as he says her name and takes a deep breath. 'Finding the love of your life is not always easy …'

Toby pipes up, 'Delsie was, though. If my memory serves me correctly it only took you one dinner and two cheeky bottles of *vino blanco* before you got a peep at her lady garden.'

Anyone who knows Toby roars with laughter. Everyone else shifts awkwardly in their seat.

Mrs Pritchard nudges her husband. 'Hardly that exciting, I wouldn't have thought,' she whispers. 'She only had a few herb trays on the patio outside her old flat in Bayswater.'

'I think she'd had some mini bay trees put in by then, Frances,' replies Mr Pritchard, patting his wife's hand, 'enhanced with some subtle topiary.'

'Didn't take Jimbo long to plant his seed either, dirty bugger!' adds Toby, entirely but predictably unnecessarily.

I look over at Adele. She is giggling, her eyes are twinkling. I think she may have had more than her pregnancy quota one unit of Pouilly-Fumé.

James turns to Toby. 'Mate, I know it's going to be difficult, but please, just for today, don't be a *complete* plum.' He grimaces, and everyone laughs again. 'Anyway, back to Adele; my beautiful wife …' He stares down at her as she drains her glass. 'Or rather, my beautiful and apparently-not-concerned-about-getting-a-bit-tiddly-despite-carrying-our-offspring wife.' More laughs and giddy woops. 'To be honest, there isn't anything I need to say now that she doesn't know already, but today is all about letting everyone *else* know how I feel.'

'James!' Adele grabs his arm. 'Don't get too mushy …'

'Bad luck, hon,' he says gently. 'You got a Barbadian steel band reinterpreting classic pop songs with a Caribbean flavour *and* ice-shaped unicorns, so I get to be slightly sentimental.' He looks back out at the room, this time with confidence. 'The thing is, I love Adele. Understandably, a few of you may have thought we were rushing into things getting engaged after six months, but I didn't see the point in waiting. The moment we met, I saw my future …'

I pour myself a glass of San Pellegrino agua mineral.

'… and suddenly, my past made sense. Because I realised that *all* of it – the good stuff,' he smiles at his foster parents beside him and his brother on a table at the front, 'and the bad – had been leading up to that point. As a child I never thought I would get the chance to be so happy. For that, Mrs Pritchard-Hart,' he sits down and takes Adele's hand, 'I thank you.'

Adele grabs James's face and kisses him. There is a lot of clapping and cheering. Most of the women in the room are dabbing at their eyes with their napkins. Melanie is steely faced, twisting a tassel on one of her pashminas. I drink my water and tentatively tap the sugar work over my pudding with a fork, wondering how much pressure the brittle cage will take before it crack. I'm sure the room is getting hotter. It must be all the candles.

Toby jumps up. 'Right,' he bellows. 'That's the namby-pamby stuff out of the way, let's get this party started! Awoooaaaggghhh!'

Adele lets go of her husband. 'Sit down, Toby,' she says, and waves over at one of the wedding planner's assistants hovering at the side of the room. 'We're doing Skype messages from absent friends before you. Is everyone cued up ready to go?' The assistant nods at her.

'Skype?' Mrs Pritchard is puzzled. 'Whatever happened to a good old-fashioned telegram?'

Adele tuts at her mother. 'No one does telegrams any more, Mops. Skype is so much easier. Besides, I haven't spent six thousand pounds on a wedding dress and another one and a half on a hair stylist and make-up artist recommended by *Harper's Bazaar* for *only* the people who bothered to show up to see how I look.' The assistant places an open laptop in front of her and James and then Adele nods at a waiter. 'Can you lower the projection monitor and dim the lights, please?'

The restaurant is gradually seeped into darkness, bar the flickering candles on each table and the artificial glow beaming out from the laptop in front of the wedding couple. I turn my chair round to face the screen on the wall. Of course, Adele was fibbing to her mother. Skyping wedding messages in real time isn't easier. But as well as the bride getting to show off, so do the people sending the message by speaking in front of an impressive backdrop.

And my opinion is *more* than justified over the next ten minutes as Adele and James are congratulated *live* by a succession of loud and confident thirty-somethings and/or (even worse, *just*) their loud and confident children at the forefront of: an entirely marbled kitchen, a wintry French olive grove, embossed Designers Guild wallpaper, a Shetland pony adorned in red rosettes and a miniature Banksy. The messages may have a different script but the subtext is the same: *We're EXACTLY where we want to be in life. Are you?*

By now, I'm boiling. I can feel sweat gathering in the underwiring of my strapless bra. I take a sideways glance at Adele's father but he doesn't seem to be affected by the temperature despite wearing a three-piece morning suit. Then again, he probably isn't functioning in the shadow of insomnia and freshly prescribed pharmaceutical drugs. I ought to go outside and get a blast of cold air. On the monitor, the owners of the Banksy (a hedge fund manager and his wife: a mother of three and part-time pilates instructor 'currently dabbling' in cranial massage therapy) are apologising for not being present because they are at their ski chalet. (Additional subtext: *We're SO exactly where we want to be in life – DESPITE THE TRIPLE DIP RECESSION! – that we don't even keep all our key pieces of contemporary urban art in the primary home.*) Furtively, I push my chair back.

'*Pssst,* Vivian!' Adele – the hawk bride – spots me before I have even got round to lifting my bum off the seat. 'Where are you going?' she whispers.

'Outside … only for a bit,' I whisper back. 'Sorry, I'm overheating.'

'You can't go.' She gestures at me with a flapping hand to turn back round. 'Not yet.'

'I'll only be a minute, I promise.'

'*No!*' she squawks, pointing towards the wall. 'It's *my* wedding present to *you …*'

'What is?'

She points at the screen. A new link-up has started. This particular absent friend is standing in a lounge between a foosball table and a large speaker. I feel the atmosphere behind me change; a few coughs, mainly pinched gasps. I glance back at Adele, my eyes wide and jaw rigid, an expression she clearly misinterprets in a positive sense because she beams at me.

'Look!' she whispers. 'It's *Luke!*'

Yes, it is … and he looks different. He looks different because he actually has a *look*. He is groomed. No, more than that. He could actually be starring in an advertisement for a grooming product – one where he is driving a vintage Lambretta through the back streets of Paris and the voice-over artist has an overly blokey lilt to his voice so he can make the word 'fragrance' sound masculine. His skin looks supple, as if it has definitely seen some moisturiser in the last twenty-four hours. It is also still tanned, so clearly he must have succumbed to using sunbeds after he left Ibiza. The stubble on his head has grown out a few inches and has been subtly waxed into something verging on a hair *style*. I find myself snorting disparagingly at his apparent new-found vanity; presumably something that has been financed by the proceeds from *that* video – *our* video – to please some sappy new girlfriend. I take in the clothes he is wearing: a pair of those drop-crotch utility trousers with a snug low V-neck T-shirt and a …

'Yeah, I know what you're thinking, people.' He grins at the camera, before Adele and James can say hello. 'And yep, this is a cardigan…' He rubs the woolly fabric. 'A *chunky* one. Oh, and the colour's *charcoal*, before any of you think it's bog-standard dark grey or nearly black. It's the new me … *smart casual*. All part of my cunning plan to deceive people into thinking I lead a life that requires me to move effortlessly from formal situations to more laidback ones, and can do so at any given moment without having to waste crucial time assessing whether or not I've got on the right clothes.'

The whole room bursts out laughing. Adele looks across

at me again and this time scrunches up her face when she smiles, as if this was the best possible gift she could have bestowed upon me. I am so utterly appalled that I force a smile back. Any honest reaction from me would inevitably lead to Adele and I having the worst row we have *ever* had. I don't know much about being a bridesmaid, but I'm guessing it's not 'wonderful' to reduce the bride to tears in the twenty-four-hour period either side of her vows.

I glance back up at the screen, making sure I avoid looking into Luke's eyes because I know how much more resentful they will make me. I briefly wonder where he is Skyping from. I don't recognise the room. It definitely isn't Wozza's place in Shepherd's Bush. Maybe it's Kevin's from the building site, that flat he suggested we move into … in Streatham.

'Anyway,' Luke continues, 'enough about my wardrobe, and let's get back to why I'm really here. To congratulate you two.' He points at the camera. 'I was surprised but totally ripped when you asked me to contribute to your day. I wanted to get what I said exactly right, so I turned to two foremost professionals on the subject of "getting hitched": my parents. They always said th—'

Christ, here we go … inspirational fridge magnet time. I start folding my napkin into a fan shape and hope I sleep better this evening. Before I go to bed I'll order something from Room Service. [Empty] stomach cramps kept me awake last night. I'll probably go for a steamed chicken breast. The kitchen won't think this is weird. That famously tiny (almost bird-like) French actress stayed in the same place last week. I saw pictures of her on the *Daily Mail* website entering the hotel with lots of Christmas shopping. She was working her usual Parisian-style 'ethereal peasant' look with lots of lace and velvet layers, but I could see how gaunt she was by the fragility of the section of skin that stretched over her knuckles as she gripped her bags. Don't tell me *le petit oiseau* went up to her suite and ordered a *croque monsieur avec les frites.*

Briefly, I gaze up at Luke's face. I watch his mouth moving but don't listen to a single word he is saying. Now, the room fills with 'awww's.

'Fucking crowd pleaser,' I mutter under my breath, as I continue with my linen origami and notice that Toby's seat is empty.

The room is back to 'ahhh'ing. I glance up at the screen to see Luke raising his fizzy drink can at the camera. He has come to the end of his speech. Suddenly, the image judders and freezes. Something must be up with the broadband. The quivering pixels blur Luke's face. I look away.

Then I look back. I keep on looking. His face blurs even more.

It was blurred the very first time I met him.

Saturday afternoon at The Red Lion. I had been out the night before with that overly trendy manager of a retro sneaker shop I was seeing. We were getting 'on it'. Again. We hadn't been to bed. I felt queasy, the room started to swim … so I put on my shades and headed out into the sunshine for a refreshing, stomach settling Lucky Strike. (The pub's vending machine has been out of Marlboro Lights since the old king died.) That was when I sort of saw … *him* … sitting at one of the wooden tables on the pavement, drinking Pepsi and reading a manual for some sort of electronic equipment. As soon as I glanced over he looked up and smiled in my direction. I could feel myself swaying.

Him: (Pointing at my cigarette) Are you sure you want to smoke that? (I ignored him.) Why don't you sit down?

Me: Do I look like I need to sit down?

Him: Mmm … you're a bit green, but then I don't know what colour you are normally.

Me: Orange.

Him: (Laughing) Actually, yeah, come to think of it you were deffo more in that ball park when I saw you at the bar earlier. I presumed you were sitting under a dodgy bulb. Is that your boyfriend in there?

Me: (Shrugging defensively but weirdly pleased he was asking) Er, kind of.

Him: (Staring right at me) Good. I'll take that as a 'no' then.

Me: (Sitting down opposite him) But that wasn't a 'no'.

Him: Yes, it was. I also had an '*er, kind of*' in Sydney, but we're not speaking any more. She didn't want me to leave for London and, well, here I am. I'm an Aussie, by the way.

Me: Really? I'd never have guessed from your strong Australian accent.

Him: Look at you … beauty *and* brains.

Me: (Taking off my sunglasses and trying to focus) What are you doing over here then, princess?

Him: (Ignoring my patronising term of faux endearment) Deejaying. Well, that's the plan.

Me: (Bursting out laughing) Of course it is.

Him: What's so funny about that?

Me: What isn't funny about that? Everyone wants to be a flipping DJ. I hate to tell you though, there are already enough of them in the capital to fill every club tenfold and there certainly isn't any money in it any more. It's called supply and demand, princess. Trust me, everyone knows some monkey with a laptop prepared to spend eight hours sweating in a DJ booth for fifty quid and a few free bottles of Stella.

Him: Is that a fact? Well, I'm much better value than that as I don't drink much alcohol, I also work harder as I play vinyl, and I'll do a free gig if it has the potential to lead to something bigger. Oh, and as part of this top-value package I also always promise *never* to say, 'It's all about the music …' or refer to the decks as 'wheels of steel'. You can't put a price on that.

Me: True. But do you ever walk around in public with your headphones dangling round your neck like a doctor's stethoscope?

Him: Like an emergency DJ on call? (He puts on a serious voice.) 'Thank God you're here. It's serious – we need you. The dance floor is emptying!' Never.

Me: What about calling records 'platters'?

Him: Nah, I don't do 'plates' either.

Me: (Smiling) I'd still give up now if I were you.

Him: Well, thanks for the encouragement. It's always a real pleasure meeting people who are so enthusiastic and supportive – when I first decided to come to England I promised my rellies I'd only make positive friends who would push me in the right direction.

Me: Looks like we won't be friends then, princess.

Him: Fine by me. I don't think I want to be mates with you. (Looking straight at me again.) You're not very nice. I think we'd be much better off starting up a purely carnal alliance. Functional and straightforward, so no one gets messed around.

Me: (Clearing my throat awkwardly) Actually, I'm more of a, er, 'relationship' type of girl.

Him: (Grinning) Really? Good for you. It's cool to be honest with yourself … because then you will be with other people, eh? Something my parents taught me.

Me: They got that off a fridge magnet.

Him: Amusing. Oh, but just so we're clear, if you did decide you'd give me a chance on the carnal front, I'd rather not have sex with you *today,* anyway. You're clearly wasted.

Me: I'm not.

Him: You are. I can tell you're on speedo.

Me: *Speedo?*

Him: It's what my Aussie mates call cocaine … because it speeds up time.

Me: That's ridiculous. What do they call speed, then?

Him: (Laughing) I don't actually know. My point is it would be best to wait so you can appreciate 'it' properly … in real time. Don't you reckon? (We both pause and stare at each other.) Wait there.

(At which point he disappeared into the pub and then reappeared with a pen, ripped the silver inlay paper from my cigarette box and scribbled something on it.)

Him: Here's the address of where I'm staying at the

moment. I haven't sorted out a mobile number yet. Anyway, if you do at any point get some spare time away from your hectic schedule of getting wrecked, painting yourself tangerine and pissing all over other people's dreams … then pop over and say g'day.

Exactly twenty-four hours later I pitched up on his doorstep. He opened the door wearing a hooded grey sweatshirt. I told him he hadn't removed the protective plastic off the toggles and apologised for not being very nice. He told me not to call him 'princess', because his name was—

'Luke!' I hear someone shout. *'Wait!'*

It's my voice. I jump up and stride over to where Adele and James are sitting. The room is silent. I lean in towards the laptop.

'Luke! It's me. I'm here. I can see you. Can you see m—'

James gently touches my arm. 'Vivian, this one was pre-recorded.'

Toby chuckles as he slips back into his seat, wriggling his nose. 'As if we would risk any live interaction between the two of you. This is a family event not sodding pay-per-view.'

'Be quiet, Toby,' snaps Adele, then she turns and scrunches up her face at me again. This time I find myself scrunching mine back. 'Don't worry, Luke recorded another message after that one … for you.'

'Did he explain why he did it? The …'

'Sex tape?' offers Toby, with no delicacy whatsoever.

Adele shrugs. 'I didn't watch it. You obviously need to hear what he has to say, Vivian.' She overly annunciates her words as if speaking like Rachel Weiss will make her sound more sober than she is. She passes me the computer. 'I *knew* you wanted him back.'

'That's the thing,' I whisper, taking it. '*I* didn't. I don't. Do I? I don't know. I'm not normal, so I'll never know.'

'I think *you do,*' she says. 'Go and watch it.'

'Now?'

'*Now.*'

Roger sidles up next to me. 'Use the staff changing room.'

Ignoring the confused whispering and salacious giggling filling the room, I grab the laptop. As I do, I see Melanie smile at me. I smile back and leave the restaurant. Running down the corridor, I can hear Toby launching confidently into his best man's speech, one hundred per cent secure (thanks to the 'hokey-cokey' he has obviously gone and 'tooted') that his shocking and mouthy comedic shtick – think Russell Brand with family money – is going to be a hit.

I enter the staff changing room, sit down, place the technology on my knees and take a deep breath. I notice Tabitha's duffel coat – a mitten dangling out of each arm – and her furry hat with rabbit ears attached looped round a peg. All the while, I am thinking: *Is Luke at Kevin's?* I press play.

'So, if you're watching this it must be the day after Adele's wedding. I'm sure you're chuffed – sorry, *pleased* – to be out of whatever daggy – agh! Sorry, terrible – outfit she forced you to wear.' *Yes, Luke must be there. His use of Australian slang is out of control. That would be Kevin's influence.* 'I appreciate you hearing me out, though, as I can only imagine how raging you are at me. Firstly, for not contacting you immediately after Ibiza. I should have done, but it wasn't fair on Suki. I knew how she felt … how you had made me feel, I guess …' He shrugs at the camera and I find myself nodding. 'And I didn't want to make it worse for her. Not that she wanted my sympathy. The only thing she wanted was to get her own back on me … something she was well connected enough to do fairly quickly.' He grins, resignedly. 'You won't be surprised to hear that I am no longer welcome to deejay on the White Isle. In fact, my name is *mud* as far as the dance community throughout Europe is concerned … and that's mud in the traditional mulched-up-earth sense, not that low-rent student high you were on when I last saw you.' I laugh. *I reckon Streatham is thirty-five minutes from here by cab. Well, over an hour on the bus in this weather.* 'But anyway, the day I was going to make contact with you, that footage got on the net. I thought you had sold it. Of course, *now* I realise you must have thought *I* had sold it. I hadn't. It was Wozza. He stole the tape from that video camera when I asked him to drop off your stuff at Burn's…' Whilst Luke is talking I put the laptop on the bench and open the cupboard at the back of the changing room. The box from Luke's room is still in there. '… and then he flogged it to some porn site after we'd been exposed in the paper. Apparently, he was desperate for cash to keep up the rent. Chrissy Crackers had taken my room after I left but that hadn't worked out.' I rifle through the box. 'He couldn't deal with Wozza's partying, which admittedly is like Bruce Willis complaining that Jason Statham's films are a bit samey, but he moved out leaving Wozza with double the rent, then Sammy dumped him and the bottom fell out of the illegal plant food market.' I find the camera. It is empty. 'Wozza admitted all this to me on a random phone call from Koh Samui this week. He sounded genuinely sorry … or at least, as much as it is possible to sound remorseful whilst tripping your nuts off on mushrooms.' *Maybe it would be quicker to get the tube. The Underground is open until half past midnight on Christmas Eve. Or is Streatham on an overground line? Tabitha told me she swapped numbers with Kevin's girlfriend the night of my birthday. I'll get it and ring her.* 'Anyway,' says Luke, 'I hope what I've said goes someway to helping you not hate me as much as I am sure you do …' *I don't!* 'Because … oh, hang on a sec …' He stops to take off his knitwear. He is wearing a pale grey T-shirt underneath that actually fits him. 'Sorry, I've got to get out of that thing. I only wore it because I knew it would be sub zero over in London right now … thought it would be less irritating than filming myself on the beach in my swimmers. Nothing worse than a smug video message at a wedding, is there? Not that I want to make you jealous or anything, but it's thirty-two degrees today in Sydney.'

I rewind.

'… it's thirty-two degrees today in Sydney.'

Again.

'… today in Sydney.'

Again.

'… in Sydney.'

He isn't half an hour away by cab. Or an hour on the bus. Or accessible by any sort of local public transport. He is on the other side of the world.

I watch as Luke steps forward, picks up his camera and directs it towards some open patio doors. Outside there is a decked area, beyond that the sea. I can make out some surfers bobbing up and down in the distance.

'So where was I? Because? Because … yes … *because* I'll never regret knowing you.' The camera stays trained on the view. 'Because on a scale of one to ten of things I could never live without – one being hair wax and ten being my extensive cable collection – you were definitely a nine for a while. I hope I was at least a seven for you. Take care of yourself, Vivian. Send my love to Monday. Goodb—'

I snap the laptop shut, whizz it away from me along the bench and stand up. I look in the mirror. But I find it difficult to focus on the person staring back at me. The person I *can* see is the person I am becoming. I stare harder and she becomes clearer, more animated … until she is in Bang & Olufsen high definition 3D 103-inch wide-screen clarity. I lied to Harriet earlier. I know what the future holds. I can see it.

I see *me*. I see the antidepressants kicking in. I see me getting back to partying. My abnormalities are what they are. I am not attempting to normalise anything. Life is *fine*. As it would be for *you* if you were *also* a single, thin, thirty-five-year-old living in a cosmopolitan city. In fact, your mid to late thirties may be your best years yet. You give up smoking, but continue to fire around town enjoying the lack of stretch marks and responsibility in your life whilst your initially smug pregnant friends get increasingly mottled and stressed, before finally giving birth and finding that as opposed to *having it all* every single part of their pre-baby life has been shot to pieces. You may even find these years are also your wildest. But then one night you'll have a moment. *The* moment. The one where you look in the mirror (it will either be in a puddly nightclub loo or in the wet room back at the flat of some random guy you have pulled on a forty-eight-hour bender, *not* in the security of your own home), and you will realise something: *you're getting older.*

If this devastating realisation is the equivalent of losing control at the wheel and spinning across three lanes of motorway, then turning forty is the heavy goods vehicle chugging towards you at 80 mph with a sleep-deprived driver behind the wheel who hasn't had a break since loading. It is guaranteed to finish you off. Over the next decade you'll find yourself becoming increasingly bitter as you are forced to engage in being middle aged. Weekends will be worst. Friday night simply becomes the end of the working week, Saturday is for 'chores' and Sunday is spent filled with a gut-wrenching sense of loss as you flick through the style supplements and realise you are no longer their target demographic. You may even consider moving to the country – anything to get out of the city and avoid the constant reminders that you will never be part of a 'zeitgeist' or even a bog standard 'trend' again. It's also around this time that you will *really* notice if you haven't got a.) a *great* career; b.) a *good* marriage; or c.) *any* sort of child … and will have to accept the awful truth that the majority of your adult life has been spent *getting ready to go out.* As opposed to *getting a life.*

You'll try to turn around this hollow state of affairs in

your fifties and sixties by taking up a hobby, like travelling. But even gazing out across the Serengeti at sunset you'll still be more concerned about whether khaki is all that flattering on your bottom half and whether the game keeper finds the divorcee/widow in the next door hut more attractive than you. Before you know it you'll be seventy and on the wane, both physically and mentally. Don't think that you'll be one of those irrepressible pensioners who swims in her local river throughout the changing seasons – you won't. Given the amount of binge drinking and drug taking you've indulged in, there will be a medical pay-off sooner rather than later. One minute you'll be behaving a little left of centre and considered eccentric, the next forgetting to shower and accusing the man behind the fish counter in the supermarket of stealing your purse. That's when *they* will start treating you like a toddler. Decisions will be made for you by hushed voices behind doors that no one bothers to shut properly and 'favourite' meals will get put in front of you on a tray – despite you never mentioning you liked any in particular. Then one day, that's it … the show is over. But the final insult: you were once the star of the whole production, but now you don't even get to enjoy the wrap party.

The clock in the staff room says I have four hours, twenty-one minutes and fifty-eight seconds of the wedding to go. I hover in the corridor for a while until I see Toby head out into the foyer, then I creep up it. As he bounds up the staircase towards the first-floor bar, I follow him. *I need to speed up time.*

As I knew he would, Toby disappears through the arched doorway towards the unisex toilets. He passes through the bar where Sophie Carnegie-Hunt is hosting her party. I spot her standing behind the decks next to the Da Goblin MC who is deejaying. She is wearing a Beastie Boys *Hello Nasty* tour T-shirt with a grey fedora and is thumping the air with a clenched fist. Keeping my head low, I wriggle through the packed dance floor and into the loo. One of the cubicles is locked. I bang on it.

'Toby! It's Vivian. Open up …'

I join him inside the cubicle. He has already crushed up four large lines of chalky textured yellowish cocaine on the ledge above the cistern. He hands me a rolled-up fifty-pound note.

He grins at me. 'I *knew* you would feel like it.'

'Yeah, I f—' But suddenly I don't. I don't feel like it. I feel *nothing*.

The nothingness is *acute*. It is on a level I have only ever felt once before: the day I hit my goal weight. But that was a *good* nothingness. The moment I looked down at those scales I knew I had escaped from my cognitive prison, and I made a promise to myself never to go back. I couldn't wait to make the most of my life post-jail … but maybe all I have been doing is living in fear of getting caught or re-offending. Maybe I shouldn't have been so hard on that inmate. The crime she committed may not have been worth the punishment I gave her. More to the point, what was the point in her escaping if she was going to spend the rest of her life on the run?

If you run for that long, you're bound to get lost.

I reach for the lock. As I do, the main door opens and I hear people enter the loo.

'I'm so glad you decided to come, honey,' purrs a girl's voice, with a familiar UK West Country via US West Coast drawl. 'It's the best birthday and Christmas present. You're so special to me, you know. I feel like I've shown you the *real* me. The real Noelle Bamford.'

Christ, not *her?* A male voice mumbles something in agreement.

'I think we could really go somewhere. But for that to happen,' says Noelle, '*you* need to let *me* in, honey. You need to let me in *there*. In your heart.' I hear her tapping the man's chest with such force she could be performing a surgical puncture of the thorax. '*I* want to be in there, with *you*.'

Toby nudges me. 'Do you want a hoof up or not?'

No. However, I want to see Noelle even less. I telepathically *will* her to leave or enter a cubicle … but the stench of chemicals mixing with brandy and damp dog on top of the clear stink of my utter failure to live normally (*or* abnormally) is becoming too much. I need to get out *now*. I push Toby to the side with a little too much force. He falls awkwardly, grabbing on to the shelf for support and ploughing into the carefully organised lines of coke. I stumble out of the toilet and trip over onto the floor. My face lands next to a pair of monochrome brogues. Next to them, a pair of perfectly scuffed hiking boots. When I lift my head, a man's hand extends to help me up. There is a 'Z' tattoo inked on his wrist. Or rather, it is an 'N'.

CHAPTER FORTY-THREE

Maximilian says nothing.

'Veronica!' carps Noelle. 'I didn't think you worked here any more.' She twists to make a face at Maximilian. '*Honestly*, honey … I never would have okayed it with Sophie if I'd known she still …' She waves her hand in my direction.

'I don't,' I tell her, and get up without using Maximilian's hand.

'So, how did you get on my guest-list?'

'Oh, fuck off, Noelle.' I sigh. I can't be bothered to put any effort into retaliating. 'I'm at a wedding downstairs.' I hear Toby snuffling around in the loo. 'As if I'd want to celebrate another year that you're alive.'

Maximilian turns away, but I'm sure I catch the semblance of a smile on his lips.

'You cow!' gasps Noelle, and she steps in front of Maximilian – arms outstretched – like a human bodyshield. 'Get out of here.'

'Wait …' mutters Maximilian, still not looking at me. 'I want a word with her.'

'What for?' Noelle asks him. 'You've moved on …' She turns back to me to make her point. 'Maybe *you* should too.'

'Move on from *the* Maximilian Fry?' I almost laugh. 'Don't worry about that, *honey* ... I have.'

That's when the cubicle door swings open and Toby strolls out. He glances in the mirror, blows his nose directly into the sink by pressing a sausage-y index finger against his right nostril and wipes his hand on his trousers.

'You're one difficult, jumpy filly, Vivian,' he says, slapping me on the behind. 'But you know what, sometimes they're the ones that handle the course better over a distance. More spring in the haunches ...'

He exits the toilet and Maximilian stares at the closing door. Then he looks at me. Now, it is me who looks away.

Noelle taps Maximilian sharply on the shoulder. 'We should get back to the party, honey. Sophie's got some photographers due any second. I can't have them arriving and the only marginally cool kids available to photograph are those two "yes" monkeys I worked with on *The T Zone* ... and that's only by association.'

'In a minute,' says Maximilian.

'No, *now*,' snaps Noelle, her LA drawl suddenly almost undetectable. 'This is *my* fucking party, and I will not have it ruin—'

But then she stops. I can visualise the cogs turning in her head, weighing up if she should risk exposing Maximilian to her black-and-white shoes *and* split personality so early in their relationship. Sensibly, she decides she can't.

'I'll wait outside, *honey*,' she half-hisses half-chirrups in his ear. She caresses his face and rubs her other hand up and down his neck. She may as well have cocked her leg and weed on him given the loaded territorial subtext.

She stalks out and as the door swings shut, Maximilian faces me square on.

'Before you say a word, Vivian, I do not want to argue with you. Everything you *thought*, anything you're *thinking* … it was and is true. I know that I have taken advantage of certain individuals … affecting their lives with my ambition, but I want you to know that I do not intend to cause any more damage. I accused you of having no depth, but it goes to show how lacking I am that I failed to do anything to save our friendship. But I knew I needed to work on myself – on the man I want to be – before I attempted to.'

I am wrong footed by his gushing admission of culpability. So much so, I don't accept it.

'Clearly, that's going *fabulously* well,' I mutter, glancing in the direction in which Noelle departed. 'You won't be the man you want to be by solely admitting who you are to your*self*. You have to show *other* people.'

Maximilian shakes his head. 'What do you want me to do? Travel the length of the UK on a giant rainbow-shaped float lip-syncing my way through the greatest hits of … of …' He searches for a name.

'Gloria Gaynor? Kylie Minogue? Lady Gaga? Abba? Liza Minnelli?' I offer sarcastically, and sit up on the counter next to the sink.

'See?' He rolls his eyes at me. 'I don't even know the basic fucking clichés. Look, I know you think I've probably taken a few steps back …'

'*A few steps back?* Ha! You've hotfooted it to the Jurassic era and gone insane in the process. You have *chosen* to get it on with Noelle Bamford … that's lunatic behaviour. It's like deciding you want some household storage tips and befriending Jeffrey Dahmer.'

'Who's he?'

'A prolific serial killer … he stockpiled his victims in the freezer.'

Maximilian rubs his forehead and leans against the counter next to me. Close up, I can see how exhausted he is. The wrinkled crow's feet at the corner of his eyes have developed since I last saw him. Before, they made him look sexily weathered, now he simply looks 'eroded', battered by the media storm.

'For your information,' he retorts, '*I* didn't choose *her*. *She* chose *me*. A few weeks ago, Nicholas got a call from Noelle's manager saying she wanted to hook up for dinner. MTV are interested in taking her new show to the States. The Yanks think she's one to watch, and since I am currently someone who *no one* is even getting an opportunity to watch, getting photographed with her on a regular basis was an offer I couldn't afford to refuse.'

'Don't exaggerate, Maximilian,' I correct him. 'What you mean is it was an offer you didn't *want* to refuse. You could *afford* to. You've got loads of money. The only breadline that you'll ever live below is an olive, fennel and rosemary infused handmade focaccia.'

He continues rubbing his head. 'That's where you're wrong, Vivian. I've blown most of my cash. Turns out I'm pretty convincing at playing a whole range of characters bar "financial expert". I have learnt the hard way that dealing with the stock market is not like making a movie: you don't get the chance for a second take. It's more like being on the stage: if you consistently under perform the show will close … especially if you don't take your director's advice. I'm selling the house in Primrose Hill.'

'Are you serious? But you were *mint*ed. What about your place in Ibiza?'

'I'll never sell that. I couldn't do it to Pedro. As you pointed out to me … along with some other genuinely nice people, I haven't treated him particularly well.'

I feel a flash of remorse for being so hard on him. 'I would give you back that money you gave me, but I don't have it.'

'You've spent *all* of it?'

'Well, er, no, I leant it to Clint.'

'Clint Parks?'

'Yeah, for rehab. He's doing well. He's still in there but already writing again – he's got a publishing deal for his autobiography. It's called *You CAN Polish a Turd: The Memoirs of a Celebrity Hack.*'

Maximilian groans. 'For fuck's sake, Vivian, you paid for his treatment? That's like feeding a Gremlin after midnight.' Now, Maximilian gets a semblance of a smile from me. 'By the way, you look dreadful. Look at your collarbones …'

I don't need to. I am aware they have morphed from 'prominent' to 'jutting'.

'Impressive, no?' I laugh. 'Flesh-deprived clavicles are very "in" right now. Apparently, some joker has even set up Twitter fan page for Rachel Zoe's.' I laugh again, but Maximilian and I *both* know the joke has worn thin. 'Listen, thank you for getting those pictures back from *The First*. How did you do it?'

'I gave them an exclusive – and *obviously* execrable interview – about how I'm "moving on". It was the least I could do to help you do the same.'

I look away, so I don't have to admit I am still immobile. 'So, Barb's got a plan to get you acting again?'

'No. She doesn't do my PR any more. She had some random midlife – I'm obviously being generous there – crisis of conscience after we got back from Ibiza. *Silver's Golden Rule – the penultimate one…*' He mimics Barb's New York accent. '*There's only so much bullshit you can handle before you begin to smell it on it yourself.* Although, I've since discovered she's in LA with Achilles so clearly that was *bullshit* too. It was more a case of her wanting to back someone younger … and presumably, straighter.'

I take a deep breath. 'Actually, Maximilian … I doubt she was lying. It's likely she was feeling genuinely guilty.'

'About what? Have you spoken to her?"

'No, but …' I take another breath and jump off the counter to face him. 'Before I begin, you *must* know I wanted to tell you this at my mother's house, I tried to, but you interrupted me … then I was too angry because you said I could be bought … and, well, I guess I did exactly what you said I *always* fail to do: pull out that truth … but this time it wasn't my truth, it was *yours* …' I trail off.

'Go on.' His eyes narrow.

'The thing is, Barb lied. Nathan did *not* attempt to sell a story about your relationship. She told you that to make you dump him. She knew it could ruin *her* career as well as yours if the relationship was allowed to continue. Nathan was in …' I pause. 'He was in love with you.' I pause again. 'You were in, er, love with him too, weren't you, Maximilian?'

I brace myself for him to either break down or blow up. But instead, he looks straight back at me and shrugs.

'Does it matter?' he asks.

'Of course, it does. It means Nathan was *that* someone worth coming out for. You should ask him for another chance.'

Maximilian emits a sad laugh. 'Don't be ridiculous, Vivian. I beat the living daylights out of him. You can't come back from something like that. It's called domestic fucking violence. How would we move forward? A couple is meant to live together in harmony, not one of them cowering *in fear.*'

'But he didn't grass you up to the police, did he? Surely that shows he *may* forgive you if you explained everything. You still want him, I know you do. It's obvious.' I grab Maximilian's hand and point at the 'N' tattoo. 'Take some of your own advice. *Reach inside and pull out that truth.* Find Nathan. Do it, no matter how far you have to go.'

He raises his eyebrows at me. 'That's rich coming from you, Vivian. You're hardly Phileas Fogg when it comes to matters of the heart. I doubt you'd even bother with an Oyster card outside of Zones One and Two.' He manages a weary grin. 'See? Evidence that I *am* skint: I've been looking into the options available on public transport …'

I drift off as he is talking and look at myself in the mirror again. But this time I see me *now* … not in the future. I look at each part of my body that is not confined to my dress: the bones nudging the shallow layer of flesh surrounding them to exactly the degree of tautness I had always hoped to achieve. As a teenager, lying in my self-imposed coffin at home I used to dream that one day I would be as good at being thin as I was at being fat. Well, my dream has come true. I have found the pot of (zero fat) gold spread at the end of the rainbow. But a rainbow is an optical illusion caused by reflection and refraction of light. It cannot be physically approached. It is only real in the moment you see it and when you do, you only ever see the upper arc. A rainbow is actually a full circle.

'You're wrong about that,' I blurt out. 'I would.'

'Would what?'

'Go far.'

'Go far for what?' repeats Maximilian. 'Love? Ha! Yeah, course you would. To the ends of the earth …'

I look away from the mirror back at him. 'That would be impossible without space training and heavy sponsorship … possibly by Red Bull. But I'd go to the other side of the world.'

'Would you?'

'I *would* because I *am*. I'm flying to Australia … to see Luke.' There is no hesitation in my voice, even though I had no idea I was about to say those exact words until I did.

Maximilian peers at me, unconvinced. '*When?*'

'I'll aim for Boxing Day.'

'Does he know this?'

'No. Neither did I until a few seconds ago.' My head is whirring. 'But he will.'

Not now, though. I will wait until I have collected some of the money Clint owes me, booked a flight, packed a bag, travelled to Heathrow, checked-in my luggage, got through security, bought some DVT socks in Boots (to prevent long-haul-flight cankles), ridden on the tram to my allocated departure gate, got checked off for boarding and be sitting in my seat ready for take-off. Then I will grab my phone. Actually, I may even wait until the aircraft doors are shut and the cabin crew have got to the stage in the flight safety demonstration between pretending that the oxygen mask has fallen out of the ceiling and them not quite blowing that whistle on the life jacket. This way, even if Luke tells me *not* to come, I'll explain that I have no choice – I can't get off the plane. I will call him again when we stop off to refuel in Japan to let him know I am continuing on to Sydney. Surely, he will agree to meet me if I have got that far. There is no way he could be so cruel as to make me stay in Tokyo, the birth place of all things *kooky* … including Hello fucking Kitty.

Maximilian is still staring at me in disbelief and my head is still whirring, when the door opens. Nicholas strides in. His lip curls as soon as he sees me.

'Good *God*, look who it is. The breakaway insurgent who singlehandedly blew apart my client's career. You're PR Semtex, darling … detonate and destroy,' he snarls. 'Forgive me if I'm not exactly thrilled to see you. Although I am mildly entertained by the appalling dress you're wearing.'

'Go away, Nicholas,' I snap back. 'I'm having a private conversation with Maximilian.'

Maximilian says nothing. He is leaning over the sink, splashing his face with water.

Nicholas clicks his tongue at me. 'Well, that's *sweet*, but I'm afraid Fry hasn't got time for a touching reunion with you, darling. He needs to get his arse out of here for the photographer.'

Maximilian grabs one of the folded beige towels on the glass shelf and pats his face dry. 'Give us five minutes,' he says. His words are muffled but I can clearly hear anger now overriding the exhaustion in his voice.

'You are required *now*,' Nicholas tells him. 'Besides, I can't imagine that anything Vivian has to say will be in your interest. Let's face it, she was hardly thinking about your welfare when she spiked your drink and you nearly died. Although,' he smirks to himself, 'I suppose it could have been worse: you could have gone round offering out shoulder rubs or a Vicks inhaler.'

Maximilian chucks the hand towel into a wicker basket and faces Nicholas. His jaw is clenched, making him look even more strained. 'What happened out there was an accident. Vivian never purposefully set out to deceive me. She never has done. Unlike some people ...' He scans Nicholas's face for a reaction.

Nicholas doesn't flinch. 'Is there a point I'm meant to be getting here, Fry? Because if there is,' he glances down at his watch, 'can you get to it?'

'The story that Barb told us about Nathan going to the press ... it wasn't true. He never had any intention of fucking me over. Did you know that?'

'Well, I ...'

'Well, *what*?' Maximilian fumes.

'Well, of *course*, I did.' Nicholas shrugs. 'I fully supported it, too, because it was the most sensible course of action. Anyway, I'm really not in the mood for an in-depth discussion about some twink whose sole purpose in life was to look good on a treadmill. We're done.'

'No, we're not.' Maximilian's words come out quietly but methodically.

'*Yes*, we *are*.'

I grab Nicholas's arm. 'Don't you understand? They had fallen for each other.'

Nicholas shakes off my hand and laughs. 'Oh per-*lease*, darling. What *has* happened to you? I much preferred the emotionless shell I met at the beginning of the summer. Listen,' he nods at Maximilian, 'don't get het up. I can see how the bare facts may look a little on the inhumane side of things, but that's the problem with describing anything in a nutshell, it sounds so … *intense*. I always think that whenever they run that ticker tape on the twenty-four-hour news channels.'

I glance across at Maximilian. His face has gone grey and a small section of skin under his eye is ticking. He steps forward so that he is less than a foot away from Nicholas. I stand back.

'You knew? You *knew*? You *fucking* knew?' he shouts. 'You *knew* Barb was lying and then you stood by and let me b—'

Nicholas doesn't let him finish. 'I did not stand by and let you do anything,' he says calmly. 'I had no idea you'd used my phone to arrange doing in Eden until that copper pitched up … and it's because of *me* sorting *him* out that *you* are not rotting in a cell. You should be grateful … and to Silver also. Let's face it, her ruse would have manifested itself in the truth eventually. I knew that when I saw the box in his gym bag,' he adds.

'What fucking box?'

'The one containing a ring.'

'There was a *ring*?'

Now Maximilian is talking more quietly again, but weirdly, he sounds even more enraged. I go to touch his shoulder but he flinches.

'There was,' admits Nicholas. There is still no hint of panic or guilt in his voice. 'But let's not get overexcited. It's not as if the two of you would have gone ahead and made your partnership official, is it? You don't need a crystal ball to figure out what would have happened. It's obvious.'

'Is it?' I ask.

'Yes.' Nicholas turns to me and explains. 'Eden would have asked Fry to marry him, Fry would have to say "no" because of his job. The two of them would've muddled along together for a while but that rejection would always be niggling away at Eden. The little foibles that once endeared Fry to him would start to grate – and let's face it,' he twists back to Maximilian, 'you're not exactly the least irritating person to be around at the best of times. Eventually, Eden would become prickly and ultimately, unattractive. Cut to Fry dumping him. Trust me, at that point Eden would be blabbing to the tabloids faster than Kris Jenner after one of Kourtney's eight-week scans. It was a lose-lose situation. I needed to protect you.'

'But *he* was going to fucking protect me,' half-whispers, half-hisses Maximilian. But then, as if he has exposed and embarrassed himself with this remark, he grabs another towel and rubs his face with it. 'He wanted a future with me,' he mumbles into the fabric.

Nicholas laughs again. 'And *I* was keen on a future with Heather Locklear when I was younger, but that didn't pan out either, what with her commitment to *Dynasty* and Tommy Lee … then *Melrose Place* and Richie Sambora. For crying out loud, Fry, I can't believe we're even having this conversation. Don't think I'm feeling sorry for you either. Your life is not merely fantastic, it's fantastic*al*. You may be forced to be in the closet, but it's not some flimsy ply-wood box of dull mediocrity, it's the sodding gateway to Narnia. You know as well as I do, if you want to act in the movies you always have done, you can't come out, let alone make it official in wedlock.'

'How do you know?' I chip in.

'Oh, darling,' he sighs, 'are you trying to wind me up? Name one openly gay actor who has *ever* secured a leading man role in a blockbuster film.'

'Rupert Everett.' I suggest. But as this pops out of my mouth I know Nicholas will snort with laughter in my face.

He does. 'Ha! What a marvellous example, given that both of Everett's most famous Hollywood parts involved him playing the bent best friend of some neurotic fag hag. Mmm, he clearly gets to run the gamut from poof to …' he pretends to search for the words, '*very* poofy. The simple fact is that if a man comes out in Hollywood, the door to romance, action or thriller is slammed shut. At best, it will be left slightly ajar for him to land niche character roles in comedy and high-end cerebral productions or voice-over work for some CGI animation … but even then he won't be the wisecracking raccoon with an eye for the ladies, he'll be the giggling parrot with a penchant for Broadway musicals.'

Nicholas is beginning to lose his cool. He loosens his tie and pulls up his jacket sleeves. I glance across at Maximilian. He is staring at the floor.

'Gay actors don't even get a look-in at the decent gay parts,' continues Nicholas. '*Brokeback Mountain* wouldn't have got the financing to shoot a weekend camping trip in a trailer park, let alone a summer-long adventure in the Canadian Rockies, if either of the leads *hadn't* been heterosexual. As for getting an Oscar? Forget it. The last time an openly gay man was nominated for Best Actor – *not* just Supporting – was Ian McKellen at the turn of the century for *Lord of the Rings* … and he wasn't even fully human.' Sweat has appeared on Nicholas's brow. 'Does it make me sick that you can't have the life you want on *and off* screen? Of course, it does, but,' he clears his throat and faces Maximilian directly, 'you said to me that you wanted to work without restriction…' Suddenly, his voice is soft. It's the first time I have ever heard it like this. 'And I promised I would make that happen. When this situation arose with Eden I only had one choice.'

'What about *my* fucking choice?' explodes Maximilian, slapping the towel against the basin. 'I wasn't even given any options. You didn't do it for me. You did it for yourself.

Everything you've done for me, you've only done for yourself … and not even that well, because if it hadn't escaped your notice, I'm not working now, *am I?*'

Nicholas takes a step closer to Maximilian. I see his hand curl into a fist and for a second I think he is about to hit him. But after a few seconds it unfurls and he lets it drop back down to his side. 'If that's what you honestly think, Fry, I'm sure you'll do a lot better with me out of the picture. I'm resigning. My lawyers will be in touch so that we can tie things up as amicably as possible.' He clears his throat again. 'I'll also make sure they forward you all the details for the Davies Center.'

'What the fuck's that?' mutters Maximilian.

'The physiotherapy unit in San Francisco where Nathan is being treated. I wanted to make sure he recovered fully … it wasn't his fault he got caught up in our, well, *your* drama. We can switch the direct debit to your account. You'll be able to afford it …' Nicholas pulls out a folded-up piece of paper from his jacket pocket and thrusts it at Maximilian. Then he leaves the room.

Maximilian opens up the piece paper.

'What is it?' I ask.

'A copy of an email from JP Goldstein,' he says slowly. 'Nicholas has got him back on side … they did a deal, Nicholas said he'd work with him in LA on a three-year contract. I start shooting the sequel for *The Simple Truth* in the New Year. They're calling it *The Truth Just Got Complicated.*'

'That's gr—'

'*Great?*' he interrupts. 'Is it?' He clasps his face in his hands. 'What am I doing, Vivian? Seriously, *what am I doing*? I've screwed up my life, I've screwed up other people's lives, I get other people to screw up other people's lives … I will continue to screw up *everything*. For what?'

'Er, to act. It's your *passion,* isn't it?' I remind him, but I am aware how pathetic this now sounds. 'One that you've always made a pretty good case for.'

'But I've realised that's *all* I'm doing. Acting. Every hour of every day … it's no longer a desire, it's a necessity. Nothing is real and I don't think I can handle it any more.' He stops. 'I can't handle *me*. You were right. I'm not an actor, I'm a liar.' His voice cracks.

I go to touch his shoulder but he pulls away again and turns to stare into the mirror. His eyes are panicked. I wonder if he is seeing his present or his future.

The door opens. A monochrome brogue appears, then Noelle, flashing a winsome smile, clearly having had a word with herself. She waves at Maximilian ultra coquettishly.

'Are you done now, honey?'

'No, we're not,' I tell her.

'I wasn't talking to you.' She nods over at Maximilian. *'Honey?'*

Sophie Carnegie-Hunt appears in the doorway too. 'God, it really *is* you,' she sniffs at me, whilst rearranging her hat at an angle verging on perpendicular, as if that will protect her from my fallen-celebrity Z-list aura. She turns to Maximilian. 'Can I have you, angel? Really want to get some bloody *ama*zing shots – something candid, yeah? –

of you and Noo-Noo with some of the other personalities who've arrived.'

'Personalities? Ha!' I laugh. 'That's probably pushing it.'

'I'm not having my picture taken,' says Maximilian, still looking in the mirror.

'Now, now, don't be thillywilly,' chides Sophie, using her baby voice. 'I agreed with your manager th—'

Maximilian turns round. 'We no longer work together. I'm leaving now.' He nods at Noelle. 'Sorry, but it's best if we call a halt to things, er, between us. Many happy returns. Good luck in the States.' He walks out of the loo.

'You can't go, honey!' Noelle gasps, stamping on the floor with her right brogue, before spinning to face me. 'What have you said to him?'

Sophie rubs her shoulder. 'Let me deal with this, Noo-Noo, he'll listen to me. It's what I do. I'm an unsurpassed mediator. It's what everyone says.'

'No, Sophie,' I tell her, 'you keep mishearing because your pretentious millinery gets in the way. Everyone says you're an unsurpassed *media whore*.'

I dash out of the loo and down the corridor after Maximilian. He is descending the stairs to the foyer three marble steps at a time. Two- thirds of the way down he passes Adele. She is holding her bouquet in one hand. James is gripping onto the other to steady her balance. The rest of the guests are packed into the foyer waiting for her to throw the flowers. Adele is too giddy to realise that it is Maximilian Fry who has hurtled past her. But everyone else clocks who it is. They point at him and nudge each other as he heads towards the exit. I follow and catch up with him by the revolving doors.

'Don't leave on your own, Maximilian. I'm worried about you. Wait with me here.' I check the time on the clock above reception. It's after nine. 'I can leave in less than four hours.'

'There is no need for you to worry, Vivian. I'm fine.'

'That was about as convincing as my audition for *The Wizard of Oz* … and we know how that panned out.'

He looks down at the floor. 'Yeah, well … maybe I'm not very good at what I do after all. If I really was one of the best actors of my generation, then I'd be able to play *any* part. But clearly, the one role I will always struggle with is "me". Ironic really, when you think about how hard I have studied it.'

'I think we all struggle with that one,' I reassure him. 'The script flummoxes me every time.'

'Speaking of which,' he pauses and looks up, 'tell me, Vivian, what will you say when you see him?'

'To Luke?' I feel a sudden blast of cold air as the revolving door rotates.

'Yeah …'

'Christ, er, well… there's loads of stuff that needs to be said. No doubt, I'll figure it out in detail on the twenty-three-hour journey … and then freeze the second I face him. I suppose "I'm sorry" might be a good start.'

'And then what?'

'You *know* …'

'I love you?' Maximilian stares at me.

'Yes, that would be advisable.'

'Say it then.'

I take a long, deep breath. 'I love you.' It is a lot harder to say when you mean it.

'I know you do. After all, you're only human, Ha! Got you again.' Maximilian manages a brief flash of his award-winning smile. 'I love you too, Vivian ...'

He hugs me and I hug him back. As I do, I think how I likened him to Ziggy Dunhill when we first met. Someone who was totally at ease with the person they were and wanted everyone to know it. But actually, Maximilian was always more like me. I didn't want anyone to find out the person I once *was*. Maximilian could never let anyone find out the person he wanted to *be*. As we hold each other, I get a sense he's thinking the same.

Finally, we both pull away. The foyer is quiet. I look over to the wedding guests. There seem to be more of them. I think partygoers from upstairs have joined them. But no one is looking at the bride on the staircase, they are gawping over towards me and Maximilian by the entrance. Adele – who has suddenly regained some sort of focus – flaps her flowers at me and grimaces. I glance at Roger standing by reception. He mouths at me to turn round. So I do. Terry is standing in the aperture of the revolving doors.

It appears he has bought me a Christmas present. It is hovering next to him in a chunky charcoal cardigan.

'Luke ...' I step back. '*Luke*. Luke! I was just *leaving* ... to come and see you ...'

'*Were* you?' begins Terry, before Luke can say anything. 'I tried to call you but your mobile is sw—'

'It doesn't matter now, Uncle Terry, does it?' I shout. 'Because he's here. Thanks so very much.' I stare at Luke. 'You're *here*. But I *was* going to come and find you. I swear. I was just telling Maximilian … *literally* minutes ago. I was about to head for Australia.'

Luke laughs at me, no way near delightedly but not bitterly either. He looks calm, as if he was expecting disappointment but simply wasn't sure of the level.

'Yeah, course you were, Vivian,' he says. 'You've always been so keen to visit my homeland. Didgeridoo and cork hat packed, are they? So, when did the two of you,' he nods at Maximilian, 'get back together?'

Now Maximilian steps back. 'Nothing is going on.'

'D'you think I would have got you over here if they were doing any such th—' Terry attempts to explain to Luke.

I interrupt him again. 'We should go somewhere and talk, Luke, so that I can tell you …' Then I lose my train of thought. Because all I can think is how glad I am to see him. But then I think how sad he is going to be when I tell him about Monday.

'So that you can tell me *what*?' prompts Luke – there is still no judgement in his voice. 'Do you *ever* know what to say, Vivian?'

Ironically, I don't even get a *chance* to answer this as Noelle Bamford barges past, weeping.

'You can have him,' she says, pointing her finger at me before turning to focus her attention on Maximilian. 'She cheated on you once before and she'll do it again, you know. But more fool you if you want a *no*body over *some*body who's in the process of creating an assured presence for herself across the pond.' She adds this as if she was about to take over CNN's prime-time chat show.

Sophie catches up with her client, one hand clutching her hat to her head, the other applying Bobbi Brown lipgloss. 'Calm down, Noo-Noo, let's do the offski and nip to the Groucho. You're looking bloody ama*zing* tonight …'

'That's true,' she sniffs.

'So, let's not waste that …' Sophie nods at her to leave the club.

As they walk out Luke sighs – not exasperatedly, it is more a resigned release of breath.

'I can't be arsed with this,' he says. 'You lot are completely nuts.' An addition that is entirely reasonable. He turns to go too.

Maximilian grabs at Luke's arm. 'Listen, I'm categorically *not* with Vivian. Whatever he,' he nods at Terry, 'said to get you over here it's true. We were never …' He trails off, aware that everyone in the foyer is hanging on his every word. 'It's always been you that she wanted; she just had a hard time admitting she needed *any*one. We're only friends.'

'That's all, is it?' asks Luke, in the acquiescent manner of a high court judge enquiring whether Lindsay Lohan feels she can keep to the terms of her parole.

'It is,' confirms Maximilian.

'But I heard you … saying you loved her.'

'I do. I love *who* she is. I don't love her like *that*, because I'm …' He pauses and turns round, acknowledging the amount of people who are listening. His skin colour has gone grey again and that piece of flesh under his eye is ticking. I assume he is about to trail off again, but he doesn't. He starts over. 'I don't love Vivian like that because … well, because … because I'm g—'

I can sense the word about to be expelled from deep with in him. I jump in before it can be.

'Becausc he's *going to find his ex …*' I shout. 'Who he still has feelings for and always has done. We haven't seen one another in months.' I glance at Maximilian and whisper under my breath, 'Don't do it. Thank you, but *don't*.'

'I said I would do it for the right person,' he says, without bothering to whisper.

'That's not me, Maximilian,' I tell him. 'But hey, I'm proud of you. Really proud.'

'And I hope you are proud of yourself, Vivian,' adds Luke. 'But I'm going now.'

'I …' I begin to reply, but then I stop, because I am processing Luke's penultimate sentence, wondering just how rhetorically the delivery was meant. Because the upsetting thing is that once, Luke did genuinely want me to be proud of myself and encouraged me to make it happen. The only person who ever really did. I shut my eyes for a second to consider the likelihood of him wanting that for me again. Or that I would ever be able to achieve a sense of pride in myself even if he did.

When I open my eyes Luke is gone. I jump into the revolving doors and outside onto the pavement. He is trudging through the snow up the road, away from Burn's and into the night. For a few moments, I stop to watch him; to fully experience what it is like to see him leaving my life for one final time. I think I need to examine this image to be able to say what I know he needs to hear, but then I realise I am already yelling …

'I don't blame you for walking away, Luke, but at least let me tell you this. The answer is "no". I'm not proud of myself. I never learnt how to be.' He carries on trudging so I follow, the snow now seeping in through my stilettos and round my toes. 'I'll tell you why. Because the years that I should have spent learning how to appreciate the person I was and the person I wanted to be or *could* be, I spent *ashamed* … because I was *fat*. There, I've said it. *I was fat.* No, in fact, I am going to scream it … I WAS FAT!' I shock myself at the volume with which these words launch out of my mouth. Finally, Luke stops, but he doesn't turn round. 'And for your information, there is no such thing as being *fat and proud.* You *never* feel pride.' I intend to stop here, to give Luke a chance to respond, but I find that I can't. 'Who cares what you are *feeling* if you are fat? No one tries to understand who you are on the inside, because no one wants to know. They've already made their judgement the moment you hauled yourself into view. You're fat. End of. That's all you are. Being large has no allure behind it. You're a faulty Kinder egg … an outer shell with nothing on the inside worth investigation. It is not like other flaws, like being a bit of a tart or a junkie or a boozer. No one wants to find out what is making you *tick* because they have made the assumption already that all you do is wait for the clock to *tick* round to the next mealtime or snack break. I can't even imagine how hard it must be for fat kids today. They either get ignored or bullied all day at school … only to get home and face the same treatment on Facebook. Or they simply torture *themselves* instead, by going on to Instagram or Snapchat or Vine or Tumblr or Flickr to see the endless plates of fattening food posted by skinny celebrities … which are clearly not being eaten by them. Their world is warped by cheap PR … with expensive consequences. At least, when I was fat I could hide from the world in my coffin to acknowledge my status as a person of *no* interest … *on my own.*' I pause, but only to take a breath. Now, I have no intention of stopping. 'But when I started to lose weight, I became a person of interest. It made me uncomfortable. I couldn't handle it, so I made sure that I only let people scratch the surface. I found it was entirely possible to function like this. But you …' I point at Luke, even though his back is still turned. '*You*, Luke, didn't want to scratch the surface. You wanted to go deeper and I didn't like it, because I knew what you would find: *all that shame.* I didn't want anyone to see that. I had come too far and I was fully intending on making more progress to be … perfect. Because the more imperfect you have been, the more perfection becomes a necessity.' I briefly think of Kate Summers and realise for her it was the other way round. She had the perfect life until I added that hint of imperfection by allowing her boyfriend to cheat on her. Suddenly, she was no longer perfect. No wonder she wanted payback. Revenge. 'The thing is, Luke, the only person you can rely on to reach that perfect place is yourself, because everyone else has the potential to hinder your journey. So, what ends up happening? Well, you don't ever let anyone inside, but you learn to live with this emptiness because it is so much better than feeling *full* …'

Now I stop. I can see Luke's breath rising in the cold air.

'Congratulations …' says Maximilian. I hadn't even realised he was standing beside me. He takes off his jacket to put round my shoulders. 'You did it.'

'Did what?'

'Reached inside and pulled out your truth.'

Luke turns, but he is staring at the ground. I watch the snow drift down onto his head, dissolving as it hits the styling product in his hair and wonder what he is turning over in his head. I wonder how I would approach all this if I were him. Would I focus on the microcosm; all the little things that have happened between us from the moment we met until now … or focus on the macrocosm: quite literally, the *larger* picture and how that will always affect who I am and who I can be within a relationship. Either way, it is a *big* ask to expect anyone to take that on. Yes, I know there are men who actively seek out women who clearly have 'issues'. I mean, there is a reason why Taylor Swift is never without a date, right? But at least there are *other* perks to be had as her boyfriend: luxury private travel, front-row seats at the Grammy Awards, a guaranteed Billboard hit written about you after you've split up … but I can't offer anything else, except me. Only *ever* me. No children. I would never forgive myself – nor expect them to forgive me – if they went through what their mother did. Or what *my* mother did. So, that's it. *Me.*

A cab turns into the cobbled mews and halts about thirty foot away. A small figure lowers herself out of the back wearing a full length fur coat and moonboots. As it steps into the glow of a streetlight I recognise the fur as fox. The footwear as Chanel snow wear. The owner as … Barb Silver. She picks her way through the snow, reaching Luke first.

'What the hell is he doing here?' She is halfway through acknowledging Luke, but then she points behind Maximilian and I. 'And who the freakin' hell are *they*?'

We both turn round. The entire wedding party and everyone from the abandoned birthday bash upstairs have followed us out of Burn's and are huddled together, transfixed by the show.

I ignore Barb's question. 'Maximilian knows everything,' I tell her.

'Ah. Okay, kiddo, I *hear* you.' She nods at me and slowly twists to face Maximilian. 'I'm sorry,' she says simply. '*Real* sorry, Maxy.'

He displays no emotion. '*Silver's Golden Rule Number Thirteen*,' he replies. '*Apologies are like get out of jail free cards in the Monopoly of life. They enable you to move forward but ultimately mean nothing*.'

'Yeah, well, you can ignore that rule,' concedes Barb, 'along with the rest of them. I never did tell you the most important one of all, did I? *Silver's Golden Rule Number One. Don't listen to a freakin' word I say, I'm Barb Silver: sixty-five per cent bullshit, thirty-five per cent commission.* But this time I'm not expecting anything back from you, Maxy. It's *me* that owes *you*. I owe you the opportunity to apologise too.'

'*Me?* Apolog—' begins Maximilian. 'Are you having a fucking laugh? As if I n—'

Barb interjects. 'Not to me.' She turns round and points at the cab, which has remained parked further up the road.

As she points, the back door swings opens again. This time a man gets out. He steps onto the pavement. I squint but I don't recognise him. I glance across at Maximilian. He is staring ahead. I watch as his eyes narrow and then he smiles. But it's not *that* smile, the award-winning grin. It's a smile I haven't seen before; he merely seems … at peace. He takes a step forward. The man by the cab takes a step forward too. Then Maximilian moves off at speed through the snow – his hiking boots finally being put to the use they were originally intended. That's when the man steps under the streetlight and I recognise him. It's that lift porter from the Rexingham Ho tel. This was who Maximilian saw that day: Nathan Eden, Marjorie's son. Or as Maximilian knows him: the love of his life. As Maximilian comes to a neat halt – no skidding – in front of Nathan, he kisses him with such passion that one thing is for sure … he is not acting.

The sound of someone clapping breaks through the stunned silence. I glance over to the other side of the road. Nicholas is standing by his Porsche applauding his ex-client. Barb waves at him and starts to clap too. Then everyone else behind me starts cheering and wolf whistling as they surge forward up the street to where Maximilian and Nathan are standing.

As they slip and slide past me, I shut my eyes and suddenly, I am thinking about Kate Summers again … and the night of our school disco, when (pissed on Thunderbird and stuffed full of cheese puffs and Twiglets) I told her and the rest of our year what I had been doing with Ziggy … just as he was proposing to her. As she burst into tears, an involuntary yowling noise shot out from the depths of my stomach and I projectile vomited all over her. Her hair, her face, her dress … were dripping in my rancid regurgitation; eighteen per cent proof lemon-flavoured port and undigested lumps of cheddary and yeasty flavoured wheat snacks. To me, she had never looked more beautiful … but I knew that I would never be so ugly; on the inside and out. As Kate screeched at me that one day she would have her revenge, I was led away. Ziggy gave me the kind of look usually reserved for a murderer being escorted out of court with a blanket over his head. Which was rather apt, as in a way, I had killed something. My future. Because the memories of Kate, Ziggy, school, my father, being fat … they were always going to haunt me and kill whatever chance I had of living a normal life. But now it's time – finally – to lay all of them to rest and give them the burial they deserve.

When I open my eyes Luke is standing in front of me.

'And the award for most long awaited but admittedly much appreciated monologue goes to … *Vivian Ward*,' he says. 'You didn't have to say all that.'

'Didn't I? For Christ's sake, don't say I had you at "hello" …' I mutter. 'It's *such* a cliché.'

'No, you had me anyway. I was only leaving to get my jacket from Terry's car.' He raises his eyebrows at me and I know he is fibbing. 'But don't worry, your hidden emotional depths and clear strength of character can be our little secret.' He smiles at me. 'So, what's next?'

'*What's next*?'

'Yeah.'

I inhale deeply. I need to speak carefully, to prove I

am ready to bear the weight of responsibility that comes with being in a relationship; that I accept my life is not just about me any more. In cinematic terms, I must show I am ready to relinquish my sole star status. Because I am. The pressure of carrying the production all by myself has become tiring. I am looking forward to sharing the billing. Something we all have to do eventually. Even Cameron Diaz. She spent a decade making *her* name, a decade being *the* name … now it's time to let someone else shoulder the box office stress. If she picks carefully (i.e., says 'no' to *Knight and Day 2*), she'll still have the fulfilling career she deserves. She just won't be the *only* name that appears before the title of the movie. I take another breath.

'There are a number of things to discuss, aren't there?' I tell him. 'The most pressing is deciding where we are going to live. Because if we were going to even *attempt* some sort of reunion then inhabiting the same country is a necessity. I don't know what your new smart-casual lifestyle entails, but if it makes it impossible for you to leave Sydney then maybe I could give life in Australia a whirl.' I pause and peer at him. 'Baz Lurhmann always makes it look, er, *awesome*.'

'Stop trying to say the right thing, Vivian.'

'Hang on, let me fin—'

'No, it's far too painful,' he laughs, and smiles at me. 'Besides, I meant *tonight*. What's next tonight? Not until the apocalypse. What stage is the wedding at?'

'Oh, *right* …' I smile back. 'Well, er, cutting the cake, I guess.'

'You'll be swerving that, then?'

'Actually,' I consider this for a few seconds, 'I think I could manage a slice. I'm fucking *starving.*'

* * * * *

ACKNOWLEDGEMENTS

My biggest thank you goes to Ben Mason, fabulously dynamic boss of Fox Mason Literary Agency, who has made it possible for me to be a) an *actual* writer and b) able to shout, 'Well, my *agent* says...' loudly (and a lot) in public places. In addition, a waggy tail of gratitude to Silvio, his equally nimble canine cohort.

Next up, I am hugely appreciative to publishing wonder woman Donna Hillyer and her crack team at Harlequin. (That's 'crack' in the expertly insightful and brilliantly motivated sense, not the junkie one. Obvs.) The peeps at Cherish PR have been absolutely splendid too.

Then there's my brother, David. He's ace and my life has been made infinitely better by having him (and occasionally his cheque book/PIN number) in it for all these years.

As well, shout-outs must go to my oldest buddies, who I will obviously disregard entirely as soon as I am summoned to Los Angeles for discussion of movie and/or TV serialisation rights of my novel. They are: Sean 'Barbara Jean' Varley and The Drag Queen Massive (Faris, Otto, Mazza'n'Rosie); my USofA family, Scott, Val, Noah, Alex and Jack Sapot; Suzette 'The Schnitzelator' Allcorn; my gurrrrrrrrrrls, Hugh McPhillips'n'John Tippens; Anoushka 'Wheely' Healy; Felix Bowers-Brown (fancy an international mini-break?!); the West London legend that is Misty Gale; Sandra 'Crofty' Carter; and The Carlisle-Griffiths unit, Fi, David and Ruby... and of course, at numero uno, Martyn Fitzgerald—my worst friend in the best possible way.

I'd also like to give maje props to Ben Raworth, Rob Fitzpatrick, Annabel Brog and Grub Smith (although the latter will be appalled at the expression 'maje props'), who all inspired me to do a book, like, totes *way* back, innit.

On a more superficial note, my Dior Homme grey beanie hat is doffed to the peeps I rely upon to keep me clinging on to 2007. They are: Pete and Nathan at boxcleversports.com (big upz da lunchtime krew!); Dr John Quinn at Quinn Clinics—'cos who actually *needs* to frown?; my DC10 Ibiza *amigos*; the gang at Aveda Notting Hill; and supersnapper Darren Orbell.